The

"I LOVED this book and did not want it to end…It has mystery, adventure, romance and fun. This is a book of guilty pleasure."

—Reader Review, *Stitches*

"She had me in the first chapter. I loved it and recommend it to everyone who likes a good story. Simple as that. Suspend all disbelief and simply enjoy the ride!"

—Reader Review, *Stitches*

"*Stitches* is a treasure of simple story telling at its best…Courtney's ability to describe her characters and the places they live and visit is second to none, in my book. I can think of many lauded authors who should have her ability…Courtney had touched a place in my heart with her characters.

—Reader Review, *Stitches*

"The way she describes the painting absolutely brings it to life in my mind's eye. I enjoy being transported into a life of magic, fun, and adventure with Courtney Pierce leading the way."

—Reader Review, *Brushes*

"The story telling is first rate…suspend any need for reality and just suppose it's all possible. What a fun concept. Thanks, Courtney for a fun ride…couldn't put it down…finished reading it around 4 a.m."

—Reader Review, *Brushes*

"All the characters are well developed and that is what really makes this book for me…definitely worth the time to not miss any of the details. All I can say is, I want an immortal dog too now!"

—Reader Review, *Brushes*

"I LOVED RIFFS! As the third volume, it was like visiting old friends and going on their adventures with them. It reminds me of HART TO HART with a magical side. I would suggest this book to anyone who likes, adventure, romance, intrigue, and wonderful characters. I will miss them."

—Reader Review, *Riffs*

Karen, thank you so much for your support and friendship! ♡ Courtney

The Executrix

Courtney Pierce

Courtney Pierce

Windtree Press
818 SW 3rd Avenue #221-2218
Portland, OR 97204-2405

THE EXECUTRIX is a work of fiction. All of the characters, organizations, and events portrayed in this novel are either products of the author's imagination or are used fictionally. Any resemblance to actual events or locales or persons, living or dead, is entirely coincidental.

Windtree Press
818 SW 3rd Avenue #221-2218
Portland, OR 97204-2405

Cover Illustration:

Jake Pierce

Oil on canvas
Used by Permission

ISBN-10: 0988917564
ISBN-13: 978-0-9889175-6-9

Dedication

To Mom and my two sisters.

"When sisters stand shoulder to shoulder, who stands a chance against us?"

~ Pam Brown

Acknowledgements

Thanks, as always, go to my husband of thirty-five years and to my entire family for their support and encouragement. No brain cells were harmed in the creation of this book as my Mom and two sisters provided inspiration on a silver platter. And speaking of family, I'm so indebted to my nephew, Jake Pierce, who interrupted his studies at the Kansas City Art Institute to create the naughty poodle on the cover.

Kristin Thiel is not only my editor but has become a dear friend on my literary journey. She completely gets my sense of humor.

Special applause goes to Carole Florian for her suggestions and attention to detail. No one could ask for a better language technician who thinks like a reader. She laughs when I call her my literary Swiffer.

Big thank yous go to Helen Dupre, Christina Dupre, Debbie Gerber, Tina Jacobsen, Annette Beck, and to the lovely members of my "Sisters in Scene" critique group: Elyse, Joy, Marla, Marilyn, Susan, and Nancy. As first readers, your generosity, suggestions, and encouragement were greatly appreciated. That I made you all laugh makes me happy.

This story took an amazing turn from its original track because of Jennifer Lauck, teacher, mentor, and best-selling author. Her writing workshops at the Attic Institute offer dishes of literary nuggets and huge helpings of inspiration. She kept me on point to sharpen my craft.

The Windtree Press family of authors offers a haven in the exhaustive quest to sell books. I'm so fortunate to be part of this supportive collective. In particular, I'd like to thank Maggie Lynch for keeping me up to date in this ever-changing technical world.

Three independent bookstores deserve kudos for their support of indie authors: Jacobsen's Books & More in Hillsboro, Jan's Paperbacks in Aloha, and Another Read Through in North Portland. They not only stock my books but work tirelessly to bring readers together with writers. Please support your local independent bookstores!

Chapter 1

Luck?

Her book signing at eleven o'clock didn't stop Olivia Novak from dashing to the grocery store at nine for Swiffer duster refills. The compulsion to clean came from her mother. She was down to one sheet, and a cloth and spray didn't cut it anymore. *Never run out of anything to keep up a house.* The timing of this quick jaunt proved fortuitous. As Olivia emerged from the Safeway, her red heels clicking on the asphalt, she spotted a white Suburban parked next to her Lexus sedan in the lot scattered with carts. Of all the available empty spaces, the driver chose that particular spot. Tossing the box of dusters on the passenger seat of her car, she slipped the ever-ready black leather journal and pen from her purse.

Olivia thumbed to one of the remaining blank pages and skulked like a cougar toward the behemoth of an SUV, waiting for an eruption of gnashing teeth from a protective dog. All quiet. She noted details that would indicate the possible model year, license number, and any dings or dents. Olivia's pulse quickened at the slight crunch in the front bumper, not a big one but a dent nonetheless. The customized Oregon plate was only letters—*AVN-CLNG*—easier for Officer McClosky to remember. A peek through the windows revealed a child's car seat in the back. A pink sippy cup lay on its side on the floor mat. Two barrettes with Hello Kitty faces stared at her from the center console. She noted those details too. Olivia got into her car and backed out of the space with a new mission, a mission more urgent than dusty ceiling fan blades.

After the five-minute drive home to her 1920s Tudor in Eastmoreland, a storybook neighborhood on the southeast side of Portland, Oregon, Olivia pulled the car into the garage and reached for her cell phone. She'd learned to give herself a cooling off period of at least a few minutes before making these calls, to think about the details without emotion. The door rolled shut as she called McClosky's office number at the precinct, a number burned into the tip of her forefinger. On the fourth ring, the voice mail kicked in. She closed her eyes and sighed.

"Olivia Novak again. I spotted a white Suburban in the Safeway parking lot in Eastmoreland, off Woodstock. The front bumper shows damage. Here's the license plate number: *AVN-CLNG*." She did a double-take as speaking the letters helped her hear what they were saying. "'Avon calling.'" Out of habit rather than hope, she added, "Call me if you find anything. Oh . . . and the owner has a female child, maybe a toddler." She disconnected and sat in silence, staring at the Day-Glo green numbers of the digital clock on the dash. Twisting the thick gold wedding band she still wore, Olivia waited for the last digit to change from eight to nine. *Pathetic.* Every *white Suburban, Olivia? When is this going to stop?*

The darkness of the garage accentuated the sealed silence of the car. A puff of breath escaped her lips, a scoff at the irony. Here she was, a best-selling author who sold millions of books around the world, a woman at the very wise age of fifty-five, but she couldn't find her husband's killer in her own backyard. Her situation sounded like the tease of a logline for her next book if she had the guts, but a real ending still waited, unknown.

Did Officer McClosky listen to her messages? Did he follow up on any of them? Hard to say. McClosky had stopped returning her calls. Mid-July. The three-year mark since losing Adam teetered over her head like unhinged scaffolding.

Olivia slipped her cell phone and the journal into her purse and tucked the box of Swiffer dusters under her arm. As she opened the mudroom door, a lazy bong from the farmhouse clock in the dining room—an heirloom from Adam's family—reverberated through the house. Its ever-swinging pendulum reminded her of the time: Friday morning, nine thirty. She had an hour before she needed to head downtown for her appearance at Powell's Books.

~ · ~ · ~

Ryan Eason ran his hand through his dark wavy hair and knocked on Sergeant Everhardt's door at police headquarters. No response. He moved to the wire-mesh window and tapped on the glass. Sarge was on the phone, and from his frustrated expression, he was talking with the lieutenant. The extra skin on Sarge's forehead formed three deep lines on his bald head. No doubt a stinker of a problem was being dumped on the department without enough staff to meet the demand. Sarge churned his hand in a circle for Ryan to come inside and pointed to the wooden chair in front of his desk. Stacks of manila folders lined the perimeter, misery squashed in their pages. Once he sat, Ryan needed to bob and weave to get a full view of Sarge's face.

"Right. One week. *One week*. All we can do." Sarge slammed down the phone. With his hand still gripping the receiver, he turned to Ryan. "You know what I wanna know?"

"What's that, sir?" Every time Ryan came into this office, he thanked the stars he didn't deal with the political side of protecting the public.

"How they think there's a secret warehouse busting with officers just sitting around with nothing to do." He waved his hand and pointed at Ryan. "I need *fifty* more of you."

Ryan's chest expanded. "Thanks, but speaking of too much to do . . . you wanted to talk to me? I'm headed out to check on the graffiti mess in Northeast from last night. Tons of calls about it this morning."

"Forget the graffiti. All this cyber crap is more than I can handle." Sarge blew out a breath. "Some nerd sucking on a Red Bull somewhere, probably China, hacked into the Witness Protection Program database. We have a new kind of war on our hands, my friend. Now the Feds' problem is our problem. An officer has to be assigned to every protected witness living in Multnomah County for the next *two weeks*. Only four of them, but still. The Fed boys want to make sure the hack didn't target anyone specific."

"I could use something low-key for a week." He usually took domestic abuse and drug calls. Traffic stops weren't all that benign, either.

The sergeant swiveled his chair to the computer and pulled up the list of four protected—once protected—addresses. His forefinger trailed down the screen. "You want low-key? Fine, you get this witness: Robert Douglas Griffin. Goes by the initials R. D. It's the name the Feds gave him over twenty years ago. Says here he's got a dog. No wife. No kids." Sarge glanced at Ryan. "Get ready for a dose of boredom. Anyone who could be after him is rotting in the slammer or dead. Griffin is ninety-three years old. Still a prize at that age. I should be so lucky."

"Simple enough. What did he do to get into Witness Protection? What am I looking for?"

"Confidential. You just let him know you'll be in the neighborhood on and off throughout the day, every day, for two weeks. Take some breaks for an hour or two. In turn, Griffin needs to tell you when he's leaving the house and where he's going. He's been notified an officer will be assigned to him today." Sarge plucked a business card from its plastic holder and wrote on the back. "Program this number into your phone. It's a secure line. Call if you spot anything suspicious. These two Fed guys will take over: Eduardo Riojas and Don Skidmore." Sarge held out the card with his first two fingers.

"What's Griffin's address?" Ryan took the card.

"Off Woodstock, near Reed College. Southeast Thirty-Fourth Street. I wrote it on the back with the Fed's information."

Ryan studied the names. When he got to Griffin's street number, he smiled for the first time all morning. Flicking the corner of the business card, he stood and moved to the door.

"Don't say I didn't do you any favors," Sarge said behind him. "Good luck, Eason."

Luck. He'd need more than a little luck.

Chapter 2

Hope Comes in Many Forms

With the box of Swiffer dusters in hand, Olivia stepped into the kitchen, remodeled five months ago as a personal reward after receiving the advance for *Tex-Mex Nights*, the latest installment of her romance series. Although an expensive distraction, the construction had been worth the upheaval. The kitchen enjoyed all of the modern appointments while maintaining the charm of salvaged antique details to match the character of the house. The kitchen now lived up to the part it had always played—it was the heart of her home. The expansive granite island, with its four leather chairs, invited guests to relax while she cooked.

Cooking still offered a peaceful respite, despite the memories that could have been associated with it. Her hands had been coated with cornmeal from dipping fish when she'd received the phone call from the police. Adam was dead. A month went by before she found the nerve to clean the hardened crumbs from the buttons on the phone receiver. There had been no sitting by her husband's bedside, holding hands with final words of devotion, or huddling in whispered discussions with doctors about hope. Adam had only gone to the store for a stupid lemon—at her request—and never come home.

The answering machine flashed a red *one*. Negative conditioning gave her cause for pause: her younger sister, Danielle, sending up an alarm about a new health issue with their mother, her older sister, Lauren, bitching about a recurring health issue with her mother, a tip about spotting a Suburban from her mother, or her literary agent requesting the new manuscript she hadn't even started yet. She didn't hold high hopes for new information about Adam's case. She pressed the speakerphone button.

"Olivia . . . McClosky here. I'm sorry we haven't talked in a while, but I need to let you know that I was reassigned earlier this week and won't be working Adam's case. The sergeant will call you with a new investigations officer's name once he identifies one. It won't take long. Please know that I've been tracking the information in your messages. Hang in there. We'll find him. You just have to be patient."

Olivia hit the stop button and stared at the answering machine. *Be patient.* Deep down, she'd suspected something like this had happened. But one day of inertia could let a perpetrator slip by, drive by, park nearby. She couldn't be everywhere, their eyes and ears. *Hang in there.* That wasn't going to happen, not today.

Olivia retrieved her address book from a drawer in the granite island. On a yellow sticky note inside the cover, in blue ink, was Ryan's cell phone number. He was a cop. He could find out where the investigation stood. She slapped the paper on the cabinet over the phone. The note stuck to the white wood like a piece of police caution tape. Her mink-brown Himalayan cat, named Freesia, sat on the counter, her crystal-blue eyes studying Olivia as she would from a jury box. Freesia's muzzle drooped in a pout of disapproval.

"Stop looking at me like that," Olivia scolded, pausing with her hand on her hip. "Okay, what would you do then?" Swishing her feathery tail, the cat appeared to be judging Olivia's red outfit more than her actions.

Maybe after the signing. Maybe after some light cleaning . . . She dampened a microfiber cloth and wiped the chocolate-veined counter around the cat to a brilliant shine. The curved steel handles of every bright white cabinet got a swipe as she moved closer to the phone charging stand.

"I don't care what you *or* Danielle thinks, Freesia. I'm calling him."

Tossing the rag in the sink, Olivia snatched up the phone and called the number.

One ring . . . two rings . . .

"Olivia? Hey!" Ryan's voice sounded upbeat. Promising.

"I need your help."

"Is Danny okay?" His exuberance faded.

"Danny's fine . . . I guess."

"She still living with your mother?"

"Uh-huh." Olivia inspected the stainless Sub-Zero refrigerator door for fingerprints. "A codependent relationship made of steel."

"What's going on? I doubt you called to chat."

She hesitated, promising herself to stay behind the line of begging. "Can you help me find him? I don't want this to reach three years."

Ryan paused. "Liv . . . Adam's accident isn't my case."

"It is now . . . *please*?" She'd sprinted across the line. Definitely begging. "Four different officers have worked on the case and found nothing. McClosky left me a message. He's been reassigned. Right now, nobody's working the case."

The connection seemed to distort under Ryan's sigh. "Look, I can't dive into the investigation. I need permission." His silent pause was more serious than his sigh. Before he asked, Olivia knew what was really concerning him. "Does Danny know you're calling me?"

"I'm trusting you to work on my behalf. Nobody's on *my* side, Ryan." Olivia's eyes filled. She grabbed a napkin from a holder on the counter and dabbed under her eyelashes. Two curved wisps of melted mascara, like butterfly wings, fluttered back at her.

"Liv?"

"Yeah?"

"Does Danny know you're calling me?"

"No. I'm not going to tell her. Keep this between you and me."

"Jesus . . . "

"Ryan . . . " Silence loomed in the receiver. She couldn't take in a full breath.

"Let me sniff around. At the very least, I can find out where the investigation stands."

"Thank you."

Olivia pressed the END button and inhaled. Hope came in many forms. Today, hope came in the form of Ryan Eason, her younger sister's ex-fiancé. Olivia smoothed the jacket of her red linen suit and adjusted the brass buttons to eliminate the gap. Time to fix her mascara and get ready to face her fans. Olivia sensed Freesia's gaze following her out of the kitchen.

~ · ~ · ~

Ryan set his phone on the passenger seat of the cruiser. He hadn't talked to Olivia since Adam's funeral. He'd need a boatload of luck to tackle finding the person who killed Adam. No, he told himself, his commitment only entailed finding out where the investigation stood. No harm in that, really. His heart met his mind. But if he did come up with a tangible lead, closure might give Olivia some peace . . . and get him back with Danny.

Turning to the laptop mounted on the dash, Ryan pulled up the records. The search languished without leads or a leader.

He called the sergeant.

"I'm going to dig into an investigation while I keep my eye on R. D. Griffin," he announced, turning onto McLoughlin Avenue toward Eastmoreland.

Silence.

The sunlight blinded and released him, rather like a strobe light, as it flickered through the canopy of tree leaves. "Sarge?"

"I'm listening."

"A hit-and-run. Almost three years ago. This particular case needs attention."

"Death involved?"

"Yeah. And personal."

"Which one?"

"Adam Novak. Killed on McLoughlin."

Ryan pictured Sarge narrowing his eyes. Their steeliness was just one of the things the man had kept from his military days. "I haven't reassigned the case yet."

"Let me take it on while I'm watching Griffin. Only an hour or two during the day. I'll sniff around when I take a break."

"Well, since you're already going to be in the area." Sarge hesitated. "Is this the—?"

"The deceased's wife is my ex-fiancé's sister."

"What do you wanna to do?"

"Pick up where McClosky left off. Let me take over the case. He completed the DMV list of white Suburbans and started on the body shops before he got reassigned. I checked the records. Olivia Novak called me. She's pretty frustrated."

"Couldn't be helped, but I owe this woman a phone call. Do you have any idea how many hit-and-runs happen every month? Hundreds!"

"Felony manslaughter. His wife needs closure."

"All right. You can work on the case while you monitor Griffin." Sarge paused, tapping his desk blotter with a pencil, or maybe a pen. "Stay objective, Eason. Adam Novak was almost your brother-in-law, right?"

"Yeah . . . almost."

"Where's she live again?"

Ryan's gaze drifted to the cyclist in racing gear pedaling with a mission. "You're not going to believe this but Olivia Novak lives next door to Old Man Griffin."

Chapter 3

The Favor

Olivia plunked her red leather satchel on the passenger seat and backed from the garage. In the rearview mirror, she spotted her codger neighbor, Ardy Griffin, starting up her driveway with his enormous jet-black standard poodle, like a bear nudging a cub. He went by his first initials, R. D., but Olivia always heard them as a word, Ar-dy. Though she had a soft spot for him, she didn't interact much with Ardy, just taking him cookies on holidays and the occasional container of leftovers. Ardy was a tough old guy who went ooey-gooey over his poodle, his pride and joy, but to Olivia, his dog, Pogo, had proved to be an unruly pain in the ass. A jumper. The dog would ruin her red suit if she dared to open the car door. She whirred down the window, but her finger remained poised on the switch.

"Olivia! Before you go—" Ardy called, raising his hand as if the gesture would help to propel him toward the car.

"Hey, Ardy. You doing okay?" He lived alone. She didn't recall if he'd ever been married.

Ardy shuffled to the driver's side with Pogo straining on the leash to reach Olivia first. The dog's ID tags jingled out a reminder that life centered on him. Thank heavens she'd left her disconcertingly similar-sounding charm bracelet behind in the jewelry drawer.

"You'll draw some eyeballs in those red threads." he commented, peering through the window.

"Hope so. I'm off to a book signing." She threw him a tight smile.

"Gonna be a hot one today. Weatherman on channel eight says we might kiss a hundred by five."

Olivia chuckled about Ardy's thick East Coast accent, an anomaly in the Pacific Northwest. Her writer's imagination pegged him as a whiskey runner during Prohibition. Ardy's olive-skinned features smacked of an Italian heritage, which didn't quite jibe with the last name of Griffin. If his name were Griffinelli or Griffinini, or something more stereotypical, she wouldn't be so curious. His dark, watery eyes held a heavy burden of regretted deeds. Ardy hadn't offered up personal details, but she suspected his colorful life included nefarious plans cooked up over delicate calamari served in the back rooms of dark restaurants. But Ardy had moved into the house next door right before she and Adam arrived, back in 1992. Other than being cheap and throwing his overflow recycling into her bin every Sunday night, the man appeared to be pretty harmless.

"What's up?" Olivia asked and glanced at her watch. If she didn't leave in four minutes, her schedule would be cut to the bone. She'd need to catch all green lights on McLoughlin Avenue.

"Need a favor," Ardy hedged, pushing down the dog's rump. "Sit, Pogo." The monster-size poodle didn't.

"Sure." Olivia reached to the dash and upped the fan speed on the air conditioner, but with the window open the vents didn't blow much but noise.

"Going into Milwaukie Hospital for one-a them procedures on Tuesday. Been having some pain in my legs." Ardy rubbed the silver stubble on his chin as if his jaw ached too. "Can you take care-a Pogo for me? Just a couple-a nights?" The dog pawed his leash, acting as though Olivia were chewing into his walk time. Pogo let out a bark of protest.

Rrrr . . . ruh . . . ruh . . . ruh.

"Hang on, boy." Ardy set his gnarled hand, deformed from

arthritis, on Pogo's head. The dog nipped at the sleeve of his checked shirt, clearly a habit since the one cuff was frayed. An image of the dog tearing up her clean house and torturing Freesia appeared in a bubble above Olivia's head.

"Of course. Happy to." She winced inside.

"Will give me some peace to know he'll be all right."

"Can he stay at your house?" She threw Ardy a hopeful smile. "I'll come over to feed him."

"Better if he stays with you. Wouldn't want him to get lonely. Gnaws on stuff when he needs attention."

"Uhhh . . . yeah. Okay."

"Come on over Monday night and get him. You don't need to worry about nothing. He got toys and special food to keep his coat shiny. Don't even need to walk him, 'less you want to. Your yard's fenced."

The bubble over Olivia's head filled again: now, not only was Freesia cowering under her bed but her pristine back garden was being bombarded with dog poo. She glanced at Pogo, his coal-black eyes full of mischief. The mounded puff of curly hair rested on the top of his head like a Chia Pet hitching a ride. The poodle's floppy ears lagged a beat behind the turn of his head as he gazed from her to Ardy as if saying, *Do I* have *to?*

"Monday then. I need to go," she urged. "I can't be late."

"Good luck." Ardy turned and raised his hand. "'Preciate it!"

Olivia whirred up the window. Her gaze trailed the pair out of the driveway and down the sidewalk, the dog pulling the old man and knowing exactly where he wanted to go.

"Damn," she muttered and put the car in reverse.

Chapter 4

The Signing

The annoyance of committing to dog-sit faded as Olivia crossed the Burnside Bridge into downtown Portland. At the stoplight, she plucked the *Romantic Times* magazine from the pocket of her red leather satchel. The review bashed her latest romance, *Tex-Mex Nights,* and said her character, Ricky Martinez, wasn't "Latin enough." This particular reviewer appeared to have a beef against women who wished for a protector.

Olivia's books enjoyed a regular place in the top fifty of the best-seller's list, but the literary critics hadn't been as kind as her readers. Outside of the romance circles, the establishment shunned her novels as drippy genre fiction.

Die-hard fans loved Ricky. Today's signing at Powell's Books would draw women from across the state. The review, though, stuck to Olivia's insides like over-chewed, indigestible gum. She wanted to write something the critics would applaud, something to touch more than women's private yearnings. Writing from the heart didn't always guarantee an invitation to sit at the big authors' table.

The driver behind her honked his horn. Olivia flinched and waved, having no idea as to when the traffic light had turned green. She hit the gas.

The attack on her character, her actual fictional character, stung not because she created him but because the soul of Ricky was Adam, her husband for thirty-two years. She and Adam hadn't been blessed with a warning—dreams of what they wanted to do together had been wiped out without a moment's notice—so Olivia kept Ricky moving forward, touching and kissing his leading lady, spooning her in bed, and tossing out a warm smile over ceviche in a quiet cantina. As she wrote the words, Adam came back to life.

Well, that critic wouldn't be at her signing, and it was time to focus on the task at hand. As a regular speaker at writer's conferences, many events required boarding a plane for appearances. But Portland was home, which meant her fans held higher expectations for chit-chat and personal conversation. They considered her a friend and neighbor. Olivia hoped her audience base would follow her when she strayed from the comfortable cocoon of romance. Maybe she'd write something serious, about a crime perhaps, under a pen name. Her literary agent might have a few choice words about that plan . . .

Olivia pulled into a space in the parking garage adjacent the bookstore. For a change of mood, she cocked the rearview mirror and flexed her face muscles in preparation for a smile-a-thon.

After applying a fresh shine on her lips, Olivia checked her bright white teeth and secured her long dark hair in the tortoiseshell clip. The red linen suit and matching three-inch heels were a good choice for a romance writer, but respected authors wore smart, sophisticated knits in serious tones of blue or black, with only a flash of something bright. Serious writers wore hand-crafted, chunky jewelry and expounded upon heady topics at cocktail parties. Ardy was right; at least her outfit wouldn't be missed by the people who mattered most: readers.

"Showtime," she muttered, tucking the folded magazine between the seat and the console. She plucked a tissue from a small packet and dabbed away the remnants of any sadness. An idea for a fresh direction could come today in the faces of her fans. A name might spark a whole new character. An expression might tell a tale.

July in Portland was a weather crap shoot, and the dice today had turned up steamy. As she clicked around the corner in her heels, Olivia ran into the line of fans hugging the side of the building to the front door of Powell's Books. *Move fast so these poor souls don't bake.*

"Here she comes!" squealed a jovial woman with an explosion of wiry silver hair. The fan reached out as Olivia went by, bouncing as if her espadrilles were spring-loaded. Olivia stopped and pumped her hand. No matter how much she bitched, Olivia loved this moment. Excited faces turned in sequence as she passed. A public entrance built excitement.

"Hello, hello! What a turnout!" Olivia shouted, raising both arms in a two-handed wave. "I'm anxious to meet you!"

Upon her approach, the first fan in line held open the front door. The instant Olivia crossed over the threshold into the bookstore the air changed. The pulpy aroma of stories filled her senses: musty used ones with broken-in pages; fresh new editions with crackly spines; hardbacks and paperbacks. Her staff handler waited for her to take a seat at the signing table. A vase of red roses and a bowl of Ghirardelli chocolates sat next to two stacks of *Tex-Mex Nights*. Nice touch. And everyone would receive a laminated bookmark, one for each of the entire four-book Ricky Martinez series, fanned in perfect order next to the chocolates. She took her seat behind the table and retrieved her favorite Mont Blanc signing pen from her satchel. She presented the last-minute choice of the new-best-friend smile to the first woman in line.

After forty-five minutes of signing, chatting, and handshaking, the faces in front of her salved the sting of the bad review and erased the morning's unspeakable Suburban episode. These women weren't buying a book, or even Olivia Novak; they desired a protector like Ricky—like Adam. Every signature filled her with trepidation about leaving the romance genre behind. But to go to what? Mystery? Literary fiction? Today, only one book existed. A new, serious book needed to wait in the shadows.

Olivia grasped the hand of the next fan. *Time for a break after this one.* Releasing the handshake, she signaled a staff member to hold the line for fifteen minutes after this woman. She took another copy of *Tex-Mex Nights* from the stack and opened the cover. Olivia raised her eyes to make real contact and spotted something that stripped her of pretense. This woman wouldn't dash home and consign her autographed book on an Internet auction site. Olivia searched the woman's expression for what intrigued her so.

"Your name?" Olivia asked with her pen suspended over the title page. Always on the hunt for a new character name, she'd not yet heard one that sparked inspiration.

"Valerie," the woman blurted out, emphasizing the *V* and licking her lips, void of lipstick and dry from nerves.

Olivia recognized the expectant expression; she was about to receive a request to attach a personalized inscription. She leaned to peer around Valerie's wide hips. The line snaked back to cookbooks, but people were talking among themselves; the aide had bought her some time. *Oh, what the heck.*

"A note for you or someone special?"

"I'm your biggest fan."

By the size of her stretchy Capri pants, Olivia thought she might be right. "To Valerie. I wish you many hot *Tex-Mex Nights.*"

"Perfect! Can I get a hint about your next book?"

Olivia paused and signed her name in flowing script. She handed over the inscribed book. "You'll need to wait, Valerie. Some of my best characters come from people I meet." Olivia paused and went thoughtful. "Might be you. Thanks so much for coming."

Something about the droop of Valerie's eyes made her appear sad—a longing to connect or reflecting some kind of loss. The woman made a move toward the cash register, but she stopped and turned. She padded back to the signing table, wanting to squeeze out one more question.

"I'm so sorry about your husband," Valerie said, tentative. "I remember seeing the accident on the news a few years ago, but they never followed up about what happened. Did the police ever catch the culprit?"

Olivia's throat tightened. The woman's sad expression didn't reflect Valerie's own experience; the pain in her eyes was a sympathetic mirror of Olivia's pain. Fans didn't bring up the accident often, but when they did the words took on their own version of a hit-and-run. The link between Adam and her character of Ricky was a private world, and was cathartic. Even in interviews she didn't talk about the connection, but the two worlds she'd tried so hard to keep separated sometimes collided with an innocent question. Olivia reached for the woman's hand with both of her own. She didn't want to let go. "Thank you, Valerie. I appreciate your concern—really I do. But no, they never did."

With her lips pressed in disappointment, Valerie released Olivia's hands. Before she turned to pay for her book, Olivia offered the woman one last appreciative smile; as she did so, a muffled chirp escaped from her satchel. Olivia dug out her cell phone and checked the caller ID: *St. Margaret's Hospital. Danny.*

She moved to a quiet spot in an empty aisle labeled *Self-Help*. Only four people knew her mobile number: her eighty-four-year-old mother, Ellen Dushane; her younger sister, Danielle; her older sister, Lauren; and her literary agent, Karen Finerelli. Danny lived with Mom, and the only time she called Olivia's mobile was with a Mom-related emergency. She must be at the hospital. A familiar drill for the past two years.

"Danny? What's going on?" Olivia squeezed her eyes, waiting for the incoming missile.

"I'm at St. Margaret's," Danny said in a veiled tone. "Mom fell with chest pain early this morning. We just got the room."

"Why didn't you call me or Lauren?"

"I didn't want you to freak out if it turned out to be nothing. But this time's more serious than I thought. Plus, I'm exhausted."

"How is she now?" Olivia ran her fingers over the spines on the bookshelves. Her gaze settled on a pink paperback, Deborah Tannen's *You Were Always Mom's Favorite!* She closed her eyes and turned her back to the shelf.

"The doctors are conferencing. They haven't come out yet. They pumped her full of morphine. She's asleep."

Olivia exhaled with relief. "I'll be there as soon as I can, but I'm doing a signing." She hesitated. "Is this an emergency-emergency or a normal one? Can you give me an hour to finish here?"

Danny started to whimper. "Liv, you and Lauren need to come. What am I going to do?"

Olivia didn't want to panic. Her sister had done this before, but a new edge had crept into Danny's voice that stopped Olivia cold. "I'll call Lauren. Room number?"

"Eight-oh-nine."

"We'll be there as soon as we can." Olivia ended the call and emerged from the aisle, whirling her hand at the manager. He rushed to her side.

"Everything okay?" he asked.

"No. I need to leave." Olivia made a quick count of the line: twenty or so. "I can't stay. Family emergency. Let me finish signing these books. I'll hand them out."

"But the line keeps getting longer."

"Gather their names. I'll send books for free to anyone I missed, but I *have* to leave." *Mom, I'm coming. I need to get out of here.*

After a hasty signing of twenty books, Olivia dropped her pen and phone in her satchel. Moving toward the entrance, she shook each fan's hand as two staff members dished out copies of *Tex-Mex Nights*. "I'm sorry, but I have to leave early. I'll set a date to come back."

Ten feet away from her car, the heel of her red leather pump stuck in a crack in the concrete, twisting her ankle. Olivia regained her balance and limped toward the car, beeping the key fob. She sunk into the seat and called her older sister. To catch the promise of a breeze, Olivia left the car door open with one high-heeled foot planted on the pavement. *Hot flash in July heat. Torture.* It didn't work. Olivia pulled the door closed and started the engine to get the air conditioner revved.

"Lauren, it's me. Danny called. We have to go to the hospital. She says Mom isn't good. Can you meet me at St. Margaret's?"

"Are you serious?" Lauren blew out a breath into the receiver, a signal she was buried in her office manager job at a real estate company. The buying season was in full swing. "All right, but I need to ride with you. My brakes are shot."

"I'll pick you up. We'll go together in mine."

"No, let's meet at your house. I don't want to leave my car at the office. I think my car can limp to your house without wiping out anybody—maybe."

"I can be home in about twenty minutes. Hurry!"

"You try telling my piece of crap car to *hurry*. Wait for me. What's Danny doing?"

"Freaking out."

"And you?"

"Not allowed to freak out. My house in twenty minutes."

"Give me twenty-five."

Olivia set her phone on the console and popped the latch on the glove compartment. A trickle of perspiration ran down the back of her neck. Three hard pumps of hand sanitizer filled the car's interior with the aroma of mango-infused alcohol. She flapped her hands in a blur to dry them. A sensation of lift off rolled in her stomach.

She, Olivia, was her mother's executrix.

Chapter 5

Olivia's Muse

Lauren called to say she was on her way to the house—now late. Twenty-five minutes turned to thirty-seven since they'd talked. Olivia had already packed up a bag of books and put them in a car, and now she made a third pass in bare feet through the small formal dining room. The picture window offered a front view of the driveway and of the historic neighborhood, chock-full of distinctive two- and three-bedroom Craftsman and Tudor homes within a maze of quaint, winding streets. She hadn't moved after Adam's accident. No kids—just an unchecked ambition to survive. The house didn't become a home again until she marched into the Oregon Humane Society and adopted Freesia, a floppy, seemingly boneless Himalayan with an attitude.

Now, Freesia followed her every step, sensing Olivia's discomfort. Their normal routine had been interrupted. Olivia picked up the cat and ran her hand over the soft fur. Freesia stared up at her with bright blue eyes, masked in a burst of chocolate brown.

"Love you, baby girl," she cooed, "but today's not a writing day. I have no idea what today is. We're going to find out."

Every possible scenario had to be thought through. Was this drama unwarranted? She'd be relieved, yes, but also pissed. What if her mother became incapacitated? Needed 24/7 care? Life interruptus.

What if—?

Lauren would help. In adulthood, as in their youth, she and Olivia operated with the opposing polarity of two magnets. But they had some common understanding now. Lauren too had lost her husband, Mark. They had both entered widowhood in the same year from opposite directions: Lauren's journey slow and painful with Mark's cancer; Olivia's arrival announced with a phone call. Their shared pain became a bond after years of lost touch. Now, having also gone through menopause together, they each suffered equal amounts of wine bloat. And neither one of them had a clue as to how to relate to their younger sister, Danielle, an emotionally fragile, dark-haired beauty, still so at forty-five. Danny had been born late in their parents' lives, an *oops* baby timed between her sisters' generations and the next.

Clean. Scrub something. Olivia wiped down the glass cooktop on the granite island. The stove knobs got a swipe too. She opened the oven door and shut it. Already clean.

The phone let out a chortle. Olivia lunged.

"All okay?" she asked, neglecting to check the number first.

The caller wasn't Danny.

"What the hell, Olivia? You walked out on the signing?" Karen Finerelli. Olivia might have known the news of the botched event would get to New York faster than she could drive across the Willamette River.

This was Friday, so Karen was fired-up in the cooking frenzy for tomorrow's huge family meal, an event held every Saturday in the Bronx. Over lasagna and countless side dishes, three generations of Karen's family fought across the table, then hugged their "I love yous" on the way out the door—every weekend. Olivia attended one of those get-togethers . . . once.

"My mother might *die*, Karen," she snapped. "I'm leaving for the hospital in a few minutes." The *D* word made the possibility real. A moment of silence hung on the line before Karen responded.

"You've been through this before . . . many times. She's a trouper, Liv."

"I hope so. I'm waiting for Lauren to get here now. Danny's already at the hospital."

"A Powell's event is pretty important . . . never mind that it's in your home town. The manager called the publisher, who called me. A huge turnout."

Olivia tried to wedge in a word, but succeeded in only opening and closing her mouth. What eventually came out was lame. "We'll reschedule." Olivia smoothed the back of her skirt to protect her offense. Karen's skill included the ability to tear through the linen for a juicy bite.

"This is a *disaster*."

Olivia rolled her eyes. "Chernobyl was a disaster; Katrina, Mount St. Helens, and 9/11 were disasters. Rescheduling a signing at Powell's Books doesn't qualify as a disaster."

Some kind of meat sizzled as Karen banged pots and pans. "You stick that spoon in the gravy, you won't believe where I'll stick this fork!" Karen shouted.

"What?" Olivia's mouth popped open.

"Not you—my nephew." Karen knocked her weapon against a pan in rapid succession. "So, listen . . . where's my manuscript for the next book?"

Olivia darted to the dining room window and pulled back the drape, hoping to catch Lauren's arrival. The street was quiet. "I want to move in a new direction—something serious."

"Only one kind of serious exists in this business, my dear: *selling* books. Lots of selling. You're a dream client. None of my other authors crank out two manuscripts a year, but nothing's in the pipeline."

"I'm working on something new," she said, distracted. Olivia's gaze followed a Prius down the street. The car slowed to a crawl in front of her house. Not Lauren. Lauren drove a dented Ford Focus. Odd, but the brown-haired man behind the wheel, maybe in his forties, stared at her front door. He hit the gas and disappeared around the bend.

"How far along is 'working on'?" Karen's normal combative tone fried to an extra-crispy edge. The knot in Olivia's stomach indicated the sentiment was warranted.

Who is that guy in the Prius? "Just a rough first draft." Olivia squeezed her eyes. "I'm not ready for you to read it yet." She had nothing written, not an outline or even an idea for one. When she opened her eyes, Lauren's Ford Focus careened—much too fast—into her driveway. She winced as she watched her sister's car bump the garage door.

"Send me the first fifty pages! Dive into the rest and follow your *muse*."

Her muse. Lauren got out of her car, slammed the door, and marched up the steps with a box of white zinfandel. Her work clothes turned her shape into a funnel: a blousy top to hide her upper body and huggy pants that accentuated her chicken legs. The long melody of the doorbell rang as the handle twisted. With the hot phone in her ear, Olivia fluttered her hand for Lauren to stay quiet. Instead, Lauren huffed past her to the kitchen. Keys clattered as she tossed them on the counter, along with her overloaded purse.

"Give me a few weeks, maybe longer if something . . . happens," Olivia said to Karen, her gaze trailing Lauren. "My sister's here. I gotta go." She hung up and bared her teeth at the phone.

"Nice!" Lauren teased. "Cool and calm Olivia Novak springs a screw. What's that about?"

"My agent. She's pressuring me for my next book. Who has time to write?" Olivia set her hand on her forehead, as if checking for a fever. "And I left a signing at Powell's when Danny called. Karen reamed me royally for that stunt. I don't blame her."

Lauren's gaze circled the pristine kitchen. "Looks like you've had plenty of time to clean your house. What do you do, take Q-tips to the baseboards?"

"I think when I clean." Olivia shifted.

"Then you ought to have a thousand books out." Lauren shoved the wine box into the refrigerator. "Sorry about the garage door. Damned brakes!"

Lauren yanked on one of the leather chairs at the kitchen island, scraping it over the tile floor. Rummaging through her purse, she finally found what she was looking for. She pulled the cellophane strip from a fresh pack of cigarettes.

"We need to get going." Olivia didn't really want to go to the hospital. She didn't want to be at the signing. She didn't want to go or be or do.

Lauren sat and flicked her chestnut-brown bangs with one hand and lit a cigarette with the other. "Five minutes. We'll be sitting around soon enough."

Reaching over the glass cooktop, Olivia switched on the down-draft fan to suck out the smoke. Being an ex-smoker herself, Olivia let family members get away with the inherited habit. Her mother smoked, and so had Danny before she quit.

"What are you writing?" Lauren asked.

"I've got nothing." Olivia sighed, waving away the white tendrils. "I'm over romance."

"Don't knock romance. Paid for your fancy kitchen. What do you want to switch to?"

"Something real."

"Real . . . what the hell does that mean anymore?"

Olivia studied her sister. "What's with your bangs?" Even at sixty, Lauren trimmed her own (after the bottle job) dark hair. Olivia pulled an ashtray from the cabinet. "Keep your cigarette over the vent. Don't stink up my house."

"I don't go to a fancy hairdresser like some people"—Lauren trained her gaze on Olivia—"and the air conditioner doesn't work in the car. Tell me about Mom."

"Chest pain, but I think this time's serious."

"Every time's serious."

"She can't keep going through these episodes." All too true. Olivia sighed and slipped her feet back into her heels. She reached for her purse. *Get it together.* Something in Danny's voice had set off an internal alarm.

"What'd Danny say?" Lauren leaned on her elbows and blew smoke into the vent. A whole conversation swirled behind her words. In the silence, Olivia knew they both zoomed back to the year when Danny fell apart and moved in with their mother, a move that changed the family dynamic: Mom and Danny versus Lauren and Olivia.

"Oh, they haven't told her anything. Danny didn't call me when she took Mom to the hospital," Olivia griped. "Pisses me off."

"Are you surprised?" Lauren pursed her lips.

"No. We'd better get moving."

Lauren grimaced at Olivia's outfit. Her gaze landed on the red heels. "You're not wearing those. They look like two demon maraschino cherries. Put on sensible ones while I finish this." She tapped the rim of the ashtray.

"My feet are killing me. I twisted my ankle in the parking garage. The price of looking good."

Lauren rolled her eyes. "Case closed."

After kicking off her shoes, Olivia padded up the stairs to her bedroom closet. She changed into black slacks and a white cotton blouse and slipped her feet into tasseled loafers. Flats made less noise in hospitals. This might be a long night. Racing back down the stairs, she stood in the kitchen doorway. "Better?"

"Much better. I hope this isn't as bad as you're making it out to be." Lauren stubbed out her cigarette and blew the last stream of smoke over her head. "Because Danny's not moving in with me."

"Me neither. Let's go." Olivia grabbed her purse and keys.

~ · ~ · ~

Buckled in for the twenty minute ride to St. Margaret's Hospital, Olivia eyed Lauren eyeing the *Romantic Times* folded between the seat and the console. Lauren waited for her to get on the freeway to ease out the magazine with two fingers, exaggerating the gesture to get under Olivia's skin.

"Is the review in here?" Lauren made a mock-horrified *O* with her lips.

"Don't you dare look," Olivia warned.

"Why not? The whole world gets an opinion, but I don't?"

Olivia's lack of argument prompted Lauren to dive in. The sound of crinkling paper filled the interior of the car.

Only blood sisters could spar so much without erupting into fisticuffs. Instead, Lauren could home in on Olivia's Achilles' heel and stick a judgment pin in the soft tissue between the fragile bones. But unconditional love lurked behind the barbs.

"Well . . . I think they're full of crap," Lauren pronounced. "I read every one of your novels, more than once, and I love them."

"No kidding?"

"They're good books when I'm stressed out. I don't need to think too hard."

"Thank you?" Olivia made sure to emphasize she was asking a question.

"Yes, a compliment. Yours are better than all the vampire nonsense on the market. Who wants to read about people biting each other and collapsing in a pool of blood? And I don't like cyber-techno garbage, either. Everybody needs a good, old-fashioned romance."

"Mom's been pretty critical." Olivia's grip tightened on the steering wheel. Her mother was one tough customer when it came to literary endeavors, preferring epic novels set in the shadow of historical events. She drank them in, as if in preparation for a college lecture, and shot out their trivia like Nerf balls.

"Yeah, well, that's because Danny didn't write them—you did." Lauren glanced at her and scowled. "If Danny were a writer, Mom would've been holding meet-and-greets at the Waverly Club."

"Mom should try writing a book. It's harder than she thinks. One conversation with my agent and she'd cower in the corner."

Lauren tapped the magazine. "I hate this reviewer. She insulted me as a reader, and she trashed you as an author. I think woman's got personal issues."

"She has a point, Lauren."

"Did you bring some signed *Tex-Mex Nights* for Mom? You can't go in the hospital without bragging books for her to give to the nurses."

Their mother's discomfort with connecting one-on-one could easily be interpreted as disapproval. They saw through it, but the behavior was an annoyance nonetheless.

"In a bag in the back." Olivia pointed to the rear seat with her thumb.

"She gushes to all the doctors about her daughter, the famous writer."

"I don't get her. She goes on and on to everybody but me."

"Welcome to my world, Liv . . . You should write a good medical romance. How about nurses who do doctors who do nurses? Mom will singlehandedly keep growing that audience for you."

Olivia laughed out loud, but her smile faded. "I hope so."

"Oh, stop! The invincible Ellen Dushane gets through these things. This isn't any different. They'll blow out her arteries and she'll be back on the bacon and cigs in no time."

"Danny's being dramatic."

"Yeah, Danny's being dramatic." Lauren paused. "Put some gas on that pedal."

Chapter 6

The Great Ellen Dushane

The parking garage at St. Margaret's always experienced a lull after lunch on Friday afternoons. By five o'clock, finding a space entailed Olivia selling her soul as most patients received visitors after work and before the dinner hour. Over the years—multiple surgeries for their mother, heart failure for their father, and spiraling cancer with Lauren's husband—Olivia had memorized the traffic patterns at this hospital for every time of day. She'd also memorized the patterns in the carpet inside—each one identified another medical specialty. Olivia had completed two of her books in multiple waiting areas. Near the walkway to the main hospital entrance, a reserved space labeled *Patient* drew her eye. She almost chuckled as she saw for the first time the word's double meaning. She pulled into it.

"Here we go," Olivia said and shut off the engine. "What round is this?"

"Ten—no—eleven," Lauren said, sighing as she opened the car door.

Olivia heaved the bag of books from the back seat as Lauren moved to the corner of the garage.

"Let's stand over here for a minute before we go in." Lauren dug in her purse. Olivia was sure that not even Lauren had a clue what lurked inside the thing at any given time, but in a natural disaster Lauren could survive for a month by using the contents. Not long ago, Olivia witnessed a pair of needle-nosed pliers, a roll of double-sided sticky tape stuck with fuzz, and a mini flashlight emerging from its depths.

"You can't smoke on the hospital grounds, Lauren."

"Oh, *please*. Spare me. Next, they're going to hang out a *No Farting* sign." Lauren grimaced and waved her hand. "Like the car exhaust in here is less toxic?"

"You'd better not get caught." Olivia scanned the rows of cars for a security guard. She didn't spot one.

"Let me tell you one thing." Lauren bobbed her cigarette. "If I'm on a plane and the sucker's going down, I'm lighting up. I don't give a damn what anybody says."

"Here, give me that." Olivia snatched the cigarette from Lauren's fingers. She took a puff and coughed. "Ugh! Like I licked the sidewalk with my tongue."

"Yeah . . . well." Lauren took a deep drag and scowled.

"C'mon. Danny's waiting," Olivia pressed, "and if Mom's awake, we'll catch hell for being so long."

"We're adults, not teenagers in the high school parking lot."

Olivia's cell phone chirped. "Where are you?" Danny choked. "She's gone."

"Where did they move her to?" Olivia locked her gaze on Lauren's.

"No, she's *gone*. She didn't make it."

"What!?" The letters scrambled as she spit out the word.

"They took her out a few minutes ago. Her blood pressure plummeted. Dehydrated . . . They couldn't revive her . . . " Danny started to sob. "A million alarms went off. They told me to leave the room."

"Stay where you are! Lauren and I just got out of the car. We're in the parking garage. We'll be right up." Olivia raised her eyes to Lauren, who stared back at her. "Oh, God . . . "

"Tell me." Lauren threw her cigarette to the pavement and twisted her rubber-soled loafer. "Is she okay?"

"No! She just died!" Olivia pulled on Lauren's arm. "Run!"

At full steam, the sisters charged through the glass doors of St. Margaret's Hospital. Lauren squeaked an arc to the right and lunged through the open steel doors of the elevator. Olivia pushed in after her.

The guilt-lined walls closed in, claustrophobic. Olivia hit the eight button in rapid sequence. Lauren remained silent, as if there were no room for words. When the doors parted, Lauren darted to room eight-oh-nine. Olivia dashed in the opposite direction to the nurses' station.

"We're here, Fran," Olivia announced to the head nurse, panting as she gripped the edge of the counter.

The nurse turned from the computer with a tender expression, infused with her own sadness. In her forties, Fran's endless positive energy had become a life jacket in a boat of dire circumstances. Patients on the eighth floor required serious nursing. Today, though, the always-smooth bun on the back of Fran's head frayed with escaping hair. A long day already.

"I'm so glad you're here," Fran said, setting her hand over Olivia's. "I'm a little worried about Danny. I got the doctor to approve a Valium for her."

"Where is she?"

"In the contemplation room by the elevator."

"Did Mom suffer? Please say no."

"No, honey." Fran's voice softened with assurance. "A pretty high dose of morphine prevented any pain. Very peaceful. The doctor briefed Danny. Do you want me to page him to talk with you and Lauren?"

"Not necessary. He can't soft-sell the truth." Olivia set the cloth bag of books on the floor. "I'm glad he talked with Danny."

"Are you sure?"

"Thank you. You've done a lot for Mom over the past few years. If not for you and your staff, she wouldn't have lived as long as she did."

"I'll miss her, Liv. I hate to say this, but you need to address some paperwork."

Olivia blew out a breath. At this moment, the heartless details of death came close to the death of a heart.

Lauren appeared at her side, eyes swollen. "The room's empty. I couldn't find Mom's stuff? Where's Danny?"

Olivia patted Lauren on the shoulder and turned. "Fran, I'll come back in a few minutes, but we need to find Danny." Her own tears needed to wait. The process had only just begun.

The small contemplation room, lined with picture windows, offered a panoramic view of evergreen treetops to inspire deep thought. Olivia and Lauren stopped at the glass door to study their younger sister. Danny stood stock-still at the window. Her shiny dark hair had been cut into a smooth pageboy. Highlights of chestnut reflected the light. At forty-five, Danny was slim with natural good looks that held without makeup. Her emotional meltdown after splitting up with Ryan, though, had taken a toll, leaving behind a stiff demeanor.

Lauren pulled on Olivia's arm. "Wait for a second. What if she flips out?"

"This day's been coming for a while," Olivia whispered, but kept her gaze on Danny. "I got back in touch with Ryan this morning to work on Adam's case."

"You called Ryan? Why are you whispering?"

"This feels conspiratorial."

"Because it is. You're meddling, Liv. Ryan's moved on."

"If he finds Adam's killer, things might mend between those two. Mom held her back by being overprotective."

"Understatement of the century." Lauren depressed the handle.

Danny turned when the door opened. Her brown eyes appeared dry, stunned and speaking of a grown woman lost. While she was ten years younger than Olivia, Danny had the cast of someone much older from living with their mother. Today, her normally rosy cheeks lacked color. Danny's world had been reduced to fear of this moment.

Olivia and Lauren both wrapped their arms around her. Danny's shoulders collapsed from the toll of relentless worry.

"We had a good last day yesterday," Danny said, pulling away. "Picked tomatoes."

"What else happened?" Olivia searched her eyes, as if trying to share her mother's last hours.

"We made BLTs last night. Mom didn't eat. My radar went off because she *loves* bacon." Danny blew out a breath, struggling to roll back the clock. "Early this morning, about four o'clock, she woke me up with chest pain. I raced her here when she wouldn't let me call an ambulance. It's like I'm still not awake."

"What did the doctor say?"

"Blah, blah, blah." Danny rolled her hand. "I have no idea what he said. The details didn't matter. He told me the technical stuff so he didn't have to say she died. He buried the lead, Liv, like they do on the news. I just stared at him."

Olivia wished she'd taken Fran's suggestion to meet with the doctor. Now, she wanted to dissect every detail. She made a mental note for her and Lauren to follow up for a private discussion, but not today.

"Let's get off this floor and go down to the coffee shop," Lauren suggested, wiping her cheek. From her expression, Lauren wanted to run to the parking lot and scream. Danny, on the other hand, appeared somewhat hollow, void of emotion. Concerning to Olivia.

"Okay . . . "

Olivia nodded her head toward the elevator. Lauren picked up the silent message. "I need to do some paperwork, Danny. I'll meet you two downstairs." Olivia had an urge to flee from the room. She might as well have been an outsider, an invader into Danny's and Mom's world.

Returning to the nurse's station, Olivia set her hands on the counter. "Fran, let's deal with the paperwork."

"Only a few forms to sign. The rest gets done by the funeral home," Fran said and pulled a note with Olivia's name from the papers in a clip. "Using the same one as your dad?"

"Of course."

Funeral home. *Not Mom.* Not *the* Ellen Dushane, mother of three. Mom was like a surgeon, dissecting each of her children to peel back their inner layers, hidden ones only she could see. Olivia stared at the forms, familiar because she'd seen them before for Adam and her father. Lauren and Danny counted on her to handle the ugly details. Grief needed a manager, despite cracks in her own shell. Heat flushed her face as her throat itched, a harbinger of tears.

"I'm not sure I can do this," she muttered.

Fran gazed at Olivia with empathy; an added sliver of insight crept into her eyes. "Ellen gave me all your books. I loved them. She never stopped talking about you. Your stories took me where I wished I could go." Fran reached across the counter and set her hand on Olivia's. "Of course you can do this."

"She did?" Olivia raised her eyes, having picked out only the select words of her mother's opinion of her. Her hand lingered under the warmth of Fran's words. Olivia pulled away and reached for the bag of books she'd set on the floor after their arrival. "Here, Fran. I brought these for Mom to give out to you and the other nurses." She handed the cloth bag to Fran. "Four copies of the new release. I can't bear to take them back to the car."

The boxes on the form magnified through tears as Olivia wrote her mother's name. She let them drop to the paper, splashing the ink to transform her mother to watercolor art.

~ · ~ · ~

Olivia wandered into the coffee shop in a daze, passing the veggie wraps, yogurt, and sandwiches in the refrigerated case. *Food for the uninspired to fill an emotional void*, she thought. She slid into the booth next to Lauren, across from Danny. Her sisters each stared at the plate in front of them, an untouched turkey sandwich resting in a cellophane nest.

"This day's been coming," Olivia declared, "but I wasn't prepared for it to be today." Releasing her hair from the clip, she ruffled the dark tresses and re-secured the mane in the teeth of denial. "A lot to do." She reached over and picked a piece of meat from Lauren's uneaten sandwich. "I'm not hungry, but I'm starved."

Lauren pushed the plate toward Olivia. "Okay, Ms. Executrix. Now what?"

"What am I going to do?" Danny whimpered. Her gaze settled on Olivia, as if a simple answer could be purchased on her credit card.

"Because you fell down doesn't mean you can't get up." She reached out and grasped Danny's hands. "Do you think I curled up in a ball after Adam died? Dushane women don't fail. We do something different. We change. We *roll*."

"You'll get yourself together," Lauren added, "and live your life—not Mom's. You've been in limbo for the past three years. No more watching TV or taking naps." Danny's eyes watered in response. Lauren kept going. "And Mom's death didn't just happen to you."

Danny pulled a tissue from her purse and dabbed her nose. "Are you deciding everything, Liv?"

"Not for you. I can sort through the details of Mom's affairs, but other decisions need to be a unified effort. When it comes to your life, you need to take charge of your decisions."

"What should I do?"

"The first chore for me is to get the paperwork from the safe: birth certificate, insurance papers, account statements, and whatever else is in there. Then, I'll call Fred Willoughby at the funeral home."

A white plastic drawstring bag, containing her mother's personal effects, sat on the seat next to Danny. Crinkling the bag to her side, a *whoosh* of Mom escaped with the squeeze: a powdery aroma of White Shoulders perfume and stale cigarette smoke swirled over the table like a genie.

"Mom's purse and jewelry . . . and her sweat suit . . . and her books," Danny muttered, her tone defensive. "She didn't get to finish the third Outlander."

Olivia's closed her eyes. Lauren put her head in her hands.

Unthinkable. Mom had insisted that a book started must be finished.

"C'mon, let's get out of this place," Lauren suggested. "No healing's going on here. We need to go to Mom's. Danny, did you drive the Blazer or your Sebring?"

"The Blazer . . . because it still has Dad's handicap tag. Mine is in the garage."

"Seriously?" Olivia blew out a breath. "Well, there's one easy thing we can do: why not give one to Lauren? Her brakes are shot."

Danny shrugged. "I can't drive anything right now."

Lauren held out her hand. "Give me the keys. I'll follow you guys."

Chapter 7

The Not-So-Safe Safe

Olivia pulled into the driveway of her mother's one-story seventies ranch house, a house that, as of today, belonged to the three sisters. She glanced at the digital clock on the dash: three o'clock. Such a long day already and more to come. Lauren shut off the engine of their father's blue Blazer, parking next to her. Lead weights appeared to pull down Lauren's eyes as she dragged her purse from the front seat, and her shoulders slumped. The solo drive hadn't been an easy one. Not since the death of her husband, three years ago, had Lauren looked so drawn. The box of white zin must be sounding pretty good. Olivia, herself, wouldn't mind just sticking her mouth under the spigot.

The ride home with Danny revealed nothing new. Olivia tried to come up with a way to describe her younger sister as a character for a novel. It wasn't easy; she was a tapestry of contradictions. Danny could be naive and childlike, so sensitive to the mildest of words, but then she would become a tower of strength as a caregiver, handling post-surgical tasks that would have brought lesser people to their knees. Danny popped out words of wisdom when everyone had given up on answers. Today, though, she was the one who needed answers—and she needed her sisters.

Danny had so much potential, but she'd lived Mom's life over the past three years, not her own: days filled with television, doctor's appointments, and frozen dinners for two, discussing ailments even the doctors didn't understand. She probably ached to laugh and joke about life issues their mother had sloughed off as complaints. Danny's excuse for not getting back on her feet after her breakup with Ryan was that she needed to care for Mom. What used to be a cover-up had morphed into the truth. Unlike her and Lauren, Danny didn't show her heart unless Mom or an animal were involved.

"C'mon, Danny Girl," Olivia said, dropping her keys into her purse. "We don't have to deal with everything today. But I need to get some papers and call the funeral home before five." Olivia's gaze focused on Lauren at the front door, struggling in her search for the house key on Danny's ring.

"Can I stay with you?" Danny asked. "I don't want to be here by myself. Not tonight . . . Just for a few days." A familiar pleading filled Danny's deep brown eyes, a reminder to Olivia she'd not been denied anything by anyone.

"Good idea." A horrible idea but Olivia wanted to handle one crisis at a time. Danny relaxed at her words.

Living only fifteen minutes away, Olivia had gotten lazy with the quality of her recent visits to Ellen's house, mostly picking up or dropping off. She depended more on the answering machine for communication. As Olivia stepped through the front door, the distinctive aroma of her mother's life washed over her: first-edition books, furniture polish, and a lingering odor of tobacco that settled over everything like a quilt. Other than the cigarette smoke, Mom had kept a tidy house, even though most of the contents were forty years old.

To the left of the small entryway were an open living and dining room. The semicircular couch and two swivel chairs had made permanent impressions on the beige carpet. In the center of the thick glass coffee table sat a silk philodendron, its leaves faded but dust-free. No one had been allowed to sit on the cream-colored upholstery with embroidered swirls of flowering vines. The living room was used exclusively for holidays: New Year's Eve, Easter, Thanksgiving, and

Christmas. But in the past few years, the family had spent those calendar milestones at Olivia's house. Decades ago, wonderful family meals graced the pecan-wood dining table, with its six high-back chairs and plush cushions of tangerine velvet. Patterns of reverse-napped *V*s fanned the carpet throughout both rooms. Mom vacuumed yesterday. She was alive yesterday.

Grief would be a companion soon enough, just as for Adam. Olivia's only defense against the surreal centered on two tasks: retrieve the necessary insurance paperwork from the safe and call the funeral home. She followed Danny into the kitchen.

"Why don't you go ahead and pack some things while I go through the safe," she urged.

"I will, but I'm hungry. I didn't eat my sandwich." Danny's voice sounded as if an overnight stay in the hospital explained Mom's absence.

Olivia circled the kitchen: all white cabinets and appliances, tile counters spanking clean. A splash of color popped from a ceramic bowl filled with ripe tomatoes, fresh basil, and a fist full of rosemary picked from the planter barrels on the back deck, picked for a meal that hadn't been prepared.

"I'll take the sheets off her bed and start a load of wash," Lauren offered and disappeared down the hall to their mother's bedroom. The Dushane response to any emotional crisis was to change the sheets, as if linens absorbed bad juju.

"Good idea." Olivia followed Lauren and stopped her in front of the linen closet. "Get all the prescriptions out of the cabinet in Mom's bathroom," she whispered. "They shouldn't be in the house. The police station has a drop-off for safe disposal." Lauren nodded in agreement, unable to speak as Olivia squeezed her arm.

Olivia returned to the kitchen. Danny pulled one of many packages of bacon from the freezer to thaw.

"Can I stay in the house?" Danny raised her eyes, anticipating the answer she didn't want to receive.

"Everything—which isn't much—is split three ways. Nonnegotiable," Olivia declared. "You can't afford to pay the mortgage and buy Lauren and me out. Mom left something but not enough for you to not work."

Danny opened her mouth in shock. "You're kicking me out?"

"Not quite yet. One person doesn't need a three-bedroom house. And this house now belongs to the three of us."

"You have a three-bedroom house."

Olivia hesitated. "Intended for two people."

"I'm sorry. I didn't mean it that way."

"No offense taken, Danny." Olivia's expression softened. Danny turned and took a tomato from the bowl. She sliced it, slowly and carefully, with a serrated knife.

The white plastic bag, printed with the St. Margaret's Hospital logo, sat unattended on the counter. While Olivia dreaded the process of going through its contents, the most personal of Mom's effects required careful attention. She pulled the jewelry from the inner pocket of her mother's purse. Three of Mom's most beautiful pieces.

"Lauren? C'mere," she called out. Danny abandoned the tomato and wiped her hands with a bright white towel.

"What?" Lauren emerged into the kitchen with a bundle of sheets in her arms and opened the louvered doors next to the pantry, behind which were the washer and dryer. As she stuffed the linens into the machine, Lauren turned.

"Lauren. Danny. There's no sense in putting these away, or taking the chance of them getting lost. Three pieces, three sisters—who wants what?"

Lauren's face fell. "Do we have to do this now?"

"Better now than later." Olivia held out her hand. "Pick. You're the oldest."

"Thanks for the reminder, Liv. I'm never getting married again, so I'll take the watch." The weighty gold glinted as Lauren clipped the Rolex around her left wrist. "Don't you think it's weird that Mom wore this to the hospital? She never wore this watch because she said it was too valuable." Lauren rocked her arm. "Not even wound—says nine o'clock."

"Rolexes are self-winding. Keep moving, and it'll start up again. But you're right—I only ever saw her wear that cheap Timex." Olivia sighed. "Do you think she knew she wasn't coming home and wanted to show it off?" Not waiting for an answer to her answerless question, Olivia picked the simple one-carat solitaire ring and complementary thick gold band from the tissue. "Here, Danny. I'm not getting married again, either, but you should." *To Ryan,* she finished silently. "I'll keep the necklace Adam and I gave her."

Danny remained quiet as she slipped the band and solitaire on the ring finger of her left hand. Regret filled her expression as she admired the flash of a missed opportunity. Olivia clasped the serpentine gold chain, from which hung a mounted round amethyst, around her neck. She and Adam had given Ellen the necklace for her birthday, years ago. The birthstone of a life now completed.

The wallet contained their mother's laminated identification, credit, Medicare, and social security cards. Instead of cash, the bill compartment was packed with coupons. She pawed through the kitchen junk drawer for a rubber band. Fifty or so were banded in a clump, aside balls of remnant thread, an eyeglass repair kit, and a film canister of tiny screws; their mother did have the raccoon-like saving habits of a World War II baby.

"Count on Mom to have what you need in all this crap," Olivia said, rearranging the drawer's contents. As she snapped a band around the cards, the ID drew her gaze.

The picture on the Oregon Identification Card showed Ellen smiling with pride, as if she'd been awarded with an identity. Staring back at Olivia was the face of a woman before she'd weathered the loss of her husband and endured the pain of a quadruple heart by-pass, colon cancer surgery, intestinal blockages, and pins being inserted into her fragile ankle bones, eroded from osteoporosis. Also before she'd lost two sons-in-law. The ID wasn't a real driver's license, because Mom had never learned to drive. Ellen didn't have even that minimal level of independence. She'd insisted the DMV take multiple shots to get the picture right. A nuisance chore for most people meant the world to her. Olivia glanced at Danny, her mother's spitting image, only forty-five years younger.

"Never learning to drive is so odd. Not when we were growing up but—" Olivia shook her head.

Lauren started to laugh. "That's why she liked to ride in the motorized scooter at the grocery store. She pretended to drive."

Danny cracked a smile, her first of the day. "Yeah, going forward was one thing, but you should've seen her try to back up. Mortifying. She took out a whole display of Lucky Charms once at Walmart."

The three of them managed no more than sad smiles. Lauren tipped a capful of detergent into the washer. Danny tossed the package of bacon into the microwave to speed up the thawing process.

Olivia pulled the current bills and checkbook from the cabinet over the coffeepot. An inch of yesterday's cold brew sat in the carafe. Ellen drank coffee all day long and well into the evening. Olivia set the envelopes next to her purse on the counter and headed down the hall to her mother's bedroom. Danny clanked a pan on the stove.

Behind the mirrored sliding doors, the three-foot-high safe sat on the floor of Ellen's closet. Olivia never violated this private parental space, and unlocking its door remained a violation today. The key peeked over the edge of the closet's top shelf. The combination, printed on a small tag, tied to the key with kitchen twine, gave her pause. The washer in the laundry room started to fill; the water ran from the kitchen tap.

Sitting crossed-legged in front of the steel case of private markers in her mother's life, Olivia opened the safe. She reached inside, pulled out a stack of documents, and thumbed through them. All in order: the will, car title, house papers, bank accounts, life insurance, and their father's death certificate. The list of calls she needed to make whirled in her mind as she set the pile aside. The Chock Full o' Nuts coffee can, filled to the brim with silver dollars sat in front of her. One of those shiny coins had been placed under her pillow for each lost tooth. The ritual launched a thrilling initiation into little-girlhood. Fifty years later, Olivia's unspent collection sat tucked away in her own closet. She hauled the can from the safe and set it on the floor next to Mom's rubber-soled fuzzy slippers. A small box contained her father's wallet, wedding band, and Masonic ring. In a recess way in the back, the last item was a thick manila envelope. She slid the package forward.

"I'm making some BLTs," Danny called out from the kitchen "Ten minute warning."

"Okay . . . " Olivia answered, her eyes trained on the tattered packet.

The envelope was old. The corners had separated from deterioration and its contents were labeled in frilly penciled script—her mother's distinctive style: Indigo to Black *by Ellen Dushane.*

What the hell?

Olivia's concentration faltered when Lauren charged into the bedroom. She brushed past Olivia and continued into their mother's bathroom.

"Find everything you need, Liv?" Lauren asked, her voice echoing off the pale green tile. The metal door on the medicine cabinet squeaked open.

"Yep . . . " Olivia's heart hammered. The mother-of-pearl buttons on her blouse visibly pulsed in rhythm.

Pills rattled like maracas as Lauren collected medicine bottles. "Jesus, she takes a lot of crap. I can't even pronounce half this stuff. Do doctors check what other doctors prescribe?"

The present tense of Lauren's words stabbed at the tightness in Olivia's chest. The aroma of bacon floated down the hall and crept into bedroom. She hoped the savory scent wasn't a sign of a stroke. "I think they do."

A plastic bag crinkled as Lauren rushed from the bedroom with the pills in hand. A minute or so later, Olivia heard the dryer door open and close—Lauren likely emptying it of the last load Mom had run.

Olivia lifted the flap on the envelope. The brittle glue dusted her black slacks as she slid out an inch-and-a-half banded stack of yellowed onionskin paper. Thick rubber bands, petrified with age, fell away with exhaustion. The amethyst around her neck swung over the cover page like a pendulum: Indigo to Black *by Ellen Dushane.*

A manuscript.

The sound of the hall closet door opening jumped her back to reality. Olivia tucked the manuscript under the legal papers, fighting the urge to flee her sisters and this house to read. If her mother had written a book, she wanted to be the first to read the story. Something private between her and Mom. As Olivia came out from the bedroom, she ran into Lauren's rump sticking out of the hall closet.

"What are you doing?" she asked.

"Look at this, Liv." Lauren's voice sounded muffled by the stacks of cotton linens. "I found the typewriter." With a grunt, she emerged from the closet with a manual typewriter. The insignia on the front of the gunmetal-gray casing was the word *Royal.* The keys were an unusual shade of hunter green. "I haven't seen this since I was a kid. Mom ignored me while she clacked away on it."

Olivia shifted, self-conscious. "I don't remember her typing."

"Mom never wrote after you came along. I remember a hellacious fight with Dad about what she was writing." Lauren dipped her head at the typewriter. "She used to swear like a sailor because the *L* key stuck. I'm keeping this."

"Did she ever tell you what she wrote?"

"No. Mom said she burned the manuscript. You know how she set her jaw when a subject was closed."

"Oh, I got the jaw too. What do you want that old thing for?"

"I love the sound. Plus, this is something personal between Mom and me."

Olivia debated whether she should mention the manuscript she'd found, but something stopped her. She, too, wanted a private and personal memento of her mother's. "I need to call the funeral home and set up a time for the three of us to go over the details. Can you take a few days off work so we can sort this out?"

"Yeah, I think so. I'll call the office."

"Danny! Get those BLTs ready," Olivia called out. "We'll all go back to my house. I need to feed Freesia."

"I'm putting this in the car. I can't wait to listen to the *clickety-clack*." A smile erupted on Lauren's face. She even batted her eyes.

Olivia glanced at the manila envelope under the pile of papers. Her stomach rolled. Something deep in its pit released a warning: the *clickety-clack* of that typewriter might become a runaway train.

Chapter 8

Ryan's New Assignment

The first few hours of monitoring Griffin's house had been uneventful. Not everyone liked having a cop parked in their neighborhood during the day, as if his presence signaled brewing trouble. But despite the deep scar on his left cheek, Ryan had one of those faces people trusted: penetrating blue eyes, dark wavy hair, and a smile that lit up his serious expression when he chose to dish one out. Ryan didn't get bored with the two-hour breaks of calm and quiet: mothers walking with strollers, bikes gliding by, and squirrels giving chase around tree trunks. Better than his usual.

At forty-five, Ryan was the oldest on his squad to never have been married. His colleagues had urged him to marry Danielle, whom they all liked. One of the female officers even pointed out his smattering of gray—how "time's a-wastin'." So they had been stunned when the relationship fell apart after the traffic incident. Ryan rubbed the thick scar on his left cheek. It served as a reminder of how dangerous his profession could be. All the talk about guns be damned; knives were just as menacing.

Some labeled Danny shallow and selfish, citing his disfigurement as the catalyst for her flight. But Ryan knew what lurked behind her rash break-off of the engagement: fear. She loved too much . . . felt too much. She couldn't see beyond the worst-case scenario. And her mother, Ellen, didn't help matters by shielding her.

Now he had an unobstructed line of sight to R. D.'s driveway—and to Danielle's sister's house. These houses from the twenties had their own distinctive style: Olivia's was a quaint Tudor with a sunburst pattern in the front windows; R.D.'s was smaller, with severe roof pitches.

R. D. knew he was watching; Olivia of course didn't. Ryan hadn't called to her when he saw her come home around lunchtime appearing stressed. Same Olivia: her shoes matched her outfit, and her Lexus was sparkling clean. He wanted to approach her, but she'd want to know why he was there, and he couldn't tell her about her neighbor. Besides, she appeared really frazzled, so much so that she didn't seem to notice the cruiser. Half an hour later, Lauren had arrived in her old beater with her wine box in hand. He imagined Olivia was still bitching about the dent in her garage door. Some things hadn't changed. But no Danny.

Now, Ryan straightened when Griffin lumbered down the front steps with his dog. The two of them approached the cruiser.

"You Officer Eason?"

"The one," he confirmed. "I'll be here for a few days, keeping an eye out."

"Wanted you to meet Pogo. He's my poodle." The dog jumped to put his paws on the edge of the window. Ryan ruffled the top of the dog's head.

"Did I tell ya I'm going in the hospital on Tuesday?"

"You told me when we talked on the phone."

"Give you a day away from watching me. Pogo here's not going to be happy, though. Neighbor's taking care-a him."

"Which neighbor?" Ryan asked. "Olivia Novak?"

R. D. pointed next door. "Yeah, the writer. Nice lady."

"I know her."

"We're going for the last walk of the day. Only down the street. We'll stay in sight."

"I'll take off when you both come back."

The dog walked Griffin, really. With one eye on that comical progress, Ryan also studied the case file on Adam's accident. On McLoughlin Avenue, Adam had been turning left in his yellow Volkswagen beetle from the center turn lane. Per the one witness, who sat at a window table in the Burgerama, a white Suburban pulled out from the side street in front of Adam. *Bang!* The Suburban T-boned Adam's car on the driver's side. Killed him upon impact. A quiet Sunday evening; not many people around. The witness said the Suburban had been driven by a young girl with long brown hair. Didn't get a license plate. An exhaustive search of the surrounding neighborhoods turned up nothing. A few possibilities emerged from running the description through the DMV, but they'd led nowhere.

The hardest phase of the investigation had been slogging on for two years: visits to body shops in the area, in widening concentric circles, to review the books for work done on a white Suburban. The notes indicated most were honest, but some were cagey about the documentation: make, year, color, and license plate. Not all body shops complied.

Tomorrow, he'd tackle the list where McClosky, the last officer to work the case, left off. McClosky was a good guy, but with over fifty-two hundred hit-and-runs each year to investigate, time was the enemy, and most of the cases lost that battle, unless a tip renewed media attention. On-air interest in Adam Novak's case had waned long ago without a suspect in cuffs to parade in front of the cameras.

Ryan checked the long printout of the more than two hundred body shops. McClosky had stopped at Rick's Auto Body, number eight-seven. Ryan skipped past the big chains to the independent shops on the list. Number one-forty-two: Bud's Crash 'n Dash in Oregon City. He tapped the paper. This shop was about twenty minutes away. Might as well be called Bud's Hit 'n Run. He circled two others: Lou's Ram and Jam and Urgent Car Care, both on the way to Oregon City.

Ryan glanced at his watch: five o'clock. Time to call it a night. "Okay, you guys. Make me a lucky man tomorrow." Saturday was a busy day for body shops.

R. D. returned with his dog and a plastic grocery bag swinging with waste. The old man gave Ryan a wave as he disappeared into his house. He returned the gesture with a thumbs-up. Shifting his gaze, Ryan spotted Olivia's car turning into her driveway.

Chapter 9

The "I Love You" Claws Need a Trim

Olivia pulled into her garage at five o'clock on Friday evening. Lauren and Danny promised to be twenty minutes behind her after they finished drying Mom's sheets, but anticipating Danny's need to pack a suitcase, Olivia pressed for her need to get back to the house. Plus, she wanted a few moments of privacy to put away the manuscript.

Four hours since her mother died. Olivia gathered up the folders and the manuscript from the passenger seat. She paused from closing the garage door and stepped to the driveway. A police cruiser sat across the street. Her stomach jumped. Somehow, parked cruisers signified trouble, as if waiting to deliver bad news. She shaded her eyes and studied the shadow inside the car. The officer's profile appeared to be familiar—too familiar.

Olivia quickened her steps toward the car. "Ryan?"

"Hey, Liv." Ryan appeared to have aged more than the nearly three years since Adam's funeral, although the deep scar on his cheek had softened. When she'd last seen him, the stitches had only just been removed. Even though he wore sunglasses now, Olivia remembered the arresting blue eyes: they took people in well before suspects were read their Miranda rights.

"I got permission to work Adam's case," he said, hanging his left elbow over the window frame. He gave his upper lip an uncomfortable scratch. "And I'll be in the area for the next couple of weeks or so. Unrelated matter."

"Thank you," she said and set her hand on his sleeve.

"I haven't started yet, but I pulled all the records to review."

"This has been a helluva day. Mom died this afternoon."

Ryan raised his dark-shaded gaze to her, reflecting her drawn face in the lenses. "I'm so sorry. I liked Ellen a lot." Ryan swallowed and turned to the windshield. "How's Danny taking it?"

"Lauren and I are going to find out, aren't we? On top of everything, I have to babysit my neighbor's crazy dog."

Ryan shifted in his seat and turned back to her. "Which neighbor?"

Olivia detected an instant change in his demeanor, as if he was testing her with the question. Uncomfortable. She pointed to the small house next door. "Ardy. Sweet old guy. He's going into the hospital on Tuesday for some minor procedure on his legs. Only an overnight, but the timing couldn't be worse."

Odd, but Ryan didn't respond with further inquiry.

"Danny's on her way over with Lauren," Olivia continued, trying to monitor his expression behind his sunglasses. "They'll be here in a few minutes. You want to come inside?"

As if sensing her thoughts, Ryan adjusted his glasses. "No, I'm on duty. I have a lot of catching up to do on Adam's case." He turned the ignition on the cruiser, a signal the conversation was over. She gave up on the niceties.

"This is so stupid, Ryan. You and Danny need to fix this between you."

"I'm not her mommy. She's forty-five years old."

"Mom's gone," she muttered, more to herself than to Ryan.

"Good to see you, Liv. I promise I'll do what I can for Adam. Sorry about Ellen."

With her hand suspended in a frozen wave, Olivia's gaze tailed the cruiser as it disappeared from view. She'd been so sure Ryan and Danny's relationship was fixable. Now she wasn't.

~ · ~ · ~

At five fifteen, Freesia waited in the entryway and gave Olivia a scolding scowl. The cat turned and marched to the kitchen, miffed that she'd been cheated out of a normal day of uninterrupted tickling and treats. Olivia set her purse, the papers, and the manuscript on the library table by the stairs in the entryway.

"C'mere, baby." She picked up the cat and nuzzled the side of her soft face. Freesia started to purr, rubbing against Olivia's chin in return. "Mommy needs a hug."

After feeding Freesia, Olivia slipped the tattered manila envelope from the stack and dashed up the stairs to her bedroom. No need to prompt questions or cause a stir with her sisters. Resisting the temptation to flop on the bed and start reading, she set the manuscript beneath her nightstand. Her mother's abandoned words would be a gift saved for tonight, a start of the inevitable process of letting go. Not yet.

At six thirty, the sound of two car doors quickened her steps to the kitchen. Her sisters were supposed to be twenty minutes behind her but ended up being over an hour. No doubt Danny puttered with indecision over what clothes to pack while Lauren huffed and puffed. Olivia filled a blue plastic tumbler with ice and pulled two wine glasses from the cabinet—the tumbler for Lauren and the goblets for her and Danny. She uncorked a bottle of Merlot as the front door opened.

"I'm in the kitchen," she called out.

Danny's steps pounded straight up the stairs to one of the two guest rooms. Lauren emerged through the doorway, her expression grim.

"She doing okay?" Olivia asked, trying to keep her voice low.

"No, not any better than I am." Lauren grasped the iced tumbler on the counter like a safety handle and opened the refrigerator door.

The nozzle on her box of white zinfandel gurgled as she released the pink juice to the brim of the glass. She took a large swallow and announced, "Can you believe we're goddamned orphans?"

"Widows and orphans . . . I wish I could uncheck at least one of those status boxes." Olivia splashed wine into her goblet. "Can I uncheck this day too?"

"This sucks." Lauren scooted out a chair at the island. "I can't wrap my head around it. Less than six hours ago I was bitching about having to wait around at the hospital. I shouldn't have had that cigarette in the parking lot."

"I shouldn't have stayed at the signing to dish out books. I put my readers ahead of Mom. And before I left this morning . . . Mom was already in the hospital while I was stalking a white Suburban. Boy, had I known." Olivia gulped and wished she could take back her last words. The admission just slipped out. Well, someone besides Mom had to know. Full steam ahead.

Lauren raised her eyes. "What?"

Stepping to her purse hanging from the back of Lauren's chair, Olivia pulled out the black journal and placed it on the counter in front of her sister. "Now let's talk about guilt." She returned to her wine goblet and took a sip of solace. She monitored Lauren's expression. "I should have been with Mom and not doing that."

Lauren opened the journal. As she flipped the pages, she studied each entry in silence and closed the notebook. She stared at the worn cover. "Liv . . . you need help."

"Damn straight I need help. That's why I called Ryan to work on Adam's case."

"That's not the kind of help I'm referring to. Did Mom know that you did this?"

"The only one who knew, except for the police. Mom would call me when she spotted a white Suburban to give me the license plate number. Some of those entries are from information she gave me, but most are pretty much a product of my own dysfunction."

"Liv . . . no. You have to let this go."

"I can't. Somebody has to do time for what happened."

Danny rounded the corner to the kitchen, her face drawn. "Who's going to do time?"

Lauren slipped the journal back into Olivia's purse.

Olivia glanced at her to keep quiet. "Coming up on three years since Adam's accident. I'm pushing." She didn't want Danny to get the wrong idea about her contact with Ryan. If he came up with a lead, Danny would find out soon enough.

"What am I going to do now?" Danny's lip started to tremble. "My whole life was wrapped up in Mom."

"Here. Have a glass of wine." Olivia handed her a goblet. "This hasn't hit me yet, either."

"I can't believe Mom's gone." Lauren shook her head.

"I feel so alone," Danny added.

Olivia lifted her gaze. "I've been alone."

The counter chair scraped as Lauren stood and stomped to the refrigerator. "And I'm not?" A cascade of fresh ice cubes dropped as she jammed her glass against the lever.

"Slow down, Lauren." Olivia threw her a warning look.

"I haven't had much. It's mostly ice."

"No, I mean we're not in a competition about who's more alone."

Lauren's shoulders dropped, regretting her outburst. "I'm putting on a muumuu. I took one from Mom's closet. If I'm going to be miserable, I might as well be comfortable." She trudged toward the entryway and up the stairs.

After topping off Danny's glass, Olivia refilled her own. The wine circulated in her veins like warm ink. Alone with her younger sister, she took the opportunity to introduce the subject of Danny's future.

"You're free to do whatever you want," Olivia said.

"I can't see past this morning. I should have called the ambulance. I should *not* have listened to Mom."

"You know what? Mom's biggest fear was ending up incapacitated and on life support. She *knew*, Danny. She went in the safe and put on her Rolex to go to the hospital. People, like all animals, have instincts when facing their own death. And while Mom had her wits, she was calling the shots. Her death is not your fault."

"Thanks, Liv."

"Danny . . . you have a whole future ahead of you. You're only forty-five."

"Doing what?"

The bright light was Danny's love of animals. On more than one occasion, Olivia had urged her to cultivate her talent as a pet whisperer. Animals, of all kinds, trusted her.

"Do something with animals. And . . . " Olivia hesitated, rehearsing her next words, "maybe open the door to reconnect with Ryan."

Danny's brown eyes turned glassy with tears. "He almost died, Liv." She grabbed a napkin from the holder on the counter. "He risked his life every single *day*, which means he risked mine, too, if we were together."

"Life is a risk. We never know what can happen from one day to the next. My situation is certainly a testament to that. And Ryan didn't die. Not even close."

"But . . . I could end up a widow like you."

The words smacked of an insult. She doubted Danny appreciated how they came across. The wine would talk if she opened her mouth—one of the not-so-good Dushane habits—but Olivia couldn't leave the comment alone. "I didn't want to end up like me either."

"No—I mean—" Danny stopped as Lauren came back into the kitchen.

Lauren had a look, the stewing one when her upper lip stiffened. She took a sip from her sweating glass and planted her hand on her hip. "Mom had a different way of saying 'I love you' to each of us."

Like a slingshot, Olivia glanced at Danny. Each of them was well aware of that particular trait of their mother's. The subtle variation in the sentiment's delivery defined the sisters' relationships—with her and with each other.

"Don't start," Olivia warned. "Going off doesn't change anything."

"No! I think I have a right to go off—because I *can*." Lauren took a long pull of her wine. "Once—just *once*—I wanted an 'I love you' without a slap attached." Turning in a circle, the ice bumped in her glass. "'How do I look, Mom?' And she'd say, 'I love you, honey, *but* why don't you let me give you some of my clothes before I lost weight.' *That's* what I got."

"Not true!" Danny countered.

"Yes, it is," Olivia muttered under her breath. "I got my own, with expectations attached. Mine were qualified with instructions: 'I love you, but don't forget to do this; don't forget to do that.'"

Lauren continued her hay ride, zeroing in on Danny. "Yours were always unqualified, Danielle. The only thing Mom said about you was 'Isn't she beautiful?' and, 'The poor girl, she's trying to do too much."

"She didn't . . . " Danny argued. "You're both full of crap."

"The hell we are! You got a get-out-of-jail-free card for everything you did."

"Okay. Okay. We're grown adults!" Olivia held up her hands, but Lauren kept going.

"Do you remember when Mom sent me a box of cast-offs after she cleaned out the pantry, thinking she was doing me a favor? All the food was *expired*: open boxes of stale crackers, cereal, and cornmeal with dead weevils. Even the canned crap was past date. Tell me *that's* an 'I love you.'"

"Why are you doing this, Lauren?" Danny asked. "Of course she loved you—both of you. I had to hear about it every day while I was driving her to the doctor's office, the pharmacy, the grocery store, and the damned doughnut shop. She'd go on and on about Olivia being interviewed and you doing so well at the real estate company after Mark died. I've done nothing for her to be proud of."

"Except be Danielle," Lauren added.

"I put my life on hold to care of her." Danny rubbed her forehead.

Lauren eyed her like an eagle. Weakened prey. "C'mon, Danny. The other way around, don't you think? Mom's goal in life was to take care of *you.*"

"Enough!" Olivia blistered. "Look at us—three Pitiful Paulines—whining about their mother, and she hasn't even been dead for twenty-four hours. Mom didn't want this."

Lauren's armor crumbled as she covered her face with her hands. "I just wanted to tell Mom I loved her before she died."

Behind the run of bluster lurked the real Lauren, the sensitive one. Her tirade had led to its ultimate destination: Lauren wanted to be by Mom's bedside, not being assaulted with the news in a parking garage. One last connection was all she'd wanted. Olivia shared her guilt. She held out her arms to Lauren and nodded for Danny to do the same. Defeated, Lauren relented to their hug, then sniffed and raised her tired eyes to Olivia.

"Now what? You're in charge." Lauren swallowed hard. The responsibility their father had designated to Olivia, years ago, stuck in Lauren's craw. Danny's too.

"Why didn't Mom and Dad make me the executrix?" Danny asked. "I took care of Dad in his final year . . . and Mom for the past three."

Olivia sighed. "You think having to wrap up an estate is some big, fat reward or something?"

"Don't say fat," Lauren muttered.

"We can't forget that Mom had a really good sense of humor," Danny said. "She loved the ridiculous. She would want us to laugh about the crazy stuff."

"And Mom did some crazy stuff."

Olivia took a breath. "We're all going down to meet with Fred Willoughby at the funeral home on Monday morning. We need to make arrangements and plan Mom's service. I made the appointment for ten o'clock. We're doing this *together*." She held up her goblet. "But right now we're going to toast to Ellen Dushane. She is, was, and always will be our mom."

Lauren and Danny raised theirs and took a drink.

~ · ~ · ~

Olivia gave the countertops a final swipe with a sponge at nine o'clock and set the timer on the coffeepot for seven in the morning. She changed the setting to eight when she assessed the manuscript's almost three hundred pages. Then she turned off the timer altogether when she remembered that Lauren was an early riser. To the accompaniment of her nightly promise to Adam, she locked the front door and flipped off the porch light. The house rested in emotional exhaustion.

Every bedroom was full: Lauren snoring in one guest room, Danny sleeping soundly in the other. Olivia climbed the stairs to her own room, an emptiness rising with every step. Tomorrow would be the first full day in a world without Mom. The private pages of her mother's manuscript would be like a hug to keep her company.

Olivia had redecorated her bedroom after Adam's death. As a form of therapy, she made the room hers alone. A Mackintosh pattern of swirling red tulips and green vines graced the thick tapestry of the drapes and continued to the quilted bedspread. Cotton velvet pillows in a hue of lush sage invited romance. But no romance lurked here. Freesia liked to back up in them as she waited for Olivia to come to bed. As Olivia expected, the cat raised her head in anticipation of being moved, as if making the concession to share required negotiation.

Three identifying scents lingered in her blouse from embracing her sisters, a blend of sibling perfumes that created something unique and new: her own sweet citrus, Lauren's fresh ginger, and Danny's complex floral mixture of hyacinth and lily. Olivia inhaled the complex aroma to remember it and slipped an oversize T-shirt over her head.

After washing her face and brushing her teeth, Olivia studied her features in the mirror. A webbing of pink rimmed her brown eyes. The sag of her upper lids was an unwelcome new addition to the summer of aging. Without makeup, every emotional blow of her fifty-five years showed like mile markers on a highway. The lack of layers and drawn lines between her and the world nudged her over the edge to old age. *At what point does makeup look ridiculous on a woman, as if advertising that she's trying too hard?* Olivia rummaged in the drawer by the sink for something emollient and expensive, but had to settle for a sample tube of emollient and cheap. At this point, vanity didn't matter. She switched off the bathroom light so she didn't have to face her face.

Olivia pulled out a pad of paper and a pen from the nightstand to make notes. She didn't dare deface the original manuscript with comments. Preparation for reading a manuscript required taking inventory: cheater glasses, sticky tabs (in a variety of colors), pencil, notepad, and an aspirin to get in front of the headache from tense neck muscles. She positioned the box of tissues within arm's length, in anticipation of a good cry.

Before she climbed into bed, Olivia retrieved the manuscript from beneath her nightstand. Freesia stretched to stake her claim of feline real estate.

The cover page read, *Indigo to Black* by Ellen Dushane. She pictured the words on a book spine. Not many books started with the letter *I*.

"Oh, Mom. Why did you keep this a secret?" Her throat swelled tight. "All those years." The extra moisturizer stung her eyes with clouded vision. She snatched a tissue from the box. "Damn, Mom, I haven't even read the first page."

Freesia curled up at her side and tucked her head under, blue eyes sparkling as the brittle paper crinkled. Olivia raked the soft spot under Freesia's chin and turned to page one. The cat purred . . . Olivia wanted to.

Chapter 10

Mom's Words

On Saturday morning, the aroma of coffee unstuck Olivia's eyes. She squinted to get her bearings. The bedroom was aglow in warm light. She'd never turned off the lamp. The last page of the manuscript still floated in her hand, released from a fifty-year sentence in the prison of a safe. When had she fallen asleep? An hour ago? Two?

Olivia's limbs refused to move; only her gaze scanned the ceiling of her bedroom. How would Mom have described the architectural details of the curved crown molding? The patterns in the plaster? Soft-green paint? No. Her mother would have described the color as that of a fern after a rain, the shafts of diffused light like those plunging through an umbrella of soaring cedars. The fragrance of her sachet in the closet: spicy Spanish lavender with a delicate finish of sweet peonies.

Indigo to Black had been a coming-of-age novel mixed with a young adult thriller. Back when her mother wrote this book, the genre didn't even exist. Becky Haines, seventeen, fell in love at a summer camp in Vermont, sure of her future with this man of her dreams: tall, handsome, wanting to be a doctor. The hook was a promise to stay in touch, to meet again next summer on a certain day at a specific time. The result was a torturous fall, winter, and spring of anticipation, letters, and mutual vows. And at the most important moment of her young life, her beau didn't show. Becky sat alone on the shore, waiting as the water of Indigo Lake lapped at her freshly polished toes, a color of rose applied in vivid detail. The abandonment had turned her into Killer Becky, hunting her boyfriend down to make the slight right. And Becky, in the end, got away with the crime.

Not only did the story bowl Olivia over, it transformed her too. Her mother's prose was poetic, more literary than genre fiction. She recalled one of her favorite passages:

Becky's hand skimmed the water as the canoe glided over the still glass of the lake, creating a tension of ripples. Warmth at the water's surface turned cold as her fingertips penetrated the cool layer below, echoing how she felt in her own core—cold inside.

Olivia smoothed her hand over the sheets to replicate the touch. No Freesia to reach for. No grounding. The relentless imagery of every paragraph bathed her with that warm and cool lake water. She'd rooted for Becky, even though she got away with a crime. Flawed, determined, and sympathetic—a monumental and tricky achievement that the hero doubled as the antagonist. Inner demons settled the score, not sweet Becky.

Who was this woman—her mother—and what did she think about to write something like this? Olivia understood her from only one side, a child side. Mom had hopes and dreams too. Their relationship had been filled with competition, rebellion, and expectations. *Never good enough.* To break free of parental chains over the decades had been a goal. At this moment, though, Olivia longed to be bound in shackles if the sentence gave her the ability to talk with Ellen about this story as a fellow writer. Pure fictional fantasy? Autobiographical? Did this happen in real life? Olivia almost didn't want to know, but many of the details were real—too real.

Ellen Dushane's words would never have been published in the fifties. Girls only did good things in books in the fifties. They wore pearls and entertained, while choking on unhappiness in private. Did their father read this? Was this manuscript the source of the fight

Lauren witnessed as a child? If so, Ellen's attempt at being a novelist must have been silenced by their father. Or perhaps her female character proved to be too strong. But today? Readers cheered characters like Becky.

Olivia glanced at the alarm clock. Seven fifteen. A waft of cigarette smoke rode above the aroma of coffee. Lauren was up. And from the overtones of bitterness, the coffeepot had been steeping for a few hours.

Willing herself to move, Olivia gathered the pages in perfect order. She sunk back into the pillows with her mother's work pressed to her chest.

Mom's book needed an audience. Her agent needed a manuscript. And a helluva manuscript is what Karen would get.

~ · ~ · ~

Olivia grabbed the rail on the stairs for support, as if suffering from the gravitational pull of reentering Earth's atmosphere. The cartilage in her knees clicked with every heavy step. At least she'd clamped a clip in her hair to disguise the flat spot on the side of her head. She shuffled into the kitchen.

Lauren sat at the island, checking e-mail on her laptop. No Danny. She must still be asleep.

"How long have you been up?" Olivia asked in a scratchy voice. She reached for a mug in the cabinet above the pot. At least the brew was hot.

"Since five. You were snoring," Lauren said, distracted. "I heard you sucking those tulips off the drapes from down here. Even Freesia wanted to escape the noise. I fed her, by the way."

"You're her new best friend."

"You drink fancy coffee, not the two-buck jitter juice I buy."

"Three-buck jitter juice."

"You look like hell."

"Thanks. I feel like hell. I couldn't sleep, so I read most of the night."

"Anything good? I need a new book."

Olivia stared at her sister. *Sweetheart, you have no idea how much the book I just read will change your life.* She switched direction.

"Hmmm . . . you'll have to wait," she teased. "I can give you an advanced reader's copy of the new Greg Iles. That baby's eight hundred pages."

"I love ARCs. Finding typos is my specialty."

"Mom liked them too." Olivia blew out a breath. "She's good—was good—at panning for mistakes in mine. So are you."

"Hire me as your editor so I can retire, will ya? I don't want to go back to the grind. I'll sit my butt right here and edit while you feed me chapters." Lauren shook her forefinger at the stove as she lit a cigarette. "Turn the fan back on."

Olivia started the fan on the cooktop and pushed the ashtray in front of Lauren. She burned to tell her sister about Mom's book. Too soon. "We need to stop by Mom's bank, before they close at noon, to transfer the accounts into our names. The three of us are trustees."

"Then you'd better wake up Her Highness," Lauren scoffed. "I wish I had the chance to sleep late."

"You always get up early."

"Yeah . . . well." Lauren leaned over the countertop and blew smoke into the vent, smashing her boobs in her mother's zipped house dress.

"Tomorrow, I'll make lists. We'll go back to Mom's house and start sorting through stuff. After we go to the funeral home on Monday morning, I'll meet with Ted Beal at his office. Only a formality. Mom and Dad had everything buttoned up. Thank God."

"I hate lawyers. You go. You're the executrix."

"You and Danny can have lunch while I meet with Ted." Olivia took another sip of her coffee, eyeing Lauren as she blew into the cup. "Mom grew up in New Hampshire, but did she ever spend time in Vermont before she married Dad?"

"Yeah, she was a counselor at some swanky summer camp."

"Are you sure?"

"She told me when I visited colleges back East. She wanted me to go to UNH and talked me out of Boston University. Why?" Lauren tapped on her laptop, multi-tasking, as her cigarette smoke streamed from the ashtray. Olivia moved it closer to the vent.

"Oh . . . no reason." Olivia tried to keep her voice casual. "I was awake last night thinking of things we used to do. I loved spending summers in New Hampshire on Lake Winnipesaukee. They never took us to any other state, though."

"I did the same thing." Lauren closed her computer and met Olivia's gaze. "Remember when we used to camp, before Danny came along?"

"A lot of mosquito bites is what I remember." Olivia scratched the back of her neck. Her phobia of spiders in the tent forced her to sleep with one eye open.

"But fun. The lake was like bath water in the summer. I loved the old creaky hardware store in Wolfeboro. And the Yum Yum Shop . . . mmm-mmmm."

"I remember too." Olivia shifted, uncomfortable. In the book, the character of Becky had gone inside the hardware store and into the bakery too, every vivid detail coinciding with Olivia's childhood memories. Becky carried rat poison in an old bottle she'd snatched from her father's windowsill. Olivia recalled those same blue bubble-glass medicine bottles her grandfather kept by his kitchen window, one of the many treasures he found digging on his farmland.

"Remember all those old bottles Gramp had lined up in the window over the sink?" Olivia asked. "They were all bubbly and blue?"

Lauren shook her head. "I haven't thought about those in years."

"Shiny when the sun hit them. Lydia Pinkham's Elixir bottles."

"Yeahhhh . . . Lydia Pinkham's Elixir! That stuff was practically poison—almost pure alcohol."

Olivia choked on her coffee and set her mug in the sink. "Help yourself if you're hungry. I'll get ready now so we have plenty of hot water. Remember: the bank before noon."

~ · ~ · ~

At ten o'clock on Saturday morning, Ryan pulled the cruiser into Bud's Crash 'n Dash in downtown Oregon City, only twenty minutes away from Eastmoreland. The first two stops, Lou's Ram and Jam and Urgent Car Care, yielded no results. At least both businesses had kept decent sales books.

Typical body shop, except for the cars. Two high-end sedans filled the bays: one a silver Audi A6, the other a white BMW 535i, both newer models. Interesting. Why not use an authorized dealership? Bud must work cheap for customers who chose not to report damage to their insurance companies.

The garage reeked of oil and gasoline. With every step toward the bays, the stench grew stronger, making Ryan want to retreat. Two legs stuck out from beneath the Audi. A thin, older man appeared from behind the hood of the BMW; he was in his sixties, in a stained, short-sleeved blue jumpsuit. Spotting Ryan, the man approached, wiping a dipstick with a once-white rag. A scruffy mustache hid his upper lip. Ornate, Celtic-looking tattoos blanketed both forearms. Must have hurt. His eyes matched his outfit: dull blue. The whites, though, had a slight yellow cast. A drinker. Ryan figured the weakness might be gin. He couldn't detect a residual odor of alcohol. But then again, the fumes from oil and gas overwhelmed his senses.

"Bud around?" Ryan asked.

"You're talking to him."

"Officer Ryan Eason." He held Bud's gaze.

"What can I do you for?" Bud studied him.

"I'm investigating a hit-and-run. Happened on McLoughlin Avenue, shy of three years ago . . . in September. The man who was hit died. Manslaughter. A witness said a white Suburban fled the scene. Had damage to the front end. Was a car like that brought in here to be fixed?"

"Don't remember." Bud shook his head.

"You're supposed to track the license plates of all the cars you work on."

Silence. The man's eyes shifted.

"This is important, Bud," Ryan pressed. "Would have been a big ticket. Can you check your books?"

"Mmm . . . books? I think my books are in storage." A shifty expression crossed the man's face.

"You pay for storage?" Ryan chuckled, but games didn't fit his mood. "I find that hard to believe." He locked his gaze on the man's face. "White Suburban—nineties."

Recognition flashed in Bud's eyes. He'd struck a chord. Ryan's pulse quickened when expressions and gestures told a story. Bud might be a lot of things but a liar wasn't one of them. He'd talk.

Bud rubbed his stubbled chin, as if pondering how to spin a response. One of Bud's eyebrows stretched upward. "A lotta cars come through here."

"Think hard. A man was killed with a bumper you might have fixed." Ryan shut up and waited.

Bud broke his gaze and blew out a breath. Now, Ryan picked up the wake of last night's bender. "Books, you say?"

"Yeah, I want you to check your books."

"Killed, huh?"

"Don't want to be connected to a fatality, do you? Is that a cross in your tattoo, buried with all the other stuff on your arm?" Ryan pushed his chin toward the man's forearm.

Bud hesitated. "White Suburban?"

"Yeah. The victim had a wife—a pretty famous writer. If you didn't track the car in writing, I'm sure you remember the customer. I'm not after your business. I'm only interested in the white Suburban."

"C'mon inside." Bud set the rag and dipstick on a work table.

Ryan followed the man to the small office walled with hazy glass. Across three panes, hand-painted in red reverse letters was Bud's slogan: *Dings. Dents. Dash.* The laminate counter supported a cash register and a clear-plastic business card holder. Ryan plucked two from the stack and slipped them in his breast pocket. The numbered keys on the till showed stains from grimy fingers. The one, five, and nine appeared to be the most popular.

After pulling a worn black binder from beneath the counter, Bud flipped to a tab labeled 2011. Ryan figured maybe two out of four jobs were recorded. He studied the cuticles on Bud's forefinger, embedded with brown grease, as the man scanned the sales sheets and turned the pages. Bud's finger stopped on an entry toward the bottom of one of them. The tip left a brown smudge next to a name and phone number. He raised his eyes to Ryan.

"Asshole guy."

"Sorry?" Ryan leaned over the counter. His gaze moved between Bud's weathered face and the dog-eared binder.

"Asshole." Bud tapped the page. "Hounded me every day for a week. Said his daughter hit a tree. Looked more like the tree hit the car. Repeatedly. But, hey, I don't stick my nose where it don't belong. Smelled bad, though."

"Insurance?"

"Uh-uh. Didn't want his rates to go up. Paid cash."

"How much did you charge him?"

"Twenty-five hundred. Says right here." Bud pointed to the dollar amount, higher than the rest of the entries on the page.

Ryan let out an arcing whistle. "What'd you have to do?"

"New bumper. Grill. Hood. Headlights. Don't make Sububbas like them anymore. All steel."

"Big tree." Ryan craned his neck to read the description. "Name?"

"Jeff. He only gave me a number to call when the Bubba was ready."

"Give it to me." Ryan clicked the end of his pen.

Bud turned the book around and pointed.

Chapter 11

Death Is All in the Details

On Monday morning, quiet filled the Willoughby Funeral Home. Muffled by carpet, silk, and velveteen upholstery, the business sounds of death chugged along. The administrative office, adjacent to the family conference room, bustled with rustling paper and the clicking of a ten-key. Olivia swiveled in the cushy chair next to Danny at the conference table. She checked her watch—ten fifteen. Of course, they were late. After hauling herself out of bed at nine, Danny raced to get ready and then puttered. Lauren figured Danny wanted to avoid the next round of tasks, as if the responsibilities would magically go away. After Danny complained she couldn't find the right color of lipstick, Olivia had given up and waited in the car with Lauren.

Fred Willoughby entered into the conference room with a notepad, appearing rushed himself.

"Sorry we're a bit late, Fred," Olivia said, glancing at her younger sister. But she had to admit, Danny looked stunning with only mascara and the touch of mauve shine on her pouty lips. Good choice. At the other extreme, Lauren zoomed through getting ready in five minutes, and her shoulder-length chestnut hair was still wet and pulled back in a pilled scrunchie.

No doubt Lauren positioned herself across from Olivia in order to shoot gestures and grimaces, her targets including the decor. Willoughby Funeral Home sported every stereotype in the funeral industry: feminine colors, recorded music, boxes of tissues, and little cards on stands with sayings of comfort for the bereaved. The pale-pink walls were interrupted with cream stripes, like a dowager's garden porch where tea was served in flowered porcelain cups. The plush carpet, in an odd shade of grayish-brown that took on a lavender cast, clearly had been vacuumed before their arrival. As with most decorative patterns, Olivia tried to make out humorous images from the vacuum tracks to help ease the tension. But the most humorous image was behind Lauren's head: an expansive video monitor on the back wall displayed an endless loop of a babbling stream cascading over rocks. Transfixed, Olivia couldn't stop staring at the flowing video. As her gaze followed the whooshing water's path off the flat screen, she fought the urge to pee.

Fred Willoughby, the funeral home's owner, pulled out a chair and sat at the head of the table. As a family friend and their guide through the business of death, Fred handled the arrangements for their father, Mark, Adam, and now, their mother. A pillar of the community, Fred shepherded countless upstanding citizens through life's exit turnstile. His kind face held an expression of sincerity that encouraged loved ones to expound on the past glories of the departed. His full head of silver hair had been set in place by spray. He could not be ruffled.

But Fred patted on way too much Old Spice. The cologne tickled Olivia's nose. She reached for one of the three convenient boxes of tissues placed in the center of the table. Olivia gulped back a sneeze. Danny took one, too, and made origami with it, then held the point of a mangled triangle to the corner of one eye as she sniffed.

"I know. I know," Fred soothed and set one hand over Lauren's, the other over Olivia's. Lacking a third hand, he allowed his gaze to rest on Danny for a couple of breaths. "I'm so sorry for your loss, ladies. I have a warm spot for Ellen because I helped her through the death of your father."

"Thank you, Fred. We can't do this without you." Olivia narrowed her eyes at Lauren, who pursed her lips. *Stop it*, she mouthed. To Lauren, the whole process of death was part of a mob racket.

"All this nasty paperwork," he continued. "Leave these details to me. Your thoughts need to be with your mother. More important. Much more important."

Danny swallowed. "Excuse me," she said. "I need to get myself together."

"The restroom is right down the hall, honey." Fred's gaze followed Danny as she hurried out of the room. He turned with an expression of concern. "Is she okay? She was particularly close to Ellen. Quite close."

Olivia stifled a laugh when Lauren mouthed the likely true reason for Danny's departure: *the waterfall or Fred's cologne.*

"This is a big transition for her," Olivia covered, widening her eyes at Lauren.

"This shouldn't take too long." Fred continued, lining up several forms in a perfectly straight line. "I won't keep you any longer than I need to." He pulled one page forward and started to fill in the boxes. "Okay, here we go. Lauren Lyndale . . . Olivia Novak . . . and Danielle Dushane. You're all still Dushanes to me." Fred raised his eyes with a beaming smile. "The Dushane sisters! Sounds like a singing group to entertain the troops . . . 'Bei Mir Bist *Dushane*'."

Lauren rocked in her swivel chair. "Ohhh . . . yeah. We *roll* in perfect sisterly harmony, Fred. Don't we, Olivia?"

Olivia wrinkled her nose, but quickly pretended for Fred's benefit that she had an itch. "I think I have a lot of the answers you need here in this file," she said and opened a manila folder. "Mom was pretty organized. This wasn't unexpected. She had health problems for a while."

"Unlike Adam," Fred added, shaking his head. "A tough one for us at Willoughby too, Olivia. Any updates on the investigation?"

"No . . . not yet. I'm still hopeful, though."

Lauren's face registered surprise that Fred mentioned the subject of Adam. She mouthed, *Sorry*.

"A damn shame . . . a damn shame. I shouldn't have brought up the subject, I realize, but we've known your family for a long time."

Olivia glanced at Lauren, whose face went slack. She felt the need to support her sister. "The service for Mark was a grueling loss for Lauren, as well. She's had her share of healing to do too."

Fred nodded, acknowledging the slight. "Been two years for you, Lauren. Are you doing okay?"

"Keeping busy working," Lauren said and sighed. "I'll be working until Olivia is sitting here talking with you about me in your back room."

"Lauren, don't even go there." Olivia pulled out the Oregon identification and social security card from the folder. Last, she set the birth certificate in front of Fred. "First thing's first—Mom wanted to be cremated."

"Fine. Fine. We'll handle the arrangements. Ellen's body arrived last night. We're just waiting for your instructions."

The body in the back room doesn't define Mom, Olivia thought. From the expression on Lauren's face, she was thinking the same thing.

Danny came back into the room and sat, rolling her chair forward. Fred studied the birth certificate.

"You all right, Danny Girl?" Olivia said and set her hand on Danny's arm.

"I'm fine. Please say this gets easier."

"Olivia, it appears that February is Ellen's birth month," Fred continued, squinting, "but the day and year aren't clear."

"Oh, it's February 27, 1929," Olivia said with authority.

He handed her the creased and yellowed certificate. "Hmmm . . . I don't think so. Can you tell what those last two numbers are? We go by the date on the birth certificate."

The sisters exchanged looks before Olivia leaned forward.

She stared at the blurred scrawl, clumped with correction fluid. "February . . . Twenty-seven . . . Nineteen . . . thirty . . . *four*?"

"That doesn't sound right," Lauren interjected. "Mom changed the date to 1927 back in the eighties. She tried to make herself older so she qualified for senior discounts."

Olivia nodded and chuckled. "After she got her ID card, then Mom changed her birth certificate back to 1929."

"Not quite, guys." Danny shook her head. "After I moved in with her, I helped her change the year to 1934 to make her younger. She wanted to be seventy-nine."

"Pick a date, Fred." Olivia waved her hand, as if the decision were a normal procedure. "Use the one that matches her ID. Who *knows* what the real date is? Even when she was young, Mom told people she was a leap-year baby, which would make her—what?—twenty-something when she died?"

"Fine. Fine. We'll give it a go." Fred pressed his lips together to keep from smiling. "Quite a challenge when there's not one at all. What were you all thinking as far as a service?" He raised his eyes and searched their faces. "We're getting booked up, so I'll need to check the calendar."

"What do you two think?" Olivia asked, swiveling in her chair.

"Just us," Lauren replied. "Let's keep it private."

Silence circled the table on a breeze of air conditioning. "We need to invite Ted. He's been Mom and Dad's lawyer—and mine—for years. Olivia ran her finger along the swirly pattern in the wood. "Should we invite Ryan?"

The waterfall appeared to halt its flow.

Danny's face collapsed. "No. Too awkward. This is about Mom, and I don't think Ryan wants to be with me after what I—" She turned away, studying the plastic holder of note cards that had a spray of calla lilies in the upper left corner.

Hope did exist. Olivia assessed Danny's first sign of taking the blame for her plight.

"Small is quite tasteful. Intimate and personal," Fred said and turned his attention back to filling out the forms to escape the discomfort. "Your father was a Mason, and Ellen was Eastern Star. I'm sure the local Brothers would be happy to participate in the service as they did for your father."

Lauren adjusted her scrunchie. "Uhhh . . . I don't—"

"Yes!" Danny interjected and tapped the table. "Mom would want a bagpiper."

Lauren squinted in distaste, as if the instrument's distressed bellowing had started up in the next room.

"Everyone gets a say," Olivia assured, not wanting to get Danny upset. "Yes, Fred. Mom loved fanfare. But just one piper, please."

"Very good. Very good. I'll make the arrangements." Fred stood and glided to an accordion door. He folded back the panels—though they looked like wood, they clattered like plastic—revealing shelves of crematory urns in multiple styles to fit the personalities of prospective inhabitants, including dogs, cats, and birds.

"I've been dreading this part," Lauren muttered, her hands grasping the padded arms of the chair.

"You three pick something out while I run this paperwork and check the calendar. We can customize a stainless-steel one for you in a couple of days." Fred picked out the plain steel one, about eight inches high, and turned the urn as if displaying it on the Home Shopping Network. "Our etcher is a consummate artist. We can put anything you want on this."

When Fred left the room, Olivia drummed her fingernails on the conference table. "Let's take a look-see, shall we?"

The three of them stood and moved to the display. Several urns sported an American flag. Others showed cultural symbols from several different nationalities and hobbies. One was even in the shape of a golf club.

"Too bad Mom wasn't a veteran," Olivia said. "Military service seems most represented."

Lauren picked one from the top shelf and bounced it for heft. "She served Dad for sixty years. Counts in my book."

"We need to agree on a theme." But Olivia thought that the enormity of her mother's spirit wouldn't fit in any container.

"Let's do custom," Danny suggested. "Mom's not an off-the-rack kind of gal."

"Something upbeat," Lauren agreed, "to go with her sense of humor. Mom would be making fun of this whole process right now. Remember when she picked out Dad's urn? She wanted to put pictures of Ritz crackers and a jar of mayonnaise on it, laughing about his favorite snack."

"What did she love most?" Olivia waited as Lauren and Danny stared at her, their mother's favorite things scrolling behind their eyes. She picked up the stainless-steel urn with no decoration. Turning the heavy vessel in her hands, she said, "Okay . . . I say the garden. How about vines and flowers?"

"Not sure Mom's flowery. She loved bees, and maybe birds?" Lauren shrugged.

"Mom was allergic to bees," Danny countered, "and the birds stole our strawberries."

Olivia put her hand on her hip. "A favorite food then?"

"Jelly doughnuts!" Lauren blurted out and started to laugh.

"Noooo . . . I think bacon is a better choice," Danny said, studying the urn as though Lauren's suggestion were a serious one.

"BLTs!" Olivia announced, triumphant.

"We need tomatoes then," Lauren added, "and lettuce?"

"This is good. We can have the etcher put three pieces of bacon, three tomatoes, and a head of lettuce on this urn. Mom will have a never-ending BLT. All in favor, say aye."

"Aye!" they agreed in unison.

Fred stepped back into the room with his nose in an appointment book. "The service will need to take place this Thursday," he said, shaking his head. "Otherwise we'll have to wait until next month. The availability of the bagpiper is dictating the date. He's on vacation after Thursday. How's that sound?"

"Thursday's fine, Fred," Olivia said, nodding.

"E-mail me your write-up and a photo of Ellen. I'll create an online guest book. We'll be in luck. The new extra-large video monitor will be installed in the chapel by then. Ellen's service will be the first to benefit from the new screen."

Olivia wished her mother had written her own obituary and left the write-up in the safe. Olivia's words could never match Ellen's eloquence.

"We'll help you write the obit. Right, Danny?" Lauren said.

"Of course, I'll help." Danny waved her hand, still inspecting the urn.

Olivia anticipated the delivery of three obituaries, each for a different Ellen Dushane.

Chapter 12

The Lead

Ryan pulled the cruiser in front of R. D. Griffin's house at ten twenty on Monday morning. He called McClosky. He owed him an update, albeit a bittersweet one.

"When's the last time you talked with Olivia Novak?" Ryan asked when McClosky answered.

"I left her a message. She knows I'm not on the case anymore, but I intended to keep whittling away at the investigation on the side." McClosky sighed. "I had my teeth into that one like a steak. But damn, I haven't been able to go back to it. Do you know that Olivia calls me every time she sees a Suburban? Keeping up with her messages is a full-time job."

"She's a bit obsessive—okay, more than a bit—but I wish you had been allowed to work the case one more day, buddy."

"Why?" McClosky's voice was filled with frustration.

"I got a line on a guy who had work done on a white Suburban, right about the same time, at Bud's Crash 'n Dash in Oregon City."

"Good goin', Ryan."

"Might end up a bust."

"Hopefully." McClosky's voice turned serious. "I hope you nail him."

"Thanks, but we're not even close. Depends on what this guy says when I call him."

"If you need backup, have dispatch call me. I'll be there in a shot."

"You got it."

Ryan slipped the phone into his breast pocket. He turned and studied Griffin's house, but his gaze pulled to the right. Next door, Olivia's house appeared to be quiet, although her father's old blue Blazer sat behind Lauren's beat-up Focus. He should pay his respects.

Ryan's chest burned. He wanted to see Danny.

Rarely nervous in uniform, Ryan stiffened with tension the moment he followed the lead of the walkway to Olivia's house. He pressed the doorbell and listened to the long chime inside. No movement. He knocked. No shadow moved through the small windows at the top of the door. More relieved than he cared to admit, he returned to the cruiser.

Ryan flipped over Bud's business card and called the phone number for this Jeff guy. After leaving the body shop last night, Ryan traced the number's origin; the location came up as Cascade Bank. The odd sequence of the last four digits indicated a direct extension. Now, he woke up the laptop, mounted on a swing-arm on the dash as the number connected.

"Jeff Rovinski speaking," a man's voice announced.

"Yes, this is Officer Ryan Eason with the Portland Police Department." Ryan typed Jeff's name on the laptop. Several spellings came up. He chose the one that matched the location.

"Is Melissa okay?" The man's voice went into panic mode.

"Who's Melissa?" *Lives in Sellwood, no more than ten minutes away.*

"My daughter. Nothing's wrong, is there?"

"I'm sure she's fine, Mr. Rovinski. I'm calling in regards to an investigation." *Works as a loan officer at Cascade Bank . . . since 1998.*

Jeff blew out a breath of relief into the receiver. "Of course. How can I help you?"

"Do you own a white Suburban?"

"No."

"Did you ever own a white Suburban?"

A hesitation, a distinct hesitation. "A long time ago, but not recently."

"When was that?"

Another pause. *Innocently trying to remember or planning a lie?*

"About three—maybe four—years ago . . . I believe. How do I know you're a real police officer?"

"Excellent question, Mr. Rovinski. I'll come by the bank and show you my badge. I can be there in fifteen minutes."

Jeff hung up without a response. Ryan's adrenalin started to rush. Change of plan. He called R. D. Griffin's number.

"Hey, Officer Eason," R. D. answered.

"Will you be all right if I'm gone for an hour or two?"

"I should be okay. Won't leave the house."

"Call me if you need anything. You've got my cell number."

"Righto. Pogo's afternoon walk is around four."

"I should be back well before then, but if I get delayed I'll send a replacement."

~ · ~ · ~

Cascade Bank was a small local bank located in the retail area of Sellwood, a historic neighborhood of roundabouts, tall trees, and long-time residents who sat on their porches. As in many close-knit communities on the east side of the Willamette River, gentrification over the years had resulted in the opening of boutiques, quaint restaurants, and upscale markets with groceries stamped *organic* and *gluten-free.*

Ryan slowed the cruiser as he approached Jeff's home address. Small Craftsman bungalow. Tidy. Narrow driveway and crowded street. So there was one simple and not nefarious reason Jeff could have sold the Suburban. Parking an oversize hulk would be a challenge here. Ryan drove three more blocks and turned onto Tacoma Avenue, a lively retail street. Cascade Bank anchored the corner. At least the bank had four designated spaces for customers. He pulled the cruiser into one of them.

The turn-of-the-century brick building had been rehabbed, saved from the wrecking ball by petitions from vigilant locals, no doubt. Ryan applauded the tenacity required to preserve the past. He took a breath of hope and sauntered into the bank.

A bank employee hustled up to Ryan as he opened the glass front door. The man appeared to have been waiting for him. *Jeff.* Ryan studied his pale skin and freckles under a gelled cap of precision-cut, reddish-brown hair. His hazel eyes appeared wary, with the beginnings of crow's feet. Ryan estimated Jeff to be in his mid-forties. He had an honest face. Either Jeff was an award-winning actor or this was an exercise in futility.

"You Officer Eason?" the man asked, extending his hand.

"Yes. Jeff Rovinski?" Ryan assessed the man's grip. Firm. Ryan pulled out his identification. "I appreciate your asking, by the way. More people should."

"Let's go in here." Jeff smiled, shrugged at one of the tellers, and led Ryan across the lobby to his private office.

Ryan scanned the office. The surroundings were those of a man who earned about fifty grand a year, with the promise of a Christmas bonus. The generic furniture consisted of a clean teak-wood desk with an ergonomic rolling chair, a matching credenza, and two guest chairs upholstered in a blue pattern of the bank's ocean wave logo. Lining the top of the credenza were framed photos of a girl, from toddler to what appeared to be college age. He studied the face: long brown hair, hazel eyes, a bigger smile after the braces came off. Melissa. She had Jeff's features. Ryan's gaze stopped on the two most recent photos. She appeared to have acquired a scar on her lip, making her smile appear crooked. The flaw drew him closer. Like he did with his own scar, the young woman brandished a visual history on her face. The scar was most pronounced in the second to last picture, a high school graduation pose.

"May I sit?" Ryan asked. "We can continue our conversation." He didn't wait for agreement and pointed to the credenza. "Your daughter?"

Jeff turned and smiled. "Yes. Melissa."

"She's the one you mentioned on the phone."

Jeff nodded, standing behind his chair. "And like I also told you on the phone, I sold the car over three years ago." He scratched his right eyebrow. *Here come the physical signals of truths and lies. Jeff is right-handed.* "I don't think I can help you."

"When did you sell the Suburban?"

"Four years . . . three years . . . whatever. A long time ago."

"While you owned the Suburban, was the car involved in a collision?"

Jeff shook his head and glanced to the upper left. Visual recall. A picture formed in Jeff's mind, but he neglected to offer an audible answer to the question.

"Was that a no?" Ryan pressed. "A similar car was involved in a serious hit-and-run accident. A man died. Every possibility needs to be exhausted to find the driver. I'm sure you understand." His gaze locked on Jeff's face. "So . . . was your white Suburban ever in an accident?"

Jeff studied the back of his chair and made a noise of sucking air between his teeth. Ryan couldn't quite interpret what the gesture meant, but it was annoying. "Nope . . . not even a fender bender."

Ryan figured Jeff to be less than truthful. Jeff shouldn't have had to think so hard.

"Who did you sell the car to? Can you give me a name?"

"Some guy down in Salem. Frank Something. I don't remember."

"Do you happen to recall the license plate number of your Suburban? This is important."

Jeff let out a forced chuckle. "No idea."

"Didn't you keep insurance papers or a bill of sale?"

"I guess, but the information isn't *here*. I'm at work, Officer Eason." The buddy-buddy quality of Jeff's voice took on a sarcastic edge.

"I'm happy to come by your house so I can cross this car off my list." Ryan stood. "What time is good for you?"

Jeff hesitated. "I don't get home until about five thirty." He opened his desk drawer and pulled out a small notepad with the bank's slogan: *Your Money Stays Right Here.* Jeff wrote out his address and ripped the paper from the pad. As he handed the sheet to Ryan, he checked his watch. "Now, you must excuse me—I'm meeting with a client in about five minutes."

A familiar tension came with suspicion, reminding Ryan not to jump to a conclusion too fast. Jeff might be innocent.

But his gut told him otherwise. He slipped the note in his breast pocket, even though he didn't need it. "Mr. Rovinski, what kind of car do you drive now?"

Jeff paused. "A Prius. Why?"

"Just wondering. See you at five thirty."

Chapter 13

Delaney and Beal, LLC

"Are you sure you both don't want to come with me to Ted's?" Olivia asked, slipping on her oversize sunglasses as they left the funeral home.

Lauren groaned. "I'd rather be flogged with a dead carp."

Olivia glanced in the rearview mirror. "Danny? Want to go?"

"I need to pick out my funeral outfit. Lauren and I are planning to go out to lunch. A new Thai place opened up in Sellwood."

"You two are a big help." Olivia shook her head. "Pack up enough for you both to stay at my house for a few more days—at least until after the service."

"Danny, let's pack first and eat after," Lauren said. "I need an empty stomach to pick out clothes."

"Last call. Are you sure you don't want to come to Ted's with me?"

"No major legal decisions need to be made," Danny said.

"And we're not biting our nails to read the will," Lauren added.

"Everything's split three ways. Period," Olivia reiterated. "No waiting. No probate,"

"And no money . . . to speak of," Lauren muttered. "Yeah, I'm really not retiring anytime soon. Besides, Ted's your lawyer too. You know him better than we do."

"What if a ton of money were coming our way?" Olivia lowered her sunglasses and peered over the top of the frames.

"Then we'd go," Lauren and Danny announced in unison.

~ · ~ · ~

After dropping off her sisters at her house to pick up the Blazer, Olivia drove solo to Delaney and Beal, LLC. Ted Beal was the Dushane family attorney and a longtime friend. Not only did he handle wills, estate planning, and nonprofit foundations, Ted reviewed Olivia's book contracts. She trusted him implicitly. He'd learned the publishing business in short order when he realized how much money was at stake.

Over the past twenty years, Olivia figured she had witnessed the gain and loss of a hundred pounds on Ted's small frame. At first blush, his sandy-blond hair, freckles, and permanent tan made him appear younger than sixty-two, but the wrinkled chicken wattle from yo-yo dieting and the stress lines around his eyes from maneuvering through family dynamics sailed him past his true age. As he sat before her now, casual in a yellow golf shirt and khakis, she was happy to see he'd taken the clothes from the trim-Ted side of the closet.

One whole shelf of Ted's built-in mahogany bookcase held several copies of each title in Olivia's romance series. Ten hardbound versions of *Tex-Mex Nights* had been added next to *South of the Borderline.* Ted handed them out to his female clients.

"Want me to sign those while I'm here?" she offered.

"I wasn't going to ask, but . . . "

"Of course I will. I prefer signing books over what you have in that folder."

"What's your next book?"

Olivia scratched her lip and realized she'd not applied any lipstick. "You're sounding like my agent. I can't write with all this going on." An image of her mother's manuscript sitting under her nightstand flashed in her mind. "I'll come up with something to keep you in golf balls. Don't worry."

"How are you and your sisters holding up?" Ted wrestled with the thick, decades-old file of her parents' legal affairs. He set three forms in front of her to transfer control of the assets.

Olivia scanned them as she filled in the required information. "Mom's death was inevitable—we almost lost her seven times in the past two years—but nothing prepared me for orphan status."

"A rite of passage." Ted removed his reading glasses and gazed at her with dusky-blue eyes that appeared reflective against his tan. "Believe me; it's ten times harder when the kids don't outlive the parents."

"I'd sure find it harder—I'd be dead, Ted." Olivia chuckled and studied the forms as she counted off her own rites of passage. "So much paperwork. How do you define someone in little boxes? They never leave you enough room."

"Write small. When's the service?"

"Thursday afternoon. We'd love for you to come."

Ted swiveled to his Oregon Humane Society calendar tacked on a framed cork board. His secretary hadn't been successful in transitioning Ted away from manually tracking his schedule. "I'm so sorry, Liv. I'll be in court. Too late to reschedule. Testifying in a messy one where the family members are suing one another. Ugly stuff." He flipped over July's fluffy kitten and August's airborne owl to get to September, a cougar draped over a tree limb. "Two months, Liv, makes it three years. Any new leads on Adam's accident?"

Olivia ran her hand through her hair. "No, but I have Ryan working on the case."

"Good man, Ryan. He's an excellent cop. That knifing incident was a shocker, though. You think he and Danny will get back together?" Ted waited a beat for an answer.

"Danny needs him." Olivia glanced at her open purse on the empty guest chair. The journal poked out from an inner pocket. "Right now, I do too."

"Don't forget: give me two copies of Ellen's death certificate when you get them." Ted held up his fingers like a peace sign. "According to the terms of the trust all the assets revert to you, Lauren, and Danny. You girls won't have to go through probate to sell the house or to access the accounts."

"Not much left in them, Ted. We'll need to get the house on the market as soon as we can."

"Wasn't the case at one time, though. I think the intention was to leave you three quite a bit."

"Pffbbtt," Olivia scoffed and waved her hand. "Mom never forgave Dad for investing their retirement with that shyster fund manager. Dad was always one to be sucked in by grandiose promises." The *K* in Novak wavered in her flowing signature.

"I'll miss Ellen," Ted said, countersigning the paper, "and her tomatoes. She had a magnificent garden."

"Still does. We had some last night for BLTs."

"I was two years out of college when your dad asked me to draft Ellen's and his first will. Changed it more times than I can count. They were flying high in those days."

"So that's how you got the Mercedes." Her attempt at humor held back the sting in her throat.

Ted caught the slow fade of her expression. "This is the last one, Liv." He slipped another piece of paper in front of her. "Put your Jane Hancock on the second line."

At the corner of Ted's mahogany desk, the ever-ready tissue box sat under a silver cover. Olivia leaned forward and snatched one as she choked back tears. She signed her name and blew her nose. "We had bacon, lettuce, and tomatoes etched on her urn."

"You *didn't!*"

"We did." Olivia pointed to the shelf. "Turn off the clock and hand me down those books."

~ · ~ · ~

Olivia relished the prospect of having a couple of hours to herself when she got home from meeting with Ted. The legal process of handing off her mother's life took less than forty-five minutes. To her, Ted's generous donations to the Oregon Humane Society connected to his work. He dealt with the details of death every day. She likened the estate specialty of the legal profession to the noble responsibility of caring for abandoned animals.

While Olivia settled the legal affairs, Lauren had left a message that she and Danny were going to her apartment to pick up some additional clothes. They had all agreed staying with Olivia for a few more days, at least until after the memorial service, was a good idea. With that plus their lunch, Olivia would have the house—and the manuscript—to herself for a good amount of time.

Karen Finerelli had sent two e-mails since yesterday, not-so-gentle reminders for Olivia to forward the first fifty pages of her new novel. Karen's sympathy had melted away beneath the heat of commerce. Next would be a phone call of demands.

Olivia darted up the stairs to her bedroom. Freesia lay on the bed with an open, scolding eye.

"Don't look at me like that," Olivia chided. "I have to do this for all of us and for Mom."

The cat opened her mouth in a silent meow. Olivia grabbed the manuscript from beneath the nightstand and gave Freesia's head three quick strokes. She headed downstairs to the den which doubled as her office.

Olivia stopped. Her mother's typewriter sat on the library table in the entryway. The manuscript required a new cover page. The ribbon appeared to be functional. She fiddled with the mechanism to pull it forward to the ink that hadn't seen the light of day for over fifty years. Dark and unblemished. She dashed to the den and pulled a piece of white paper from the shelf. The font had to match the rest of the manuscript to appear seamless. *Courier.*

Every click of the roller seemed like a wind up to the release of her mother's ghostly words. "Here we go, Mom. I'm going to make damn sure you're published," she murmured.

Olivia typed, one-fingered, each letter sounding like gunshot:

Indigo to Black
By
Olivia Novak

The *L* key stuck twice. She pried the key from the paper each time. After typing her address in the lower right corner, she pulled out the paper. *Please love me for this, Mom.* Olivia trotted to the den. The pages of her mother's words sucked into the hungry scanner. She waited as they combined into a document on the screen. Attaching a separate file of the first fifty pages to an e-mail, Olivia entered Karen's e-mail address and a short note:

Karen,

Here you go! This is a departure for me, but I hope you like it. I told you I wanted to write something different. How about young adult on steroids? Breaks all the rules. The full manuscript is being overnighted. I typed on my Mom's old typewriter.

Let me know what you think.

Liv

Olivia printed out the entire manuscript, replacing the former cover sheet with the new one. As they spit from the feeder, she monitored each page for a jam, her head bobbing with the *ca-shunk . . . zzzzhh . . . ca-shunk*. She chastised herself for not purchasing a faster one; this was torture.

The post office closed at four. Olivia glanced at her watch: two thirty. Lauren and Danny would be home soon . . . well, maybe not. Danny would linger with indecision about what clothes to bring; Lauren would deliberate whether her funeral outfit made her look fat. And then Lauren would order more vegetable fried rice at the restaurant.

"C'mon, you piece of crap. Finish!" Olivia smacked her hand on the lid.

Silence.

Olivia stared at the stack. The pages radiated heat. She slipped the warm manuscript into a bubble-pack envelope with a handwritten note. A cushion of air protected her mother's words as she wrote out the address with a black marker. Karen wanted the whole story in hard copy. Done.

With the envelope sealed, Olivia grabbed her keys. Thirty minutes to make the post office.

Chapter 14

If It Smells Bad, Don't Buy It

At four thirty on Monday afternoon, Ryan waved at R. D. after he completed his walk with Pogo. He got out of the cruiser and approached the pair.

"I'm taking off for a bit." Ryan ruffled Pogo's head and let the dog lick his hand. "I'm going to call for another officer to come on watch. I'm not sure how long it will take for him to get here, but it won't be long."

"I'll keep an eye out, Eason," R. D. said. "'Preciate it."

"Lock the door and don't go anywhere. If you want to go out, wait for the other officer to get here."

"I know the drill. I'm in for the night. I gotta wash and change the sheets. Funny thing, I like coming home to fresh sheets. Then I'm turning in. Early day tomorrow." R. D. turned and shuffled back to the house. This time, Pogo's steps lagged behind Ardy's, as if the dog was buying time to delay the upcoming separation.

After Ardy closed the front door, Ryan returned to the cruiser, anxious to get back to the bank before Jeff left for the day. If Jeff got spooked, he may not go home. He turned the key in the ignition.

Ryan had checked the hours on the door; the bank closed at five, so Jeff was easily telling the truth about getting home at five thirty—

but living in the same neighborhood in which he worked, he also would have time to run an errand. Ryan would park the cruiser out of sight of the parking lot at Cascade Bank before Jeff came out to his Prius. Ryan headed toward Sellwood.

Since his visit to Rovinski's office, a scroll of images, clues, and remembered body language rushed through Ryan's mind. Two aspects of Jeff's manner bothered him: the man either hesitated at or wouldn't give a straight answer to any of his questions, and Jeff kept glancing at the scar on Ryan's cheek. The expression wasn't one of curiosity but of empathy, maybe guilt. Sure, Ryan bought the line that Jeff couldn't recall the license plate number; most people didn't even remember the one on the car they drove every day. But they remembered if their vehicle had been in an accident, especially a major accident.

Years ago Ryan recalled when he and Danny had taken Ellen Dushane to the grocery store, and she'd imparted advice that lingered with him still: *If it smells bad, don't buy it.* The woman had more wisdom than anyone acknowledged. Since then, he sniffed everything raw before he bought it. Ellen had single-handedly saved him from numerous cases of the trots. *Ellen.* Ryan shook his head and chuckled. A piece of work, but a fine lady with an enormous, fragile heart. Yes, she made his life miserable on many occasions, but Ellen was a good person.

Ryan thought of Ellen as he drove down 99E toward Sellwood—protective of her daughters, all three of them. She crowed about each of the sisters when they were out of earshot, never giving compliments to them face-to-face. Ellen had the goods on the girls. Something in Jeff's voice was also protective—too protective. The scar on his daughter's lip was concerning—not visible in the early pictures, but in the two most recent . . . obvious.

Jeff's Prius sat in the parking lot of Cascade Bank. Chalk up one point in his favor. He hadn't been spooked and fled after their discussion. Still at work. Many points, though, remained stacked against him.

Ryan called the sergeant.

"I've got a strong lead in this Novak case," he said. "I might have found the guy."

"Almost three years and you swoop in on a perp in one day?"

"I only picked up where McClosky left off. He's done a year of heavy lifting. McClosky would have been here, maybe sooner, if he hadn't been reassigned."

"Couldn't be helped, but good work. I hope this is the one. Closing these cases is good for the department and the victims' families."

"We'll find out at five thirty. I'm meeting the guy at his house. I'll call in if I need back-up. McClosky's on standby. He should be in on this one. In the meantime, can you send a replacement to watch Griffin's house?"

"Done."

"I could get waylaid if this goes how I think it will. Griffin's walked the dog and is in for the night. He leaves for the hospital in the morning, but I'll check on him again before I go home."

"Fair enough." The sergeant paused. "Be careful, Ryan. You can't predict how these people will react when they're cornered."

He chuckled and thought to himself, *Yes, Mom.*

~ · ~ · ~

Ryan waited for Jeff Rovinski to pull into the driveway of the small 1920s bungalow. As Jeff exited from his Prius, Ryan's gaze focused on the man's hands to make sure they were empty of a weapon. While Jeff appeared to be average, honest face or not, something in his manner gave Ryan pause. He let Jeff get a head start and followed him to the house.

As Ryan climbed the stairs to the porch, Jeff fumbled with the keys to unlock the front door. He apologized and ushered Ryan inside.

"Have a seat," Jeff offered. "Want something to drink?"

"No, thanks. And I'll stand," Ryan said. "I sit too much."

"Suit yourself. I think I will."

The house was clean and comfortable. Architectural details of the room drew Ryan's gaze as Jeff moved to the kitchen. He appreciated the stained-glass windows above the built-in bookcases flanking the tiled fireplace. The oak mantle, carved in a dentil style to match the crown molding, held pictures of Jeff's daughter, Melissa. These showed more casual poses than those at his office. No photos of the mother.

Jeff emerged from the kitchen with a glass of ice water. He loosened his tie with one hand. "So, what's this all about, Officer Eason?"

"The license number, remember? You were going to get me the number for your white Suburban. I need the engine's VIN number too. Should be on the bill of sale."

"Oh . . . right." Jeff set his glass on the coffee table. As an afterthought, he shoved a coaster under it and dashed down the hall, presumably to a back bedroom.

Ryan moved closer to the pictures, framed in oak wood to match the style of the house. He wanted another good look at Melissa, in particular her upper lip in the most recent photo. She appeared to be about twenty or twenty-one. Her long brown hair matched the description from the witness's interview. The young woman's wide smile had benefited from the braces depicted in the earlier photos, but another inspection of the most recent ones confirmed the uneven smile on one side. Ryan replayed the possible accident in his mind—from Melissa's perspective. Upon impact with Adam's car, Melissa would have been thrown forward from the momentum of the heavy Suburban. She'd split open her lip on the steering wheel, maybe busted some teeth or her jaw. The wound would have required multiple stitches. As he put the pieces together, Ryan relived his own skin-sewing experience. The Suburban's interior would need to be tested for blood. Too soon. Don't jump to conclusions without evidence.

Jeff emerged into the living room, fluttering a half-sheet of paper. "Here it is. Found it," he announced. Jeff handed Ryan the bill of sale. "I sold the car longer ago than I thought; back in 2010, not 2011."

The date of the car's sale drew his gaze. He rocked the paper toward the sunlight from the front window. The ink was shiny on the last *0* of 2010. The *1* had been changed to a *0* with a different type of pen. The color of blue was close, but somewhat darker than the other numbers.

"A few questions," Ryan said, taking a seat on the Craftsman-style chair. He placed the paper, face up, on the coffee table.

Jeff sat on the matching couch and took a long swallow of his water. Condensation from the warm, humid air trickled down the sides of the glass; a few drops splashed on Jeff's suit pants. Beads of sweat had formed on his hairline too. Jeff set the glass on the coaster and tapped the pads of his forefingers.

"You know, I think I will take a glass of water," Ryan said. "Hot today."

Jeff stood, looking somewhat irritated at the request, and rushed through the dining room to the kitchen. With Jeff out of sight, Ryan called dispatch for backup, keeping his voice low as he gave a rush of instructions. "May have an arrest. Call McClosky to be out in front in fifteen minutes." Ryan muttered the address. "Tell him the Novak case might blow open." He set the phone on vibrate and dropped it in his breast pocket. He turned to see Jeff standing with a glass in his hand. The man's expression reflected wariness, as though having overheard Ryan's conversation, maybe not the actual words but the seriousness of their tone.

"Here you go," Jeff said, his words stiff.

Ryan took the glass. "Tell me about Melissa. Is she in college?"

Jeff returned to his spot on the couch. "The love of my life. I raised her myself." Jeff sat up straighter. "Her mother and I were divorced when she was ten. Melissa's twenty now and an English major at PSU. Time flies."

"For some . . . Not for others." Ryan drained the water and jostled the ice. "She's in—what?—her sophomore year? Junior?"

"Junior." Jeff nodded with pride. "Quite a feat these days to get kids through school. They need a lot of help."

"I'm sure." Ryan offered a slight smile and a slow nod. "Where's her mother?"

"Remarried. She's back East."

Ryan flashed on Danny's mother, Ellen. Her lash-out in the hospital when he was getting stitched up after the knife attack had taken him off guard. Instead of motherly sympathy, Ellen had been outraged that he had caused Danny pain. *How dare you put yourself in harm's way, Ryan, with no regard, whatsoever, about what it would do to my daughter! You could have been killed! Danielle is devastated. She's coming home with me!* In his memory, Ellen had never reacted with such protectiveness over Olivia or Lauren, only Danny. Always Danny. Ryan raised his eyes to meet Jeff's. "Bet you'd do anything for Melissa. Am I right?"

Jeff's tense smile collapsed with suspicion. He didn't answer. A crack, a fissure in the lead lining he'd built around Melissa. Ryan ran his finger over the raised ridge of his own scar (a gesture he hoped was not missed by Jeff) and pointed to the receipt on the coffee table. "I think your white Suburban was in an accident while you owned it, Mr. Rovinski."

"No! I told you—" Jeff objected—too fast—and shifted his gaze to the left, away from Ryan's. Jeff was recalling something, maybe his daughter coming home with a bloody shirt, inspecting the damage, or replaying the conspiratorial discussion to align disparate versions of the story. Jeff reached for his water glass, now stuck to the coaster in a puddle of condensation. The disc clattered back to the oak table. He wiped the spill with his shirtsleeve.

"You may want to rethink your answer," Ryan warned. "That's not quite what Bud told me at the Crash 'n Dash."

Jeff froze. He stared at the melting ice in his glass, formulating a response. When he lifted his gaze to meet Ryan's, defiance filled his eyes. Jeff's pale skin flushed pink. "Are you charging me with something? Because if you are, I'm innocent."

"*You* might be." Ryan spread his hands and leaned toward the bill of sale. The license plate number burned red hot, a number he'd never forget: *424-SKR.*

Outside, a car door shut. Jeff's head turned to the front window, his protective expression—jaw muscles clenched, shallow breaths, hazel eyes wide—betraying the identity of the new arrival. *Melissa.* Jeff leaned forward as though he wanted to shout for her to stay outside. Instead, the latch on the door handle depressed.

A young woman swept her long brown hair out of the way as she bumped through the front door with a leather knapsack. She pulled an audio bud from one ear, the cord trailing to her smartphone. "Hey, Dad! There's a cop out—" She stared in shock as Ryan stood.

"Are you Melissa Rovinski?"

"Yeah . . . ? Why?"

Chapter 15

Confessions

"We're doing chicken breasts and salad for dinner," Olivia called out with two bags of groceries in her arms. Lauren and Danny were unpacking their suitcases upstairs. Olivia headed in the opposite direction, to the kitchen.

The manuscript now had a life of its own, its tethers cut. The pages once again sat in a dark steel box, waiting to be pulled out by a postal worker who would throw them on a truck to board a plane at the airport. The end of the manuscript's journey would be the desk of Karen Finerelli—before noon. By this time tomorrow night, Karen might be reading her mother's words. Olivia opened the butcher paper and took a whiff of the chicken. No odor. Fresh.

"C'mere, Liv!" Lauren called from upstairs. "I need you to check something."

Olivia set a bag of cornflake crumbs on the counter and waited at the base of the stairs in the entryway. "I'm not coming up."

Lauren appeared on the landing, flicking her bangs and adjusting a purple silk blouse. Her loose black pants gave the illusion of a long skirt. Brown orthopedic loafers peeked out from under the hem. "Does this make me look fat?"

"Is that what you're wearing on Thursday?"

"Yeah, why?"

"The color is a bit bright for a funeral service, don't you think?" Olivia winced. "And your shoes are brown."

"Purple is Mom's favorite color. Nobody's going to see my shoes. These pants will cover them." Lauren pulled closed the gap on the front her blouse. "And I'll wear a bra on Thursday."

"Thank God for small favors," Olivia said, laughing, "because you need to corral those two hopping bunnies under there."

Lauren rolled her eyes as Danny appeared.

In a black suit of soft crepe with a mango silk shift and strappy sandals, Danny moved to the rail like a fashion model. *Stunning.* "I'm wearing this," she said and turned in a circle.

"Wonderful. Come down. We have to write the obituary, and I need to start dinner."

"I'm getting comfortable. It's wine o'clock." Lauren quickened her steps back to the bedroom to change into her mother's terry-cloth muumuu.

A few minutes later, Lauren lugged the typewriter into the kitchen. She set the machine on the kitchen island with a *clunk*. "Let's write the tribute on this instead of your laptop." Lauren reached for the blue tumbler as though it had an ownership tag. "I love typing on a manual. The report makes a *clickety-clack* sound so you can feel every word." Lauren *clickety-clacked* her glass full of ice cubes from the refrigerator door. "I learned to type on one of these." She turned to Danny, who appeared anxious to contribute to the obituary process. "Get some paper from Liv's printer."

Danny bounced to the den, more buoyant than Olivia had seen her in years. Olivia eyed the typewriter, its keys gnawing at her conscience like a guilt machine.

Lauren took a deep gulp of her wine as they waited. "Her Highness had to get a pedicure after lunch."

"Why didn't you get yours done too?" Olivia took two sips of her cabernet and set a frying pan on the stove. She swirled in the olive oil.

"Right. I don't think so with my 'Fred Flintstone' feet." Lauren blew into the keys of the typewriter. Motes of dust, and a few cat hairs, floated over the island. "Everything go okay with Ted?"

"Fine. No surprises." Olivia waved her hand to protect the pan from landing lint.

"Paper!" Danny announced. "You only had five sheets left."

"I go through *a lot* of paper," Olivia muttered.

"Okay, let's talk about Mom!" Lauren positioned a blank piece of paper around the roller. "We'll do our fake version first for the stuff we can't say in a real one."

"I'm not sure this is a good idea," Danny said and took a sip of her wine.

"Oh, c'mon, it'll be fun."

Olivia cracked an egg over a plate and whipped the yolk to froth. Just as the heated manuscript had warmed her fingertips, warmth from the wine in her veins streamed to her limbs. "Mom kept secrets for all three us." She poured the cornflake crumbs into a separate dish.

"Okay, Miss Drama Queen. We'll start with you!" Lauren poised her hands over the keyboard. "Secrets revealed. Let the healing begin."

Lauren and Danny stared at her, waiting in silence.

Olivia tossed back the rest of her wine. "Okay. You ready?" She paused. "When I was seventeen, Mom went with me when I got an abortion. She rode shotgun because the doctor said I needed someone to take me home. Of course, since she never learned how to drive, I still drove myself." She dipped one chicken breast in egg, rolled it in the crumbs, and set it in the pan. "There. How's that?"

"You did? She did?" Danny said, almost whispering.

Lauren raised her eyes from the typewriter. "You would've had a thirty-eight-year-old kid right now, probably married with kids of their own. That, or a kid still living at home with no job, watching television, and draining your retirement account."

A pall settled over the kitchen island, except for the sizzle. Olivia nodded and turned to the sink to wash her hands.

"Good one, Liv!" Lauren grinned as though she had canary feathers sticking from both sides of her mouth. "You're full of surprises."

Clackety . . . clackety . . . clack. "Note to self: we need to talk more about this later." Typing too fast, Lauren stopped and unstuck the keys. "Well, that was thirty-eight years ago. Quite forward-thinking of Mom, don't you think?"

"A woman ahead of—and behind—her times," Olivia agreed. "She acted like it was just another problem to be solved." Olivia dipped the second chicken breast into the crumbs. "She never told Dad."

Clackety . . . clackety . . . clack.

Lauren stopped and scuffed to the refrigerator for a refill. Olivia washed her hands—again—and poured herself another glass of cabernet.

"Okay, Danny, your turn," Lauren said, eager to get back to the counter chair. "Give it to me straight."

Danny stood quietly and sipped her wine . . . twice. "I crunched Dad's Cadillac when he was out of town on business," she said. "Mom knew I had been out with my friends smoking pot. We took Dad's car because it had a killer stereo."

Clackety . . . clackety . . . clack. Lauren's jaw clenched. "I had to buy my own car."

"But Mom and Dad bought you your own Cadillac," Olivia said.

"This was before I had a driver's license," Danny continued. "Mom gave the body shop the business to make sure the car was fixed before Dad came home. Boy, was she mad, but Mom knew Dad would be madder. Mom had a solution for everything."

"Not quite," Lauren scoffed, glancing at Olivia. She took a sip of her iced pink juice and pressed her lips together. The keyboard drew her fingers. *Clackety . . . clackety . . . clack.* "This topic could be a whole page. Did you ever tell Ryan about that? He could have arrested you."

"You should still be with Ryan, Danny," Olivia added.

"I know." Danny shook her head and sighed. "I still love him. But I'm a coward."

Lauren lifted her gaze to Danny. "Damn straight! We all love Ryan, you big doofus."

"You're not a coward," Olivia said. "But let's not get snarky.

These are supposed to be fun." Olivia pulled the dish towel from the bar and threw it over her shoulder. "Next! Your turn, Lauren." She dipped the last breast in the egg and dredged it in the cornflakes. With all the chicken in the pan, Olivia washed her hands for a third time. "We're waiting. No holding back."

"Why don't you wash your hands once, *after* you do all the chicken?" Lauren said, more as an instruction than a question.

Olivia whirled the dish towel. "You're stalling."

"As a teenager, I rode down the middle of the street on Danny's Big Wheel tricycle. Mom called the police and had me thrown in jail to teach me a lesson. Dad knew all the guys on the force. It was a big joke, but that stunt scared me out of my wits."

"Oh, c'mon. Tell us something juicy," Danny pressed, tossing a wadded tissue in the garbage. "You were no angel. How about sex?"

"I never had sex before I was married." Lauren took a sip of her wine, refusing to meet either of their stares.

"You're so full of crap," Olivia chided. "You're reinventing history. You and Mark lived together before you were married."

Lauren tried, unsuccessfully, to change the subject. "Do you realize that Mom never had the sex talk with me? She thought the discussion happened in school, but it didn't back then. I had no idea what was happening to me—the whole period thing. It freaked me out. Honest to God, I thought if Elizabeth Taylor could get through this, then I should stop bitching. Otherwise, I might as well be dying at the age of eleven."

"Eleven?!" Olivia paused. "I did learn about it in school, but they had separate sessions, one for the boys and one for the girls. Mom didn't want any part of the life discussion. You should type that." She tapped her fingernails on the granite, but Lauren's fingers remained still. "Okay . . . here's something I have to tell you."

"What?" Danny and Lauren asked in unison.

Olivia threw her sisters a sideways glance and pointed the spatula.

"I told Lauren about the journal I keep. I write descriptions of every white Suburban I see. Mom knew about it. In fact, over the past year she's been helping me."

"How?" Danny asked, incredulous. Lauren kept quiet, but nodded in affirmation.

"Whenever she saw one, Mom called me with the license plate. She completely understood my need to find the driver who killed Adam."

"She never said a word to me about this, Liv." Danny sounded almost hurt that their mother took initiative to do something without her knowledge.

"In fact, she left me a message two weeks ago. It was funny . . . in a way."

"What did she say?" Lauren asked, as if hungry to hear Mom's voice.

Olivia closed her eyes. "Listen for yourselves. I saved it." She moved to the phone and scrolled through saved messages. She hit the speakerphone key. Their mother's voice filled the kitchen.

"Hi Honey. It's Mum. I'm sitting here in the car at Walgreens, the one on Arlington and McLoughlin. Danny went inside to pick up my prescription. I have to talk fast. A white Suburban just pulled in. Here's the license number: *226-EEK*. Just like a monkey—'eek eek.' Got it? Love you."

A series of beeps in musical tones preceded the end of the call. Olivia hit the stop button, her eyes filled with tears. "Now, *that's* a mom."

Danny grabbed a napkin and squished it over her eyes. "Mom never figured out how to hang up a call on her Jitterbug."

Lauren ripped the paper from the typewriter roller and scrunched it, her cheeks streaked with grief. She tossed the paper ball on the floor. "We're done here. I don't know what to say."

Wiping her face with her sleeve, Olivia took another sip of her wine. She froze with the spatula in her hand. "Oh my God!"

"What now?" Lauren raised her eyes.

"I forgot. I promised to babysit Ardy's dog. My neighbor's going in the hospital tomorrow."

Danny straightened and sniffed. "What kind of dog?"

"A huge poodle. All seventy pounds of him. I have to go next door and bring him back over here. Freesia's in my bedroom. Watch the chicken." Olivia raced to the front door, abandoning the sizzling pan. She shoved her bare feet into sneakers.

"No way. We'll go over with you." Danny jumped up and slipped her feet into her pink flip-flops. "I'll close your door upstairs so the dog doesn't bother Freesia when we get back." "C'mon, Lauren."

"I'm not changing out of my slippers."

Danny slapped up the stairs, taking two at a time. Lauren blew her nose as she stood at the front door. Olivia dashed back to the kitchen to turn off the burner on the stove.

Chapter 16

Desperate Situations Call for Desperate Measures

With the sun still bright at five thirty, Olivia led her sisters across the driveway and through the yard to Ardy's front door: Olivia padded in her sneakers ahead of Lauren in her slippers and Danny in her flip-flops. Ardy's old Datsun wagon sat in his driveway. The old man never kept the car in the one-car garage.

"I should have stayed at the house," Lauren groused. "I've got my goddamned slippers on."

"Oh stop. Where's your sense of adventure?" Danny chided. "And we know you don't care about your footwear. You're worried somebody's going to break in and steal your wine."

With a finger to her lips, Olivia turned. "Shhhh. Keep it together."

Lauren's slipper caught on the step. She fell forward and grabbed the back of Olivia's sweatpants. Olivia started to giggle. "Get off!" She rang the doorbell. "Don't embarrass me. This is my neighbor."

Inside, toenails clicked on the floor inside and scratched on the door. *Rrrruh . . . ruh . . . ruh.*

"Pogo," Olivia whispered. "He's not the most well-behaved dog."

"I don't think he's home." Lauren started down the steps.

"He doesn't go into the hospital until tomorrow morning. He wouldn't leave his dog." Olivia pressed the bell again. "Pogo's like his child."

No answer. Pogo whined and barked inside. *Rrrruh . . . ruh . . . ruh.*

"Let's go around to the back patio," Olivia urged. "He's got to be here." Her mother's words popped into her head. *If it smells bad . . .*

Olivia led Lauren and Danny down a path of paving stones along the side of the house. They streamed to a flagstone courtyard. The patio was void of decoration, except for a towering maple tree growing from the center of a dirt circle—and there was no Ardy. Olivia moved to the French doors leading to Ardy's kitchen. She knocked.

No movement. No lights.

All three sisters cupped their hands to peer inside through the glass panes. Pogo had joined them and turned in a circle behind the French doors. In the dusky light, the dog pawed the door, clearly a regular behavior. Swishy prints smeared the panes under the door handle.

"I'm telling you, he wouldn't leave Pogo!" Olivia insisted. The barking set her nerves on edge.

"How well do you know him?" Lauren asked.

"We don't socialize, but he's been here since Adam and I moved in."

"Did he give you a key?"

"No. He wanted me to come over tonight to get the dog."

"I bet he left early," Danny suggested.

Olivia shook her head. "Not without talking to me. His car's in the driveway." Air *whooshed* from under the door as Pogo sniffed at the jamb.

"Took a cab?" Lauren offered.

"Possible, I guess."

Danny peered inside for another look. "There's a carton of orange juice on the counter—Tropicana."

"Pulp or no pulp?" Lauren asked.

"I can't tell. Mom liked juice without pulp—too much fiber—but I would have preferred the pulp kind."

"Will you two knock it off?! What does it matter?" Olivia scolded.

"What are we gonna do? We have to get the dog!" She knocked harder on the door frame.

No response. A slight rustle of the leaves accompanied the *rrr . . . ruh . . . ruh* inside.

Lauren pushed forward. "Stand back. We have to break in," she announced, with a slurred finality in her words.

"We can't!" Olivia's eyes widened as she pictured the three of them being hauled off to jail under a glow of swirling red and blue lights. She took two steps out of the way to give Lauren a wide birth.

"Blame me." Lauren wadded the bottom of her muumuu and wrapped the terry fabric over her arm.

"Lauren, you don't have any underpants on!" Olivia cried.

"My eyes!" Danny shielded her face.

"Desperate situations call for desperate measures." With her bare rear to the door, Lauren pulled her covered arm forward and squeezed her eyes shut. "Here goes . . . " She swung her elbow and smashed the pane next to the handle. Glass shattered to the ceramic-tile floor inside.

"Oh my God. Oh my God," Danny muttered.

"We're criminals . . . " Olivia shook her head, trying to figure out how to write this situation as a scene in a book. Adjectives to describe Lauren didn't yet exist.

Lauren stuck her hand between the remaining shards. Pogo added circle turning to his continuous barking.

"Be careful!" Olivia squinted as Lauren unlocked the deadbolt. A trip to the emergency room for stitches wasn't in the plan, and neither was this situation. Pogo charged as the door swung in. All seventy pounds of dog attempted to give her a bear hug. "Back! Down, Pogo! Sit!" she ordered. The dog stood with his paws on Olivia's chest, pushing her as he licked her face. She lost her balance and fell to the floor. "Get him off me!"

"Some protector," Lauren said. "He's kissing an intruder to death."

Danny pulled Pogo by his collar and took him aside. She whispered in his ear. "We'll take care of you, sweetie. You'll come with us."

The dog calmed, but continued to whine as he sat in front her. "I'll hold him here while one of you cleans up the glass. Hurry. He'll cut the pads on his paws."

"I'll do it."

"Leave it to Beaver," Olivia said, wiping the slobber from her mouth. "Pfftooo . . . blech. That's what I'm going to call you from now on—*Beav*."

"Oh, go check the house." Lauren opened and slammed kitchen cabinets.

Did Lauren really just break in here? Olivia had, for the first time in her life, resorted to criminal behavior to meet an obligation. With the image of Lauren's hiked-up housedress burned into her brain, Olivia tiptoed from the kitchen to a short hallway that led to the front entryway. Her sneakers squeaked on the hardwood floor.

Lauren stepped behind her. "Turn on some lights. It's spooky in here. Let's get the dog and go. This Ardy guy must have left before you remembered to come over."

"Something's wrong with this whole scenario." Olivia met her sister's eyes.

Lauren turned and opened the hall closet. She pulled out a whisk broom and dustpan. "Maybe he fell and was knocked unconscious or something."

Olivia flipped on a light. A chandelier gave off a clouded, hazy glow. Beyond the plaster arches on each side of the entryway, a living room to her right and a dining room to her left. The furniture appeared to be a collection of secondhand cast-offs, simple but with no cohesive style. A white towel covered one cushion on the end of the couch, shadowed with black curly hair. A tube television sat on a rolling stand along the opposite wall. Built-in shelves were jammed with books, some placed on their sides atop those standing up

"Ardy? Olivia here," she called out, tentative.

She listened for a response. None came. The only sound was the tinkle of broken glass being swept up in the kitchen. Pogo remained quiet with Danny.

Olivia gripped the scrolled wrought-iron railing as she climbed the wooden steps, her knuckles white. A pattern of scratches ran up the center of the wood, wear marks from Pogo's toenails. Images of Ardy unconscious on the floor upstairs made her chest pound. She stopped on the landing. The layout was similar to her house except smaller, with only two bedrooms and one bath. All quiet.

The small bathroom at the top of the stairs yielded nothing. Olivia illuminated a sconce in the first bedroom. Strands of accumulated dust hung like fragile garland, swaying in the disturbed air. Several cardboard banker's boxes littered the scratched hardwood floor, along with piles of newspapers and magazines. She suppressed an urge to run home for a bucket and cleaning supplies, imagining that if she dove into straightening up this room she'd discover something scandalous. She turned out the light.

The master bedroom was clean and cheery but almost empty. Puzzling. *How does he sleep?* Her gaze stopped on the large flat panel across one wall, trimmed to match the rest of the molding in the house: a Murphy bed.

"I haven't seen one of these in years," she whispered. "Ardy? Are you in here?" A thump made her flinch.

"Liv?" Lauren called from the bottom of the stairs. "Did you find anything?"

Olivia returned to the landing. She leaned over the railing. "Nothing to report, Beav. But I think I heard something."

Lauren grimaced. "I think you've run that joke into the ground. Danny dropped a can of Pogo's food. She found his leash. We'll take him back to your house."

"I'll call the hospital. Maybe he left early because he was in pain or something."

"I'm sure that's it." Lauren's voice faded toward the kitchen. "This Beav wants get out of here."

"You really ought to wax."

~ · ~ · ~

At six fifteen, Pogo strained at his leash to get through the front door of Olivia's house.

"I think we should call the police," Olivia suggested, unhooking the clip. The dog bolted through the house, having picked up Freesia's scent.

"I can't take any more drama." Danny fluttered her hands over her head and moved into the kitchen. "I'll feed him. He must be hungry."

Lauren followed her. "Let's call Ryan."

Danny ignored the comment and pulled out a can of natural dog food from a paper bag she'd found in Ardy's cabinet. "Where's the opener, Liv?"

"The drawer by the sink," she answered, torn about salvaging dinner or chasing Pogo. Dinner won when she checked the half-cooked chicken, cold in the pan. She stared at the ruined meal. "Well, this was a big, fat waste. I'm starving."

"Cook it," Lauren said.

"Oh, right. And take a chance that the three of us will be hurling chicken all night?" Olivia scraped the contents of the pan into the garbage. "It's been sitting too long."

Pogo attempted to get traction on the ceramic tile as Olivia washed the pan. At the sound of the can opener, the poodle became a black blur as he scrambled three laps around the island. Unable to wait for his own food, Pogo vacuumed the contents of Freesia's kibble dish in two gulps. He leaped up and set his paws on the counter as Danny twisted the opener around the can.

"Calm down, Pogo!" Danny scolded. "It's coming."

Olivia set a stainless-steel mixing bowl of water on the floor and grabbed a ceramic pie plate from the cabinet. "Here, Danny, use this for his food." She turned and poured a glass of wine. "I need a drink to figure out what we're going to do for dinner."

"Good idea," Lauren agreed. "I'll join you." She leaned into the refrigerator to fill her tumbler and, as an afterthought, tucked packages of turkey breast and sliced Swiss cheese under her arm. A loaf of bread made an appearance from the bottom freezer drawer before she pushed it shut with her slipper. After a few plunks of ice in her glass, Lauren plopped the gourmet meal on the counter. "Dinner! Knock yourselves out."

"Pour me one too, Liv," Danny said, spooning out half the can of dog food with a *thwonk*. "Turkey sandwiches are fine with me."

"We need to at least toast them." Olivia swiped her forehead. "I'd better call the hospital. I hope Ardy's okay." She eyed Pogo with his head in the pie plate. A circle of splashed water surrounded the bowl. She snatched a towel from the oven door.

"While you call, I'll start the obituary." Lauren rolled a fresh piece of paper into the typewriter. "We have to get this to Fred in the morning."

"I'll toast the sandwiches," Danny said.

Olivia scooped up the wadded admissions Lauren had thrown on the floor, now unimportant, and tossed the paper in the recycle bin.

"Let's use the picture of Mom in her floppy gardening hat," Danny suggested to Olivia. "I saw it on your shelf by the printer. It'll go with the urn."

Olivia headed for the den and her computer. She sat at her desk and pulled up the number for Milwaukie Hospital. After being placed on hold and transferred to Admitting, Olivia asked about R. D. Griffin. Olivia's answers made her realize how little information she had about her neighbor. No, she didn't know what the *R* and *D* stood for. And no, she hadn't any idea who Mr. Griffin's physician was. The staff member confirmed that no one with the last name of Griffin had been admitted within the last two days.

"Damn," she muttered, taking a breath as she hung up the phone. She reached for the framed picture of her mother. Ellen beamed as she showed off a zucchini that far exceeded its ability to be called a phallic symbol, with one hand on the top of her wide-brimmed straw hat to prevent it from sailing away. "Yes," Olivia whispered. "This is perfect." She slipped the photo from the frame and scanned it.

Her sisters' voices floated from the kitchen into the den. Lauren and Danny talked about Mom. Olivia picked up a volley of "self-centered" and "generous" flung between descriptions of "secretive" and "big-hearted." Two different Moms for two different sisters. Olivia vowed to remain Switzerland.

The yellow sticky note with Ryan's cell phone number dangled from the bottom of her computer monitor. She called it. After three rings, Ryan's voice mail kicked in. Caller's regret. Olivia disconnected without leaving a message. Ardy was a grown man. This was a misunderstanding that she was blowing out of proportion. Give it another day. She refilled the paper supply in the printer, slid the photo back in the frame, and switched off the desk lamp.

Where the hell is Ardy?

Chapter 17

Cornered

Ryan studied the young woman as she stood frozen by the front door; a startled rabbit preparing to flee. Ryan caught the shift of Jeff's eyes toward the back hall, as if sending her a signal to go straight to her room.

"I'd like to talk with you, Melissa," Ryan began. "I've been having a discussion with your father. Maybe you can help clarify a few things for me." Ryan kept a steady eye on her expression. Scared. Blindsided.

"About . . . what? Can I take my stuff to my room?"

"No. I think you need to sit."

Melissa's knapsack and purse slid down her arm to the floor. With tentative steps toward the couch, she sat next to her father, but only on the edge of the cushion. She searched Jeff's eyes for guidance, drinking in silent instructions. Their fingers entwined with tension.

"Melissa, I'm investigating a hit-and-run accident that took place almost three years ago on McLoughlin Avenue," Ryan continued. "A witness described a vehicle, similar to the white Suburban your father owned, that fled the scene. The man who was hit died." Ryan monitored Melissa's face for a flinch, a tick, or a quickening of breath.

"Okay . . . " She licked her lips and inhaled. Not much air came back out.

"What does this have to do with Melissa?" Jeff interrupted. "I don't think it's appropriate for you to question my daughter."

"Yes, Mr. Rovinski, it is. The driver was described as a young girl, about seventeen at the time, with long brown hair."

"We don't have a Suburban," Melissa said, squeezing her father's hand. She twisted. "Dad, we don't have a white Suburban. Tell him."

"You did at the time," Ryan corrected and pointed to the paper on the coffee table. "I believe your father changed the year on this bill of sale this afternoon."

Shock registered on Jeff's face, but he didn't contradict the statement.

"How did you get the scar on your lip?" Ryan ran his finger over his cheek for emphasis. "I have one too. Let's compare stories."

"I . . . don't remember. Happened a long time ago." Melissa straightened and touched her mouth, more of a gesture to hide it than explain the flaw. "I fell off a bike."

Ryan pointed to the three-inch raised scar on his own face. "See this? I guarantee I remember how I got it. The experience of having fifty stitches being sewn in my skin was something else." He shook his head. "Even though I was numbed up, I'll never forget the pulling sensation of a needle going in and out."

Melissa remained quiet, but her eyes started to water.

Ryan continued pushing to open the tap. "After you pulled out to McLoughlin Avenue did you bang your mouth on the steering wheel when you hit a yellow Volkswagen?"

"No . . . not like that—"

"Did you panic and leave the scene?"

"No . . . I mean—"

"Did you run home to your father with a busted bumper and a busted lip? I need the truth, Melissa."

"Hey, don't badger her," Jeff admonished. "Don't say another word, Melissa, until we get a lawyer."

Ignoring the outburst, Ryan leaned forward. "The man who was killed had a name: Adam Novak. He was married for thirty-two years, just going to the store. What did you think when you watched the reports on the news? Did you read about the crash on the front page of the paper? Did you Google for updates to see if the police had any leads?"

"It was an accident!" she cried out.

Jeff raised his blazing eyes. "Enough!"

Ryan got what he came for. He lived for that physical twinge in his gut, when his body claimed success before his mind could take the credit.

Melissa started to shake. Letting go of her hand, Jeff rubbed Melissa's back in quick circles, as if spreading a salve of alibi.

"Look what you've done! She's upset." Jeff tightened his arms around her. A whimper escaped from Melissa's scarred mouth, which escalated to a sob as she buried her face in Jeff's shirt.

A vibration in his chest prompted Ryan to reach for his phone. With his adrenalin flowing, he glanced at the small screen. *Not yet, Olivia.* He let the call drift to voice mail as he stood and moved to the front door. McClosky waited in his cruiser at the curb. Once on the porch, Ryan stuck up his thumb and waved for his colleague to join him inside.

~ · ~ · ~

Clickety . . . clack . . . clack . . . clack. As soon as Olivia opened the pocket door in the den, the sound of pounding typewriter keys hit her. Lauren might as well have been tapping on Olivia's forehead with a reflex hammer. The typewriter's report made her jump like that damned misplaced *L* key. There was one admission she chose not to offer.

Olivia joined Lauren and Danny in the kitchen. She should have left a message when she called Ryan, but he had more important business than a neighbor who may have abandoned his dog. Wait a day and call back. She had her fair share of concerns: the funeral on Thursday, Karen reading the manuscript, and Pogo tearing up her clean house.

"A masterpiece!" Lauren announced. "Ellen Dushane was kind, generous, and full of advice for everybody else." She turned the roller and handed the paper to Olivia.

"Except the question mark for the year she was born," Danny said. "I think we should make Mom seventy-nine like she wanted."

"Obituaries are for the living, Danny." Lauren lit a cigarette. "People will say she died too young from smoking." She studied Olivia's face as she read the tribute, a white squiggle streaming above her head. "What? You're being quiet. I figured you'd want to rewrite the darned thing because it wasn't good enough—too many *-ly* adverbs or something."

"No, it's fine. Lovely, in fact," Olivia muttered.

"What's the matter?"

"Ardy's not at the hospital, that I can tell. I don't know where the hell he is."

"Not good . . . " Lauren took another drag on her cigarette.

"At least his dog's okay," Danny added, attempting to say something positive. "I'd be freaked if we hadn't gone over to his house to get him."

"Where is Pogo, anyway?" Olivia asked, eyeing the empty pie plate. She wiped up the new spill of water under the bowl.

"I let him out in the backyard so we don't need to walk him." Danny stepped to the patio doors in the small breakfast room off the kitchen. "Pogo! Come inside. It's getting dark."

In the dusky light, the jingle of Pogo's collar preceded his barrel around the corner to the side door. He jumped up on the screen, ripping the sides from the frame. Olivia lunged to untangle his paws. "Come in the normal way, Pogo!"

The dog busted through the rest of screen before Olivia could unlatch the door. He leaped up on his hind legs and, with his paws punching like two black boxing gloves, knocked over the salt and pepper shakers on the kitchen table. Like an overwound watch, Pogo circled the island and sprung toward the entryway to escape a scolding. Olivia, too, wanted to blow a spring at the scratch of the dog's toenails on her polished stairs. Sweeping the peppered salt into her palm, Olivia stomped to the kitchen sink, turned, and tossed the grains over her shoulder. *Bad omen*, her mother had always insisted.

"I swear, that dog," she griped. "Spoiled as chicken salad at a picnic. Now I need a new screen door!"

"He's a picnic all right. Damn," Lauren agreed. "I'm glad he's destroying your house and not mine."

"Pogo needs attention. He's upset," Danny defended, ripping the rest of the screen from the door. "But I'm with Liv; I'm worried about this Ardy guy."

"Then you play with Pogo tomorrow. Take him to the park or something," Olivia said, waving her hand. "I'll be on the phone most of the day, dealing with Mom's accounts and going through her address book. Isn't there a cousin in New Hampshire . . . Dotty? Dody?"

"Della," Lauren corrected. "Short for Delphine."

"Right . . . Della. Who the hell knows if Della's still alive?"

"I don't think there was any love lost between them."

"Why?"

"You know New Englanders. Doesn't take much. Yankees even snub people for not returning Tupperware." Lauren shrugged. "Mom always bitched about her. While you do the executrix things, I need to dye my glorious locks and trim my bangs." Lauren dipped her scalp forward and parted her chestnut hair. A rail of gray ran down the length of her roots. "Mom's going to pop the top on her urn and stick her head out to yell at me. Can't you hear her now? 'You could have at least done something about that hair!'"

"What are you going to do to it?" Olivia huffed.

"I went by Walmart and picked up a box of Warm Summer Breeze, but I have a dilemma." Lauren hesitated. "I need my glasses to see what I'm doing, but I can't wear my glasses when I dye my hair. Maybe I'll just do the front. Mom won't be able to see the back."

Olivia's features softened at the absurdity of the conversation. "I'll help you. I don't want you to stain the bathroom floor when you miss your head with the squirt bottle. Even better, I can make an appointment with my hairdresser."

"Noooo . . . salons are a rip-off."

"What should we put on the altar for Mom's service," Danny asked, "besides her picture and the urn?"

"This typewriter." Lauren's tone didn't invite negotiation. "It meant a lot to her."

"Okay . . . " Olivia glanced at the outdated steel lump that sat on the polished granite. A collision of eras.

"Mom had about a third of a pack of cigarettes next to her computer back at the house," Danny said.

"Ohhh no. Crossing the line." Olivia rolled her eyes.

"Line of what?" Lauren countered. "If they were important to Mom, we should get them." She nodded at Danny.

Olivia cringed. In an attempt to erase the image, she added one of her own. "I say Mom's and Dad's wedding rings. I'll add Adam's band, and Lauren, you can add Mark's."

"Nice touch, Liv. I keep Mark's right here." Lauren pulled up the chain on her neck, from which dangled a thin gold band.

A loud *thunk* upstairs prompted the three of them to raise their eyes to the ceiling. Freesia raced through the kitchen and streaked toward the den to hide. The counter chair scraped as Lauren smashed out her cigarette. "Pogo!"

In scrambled formation, Olivia dashed to the base of the stairs in the entryway, followed by Danny and Lauren. A mangled red high-heeled pump fell through the upstairs rail and landed atop dozens of onionskin pages littering the floor and the steps. More pages floated from the second floor hall like giant square snowflakes. With his snout pushed through the upstairs balustrades, Pogo sat with his jaws jammed full of paper. His eyes blinked with unleashed secrets.

Olivia froze. Danny stood with her mouth open. Lauren started laughing as she picked up one of the saliva-covered red pumps by the tip of the heel, as if a wet, dirty sock. Chew marks had shredded the leather.

"*Sharknado!*" Lauren declared.

"My favorite shoes!" Olivia grabbed the pump, but the shoes were the least of her worries. Her heart thumped at the sight of the paper strewn over the entryway.

"Good one, Pogo! I wanted to do the same thing when I saw Liv wearing those the other day." Lauren caught the last floating page before it landed on her head. She stared at the paper. As she read the words, her humor evaporated. "This was done . . . on Mom's typewriter. The *L* key. The *L* is raised right here." She pointed to the third line of text. Lauren's mouth gaped as she picked up more pages from the floor. "And this one . . . and this one . . . " The fourth was the cover page. Lauren turned to Olivia, her face burning with inquisition. Even her cheeks bloomed pink with realization. "*Indigo to Black*? By Ellen Dushane?"

"Mom? A manuscript of Mom's?" Danny said, incredulous. She grabbed the page from Lauren's hand. "Let me see."

Lauren zeroed in on Olivia. "Where did you find this?"

Olivia shifted, her mind whirling faster than her ability to form words. "I . . . found it . . . in the safe . . . with the other papers."

"Why the hell didn't you say anything?"

"Yeah, you should have said something," Danny echoed.

Lauren and Danny stared at her, waiting for an answer.

Olivia waited too. A miraculous rapid-fire rebuttal congealed with fragments of truth. "I wanted a private memento—between Mom and me. I don't have anything special of hers . . . for me." Her eyes welled as her own words ripped at her insides, knotted with moral fibers of veracity and deceit. "Danny, you might as well have been an only child; you had Mom every day. And Lauren; you got to be her only child before I came along." Olivia buried her face in her hands, pouring out guilt and relief for the charade leg of this journey to be over.

"Liv . . . " Lauren's voice cracked. She reached her arms toward Olivia. "I didn't realize how hard this must be on you."

Danny's shoulders slumped. "We've been so selfish. And coming up on the three-year anniversary of Adam too. I'm so sorry."

Olivia broke from the embrace and glanced up at Pogo. The

papers dropped from the dog's mouth as he watched the scene from above. Having lost his status as the center of attention, Pogo's face drooped with disappointment.

"Get these pages!" Olivia cried, smoothing the papers as she picked them up. "Every . . . single . . . one! I hope he didn't eat any of them." She sniffed and wiped her eyes with her arm.

On her hands and knees, Lauren gathered the manuscript scattered on the stairs, attempting to organize the pages in numerical order. "He'd better not!" She stopped and turned. "Have you read this, Liv?"

"Yeah . . . "

"And?"

"It's good . . . *really* good. You wouldn't believe how good."

"Get those pages, Danny!" Lauren shouted. "I'll get these on the stairs!"

Danny plucked a page from beneath her foot, the opening of chapter three. She studied the first paragraph and raised her eyes. "Who the hell is Becky?"

~ · ~ · ~

Ryan locked the cuffs on Melissa's wrists as tears streaked her face. "Melissa Rovinski, you have the right to remain silent . . . "

"Daaaaaddyyy!"

"Anything you say can and will be used against you in a court of law . . . "

"Daaaaaddyyy!"

"You have the right to talk to a lawyer and have him present with you . . . "

"Daaaaad?"

"If you cannot afford to hire a lawyer, one will be appointed to represent you . . . "

Melissa coughed as she stamped her foot.

"You can decide at any time to exercise these rights . . . " Ryan checked the cuffs and pulled back Melissa's arms to give the grip some slack.

Jeff Rovinski's eyes were wild with disbelief. "Meeeee . . . not her! I did it!" McClosky led Jeff down the porch steps in his own set of handcuffs, having already read him his Miranda rights. "Not one word, Melissa!" Jeff shouted. "Not one word. They have no proof!"

Ryan nodded as he guided Melissa through the front door. "Separate cars. You take him; I'll take her."

"I've got the bill of sale." McClosky patted his pocket. "I owe you one, Eason."

Chapter 18

I Need the Dog

The drive to the station with Melissa had been uneventful, except for several rounds of "I'm sorry" and "not Dad's fault." During the booking process, she'd refused to elaborate when asked about the details of the accident. She'd spill soon enough, and so would Jeff. With the license number of the white Suburban in the hands of the investigation team, the unsuspecting owner who'd purchased the car was now involved in the case. A flatbed truck was on the way to the man's house in Salem to confiscate the car.

After providing an extensive statement to the district attorney at the Multnomah County Jail, Ryan glanced at his watch: nine o'clock. He followed McClosky into the small staff kitchen.

McClosky shook a sugar packet, tore it open, and poured it into his coffee. "Why don't you call it a night?" he said. "I'll finish up the paperwork. No need for both of us to be here."

Ryan nodded. "You mind? I need to tell Olivia, and I think it's best to do this in person."

"Better coming from you. Get the heck out of here. And go out the side door. I caught some reporters in the front."

Ryan poured black, over-steeped coffee in a to-go cup. Now he had two reasons to drive back to Eastmoreland tonight, maybe three:

Danny. Before he shared the news of the arrest with Olivia, Ryan needed to do a quick check on R. D. before the old man went to bed. The Rovinskis would be held overnight until they were charged tomorrow afternoon: involuntary manslaughter for Melissa, an accessory charge for Jeff, plus a host of other charges related to fleeing the scene and intent to conceal a crime. Ryan blew into the cup before securing the plastic lid.

Both Melissa and Jeff would end up paying for their mutual protective stance. Had either one of them offered an explanation at the time of the accident, the pair might receive a more lenient sentence. The agony for Olivia might have been shortened too. He hoped Olivia's stoic control wouldn't crumble to vengeance.

Ryan opened the side door to the police car parking lot. As he took one step outside, a reporter waited to scoop the story. Ryan wished police scanners were on a private network.

The press. He had to get to Olivia before she saw developments on the news.

"You made an arrest in the Novak accident tonight?" a male reporter asked, waiting beside the back exit.

"No comment at this time," Ryan answered. "Your colleagues are in the front, not here."

"Has Olivia Novak been informed?"

"Please let us do our job tonight."

"Hey, I'm just doing mine."

Ryan didn't have the energy reserve to waste on this guy. He walked away to the quiet of the cruiser. The engine idled as he checked his messages. He pressed the listing for the missed call from Olivia to learn more information about it. No voicemail. She'd hung up. His news needed to be relayed in person. He'd find out what that call was about.

Hour fourteen of his day. Ryan drove down 99E and sipped the coffee to stay alert. The hot dog he'd eaten earlier at the station sat in his stomach like road kill. Most of the details of Melissa's story made sense; the rest would come out at the arraignment. But the real story was spoiling syndrome: parents who create the very problems in their children they seek to thwart. Ellen didn't want Danny to be alone. And where did Danny end up? Alone—a scared child at forty-five when she should have been with him, married by now. Wasted time. But her mother got what she wanted from the deal. Ellen never had to be alone.

Ryan pulled in front of Olivia's house at nine thirty. He flashed his lights at his fellow officer who waited for his arrival. He pulled up next the cruiser and lowered his window.

"All okay?" Ryan asked.

"Not a peep. This is one quiet neighborhood," the officer said.

"What time did you get here?"

"About six thirty. Didn't see anything amiss."

"I'll take it from here. Go on home."

"Hey, I heard the news of the arrest. Congratulations."

"The night's not over yet, but thanks."

Ryan watched the cruiser drive away to a home, kids, and a warm greeting of 'How was your day?' He turned his gaze back to Olivia's house. A lamp glowed in the living room behind the sheered curtain, with a sister holding down each end of the couch: Lauren and Olivia. The porch light was out, and so was R. D.'s. Much better for him to knock on Olivia's door tonight than for a reporter to bang on it in the morning. Easy one first: start with Griffin. This could be done with a check-in phone call.

After four rings, R. D.'s phone went to his answering machine. Asleep. The old man needed to get up early for his trip to the hospital. But Ryan needed assurance that Griffin was okay. He pulled a flashlight from the center console.

With the beam trained on the front steps, Ryan moved up R. D.'s S-curved walkway. Melissa Rovinski's whining cries still rang in his head, a reminder of a long day. Now it was too quiet. A dim amber glow from the doorbell drew his finger to the left of the front door. A muffled *bing-bong*, like carillon church bells, echoed inside. He waited for the hall light to come on, but it didn't. No dog barked. No thump on the stairs. Ryan pressed the bell again. Suspicion started to mix with caffeine and processed protein. Perhaps he'd been too dismissive of this Witness Protection breach, not taken the threat seriously enough. He fanned the beam over the paving stones to the back patio.

Cautious, Ryan crept along the side of the house with his hand on the 9mm Glock. Sticks and debris crunched as he stepped onto the patio and shone the light over the French doors. Glints of glass drew his gaze to the concrete. He leaned closer and followed the reverse trajectory to the broken pane next to the door handle. His stomach flipped as he reached for his wallet.

Ryan called the secure number under Eduardo Riojas's name on the back of Sarge's business card.

~ · ~ · ~

At nine forty-five, Olivia reviewed the list of outstanding arrangements for the funeral service and to-do items for the estate settlement. She sat on one end of the couch in the living room while Lauren held down the other with her stocking feet resting on the glass coffee table and Mom's manuscript in her lap. Olivia cringed every time Lauren licked her finger for the turn of a page. She fought the urge to retrieve a container of hand sanitizer. Sitting in the overstuffed side chair, Danny stared at the TV in the built-in bookcase, engrossed in an episode of *History Detectives* on cable that followed the life of an artifact from the Civil War. Freesia was stretched out on Olivia's bed upstairs, and a truce had been called with Pogo, who made a focused project of chewing on both red pumps like rawhide bones. Olivia was resigned to her inability to control the crimson carnage.

Olivia glanced at Lauren every few seconds, monitoring her expression as she read the manuscript. Only into the first twenty pages, Lauren's eyebrows rose; her lips pressed together; her mouth went up and down on each side.

The doorbell rang. Pogo abandoned the red pumps and sprang to attention. He sprinted to the front door.

Rrrrruh . . . ruh . . . ruh . . . ruh.

"I'm not getting up. Becky's my new best friend," Lauren said and turned over a crinkly page of the manuscript. "This is way too good."

"This Civil War letter is fascinating," Danny added, turning up the volume on the television. "Your house, Liv. You have to answer it."

Olivia huffed to the entryway and flipped on the porch light. She peered through the peep hole. "Quiet, Pogo!"

Olivia held the dog's collar as she opened the front door. Ryan stood in front her in uniform.

~ · ~ · ~

"Olivia?" Ryan wanted to tell her the second update, but the news of the arrest had to wait. He needed her full attention.

"What are you doing here?" Olivia asked. She restrained the dog by his collar and glanced toward the living room. She leaned in and whispered, "Danny's here."

Ryan shifted his gaze beyond Olivia and spotted Danny turning off the television. "Two things, but at this moment I'm concerned about your neighbor."

"Ardy?"

"Yeah."

"Come in. We're having a dose of Mom."

Ryan stepped inside, maintaining his official countenance. Danny stared at him, a wash of emotions in her expression.

Lauren raised her eyes from the pile of paper in her lap, surprised to see him. "Ryan! Is everything okay?" She swung her feet from the coffee table and set the papers aside.

"Ryan?" Danny smoothed her cotton blouse, well aware of the effect she had on him. "Are you here to see me?"

"Sorry, you're not the top priority right this minute." Ryan adjusted the weapons on his waist, weapons that didn't protect him against Danny. He tried not to stare, but imagined wrapping his arms around her. Instead, he said: "I need R. D.'s dog." Ryan squatted in front of Pogo and held both sides of his curly muzzle. "C'mon, boy. We're going to find your daddy."

Pogo licked his face like a treat, leaving behind a trail of shiny saliva. Ryan wiped his cheek with his sleeve.

"He's a good dog, but he needs training," Danny said, searching for something to say.

"What's going on? We're worried about Ardy too," Olivia said, though she was watching the chemistry between him and Danny. "I can't believe he left Pogo behind without talking to me. I called the hospital, but he hadn't checked in."

"When?" Ryan asked, studying her.

"Sevenish. All three of us went over to his house to talk to him about taking care of the dog. Ardy wasn't there. His car's in the driveway. Where did he go? I was worried, so I called you." Olivia threw him a sheepish look. "Sorry, I hung up. I figured I might be overreacting."

"An inopportune moment." Ryan hesitated and checked his watch. Riojas was on his way. "How'd you get the dog over here?"

"We had to smash a pane in the back door. Pogo was going crazy inside the house."

"Go ahead," Lauren interjected. She held out her wrists. "Arrest me for breaking and entering," When he didn't react, the expression on her face turned serious. "I broke the window, Ryan."

"Makes sense. Did you check inside the house?"

"I went through every room," Olivia confirmed. "Nothing."

"I'm taking Pogo over. If R. D.'s in the house, he'll pick up the scent."

"You think he's—"

"Okay?" he said, finishing the statement. "I hope so."

"Let me go with you."

"No. You three stay here."

"Uh-uh. I'm coming," Olivia insisted. She pulled Pogo's leash from the banister.

"Me too." Lauren scooped up her slippers.

"I want to go," Danny said, scrambling to find her flip-flops. "I don't want anything to happen to you, Ryan."

The statement softened his insides. *She cares.*

At the front door, Olivia clipped the leash to Pogo's collar. She raised her eyes. "Ryan . . . how do you know my neighbor?"

Ryan hesitated and avoided Olivia's questioning stare. Pogo strained at the open door. He switched on the flashlight. "Let's go, boy."

~ · ~ · ~

Twilight faded to night as the group made a trek to Ardy's back patio. Olivia knew every step and stone by heart. To the rhythmic *thwock* of Danny's flip-flops, she counted them off in her head. She peered through one of the panes as Ryan shone the flashlight on the French door, the only illumination in the courtyard. She sucked in a breath as Ryan reached his bare hand toward the broken glass next to the handle.

"Careful . . . careful . . . you'll cut yourself!" Danny warned, squeezing her eyes.

"He knows what he's doing," Olivia scolded, attempting to restrain the dog.

Ryan poised his fingers to reach past the lethal shard remaining in the broken window.

Lauren scuffed to the patio door. "Here, give me the flashlight." She snatched the heavy cylinder from Ryan and banged out the remaining glass. "There. Now stick your hand in."

"We should've paid more attention to this door," Olivia said. "Anybody could have gone in here." Her mother's scolding words rang in her head. *I didn't raise you this way. What were you thinking, girl!?*

"Liv, we were more than a little distracted."

"This is dangerous, Ryan," Danny warned. "What if a crazed murderer is hiding inside?" Her brown eyes glistened in the light beam. "And we were inside . . . "

Ryan shook his head as he reached in and unlocked the door. He turned to Olivia. "Did you take Pogo through the house when you were in here before?"

"No. Danny stayed with him to keep him calm. She did a good job."

"Thanks, Liv," Danny said.

Ryan pointed to the dark kitchen. "Let Pogo off his leash. We'll follow where he goes."

As Olivia unhooked the clasp, she hoped the props she gave to her sister might soften Ryan's edginess. Pogo bolted inside and darted toward the front entryway, sniffing in short puffs. Ryan followed him and switched on the light in the hall. Olivia, Lauren, and Danny dashed behind him to catch up. In the living room, Pogo jumped on the couch and turned in a circle to inspect his towel.

"Where's R. D., boy?" Ryan urged. "Find him!"

"I don't think he's in the top percentile of doggy IQ," Lauren said.

"Don't hurt Pogo's feelings," Danny scolded and turned to Ryan. "We shouldn't be in here, should we?"

Pogo took a leap and bolted up the stairs.

"No, you shouldn't," Ryan said. "I wanted to come in here with only the dog. You three wait down here." With his Glock trained on the upstairs landing, Ryan dashed after Pogo. He turned on the fourth step. "If you hadn't tried to protect the dog so much and let him lead *you*, we might have saved time. Why didn't you call me the minute R. D. didn't answer the door?" Ryan raced up the steps before Danny could respond.

Olivia turned to Danny. "He doesn't even know Ardy. Something else is going on."

"See? That drove me crazy," Danny complained, spreading her arms. "Always trying to be a hero. He never gave me any clues of his cases. I felt like a useless lump while he put himself in harm's way."

"Well, don't be a lump now," Lauren said.

"Head high, Danny. Back straight." Olivia stared at her little sister and pointed. "Go up those goddamned stairs and support Ryan. The future's up there, not down here. Get off the sidelines."

Danny's lip started to quiver as her gaze shifted from Lauren to Olivia. She gripped the banister and charged up the steps.

Olivia turned to Lauren and smiled. "Tough love. That kick in the butt was long overdue."

"Yeah . . . well. Mom can't baby her anymore."

They both listened to the whispering, scratching, and jingling upstairs. Lauren's eyes widened. Olivia's thoughts went right to the spilled salt.

At the top of the stairs, Danny appeared and leaned over the railing. "You two need to get up here. Pogo's picked up something in the wall. We think we heard a groan."

"Oh no!" Olivia pushed Lauren from behind. "Go, go, *go*!"

Lauren stopped short in the doorway of the master bedroom. Plowing into her, Olivia teetered as she missed her footing. Ryan stood at the wall, pressing his hands on the wooden panel.

"What the hell is this? A secret room or something?" he muttered. Ryan ran the flashlight beam along the edge of the molding.

"A Murphy bed," Olivia said. "Old houses from the teens and twenties sometimes had them."

"How do I get it open?"

"I put one of these in a setting for one of my early books. I did research about how they work." Olivia stooped and pushed along the bottom of the frame. "It works on . . . a . . . counterweight. This one seems to be stuck . . . from the house settling." She waved at Lauren and Danny. "Help me push on the bottom so the top can come down. Ryan, get ready to catch it. All together . . . one . . . two . . . "

"Freeze!" A new voice shouted from the doorway. "Don't move! FBI!"

The sisters froze. Ryan stood with his arms extended, ready to catch the bed. One dark-haired agent waved his gun at them; a second one, with sandy-blond hair, aimed his gun at Pogo when the dog started to bark.

"Don't you dare shoot that dog!" Danny shouted. "He won't hurt you. You have to whisper to him."

"What?" The blond agent backed away, still training his gun on the dog.

"Don't yell. Pogo doesn't like loud voices."

The agent pointed his gun at Danny as she lunged for Pogo's collar. "I told you not to move!"

"Oh, for God's sake. Don't shoot me," she groused. "I'll get him." Danny stooped and clapped, reaching out to Pogo as he trotted to her side.

Ryan turned with his hands raised. "I'm the officer who called: Ryan Eason. I was assigned to monitor R. D. Griffin. He's missing."

Both agents lowered their guns. Olivia let out a breath as they did so and turned to Ryan. "What do you mean *monitor* him?" Ryan didn't answer. She narrowed her eyes and set her hands on her hips. "I want to know what the hell is going on here! Who are you people?"

"Agent Skidmore," the blond one answered as he slipped his gun back into his chest holster.

The second man did the same. "Agent Riojas. We're responding to Officer Eason's call."

"Then make yourselves useful," Lauren instructed, turning toward the wall. "We don't need guns; we need hands. Help us get this damned bed open."

"We think Ardy's in here," Olivia agreed, kneeling at the base of the molding. "Ryan heard a groan."

Riojas rubbed his chin and pointed in sequence. "Who are you three?"

"Next door neighbors. I've—we've been babysitting Ardy's dog."

Skidmore joined Olivia, Lauren, and Danny on the floor, while Riojas supported the top corner of the panel, opposite from Ryan.

As Danny held back Pogo, Olivia resumed the count. "One . . . two . . . three . . . *push!*"

The combined force engaged the counterweight. As the bed launched forward, Olivia, Lauren, and Agent Skidmore scooted away to escape a head bonk.

"Ughhhhh . . . ughhhhh." Ardy bounced on the mattress as he

landed with a *bang*. Laying face up with his arms extended, he resembled a clothed version of Leonardo da Vinci's *Vitruvian Man*. Ardy let out a weak groan, but didn't open his eyes. His jeans and checked shirt were creased, as if pressed for hours in a Panini toaster.

"Ardy!" Olivia shouted. She pushed the FBI agents out of the way to take Ardy's hand. Danny released Pogo, who jumped on the bed. In a frantic reunion, Pogo licked the old man's ashen face.

Ryan pulled out his phone and called 9-1-1 for an ambulance. "Danny, get some water."

"I'm on it, honey."

Olivia's heart swelled at their words, voices filled with the understanding exclusive to couples. Then, she raised her eyes to the two FBI agents helping Ardy to sit up, convinced a new story was about to emerge from their presence. She wanted in on whatever it was.

Chapter 19

The Phone Message

At ten fifteen Ryan thumped the door of the ambulance twice. The sisters' faces flickered red with the flash of lights as they gathered on the front stoop of R. D.'s house. The siren blared as the ambulance pulled from the driveway and raced down the street. The lights faded, leaving only the glow of the porch light.

"We appreciate all you did to protect Griffin, Officer Eason," Agent Riojas said, shaking Ryan's hand. "Glad this was an accident and not a real threat." He signaled for Skidmore to start the Crown Victoria. "We'll meet the ambulance at the hospital."

"Doing my job," Ryan said, his voice weary. He took a breath and moved toward the porch. Olivia and Lauren leaned against the railing; Danny sat on the top step with Pogo on his leash.

"Is Ardy going to be all right?" Danny asked, stroking the dog's chest.

"He needs a few days in the hospital. Pretty dehydrated."

"What's that about, Ryan?" Olivia pressed, pointing to the black car pulling away.

"I can't tell you. Leave it, okay?" Running on fumes, Ryan knew he had one more round to go with Olivia about his other news before the night was over. "I've locked the place up. Let's go over to your house for a chat." He reached for Danny's hand. "You did good tonight, Danny Girl."

She squeezed his fingers. "I hope I made a difference."

Lauren yawned. "I'm going to bed." She ruffled Danny's hair and did the same to Pogo's. "This is way too much drama for me. Is life at Casa de Novak always this crazy?"

"Things are about to get crazier," Ryan added, locking his gaze on Olivia. "I have to talk with you in private."

~ · ~ · ~

Back at the house, Pogo had collapsed under the chair in the breakfast room. Freesia eyed the dog with her head drooped over the edge of the seat, stretching one paw to within an inch of his ears. Olivia set a turkey sandwich in front of Ryan at the kitchen island. An odd expression crossed his face. Words for its explanation appeared to be trying to escape, but weren't forthcoming. Danny stood behind Ryan and massaged his shoulders, perhaps sensing Ryan's anxious mood. Lauren circled the kitchen in a tight coil of nervous energy, as if she might miss something. A strange tension filled the air, and Olivia didn't think it stemmed from Ardy's ordeal.

She glanced at Ryan. "What did you want to talk to me about?"

"I changed my mind," Lauren said. She tugged open the refrigerator and shoved her whole head in. "This will help me sleep." She emerged with her ice-filled tumbler of wine and took a deep drink. Calm again, she nodded toward the flashing red one on the answering machine. "You've got a message, Liv."

Ryan straightened and sped up the chew on a bite of the sandwich. He struggled to swallow. "Wait! Before you check it, I—"

"Oh, keep your gun on safety. This'll just take a sec," Olivia said. "I left a bunch of messages about Mom's service on Thursday. I want to make sure the etcher for the urn will be done, and the florist was going to confirm they got the hydrangeas in." She pressed the speaker button on the answering machine:

"Oh, Liv . . . you made my day . . . my week! I read the first fifty pages you sent. I hope you overnighted the manuscript because I . . . "

Olivia fumbled to hit the stop button. "Just my agent," she said, relieved to have silenced Karen's voice.

"No, no, no . . . let it play!" Lauren said, bumping the ice around in her glass. "I want to hear this. You wrote a new manuscript?"

"Me too," Danny chimed in. "Go ahead."

Ryan squeezed his eyebrows together at the bridge of his nose with his thumb and forefinger. "Look. I have something to tell Olivia."

Ignoring Ryan's comment, Lauren's eyes danced with anticipation. "You told me you couldn't come up with anything, Liv. You were holding out on me."

Olivia's knees liquefied. They'd never understand her motives. Even she didn't understand her motives. The bell sounded in her head to start the second round of this debacle with no gloves. Olivia didn't move as Lauren rushed to the answering machine and resumed playing the message. A wide smile lit up Lauren's face as Karen's voice filled the kitchen:

" . . . want this. I don't know what happened to your writing since *Tex-Mex Nights*, but this is terrific! You were right. It's YA on steroids . . . suspense, maybe a thriller. Three publishing houses are interested. Yes! I already made the calls. I'll bet we'll even whip up a bidding war. You were hiding this from me, you minx. How on earth did you come up with this Becky character? Call me as soon as you can."

As Karen's voice uttered the name Becky, Lauren's smile evaporated as her mouthed popped open. Olivia kept hers closed, waiting for the machine's mechanical voice to kick in. She rolled her hand in a circle to get this over with.

"End of messages. To erase this message, press—"

Lauren jabbed the stop button, her forefinger loaded with ammunition. "Did you send Mom's manuscript to your agent?"

Ryan raised his eyes, on full alert at Lauren's acidic tone.

"This is *not* what you think." Olivia held up her hands and pumped the air.

"Oh, it's *exactly* what I think. '*Your* writing'?" Lauren's slammed the plastic tumbler on the counter and stomped to the living room.

"I . . . I . . . *wait*!"

With a tangle of feet, Pogo chased Lauren. In the dog's wake, tense silence crackled with ungrounded electricity. Danny and Ryan stared at Olivia, unable to speak.

Olivia's wedding china rattled in the dining room as Lauren pounded her steps back to the kitchen, followed by a jingle of dog tags. Freesia jumped off the chair and scurried away as if being stalked by a demon predator. Lauren slapped the manuscript in front of Ryan. "Here! Evidence!"

"What's going on here?" he asked. Danny stood behind him, peering over his shoulder with her mouth still open. "This is not as important as what I have to—"

"I want you to arrest my sister for plagiarism! *That's* what's going on!" Lauren grabbed her wine glass and took a gulp. The ice let loose from the bottom and hit her in the face, splashing a pink stream down the front of her muumuu. "Becky my ass!"

"Olivia? Is this true?" Ryan questioned, his words measured to avoid fueling the fire. "Did you pass off"—he glanced at the cover page—"this *Indigo to Black* as your own book?"

"No way is it *her* book," Lauren cut in, wiping her chin of droplets.

"I did it for Mom." Olivia blew out the stream of breath she'd been holding. "Otherwise, the story probably wouldn't get published. And it still might not happen. All the ingredients came together. Karen Finerelli, my agent, has been pressuring me for a new manuscript, and when I read this . . . " Olivia pointed to the stacked pages in front of Ryan.

"Where did it come from?" he asked.

"I found it in Mom's safe."

"Were you going to say anything?"

"Eventually . . . but not until I could get a deal." Olivia now appreciated how Ryan could get suspects to confess. "The book's good . . . damn good."

Ryan tapped the onionskin pages. "This book belongs to the three of you. Let's move on here."

"Of course it does." In defeat, Olivia folded a dish towel in thirds and rehung it. "I hadn't gotten quite that far. This is the first I've heard Karen even liked the darned thing."

"Good news, right?" Danny interjected, wide-eyed. "Liv would never screw us."

Lauren locked her jaw, just the way their mother used to do. Olivia braced herself for another tirade.

"That's not what Karen's message sounded like to me," Lauren said.

"Calm down, Lauren," Ryan chided. "I, for one, don't believe Olivia had ill intent."

Lauren avoided Olivia's gaze.

Ryan tapped the stack of paper. "Remember, this wouldn't be published without Olivia's established reputation, her connections, and her agent to get the book off the ground."

Yes, Mom could have stood on her own two feet with this book. She didn't need me to interfere. She didn't need me. She didn't need me . . . Olivia imagined herself a specter, eavesdropping on a pick-apart, gossipy conversation from another room. Her stomach rolled at what might have been said if she wasn't standing in front of them. She burned to run upstairs and change all the sheets.

Lauren pursed her lips, absorbing the truth of Ryan's words. Turning to Olivia, she jutted her chin like a demanding finger. "But it needs to have *Mom's* name as the author, not *yours*."

"I'll call Karen tomorrow," Olivia conceded. Her sisters didn't understand the uphill process the three of them faced to get the book published. At least she wouldn't be alone, crushed in a cocoon of deception. Her shoulders dropped with exhaustion, releasing a leak of tears. "I'd never screw you guys."

"Okay, are we done with the fight here?" Ryan held up his hands. "I've got one ugly scar. I don't need another."

Olivia pressed her forehead. "I hope so. I can't take much more today."

"Better brace yourself, then."

Olivia raised her eyes to Ryan. "What now?"

"I made an arrest tonight." Ryan let the words sink over her like volcanic ash. "Two . . . to be exact."

Olivia struggled for breath. Her face pulsed in rhythm to the pounding in her chest. Forcing her mouth to move, she could only form one word: "Adam?"

Ryan returned a slow nod. "You'll have reporters showing up in the morning."

"Oh . . . my . . . God!" Danny cried out. She squeezed Ryan's shoulders and buried her head in his neck. "You found him."

"*Her*. A young woman and her father." Ryan reached up and held Danny's wrists. "The arraignment is tomorrow at ten. Olivia, I think you should attend. They've requested a private meeting with you."

Olivia stood frozen. Her arms hung limp at her side as Lauren embraced her. Years turned to nanoseconds, as if compressed in a twisted, cruel joke.

"I'm sorry. Of course, you wouldn't screw us." Lauren released her and reached in the cabinet for three goblets. She grabbed the open wine bottle. "I'm thrilled for you, Liv." After splashing the insides, Lauren handed one each to Olivia, Danny, and Ryan. She refilled her tumbler. "I don't care if you are on duty, Ryan, we're toasting to closure—for all of us. Tell us every detail of how the arrest went down."

Danny took a glass. "Here's to Ryan! The best damn police officer in Portland!"

"To Ryan!" Lauren announced.

Pogo stood in the kitchen and barked to add his two cents.

Ryan didn't join the toast. Instead, he locked his gaze on Olivia.

Olivia stared at the crimson liquid in the goblet, unable to comprehend what to do with it. Shiny? Drink? The barking faded. Her sisters' voices thinned, as if squeezed through the head of a needle. In their place, a torrent of emotions rolled through her: the loss of Adam and her mother; her potential injury to the relationship with her sisters, and the fear of dying alone, as might have been the fate of Ardy. She leaned against the counter to steady her shaking limbs. The wine glass slipped from her fingers and smashed on the tile floor.

Indigo . . . melted . . . to black.

Chapter 20

The Meeting

"Olivia Novak! How do you feel about your husband's killer being caught?!" a voice shouted as she emerged from the front door at eight forty-five on Tuesday morning. The woman reporter, coiffed for an on-air appearance, stuck out her microphone like a vacuum cleaner attachment to suck up Olivia's words.

"No comment," she muttered, adjusting her black sunglasses. Lauren held Olivia's arm to lead her to the car. Danny held her purse and keys to lock the house as she corralled Pogo on his leash. Leaving the dog behind with Freesia wasn't an option. The doorbell and the barking hadn't stopped all morning.

The previous night had been a blur after Ryan revived her on the kitchen floor. Olivia vaguely recalled Danny being on one side, Ryan on the other, supporting her trek to the living room couch after collapsing. Lauren forced her to drink water as Olivia drifted through the forty-five-minute explanation of how Ryan's investigation resulted in the arrest of Jeff Rovinski and his daughter, Melissa. The words stuck in her skin like shrapnel. She wanted the Rovinskis to be evil people, on the lam and found cornered in an open field by snarling police dogs in a hail of gunfire. But Jeff and Melissa were average people who had catapulted themselves into an evil situation—by their own doing.

And now, this morning, she was on her way to sit in front of the two of them in a specially arranged private meeting at their request. Overnight, they'd both confessed. The arraignment was nothing more than a formality to document the charges.

Thick teeth of a large clip gathered Olivia's heavy, wet hair. The dryer might as well have been a boat anchor, given what little arm strength she had to hold it.

"Leave her alone! How do you think she feels?" Lauren snapped as she guided Olivia down the front steps. "C'mon, Liv, you're doing fine."

Pogo's emergence through the door caused the throng of press to step back. Danny didn't restrain him from his attempts to jump on the closest reporter. He lunged at the microphone as if it were a fetching stick, or maybe the dog's protective instincts kicked in.

A male reporter shouted Olivia's name and elbowed his way toward her. "Did you know Jeff Rovinski and his daughter lived only a few miles from here?"

"Was Melissa Rovinski texting when the accident happened?" shouted another.

"Do you think the driver being a minor will influence the charges?"

The relentless questions came in waves, making Olivia dizzy.

"What did you say to Officer Eason after he tracked them down?" A woman reporter shouted, shoving the microphone toward Olivia.

The group backed away when Olivia jerked her arm from Lauren and turned on the woman. "Ryan Eason—spelled *E-A-S-O-N*—is the best damn police officer in the city of Portland." Olivia waved the reporter's hand away. "I have to go."

Olivia climbed into the passenger side of their father's Blazer, while Danny sat in the rear seat with Pogo. Lauren didn't want the dog to tear the leather in Olivia's clean car.

"Only a one-day deal, Liv. All of this will be over soon," Lauren assured as the eighties SUV grumbled in protest when she turned the key. "C'mon, you piece of crap! Start!"

"Remember, this is your car now," Danny said.

Olivia watched the reporters drift back to their trucks. "Guys . . . I don't know if I can face the press after I meet with the Rovinskis." She couldn't save Adam with this charade. To the media, this was only a news story for a thirty-second bump. But to her, the day was about letting go. She'd held on so tightly, like a lover, to the lack of closure with no idea how to loosen her grip.

"Bull!" Lauren scoffed and backed out of the driveway. "Of course you can. You can do anything. You're a Dushane. We *roll*, remember?"

"Where are we going again?" Olivia's mind went blank.

"Downtown, the district attorney's office." Lauren voice sounded so confident.

"If you want, we'll wait outside with Pogo while you're in there," Danny added.

"No. I want you both right beside me."

~ · ~ · ~

Olivia sat on one side of a long conference table, flanked by Lauren to her right, Danny to her left. If only the leather rolling chair had a seat belt to keep her down when Jeff Rovinski and his daughter, Melissa, were ushered into the room. Ryan took a strategic place at the end of the table with a notepad, keeping professional distance to assess the emotion on both sides. Two officers waited at the door to usher the offending pair inside the conference room.

"Keep it together, Liv," Ryan instructed. "Let them do the talking when they come in. Don't forget, the Rovinskis requested this meeting. Listen to what they have to say."

Danny mouthed to Ryan: *Thank you.*

Olivia nodded as her response, unwilling to commit to anything with her voice. She figured Ryan worried about all three of them, a collective weapon of justice. While they waited, Lauren's and Danny's protectiveness strengthened Olivia's sense of control.

The bright morning sunshine streamed through the bank of windows behind her, projecting warm rectangles down the length of the maple table. When brought into the room, Jeff and Melissa Rovinski would be seated across from her with the natural light shining in their faces. The sun would double as an interrogation lamp.

Two empty chairs waited. She stared at them, realizing hers was full and, like wind-filled sails, the seats on either side of her were full too. She wasn't facing this alone. The support of her sisters and Ryan filled her with a strange calm, and despite little sleep, Olivia's mind cleared of the morning's media debris. She had waited for this moment for so long, and she'd be damned if it would become a pity party.

Ryan kept glancing at her, as if she'd combust in anger, or faint, or make a scene. He needn't have worried; this was business, albeit family business.

Olivia stiffened at the voices growing louder in the hall. With a nod from Ryan, the attending officer exited the room. She stared at the door and waited for a turn of the handle. The officer reentered with Jeff and Melissa Rovinski in yellow jumpsuits. The morning's arraignment had resulted in charges to Melissa of involuntary manslaughter, failure to perform duties following an accident, and intent to conceal a crime; Jeff had been charged with accessory and tampering with evidence. No drawn-out trial. Neither one would meet Olivia's lasered gaze.

Olivia took a deep breath as their handcuffs were removed. The tendons in Jeff's neck pulsed with tension, but his hazel eyes relaxed as he rubbed his wrists and took a seat next to his daughter. Melissa's features appeared swollen from crying. Two officers stood behind their chairs. *These people killed my husband.* Olivia wanted to pull out her journal to note the details of their faces.

Jeff spoke first. "I'm so sorry, Mrs. Novak, I can't imagine the pain I caused you."

You can't imagine. Olivia stared at the man. All the poison words she'd stored in her own version of a Lydia Pinkham's Elixir bottle evaporated, as if a brew of a mere childish rant. Jeff's manner seemed rehearsed, practiced for the past fifteen hours, maybe for nearly three years. No mention of Melissa; he was still protecting her by taking the blame.

"Mr. Rovinski . . . " Olivia paused, meeting his gaze, "you use the term *Mrs* like my husband is waiting for me at the house doing yard-work. Half of me isn't *here*."

Ryan shifted in his seat, ready to spring into action. Lauren gripped Olivia's fingers. Olivia set her other hand over Danny's and continued. "If it weren't for this officer"—she nodded toward Ryan—"I doubt either of you would've ever come forward on your own."

"It was an accident!" Melissa cried. One of the officers grasped her shoulder. Melissa recoiled at his touch.

Jeff knotted and unknotted his fingers, fighting the urge to defend his daughter. Olivia's stony stare stopped him cold.

"I want to talk to Melissa." Olivia focused on the young woman in front of her, seizing on her outburst. Melissa's eyes watered within their inflamed rims of fear.

"But she didn't—" Jeff tried to interject.

Olivia held up her left hand to Jeff. "Let your daughter take responsibility for herself. I need the details from her perspective, not yours." Olivia's tone softened. "I know this is hard, Melissa, but you have to tell me everything that happened and how. Don't give me lawyer or Daddy-speak—*your* words."

Melissa glanced at her father; his head was down, staring at the pattern of random knots in the conference table. "I borrowed my Dad's car to help a friend move," she muttered.

"The white Suburban?"

"Right. My girlfriend got accepted at U of O and rented an apartment. I was on my way to meet her at her parents' house, and then we were going to drive down to Eugene with her stuff." Melissa swiped a forefinger under her eyelashes.

"Go on." Olivia sat back in the chair. Lauren and Danny leaned forward with rapt attention. Their shield of energy swirled on a current of sibling blood. Olivia glanced at Ryan, who studied the three of them.

"I came up to the intersection on McLoughlin Avenue," Melissa continued. "I checked both ways, and nobody was there. I swear!" She ran her hand through her hair. "My phone rang when I pulled out to turn left." Melissa paused. "I reached to answer it, but it slid to the floor . . . the passenger side."

"You tried to answer your stupid phone while pulling out onto a major roadway?" Lauren interrupted. The seething question sounded more like an additional charge to the other offenses.

Olivia imagined a prosecutor shouting, *Objection!* She squeezed Lauren's forearm to stay quiet. "And . . . ?"

"The yellow car was there . . . in the center lane . . . to turn left. I was in the intersection and saw the car too late. I couldn't stop—" Melissa started to choke on her words. "I couldn't *stop*."

"What kind of car, Melissa?" *Say it.* Olivia pictured Adam in the car.

"I don't remember. A small car, a yellow blob of some sort."

"You know exactly the kind of car you hit; you watched it on the news." Olivia stifled the anger erupting inside her. *Pull back. Breathe.* "Then what?" Unspoken signals kept Lauren and Danny still, two controlled wolverines anxious to tear into skin.

"I freaked out. I panicked," Melissa said. "My mouth hit something. I don't remember what I did." Melissa put her head in her hands. "Daaaaad?"

Jeff's face registered physical pain. His skin flushed with the exposure. The protective covering he'd woven around Melissa was being ripped away by the relentless words of truth. Olivia flinched at the imagined impact.

"What did you do after you hit the car?"

Melissa hesitated and turned to her father for permission. He gave her a silent nod. "I threw the car in reverse and turned right. I zigzagged through the neighborhoods, but my mouth was full of blood. I went home and pulled into the garage."

All eyes, except Melissa's, trained on Jeff like lasers. The baton of deception had been handed off.

"Mr. Rovinski . . . what did you do when Melissa came home?" Olivia asked and stiffened for the moment when parental responsibility became a conspiracy.

"Mad as a hornet at first, but she was hurt." He raised his eyes to meet Olivia's gaze. "When your child is bleeding and in pain, who cares about a bumper?"

"Did she tell you what happened?"

"She did. Melissa has always been honest. A good girl."

"Did she tell you someone had been hurt in the accident?"

"I didn't know!" Melissa shouted.

"She's right," Jeff reiterated. "We didn't know."

"You found out in short order. The story was all over the media for at least a week."

Jeff huffed and turned defiant. "My daughter was only seventeen, Mrs. Novak. Do you have children?"

"No . . . " Olivia wanted no part of him turning the tables on her. "That is not relevant to this discussion."

"Oh, I think it's more than relevant, Mrs. Novak," Jeff countered, his voice seething. "I was *not* going to sit back and watch Melissa's life be ruined. She has a bright future. She wants to be a teacher. I want her to get married . . . and have kids of her own!"

"You should be rephrasing the description of your daughter's future in past tense," Lauren muttered. Jeff glared at her but was smart enough to not respond.

"But . . . Mr. Rovinski . . . " Olivia hesitated, "my life was ruined the moment Melissa hit my husband."

"Melissa was only seventeen," Jeff repeated.

Olivia balled her fist and pressed her upper lip. She closed her eyes. *Don't break.*

Danny widened hers and pointed at Melissa. "Are you saying what *that girl* did was okay because my sister is old?" She stopped herself and turned to Olivia. "You're not old, Liv. I didn't mean it like that."

"I know what you meant," Olivia assured.

"No—" Jeff sighed. The trench he'd dug was getting deeper.

"Mrs. Novak, do you know how many times I drove past your house? The accident ate at me every day."

"What kind of car do you drive now, Mr. Rovinski?"

"A Prius."

Olivia inhaled at the word. "A Prius," she whispered, more to herself. The vivid image of the silver car slowing in front of her house had been imprinted on her memory. "Huh . . . I've seen it go by." Olivia shook herself back into the moment. "Let's not get off track here. Did you contact your insurance company?"

Jeff hesitated. "No. Melissa's record would have been ravaged, never mind my rates being jacked through the roof. I needed to get the car fixed, sell the damned thing, and move forward."

"Like nothing ever happened . . . " Danny said and tightened her grip of Olivia's hand.

"Bud's Kill 'n Go," Lauren sneered. "Liv, you—and Mom—would never have found that car."

Olivia's chest tightened. Her search for the white Suburban had been in vain; she never would have found it. But she didn't regret her actions now, sitting here, because her mother's phone message played in her head. The hunt had become a bond of courage with her mother that countered Jeff's bond of cowardice with Melissa.

"Wait long enough and it all goes away." Danny's voice trailed off as she glanced at Ryan. "Believe me, Mr. Rovinski, time doesn't mean anything when you make an unforgivable mistake." Ryan returned a tender expression. "Deal or lose. You should have accepted blame. I hope the three years of living with what you and your daughter did were worse than getting caught . . . I guess you have to be a decent person to feel guilt."

Olivia tapped the table to get Jeff's attention. "What would you have done if my husband had hit and killed Melissa?"

"Well . . . since we're being honest here," Jeff responded, his voice measured, "I'd be in jail for murder." He turned his gaze to the wall, on which hung a large framed photo of the Portland skyline, what would be his only view of Portland for a while.

"Just what I thought." Olivia stood. Lava churned in her gut, oozing through fissures. She placed both hands on the conference table and leaned forward. "And since we're being *honest here*, my sisters and I were raised to be better people than you or your daughter. Our mother's funeral is on Thursday afternoon. I need to thank you for the reminder that I should have appreciated her more." Lauren and Danny rose to their feet next to her. They let Olivia continue. "My mother would have been the first to raise her hand, but then again"—she glanced to the left and right—"any one of the three of us would *never* have left the scene of an accident. And no matter what I think, the law says you have an obligation to help someone when you injure them—but *kill*?" Olivia paused and stared at Melissa. "Look me in the eye, little girl!" Melissa appeared to be more like teenager than a grown woman as she raised her eyes, as if struggling against the counterweights of Ardy's Murphy bed. "You should have done the right thing in *spite* of your father. Get it? You're an English major—*were* an English major. Look up *moral integrity*, you little murderer." Olivia gulped and slapped the table. "Go check your damned phone. How many of your friends are calling you *now*?" Olivia turned to Ryan. "We're done here."

Melissa buried her face in her hands. Ryan rushed to the door to encourage Olivia's exit.

Lauren and Danny clutched Olivia's arms and shepherded her from the room. Leaning into them, her chest tight, Olivia was thankful to have her sisters by her side.

Outside in the hall, Olivia took a deep breath and straightened. "I'm okay. I'm okay." She pulled the clip from her hair, releasing a sense of freedom.

"You were fantastic, Liv," Lauren gushed. "I almost dove across the table to grab Jeff's throat. I wanted to choke the son of a bitch."

"I would have fallen apart," Danny added. "You kept your composure right up to the last remark." Danny hurried to a female officer and took Pogo's leash. "Thank you for taking care of him while we were in there."

"He's a good boy," the woman said. "I was starting to get attached."

The dog pulled to get to Olivia's side and started to whine. To comfort her, Pogo leaned his head against Olivia's hip.

"All over, Pogo," Olivia said, combing her fingers over the top of the dog's head. "Let's go home." She raised her eyes to Ryan. "I can't thank you enough for all you've done. Now, I'm done. I said what I needed to say."

"Dig in your purse and give me that journal you keep," Lauren said. She held out her hand.

"What are you going to do with it?" Olivia pulled out the tattered and dog-eared notebook, hesitant to surrender the evidence of her obsessive behavior. It had become a supportive companion.

Lauren handed the journal to Ryan. "This is Olivia's little black book of dysfunction. If there's ever a need to find a white Suburban in the tri-county area, she's done all the work for you. But if I were you, I'd burn the sucker."

"The end of a nightmare for you, Liv," he said, fingering the worn cover. "You can move on." Ryan turned to Danny but continued to address Olivia. "Speaking of moving forward, do you mind if I kidnap your sister for a long lunch?"

Danny's face broke into a wide, guilty smile, as if torn between leaving with Ryan and staying with her sisters. With pleading eyes, she gazed at Olivia and Lauren.

"Go, Danny Girl," Olivia assured, embracing her sister. "I'll be fine." Behind Danny's back, Olivia stuck up her thumb to Ryan.

Ryan nodded and smiled, a signal he had more elaborate plans than lunch . . . or dinner.

"I suppose I need to go make a statement to those reporters in the lobby."

"I'll go with you, Liv," Ryan said. "Then we'll all get the hell outta here."

"Will you both be home for dinner?"

"We'll take Pogo with us," Danny said. "Can I call you later?"

Chapter 21

Lauren and the Manuscript

By nine o'clock, Olivia had exhausted her discussion with Lauren of the meeting with the Rovinskis. Lauren concluded that she wouldn't have been as calm and controlled as Olivia in front of them. No way. Lauren had wanted to smack the smug expression from Jeff's face when he suggested his daughter's age lessoned the severity of his actions. Olivia agreed. To Olivia, the unexpected gift from the meeting was the bond with her sisters and sticking up for one another in the face of tragedy. Lauren felt releasing Danny to the arms of Ryan—when Olivia needed her more—had been a difficult but necessary act of selflessness. Olivia knew she'd been selfish for too long. A tough statement, but a true one.

"I gave Danny a key. I'm locking up," Olivia called from the bottom of the stairs. "I'm dead on my feet."

"Get some sleep, Liv," Lauren answered from the upstairs guest bathroom. "I'm going to dye my hair and finish Mom's book."

Olivia switched on the lights in the living room. The manuscript sat on the couch, Lauren's place marked with a turned-over page. Chapter eighteen. Freesia lay curled up on the end cushion, waiting for Lauren's brand of attention.

"You're a traitor, Freesia," she said. "Come up to bed with me."

The cat didn't move. "And don't think I haven't noticed you sneaking into Lauren's room in the middle of the night." Olivia gave the cat's chin a soft stroke.

In the kitchen, the quiet whir of the dishwasher washed away the remnants of a dinner for two. Olivia straightened the hand towels to make sure they hung evenly on the towel bar. After this week, she'd resume her routine soon enough: cooking for one. *Routine.* What would be her routine now? The primary plot of her personal story—the obsessive hunt for Adam's killer—had an ending. But a new story was emerging with her sisters, and also with Ardy, that she couldn't have imagined only weeks ago. Olivia longed to sit with Mom over coffee to hash through the development of plot points and character arcs: Lauren taking charge, Danny coming back into the sisterly fold with Ryan, and Olivia, herself, making the egregious misplay of deceiving her agent. Ardy's story had yet to unfold.

Lock the front door. *Check.* Turn out the porch light. *Check.* "No, sweetheart, I won't forget," she whispered, heeding her husband's instructions in her head.

"Liv! Come up here, will ya?" Lauren shouted from upstairs.

Olivia trudged up the steps toward the light in the guest bathroom. She found Lauren with one eye shut, squinting the other at the instructions on the box of hair dye.

"Don't ask me to color your hair for you," Olivia said, leaning against the doorjamb. "I need to get horizontal."

"I can't see. What's this say to do? I've never used this kind before."

Olivia took the box and studied the directions. "For a more natural you . . . put the contents of the little bottle into the big one."

"I'll be more natural in front," Lauren said. "Screw the back."

To make sure her sister didn't stain the towels or floor tiles, Olivia monitored the hair show. Lauren mixed the contents of the bottles together and shook the concoction like a cocktail. After snapping on the clear plastic gloves, she squirted her roots at the crown to the ends on the front half of her head. The whole mess got a squish and a tuck under a thin plastic cap. Lauren held out her hands. Olivia rolled off the gloves and tossed them into the waste paper basket.

"Don't drip," she said. "You have *fifteen minutes*. Keep an eye on the time."

"I'll go down and read Mom's manuscript with Freesia." Lauren checked the cap in the mirror. "I wish I could take that little doll baby home."

"Nothing doing. But while you're here, we'll share her."

With her hair cooking, Lauren headed down the stairs to the living room. Olivia padded to her bedroom and climbed into bed without turning on the light.

In the dark, Olivia pictured Lauren's progress with the story. In chapter eighteen, Becky had boarded a bus, working her way from New Hampshire to Boston, plotting to kill her boyfriend. Her ultimate destination was Boston University. With a box of rat poison in a white paper bag, purchased at a hardware store in her home town of Wolfeboro, New Hampshire, Becky crossed the street to a bakery called the Yum Yum Shop. Those places were real. And Lauren was about to stumble into them.

Ellen had taken her and Lauren into that same bake shop when the family spent summers at their grandparents' house on Lake Winnipesaukee. Danny had been only an infant. The character of Becky even took a number from the red lacquered ticket machine, mounted on a pole next to the glass-fronted cases. The descriptions of the details were spot-on, just as Olivia remembered them: curved displays lined with fresh loaves of bread, puffy rolls, gooey doughnuts, chunky cookies, and strawberry layer cakes with whipped cream. A delectable aroma wafted from her mother's words, igniting a craving for a high-calorie snack of sugary carbs, maybe sea-salted dark chocolate. The story might not be real, but *Indigo to Black* flying off the bookstore shelves could be a real possibility.

Sleep threatened to swallow Olivia whole when the floor creaked in the hall, causing her to stir from a light snore. The damp spot on her pillow absorbed the evidence that she had been drooling. Lauren's silhouette loomed over the bed.

"Hey," Lauren whispered, shaking Olivia's shoulder. "Wake up."

Olivia lifted her head. "What's the matter?"

"The Yum Yum Shop? What the hell?"

"Oh . . . I know. Weird." Olivia sat up and switched on the bedside light. She squinted and rubbed her eyes. "Made me want to get on a plane for a goddamned doughnut."

"Your hair looks like somebody detonated it." Lauren plunked on the bed. "You think the book's true?"

"Noooo . . . " Olivia gave a lazy wave of her hand and smoothed down her hair. "All authors put details of their life into fiction. Makes the story more believable."

"But the hardware store is real and so is the Yum Yum Shop."

"Mmm . . . hmmmm," Olivia agreed, still grasping for her bearings. "Did you get to the part where Becky puts the rat poison and brandy in one of those Lydia Pinkham's Elixir bottles?"

Lauren's eyes widened as her mouth popped open in a long *O*. "Noooo . . . Like the ones Grampy had lined up on the kitchen windowsill?"

"Yep. Let me tell you, that'll raise the hair on your legs. Chapter twenty-five. Keep reading. Don't talk to me until you're done." Olivia sunk back into the pillows.

"We were just talking about this a few days ago. You didn't say anything."

"Still trying to digest it myself. Plus, you and Danny didn't know about the book."

Lauren stared at the stack of books on Olivia's nightstand. "Mom was an excellent writer, Liv."

"Yeah, an amazing writer. Not only because of the story, either. Did you notice how she picked the perfect words for every emotion? Her description of the aroma inside the Yum Yum Shop is incredible . . . the flavor and texture of the hazelnut square Becky bought . . . and when Becky touches something . . . wow." Olivia shook her head. "Like you're there."

"Like *she* was there . . . " Lauren grazed her fingers over the bedspread, tracing the flowered pattern. "What do think Danny will say when she reads it?"

Olivia felt herself drifting; the question dissipated.

Lauren elbowed her leg. "How the hell can you sleep?"

"It's not real, Lauren. Trust me." Olivia hugged the pillow. "Turn off the light."

"Don't forget; we're calling your agent tomorrow"—Lauren patted the mattress—"first thing in the morning."

"Right. Finish the book." Olivia rolled over, but Lauren kept talking.

"Accidents happen, Liv. Curveballs happen. We both know that. But you finding this manuscript started a serious *happening*."

"If you want a serious happening, then you'd better check what's going on under that cap on your head," Olivia said, her voice muffled by the pillow.

Plastic crinkled. Lauren sucked in a breath. "Oh crap! Forty-five minutes!"

Chapter 22

Facing the Agent

At eight thirty on Wednesday morning, Olivia ran a toothpick under the edge of the glass stovetop to remove residual cornflake crumbs. Lauren smoked a cigarette and sipped coffee at the island, her gaze following the toothpick's trek. She tossed Olivia a napkin to wipe up the debris. Lauren's eyes appeared tired from staying up too late, but the rest of her vibrated, wired on caffeine and nicotine with a head of crazy hair. A combustible combination.

"What happened to your hair?" Olivia asked, brushing the crumbs into the napkin. The lid of the garbage can banged against the cabinet when we she depressed the foot pedal. "I can't tell if you're comin' or goin'."

"Why didn't you remind me to check it earlier?" Lauren grimaced as she fluffed her espresso-brown bangs. "It's too dark."

"Uhhh . . . yeah, I'd say. Looks like you went dunking for apples in a barrel of tar."

Ignoring the comment, Lauren blew a stream of smoke into the stove fan. "I swear to God, Liv, the book is real."

"I don't think so." Olivia shook her head. "But it's a testament to Mom's storytelling. Want me to call my hairdresser?"

"No. Forget my hair. Becky had three kids and never got caught."

"Will you *stop*? You looked into those two faces yesterday, the same as I did. Melissa is a killer. Jeff could have been a killer. Mom was no killer."

"It's a best-seller then."

"*That* I'll concede.

"Call your agent." Lauren fluttered her finger toward the phone.

Olivia wiped and rinsed the sink, and even cleaned the tiled backsplash to a gleam, anything to avoid talking with Karen Finerelli. After the parting jabs she'd delivered to the Rovinskis, Lauren had taken charge of Olivia's mouth. The agreed-upon discussion points with Karen sat on a list pad from last night's lecture from Lauren.

"Everything's clean, Liv. Pick up the damned phone and talk to her."

Olivia glanced at Lauren over her shoulder. "When do you have to go back to work?"

"Not until Monday. I'm on bereavement leave, remember? Now, pick up that *phone*."

"You don't know Karen like I do. She's not in the office yet. She has to buy a mocha and complain about people in line."

"It's eleven thirty in New York. Karen's chewing on the cord waiting for your call."

Olivia tossed the sponge in the sink. "All right. Let's get this over with, so you can arrange *my* funeral." She grabbed the phone and pressed Karen's programmed number. As Lauren predicted, Karen answered on the first ring.

"Olivia! Where were you? Didn't you get my message?" Karen sounded as if she'd spun a three-sixty in her chair. "I figured you'd get a windburn calling me back."

"I got it. Did I ever." She wrinkled her nose at Lauren. "My mother's funeral is tomorrow. I had to"—Lauren whirled her hand to urge her sister to get to the point. Olivia batted at the air—"go to a meeting."

"I'm so sorry," Karen said. "My mom has four brothers and three sisters. Eight friggin' kids. I can't imagine what will happen when my grandmother goes. All claws and paws. I'm having an arrangement sent to the funeral home, by the way."

"Thank you. I'm sure it'll be lovely. Still a lot to do with Mom's house." Olivia chose not to bring up the arrest of Adam's killer. She didn't want to take the discussion in a different direction. "Let's talk about the book."

"Time to look to the future, Liv. I got the manuscript. Thanks for sending it to me so fast. I couldn't put the damned thing down. Finished the sucker last night. Incredible. Fabulous work!"

Olivia drew in a deep breath. *Here goes.*

"I didn't write it. My mother did . . . over fifty years ago." Olivia braced herself for an eruption, but the phone emitted no sound. She glanced at Lauren, who leaned forward in anticipation. "Karen? You there? On the floor, maybe?"

"I . . . what the—" Karen stammered. "You didn't?"

"No. Now, if you still want to represent *Indigo to Black*—"

"Of course I want to! Are you crazy? But your name is on the manuscript. You're the one with the marketability, the fan base, the reputation that sells."

Reputation. The letters of the word became shards, like the shattered pieces from the wine glass she'd dropped on the floor the other night.

"The name of Ellen Dushane needs to be on the book or it doesn't get published." Olivia pictured Karen's face turning red as she clicked the end of her even redder pen.

"I'm so goddamned pissed at you, Olivia! This screws me up with the publisher."

"I know. And I apologize. I put my name on the manuscript for all the reasons you just cited. Would you have been so gaga with my mother's name listed on the cover page?"

Karen's silence broke when she blew into the receiver. "You know the way this business works."

"I certainly do. Publishers want a track record and an audience base already developed. Mom had neither."

"Sloane wants it. They're prepared to pay a huge advance."

"How huge?" Olivia narrowed her eyes. Lauren spread her hands for more information.

"They threw out $2.1 million, Liv," Karen continued, "because of you. Your name sells books."

Now, Olivia went silent. She mouthed, *Two . . . point . . . one . . . million.* Lauren choked on her smoke and smashed her cigarette in the ashtray. She stood and turned a circle in her flowered house dress.

"If you think Sloane will still want to go forward," Olivia said, holding up her hand at Lauren, "they'll need to put the contract in the name of the Estate of Ellen Dushane." Lauren tiptoed to Olivia and smacked her hand in a high-five.

"Why is nothing ever simple with you?" Karen's voice faded, as if talking to herself. "How am I going to sell a debut author who's dead? Only works with celebs. Nobody knows who Ellen Dushane is."

"Hey, hey! You're referring to my mother!" Olivia bristled.

"She can't do interviews. She can't do signings. She can't write another *book*!"

Lauren paced in a circle, muttering, "Oh my God. I can't believe this."

"I'll do all the publicity, Karen." Olivia wiggled her hand for Lauren to stay quiet. "We can push the whole mother-daughter angle." She waited a beat. "It needs to be on shelves before Christmas to capitalize on the selling season."

"Christmas?! Sloane can't work that fast. Maybe next Christmas!"

"They'd better. Otherwise, I'll publish the damned thing myself. I can have the book out by Halloween on my own and hire a lawyer to arrange worldwide rights. A marketing consultant and a publicist aren't hard to come by, either. My fan base already follows me on my website."

"Extortion! My reputation is on the line. So is *yours*."

"That's why I pay you 15 percent."

"Ugh! Maybe spring. Give me some time. This was going to be so clean, so fast—bada-bing, bada-boom. Now it's is a friggin' mess! I'll get back to you." Karen slammed down the receiver.

Olivia set the phone in the charging stand, turned to Lauren, and smiled. "That was the nicest conversation we've ever had."

Lauren stared at her. "I'm glad I wasn't on the other end of the line. I wouldn't have believed you could stoop to blackmail."

"Extortion. I'll bet the book will be published by April. I threw out Christmas to scare her."

Lauren slapped her hands on the counter. "So . . . does this mean I don't have to go back to work on Monday?"

"Don't change *anything*. Act as if nothing's happened because this could blow up in our faces. Deals are never done until they're signed by all parties. Wait to tell Danny. I don't want to get her hopes up. She hasn't even read the manuscript yet."

"I'm interested in her opinion of the story," Lauren said.

"Me too. This conversation might influence whether she likes it or not. Don't you think it's odd Danny hasn't even asked to read it?"

"Denial."

"She's not in denial about Ryan. She never came home with Pogo last night."

"I'm happy for her." Lauren's face lit up with a mischievous grin. "Let's bet! If they publish *Indigo*, I'll buy the fancy lunch at Timberline Lodge when we scatter Mom's ashes on Mt. Hood. We'll coordinate the ceremony with the book coming out. If they don't publish . . . then you have to give up writing to clean houses for a living."

"That makes no sense. You think cleaning is punishment? I think cleaning houses would be fun," Olivia said and laughed. "What about you? You have to give up something too."

"Okay. I'll quit smoking and take up exercise."

"You should do both, regardless of this deal. Get dressed. We need to pick up Danny at Ryan's house and take Pogo to visit Ardy at the hospital."

Lauren raced out of the kitchen and did a dance in the doorway, as if churning a vat of butter. "Let's do it."

Olivia retrieved the sponge in the sink and shook her head. She didn't want to tell Lauren that they still had a long way to go before holding Mom's book in their hands.

~ · ~ · ~

Olivia pulled into Ryan's driveway and gave the horn two quick taps. Ryan had purchased the 1920s Foursquare in the Laurelhurst neighborhood years ago, back in the early nineties before the real estate prices skyrocketed. Gentrification crept into every distinctive residential area in Portland, especially those with canopies of old-growth trees. The house was a sophisticated shade of warm beige with contrasting glossy black shutters. When Danny had lived with Ryan, the flower beds were mulched and filled with a colorful border of summer annuals: orange zinnias, bright red impatiens, and electric-blue lobelia. Now, they were filled with weeds. With Ryan's overloaded work schedule, domestic chores had been neglected.

"The house needs Danny's touch again," Olivia said. "She inherited Mom's green thumb."

"Keeping up a house is a big job, Liv," Lauren defended. "You know how much work it is by yourself."

Olivia took off her sunglasses. "I do. I wrote nonstop after losing Adam. I ended up hiring a yard service."

"I miss having a yard." Lauren gazed at the front door. "My little apartment balcony is nice—I can throw peanuts to the squirrels in the tree and listen to the guys with blowers on their backs—but I miss gardening." She rummaged in her purse, searching for nothing in particular. "Don't tell me they're trying to find a cure for cancer. Too much money to be made. I know—Mark's medical bills wiped us out. Insurance is pretty quick to pay for erectile dysfunction but not for cancer. God forbid a guy gets a case of the flopsies." Lauren set her purse on the floor and turned in the seat to face Olivia. With her hair two contrasting tones, it appeared that three people were in the car. "You think this book deal will come through? Give me odds. Fifty-fifty?"

Olivia didn't want to answer. If no contract transpired, not only would Lauren be crushed but the blame would rest squarely on Olivia's shoulders. A lose-lose situation. "Here's Danny. Almost on time too."

The front door opened and Danny waved. She turned and clipped the leash to Pogo. With black sunglasses, sandals, a cotton summer dress of pink roses, and her hair pulled back in a headband, Danny appeared to be no older than thirty. She held out her hand to the dog, instructing him to sit while she locked the door. He did.

"I'll be damned," Olivia muttered.

"What? Danny looking like that at forty-five and me like this at sixty?" Lauren gestured to her own outfit, an oversize white blouse and blue stretch pants with the finishing touch of brown orthopedic shoes. "Where'd Danny get that small waist? You and I look like satellite dishes mounted on Pick-Up Stix."

"No. Check out Pogo. He's being an angel. No jumping."

Olivia started the car as Danny approached with the dog hugging her side. She opened the back door and motioned for him to jump in.

"Up, Pogo," Danny instructed, slipping into the seat next to him. "Good boy. Let's put your seatbelt on."

Olivia and Lauren turned, incredulous, as Danny buckled the dog in the shoulder harness.

"Time to go see Ardy." Danny adjusted the strap. "Then we've got some serious work to do in the yard."

Pogo gazed out the window and puffed through his snout, as if he were being chauffeured to an important appointment and was late.

Olivia caught Lauren's eye and put the car in reverse.

Chapter 23

The Orange Vest

"We're here to see Mr. R. D. Griffin. He was brought in a couple of days ago," Olivia said, tapping her fingernails on the information desk at the front entrance of Milwaukie Hospital. She smiled at the receptionist. The woman's pudgy jowls gave her a bossy demeanor, as if she believed only the worst in people. She'd have to remember this woman's face as a reference for a future character. The plastic pin on the woman's pink smock indicated her name: *Edna, Volunteer.*

"Mr. Griffin is in room five-oh-six on the fifth floor," the woman said. "If all three of you are going up, you'll need to check in at the nurse's station for any restrictions."

Olivia nodded and turned.

"Oh, Miss?" The woman raised her salon-polished finger. "The only dogs allowed on the patient floors are those for service and therapy."

Widening her eyes, Olivia subtly gestured to Danny's sunglasses. She waited a beat before turning to face the woman. Danny got the hint and lowered them from the top of her head.

"He's a service dog," Olivia said, her words stiff but delivered with a smile.

Danny reeled in the leash and patted the air, pretending to grope for Pogo's collar. "He's mine. I'm blind."

"I'm sorry. I'll need for you to show me your verification of the dog's status. He's supposed to have an identifying vest." Edna clearly enjoyed her authority.

Lauren approached the counter and studied the woman's pin. "Excuse me, *Edna*, but are you asking my sister to prove she's blind—in a *hospital*?"

"No, ma'am. She's supposed to carry service credentials for the dog."

"Then he's a healing one." Lauren set her jaw on jut.

"Therapy dogs need ID," the woman reiterated. "You three can go up but not the *dog*."

To break up the escalating argument, Olivia shooed Lauren and Danny toward the front entrance. The glass doors hissed open as they streamed to the walkway. Standing out of sight with Pogo, Olivia leaned in for a conspiratorial whisper. "There's a cleaning cart in the lobby. An orange vest is hanging off the side. I'm going in to get it. We'll strap the vest on Pogo and come back inside through Emergency. Danny, you wait here with Pogo; Lauren, you go in first and distract Edna at the desk."

"I'm on it," Lauren said. "Leave that witch to me."

"Wait! I need a black Sharpie, the thick kind. Do you have one in your purse?"

Lauren dug through her oversize handbag. "Here, hold these. I know I've got one." Both Olivia and Danny held out their hands for the onslaught. Lauren doled out a bag of almonds, a ring of keys, a wallet, a pair of scissors, a can opener, the remote control for her DVD player, and a smashed box of Band-Aids. The small round Band-Aids—the ones nobody ever uses—cascaded to the sidewalk. Lauren beamed as she pulled out a fat black marker from the bottom.

Olivia waited for Lauren to reassemble her survival gear and disappear through the automatic doors. Beyond the glass, she spotted Lauren in wild gesticulation, pointing at God knew what. Olivia slipped through the door and bolted in the opposite direction as the volunteer's voice took on a razor's edge. Dashing toward the cleaning cart, Olivia held out her hand and snatched the orange vest from a hook without breaking stride. She made a quick right turn to a short hallway with overhead signs to the restrooms. After folding the belted vest, Olivia shoved it down her blouse and sauntered back to the lobby. With a smooth move, she appeared at Lauren's side.

"You go on ahead," Olivia said, patting Lauren's arm. "We'll take turns staying with the dog. I'll meet you upstairs."

The volunteer released an audible sigh of relief, satisfied to have won. "The elevators are over there," the woman huffed, pursing her lips and glaring at Lauren. Winking at Olivia, Lauren marched toward the bank of steel doors. Moving in the opposite direction, Olivia darted to the front entrance.

Once outside, Olivia found Danny still picking Band-Aids from the concrete. She pulled the plastic vest out of her blouse as Danny held up the black marker. Across the back panel, Olivia wrote *Service Dog* in block letters.

Danny strapped the vest around Pogo's torso. Lowering her black sunglasses from the top of her head, Danny smoothed the dog's ears and announced, "He's official!"

"You take Pogo around to the other entrance. Meet you upstairs on the fifth floor."

~ · ~ · ~

Olivia waited with Lauren at the fifth-floor nurses' station, chuckling as Pogo pulled Danny from the elevator. With his curly jet-black fur and bright-orange vest, the poodle resembled a Halloween decoration for a window display. The nurses swarmed around the dog, drawing gawks from a few doctors and patients too.

"Isn't he sweet?" one of the nurses cooed. "He's a new one." She leaned over and thumped Pogo's side, changing her voice to cutesy dog-speak. "We've got a busy day for you, sweetie boy. What's your name, you big fuzzy-wuzzy bear?" The nurse tickled his muzzle, making Pogo sneeze a spray of saliva on the linoleum floor. Olivia winced, fighting her urge to request a towel and disinfectant.

"This is Pogo," Danny said. She smiled at the nurse and turned to Olivia in desperation. "He needs to visit Mr. Griffin first."

"Okay, start in five-oh-six. But not too long now—Mrs. Foster in five-ten has been asking for her session all morning. A lot of doggy rounds to be made today."

Pogo led Danny to Ardy's room. The closer the dog came to five-oh-six, the more he strained on the leash. Deep within the jumble of medical smells, he'd picked up Ardy's scent. Breaking free of Danny's grip, the dog bolted with the leash catching air behind him.

Lauren and Olivia stood in the doorway with Danny to watch the scene: Pogo had jumped on the bed and stretched out, whining and licking Ardy's face.

"Someone's mighty glad to see you," Olivia said. "How're you doing?"

Ardy appeared exhausted, but a rosy flush filled his cheeks as he stroked Pogo's ears. "Thank you for taking care-a him, Olivia. I hope I get busted out of this jail in a few days."

"Thank Danny. She's the one who babied him."

Danny stepped forward and took Ardy's hand, being careful not to disturb the IV tube taped on his wrist. The thin skin on his forearm was patchy with purple bruises from vein hunting. "We're glad you're okay," she said. "We were so worried."

"We'll get the window fixed on the back door," Olivia continued. "Lauren had to break in so we could rescue Pogo." She set her purse on the chair. "How the hell did you get caught in the Murphy bed? I went through the whole house trying to find you."

Ardy sighed. "I blacked out. I don't remember much of anything after that bed took me for a ride." He rubbed his forehead. "I was putting on clean sheets; couldn't get one corner tucked in. When I climbed on top of the bed, the damned counterweight let go. Thing never did work right."

"No more Murphys for you," Lauren insisted. "We're getting you a proper bed. Those things are dangerous."

"What would I've done without you three?"

"Let's not go down that road," Olivia said. "You're okay, and that's all we care about."

Ardy didn't offer a response as he stroked Pogo's ears. He raised his eyes to Danny. "He didn't cause you no trouble, did he?"

"Oh noooo . . . No trouble at all. We've—I've—gotten attached." Pogo lifted his head and licked Danny's fingers.

"Done some thinking while I been stuck in this bed." Ardy's weary eyes fixed on Olivia. "I came pretty close to biting the big one."

"Don't—" Olivia held up one hand. "I don't want to even think what could've happened."

"I shouldn't be trying to keep up a house at my age. I'm gonna sell and move into one-a them senior places down on the river."

"Pretty expensive, Ardy."

"Got some savings. Can you check 'em out for me?"

"Be happy to."

"Not all of them allow dogs," Danny added.

Lauren set her hands on the white cotton blanket over Ardy's feet. She squeezed his toes. "We'll help you. We need to make arrangements for our mother's house too."

"What happened to your ma?" Ardy lifted his head with concern.

"The funeral's tomorrow," Olivia said, realizing how much they'd endured since Friday afternoon.

"You don't need me added to your burden." He shook his head and hesitated. "Is Officer Eason in trouble because of me?"

"What do you mean?" Olivia glanced at Danny and Lauren.

"Ladies . . . I had a colorful life." Ardy sighed and turned his gaze to the picture window. "When I get outta here, I'll tell you my story. Olivia, with what I've done, you could write a book . . . after I'm gone. Not until then."

Olivia widened her eyes, hungry for details. Lauren shrugged.

Danny squeezed Ardy's hand and stroked Pogo's torso with the other. "Ryan's fine. He's a hero. I don't know if you've been watching the news, but he arrested two people who were involved in Adam's accident."

Ardy closed his eyes. "I saw it. Closure is good. I need it too."

"Yes," Olivia agreed. "I can't describe how healing it is. When you're released, we'll help you get settled. I want to hear your story." Olivia smiled inside. Could this be the serious book she wanted to write? Diving into someone else's life might deflect her obsessive wallowing in her own circumstances. "I think I'd like to write your memoir."

"I can tell you right now it won't be a romance. They're keeping me in here through the weekend. They got to do heart tests. Still ain't had the procedure I was coming in for, before all this nonsense happened." Ardy swept his hand. "Now they gotta wait till I'm stronger." He threw Olivia a sheepish grin. "Want to do some more time with Pogo?"

"Of course." Olivia anticipated the next question, so she saved him the trouble of asking. "And we'll pick you up when you're released."

"By the way, there's a house key under the mat by the patio door. If you want to do some cleaning up, I wouldn't squawk about it. Don't do nothing in the spare bedroom upstairs. I'd better do that myself." Ardy glanced at her. "And I suppose I need a will done too."

Olivia pulled a pen and a new notepad from her purse. *Give an inch, take a mile.* "Slow down, Ardy. Chill."

"Olivia?" Ardy hesitated. "Will you . . . be my executor? Get my affairs in order? This dose of mortality was a butt-kicker."

"Called an executrix, the female version. And, yes, I will."

Lauren burst out laughing. "Yeah, Liv, you'd better get busy. Now, you have three houses to clean: yours, Mom's, and Ardy's."

Olivia grimaced and pointed. "You and Danny are helping."

The nurse rushed into the room and clapped her hands. "Time for Fuzzy-Wuzzy Boy to move on. Mrs. Foster's waiting for her visit!"

Lauren's eyes twinkled. "Better take Pogo on his rounds."

Chapter 24

Ellen Is Ready, Ladies

At two o'clock on Thursday afternoon, Olivia waited with Lauren and Ryan in the lobby of the Willoughby Funeral Home. Danny remained outside, giving Pogo a behavior lecture. Leaving the dog alone in any house wasn't an option.

"Let's go in," Lauren griped, holding the weighty manual typewriter in her arms. "This thing is killing my back."

"We need to wait," Olivia chided, gripping the gardening photo of their mother and the original manuscript of *Indigo to Black*. She chuckled when Pogo jumped up on Danny's black pantsuit. With the dog straining at his leash, she finally bumped through the doors.

"Sorry," Danny said, rolling her eyes. "He promised to be good."

"Promises, promises. He'd better," Lauren countered.

"Ellen is ready, ladies," Fred Willoughby announced and gestured toward the open doors of the nondenominational chapel. "Two o'clock on the button. Right on time." He shook Ryan's hand. "You were quite the celebrity on the news yesterday, Officer Eason—quite the celebrity. It is, indeed, an honor to meet you, although I wish under better circumstances."

"Tough day for all three girls," Ryan said. "Danielle was close with her mother. Thank you for all you've done for Ellen. I'm sure the

Dushane sisters were quite a challenge."

"We're easy, Ryan," Lauren said.

"We get things done," Olivia added.

Danny just smiled.

"Colorful, Officer Eason. Colorful." Fred pressed a button on the wall, positioned like a doorbell at the chapel entrance. "Shall we?" The voice of Burl Ives and his folk guitar filled the chapel with "A Little Bitty Tear."

Lauren turned to Olivia. "Burl Ives? When did we decide on the music?"

"Mom loved Burl Ives. Danny suggested it."

Danny nodded in agreement. "Mom sang 'Goober Peas' when she picked beans in the garden. 'Goobers' is the next song on this CD."

Olivia poked Lauren's shoulder. "Oldest goes first. Or should I say, both the front and back of your hair can go in."

"It's Mom's book's fault," Lauren argued. "You're not far behind me, by the way."

"I'm last because I'm the youngest," Danny gloated. Pogo pulled on his leash, anxious to go inside.

"I hope you don't mind, Fred," Olivia said, leaning around Lauren, "but we had to bring the dog. We couldn't leave him at home. My cat wouldn't have been able to handle the ruckus."

"Fine. Fine. Pets experience grief and loss too."

"I'll take Pogo in and wait for you three in front," Ryan offered, taking the leash from Danny. "C'mon, you. I'm making a doggy arrest if you misbehave."

"Here we go. Got everything?" Olivia asked.

"*Yes*, Liv. That's the third time you've asked." Lauren dipped the dark side of her hair toward the chapel.

To the accompaniment of Burl Ives's strumming guitar, Lauren lugged the typewriter down the aisle, followed by Olivia and Danny with their own offerings. Ryan sat in the front pew with Pogo on his right, patting his back. From the rear, the dog looked like a mourner in a black curly wig. Olivia stifled a snicker. The only thing Pogo lacked was a short veil and a hanky, with a *P* embroidered on it, to dab his snout.

The altar, skirted in white linen, was adorned with a crystal vase of puffy blue hydrangea blooms on each side of Ellen's freshly etched urn. As promised, Karen's arrangement of a crystal bowl with a mound of tight white roses added a sophisticated touch. Mounted on the center of the rear wall, an expansive high-definition screen ran a rotation of pastoral scenes: a forest of tweeting birds, a misty morning meadow, and the trusty waterfall that made Olivia's bladder twitch.

Olivia set the framed photo at an angle next to her mother's urn. With a *thunk*, Lauren set the typewriter on the altar and unhooked the smooth serpentine chain from her neck. She slid off Mark's wedding ring and set the gold band in front of the urn. Olivia placed Adam's ring next to it and rested the manuscript for *Indigo to Black* on top of the typewriter. Danny removed Ellen's diamond solitaire and gold band from her right finger and set them, along with their father's ring, with the others. After digging in her purse for Ellen's open pack of Marlboro Menthols, Danny arranged the crumpled cellophane package adjacent to the urn.

The three of them stood in silence to the head-bobbing rendition of "Goober Peas," immersed in their private memories of love, promise, loss, and their mother. Olivia sensed Ellen whispering in her ear, telling her what to do, what to think, what to feel. Even in death, Mom had an opinion about her simplest of actions. Olivia welcomed the imagined words. This pageantry would have made Ellen laugh, a reason to make fun of the world by finding the humor in the melancholy. Mom had always hoped for something ridiculous to happen at stiff affairs—and it usually did.

Ryan stood and placed his police badge over Adam's wedding ring as the last offering. The brass star glinted in the overhead lights. Olivia's throat tightened.

Lauren sighed, the silence broken. "Well, everybody I used to bitch about is represented on this altar. I guess I need to take my bitching about you up a notch, Liv."

Olivia turned to her sister. "I feel so privileged."

"Happy to accommodate. Let's sit."

Golden light from the pin spot illuminated the assembled collection. As Olivia fingered the amethyst on the serpentine chain on her chest, she studied the items that represented a family. The joyful, humorous moments eclipsed the painful ones. She thought of the Christmas morning when their father had purchased a tank of fish, eating each other like piranhas before the gifts were unwrapped; the summer barbeque where Adam and Mark, as a joke, dragged the garden hose through the house, soaking Ellen when she opened the front door. Those were the moments she clung to and never wanted to let go.

The half-pack of cigarettes drew Lauren's eye. Olivia waited a few seconds for the inevitable smart remark. As predicted, Lauren delivered.

"You think Mom would care if I took one of those and went outside?" Lauren said under her breath.

"Don't you dare," Olivia scolded.

"The bacon came out okay," Danny proclaimed of the etching. "Kind of Picasso-looking. What do you think, Ryan?"

"The man was an artist." Ryan tried to keep his face deadpan. "I've never seen bacon depicted quite that way." Danny nodded in agreement.

Pogo sat between Danny and Ryan on the pew, as if he were a fourth sibling. He, too, stared at the urn. Maybe the images of bacon drew his attention, but Pogo had a reverent look on his fuzzy face. He emitted a low whine from his snout, puffing as he built up steam.

"Pogo, stop! You didn't even know Mom." Danny stroked the dog's back.

The rotation on the flat-screen monitor switched to the tweety birds in the woods. To the accompaniment of chirping, Burl Ives started "A Funny Way of Laughin'."

"Now what?" Lauren asked.

"Bagpipes." Olivia turned, anticipating a cue.

"Let her rip."

"I'm not sure this was a good idea." Olivia blew out a breath and smoothed an escaped wisp of hair back into the clutches of her hair clip.

"It's what Mom wanted," Danny said, her voice shaky. "She loved Scotch eggs." Danny fingered a piece of their mother's family plaid, crisscrossing shades of mauve and gray, that she'd found in the cedar chest. She stood and set the folded length of wool on the altar.

Lauren tried to suppress a snicker at the clatter of wooden pipes and regalia in the lobby. The noise sounded like a broken kazoo as the piper pumped the instrument with air. She leaned toward Olivia. "He ate Mexican last night for dinner."

Olivia burst out laughing and covered her mouth as the Highland tune sprang forth up the aisle. Lauren pressed her lips and shook her head.

Pogo started a low growl. He stuck his snout toward the ceiling and revved to a howl.

Ruh . . . rrr . . . rrr . . . Wha-ooooo-whooo. Wha-oooooo!

"Oh my God. He's distraught," Olivia cried, reaching over to stroke the dog's chest. "Shhh . . . "

"Take him out of here," Lauren urged. "He's ruining the moment."

Olivia leaned forward and held out her hand. "Give me his leash." Ryan handed her the long strap from his lap. She snapped the hook on Pogo's collar. "C'mon you. We're going outside. Ryan will haul your butt to jail for disorderly conduct." Pogo continued to howl as he jumped from the pew and trotted behind Olivia down the aisle. When he reached the piper, Pogo stuck his head under the man's kilt.

Whooo . . . whooo . . . sniff . . . sniff.

The piper did a Highland fling dance in an attempt shake off the dog. Olivia pulled Pogo toward the vestibule.

"Stop that!" Olivia admonished. She turned to Fred. "He's always wanted to know what's under there."

Pursing his lips, Fred held open the chapel door. "I'm so sorry," he said. "He must have loved your mother very much."

"Yeah . . . uh-huh." Olivia pushed the door closed, muffling the bagpipe noise but not the howling. She stooped and held her hands on each side of the dog's face, as Danny had done to calm him. Pogo's dark eyes tick-tocked back and forth. The dog-talk muffled as Olivia grasped his snout.

Rrroooo-ooo-rrroooo.

"You have to keep it together, Pogo. I know this is your first funeral, but you need to be a good boy."

The bagpipes continued their wail to the front of the chapel. The noise grew louder as the piper made the return trip to the exit. Her shoulders relaxed when it stopped.

"All done, Pogo. Now, let's go back inside."

Whoo. The dog gazed up at her after making one last comment.

Olivia opened the heavy door and ran right into the bagpiper, attempting to make his escape. The cloth bag of the pipes became a target as Pogo leaped up and clamped down, pulling on the bladder like a chew toy. A deep rip opened in the air chamber. Olivia's eyes met the piper's, both of them in shock, as the final gasp of air pushed through the instrument with a descending diatonic scale.

"I'm so . . . sorry." Olivia burst out laughing as Pogo ran up the aisle, trailed by his leash. "I'll pay for a new one. I promise. I'll bet you can't wait to start your vacation." The man's face turned beet red. He brushed past her in a huff. Fred Willoughby pressed the bridge of his nose and glanced over his fingers. Olivia tried to catch her breath as she held her stomach. "Fred, this is so perfect. Mom would have loved this moment."

"Fine. Fine." He pointed to the front of the chapel. "Better go tend to him."

Olivia plunked down on the pew, still laughing. Lauren, Danny, and Ryan were all wiping their eyes, trying to regain their composure. Laughter circled the chapel and settled to thoughtful silence as they stared at the urn.

"Let's sweep up Mom and take her back to the house," Olivia

said. She couldn't let the mood sink to grief. "Mom would have wanted the service to end on a high note."

"I gotta lug the typewriter *again*?" Lauren said.

"Yep." Olivia patted her knee. "You're the one who wanted to bring it."

Danny and Ryan stood and moved to the altar. Ryan slipped his badge into the breast pocket of his suit jacket. Danny picked up the rings, doling them out to Olivia and Lauren and saving her parents' ones for last.

"This was my dad's," Danny said to Ryan, handing him the thick gold band.

Ryan slipped the ring over the finger of his left hand. "Fits," he announced. Ryan turned to the altar and plucked up Ellen's engagement ring, its sparkles dancing in the light. "I know this is inappropriate, but will you marry me?"

Olivia's jaw dropped. Lauren's eyebrows disappeared under her bangs. For once, the sisters were both speechless.

Danny gazed at Ryan with an expression Olivia didn't recognize. "I'll marry *you*, but I can't guarantee I'll marry the badge."

"I'm a package deal, Danny Girl." He nodded to Olivia and patted his pocket. "Ask your sister. This badge can do good things."

Overwhelmed, Danny gazed at her finger, as if her mother's engagement ring looked different, new. She whispered, "Yes."

Olivia raised her hands over her head, Mom's photo in her right hand. "Yes!"

Lauren held the typewriter in her arms. "If I could put this down, I'd hug you, Ryan."

Pogo stuck his nose toward the ceiling and howled.

Wha-wha-oooooo!

~ · ~ · ~

After the service, Olivia and Lauren returned to Olivia's house. Danny had split off with Ryan, Pogo in tow.

Olivia placed her mother's urn in the center of the breakfast table, between the two vases of hydrangeas. Karen's bowl of white roses and the framed photo completed the assemblage. For the first time in a week, the walls of the house took a breath from containing wild bouts of estrogen and canine antics.

"I'll bet Fred's never had a marriage proposal at one of his funerals," Lauren said as she filled her plastic tumbler with wine.

"You got that right. He'll be talking about this for years," Olivia agreed and laughed. "Poor Fred. I feel bad Pogo tore up those bagpipes. The piper was seriously mad. I'm not looking forward to the hefty add-on to the bill, but the moment was worth it at any price." She pulled out a glass serving plate of meats and cheeses for their gathering, intended to serve four. "I haven't laughed that hard in years—literally years."

"If Pogo hadn't sunk his teeth into the thing, then I would have. Sounded like a constipated goat," Lauren said. "When was the last time you laughed like that?"

"When Adam belched really loud in the den while I was doing a phone interview. I had to mute the call. Adam forgot I was on the phone and came in to ask me a question. I about wet my pants."

Lauren laughed. "The last time I cracked up like that was when Mark imitated a Chippendale dancer in his overwashed underwear. Priceless. He could make his stomach roll like a creeping caterpillar."

Olivia laughed. "I'm happy for Danny and Ryan. They need moments like that."

"Danny has to make up for lost time. What a moment. So romantic. You should use that in your next book."

"I doubt Ardy's story will be a romance. But maybe in a different book." She gave Lauren a sideways glance. Since leaving the hospital yesterday afternoon, Olivia had cooked up dozens of possible plot lines of Ardy's life. She hoped the stories would be as colorful as she imagined.

"Pogo made the service for me."

"Mom would have loved it."

"She did love it."

Freesia rubbed against Olivia's leg for attention. She lifted the cat in her arms and nuzzled the side of her face. "We have to let Danny go, Lauren. She's on her own."

"I know, but I was getting used to having her around. There are three of us."

Olivia set Freesia on the floor and put her hand on her hip. "What were you doing at forty-five?"

"Barbecuing on the patio and listening to Johnny Cash with Mark." Lauren threw out the answer with no hesitation.

"Exactly. Danny deserves the same experience too . . . with Ryan."

"What were you doing at forty-five?" Lauren countered.

At that moment, Olivia realized how little she had communicated with Lauren in their forties. They'd left messages or had pleasant conversations on their respective birthdays and on major holidays. They were each steeped in building their own lives, living in the private world of marriage. Today, their forties could have been only a healthy dream.

"Walking the Uffizi Museum in Florence, burning off an unbelievable lunch," she answered. "Adam and I did one big trip a year."

Lauren gazed at her, all humor gone from her voice. "Will you make sure I don't get ear hair when I'm old?"

"Yes. Will you make sure I don't have hair growing out my nose?"

"Deal! But I wouldn't be able to see it, so no worries." Lauren folded a piece of salami on a cracker and popped it in her mouth.

Olivia glanced at the urn on the breakfast table. She lit a glass-jar candle set out for the occasion—pineapple-sage scent—and positioned it next to one of the vases. Her mother savored the sweet fruit and prided herself on growing organic herbs. Taking a sip of her wine, Olivia said, "Okay, let's talk about *Indigo to Black*."

"The story?" Lauren pressed her lips.

"What did you think?"

"Fantastic. A bit twisted—a lot twisted—but fantastic." Lauren gave her a wide smile. "I can't wait to hear what your agent comes back with. My guess is the book will be huge, but I don't know how these things work. The possibility's fun to fantasize about, though."

"Becky stalked and killed her boyfriend. Fiction . . . or memoir?"

"Ohhh, Liv," Lauren scoffed. "You were right. There's no way the story's real. This is Mom we're talking about." She dipped her head and raised her eyes. "Mom always did have a vivid imagination."

Olivia held up her hands in defense. "I'm a writer with her DNA pumping in my veins. And I have a vivid imagination too."

"You're flip-flopping." Lauren shook her head. "You were the one who convinced me the story isn't real."

"I know, but . . . the Yum Yum Shop . . . and the Lydia Pinkham's Elixir bottle." Olivia rolled a slice of Swiss cheese into a tube and took a bite. "I woke up the other morning smelling baked bread, like an olfactory hallucination."

"When you write notes for the back of the book, are you going to mention the locations are real?"

"Hell *no*! People will think the whole story is based on truth. We need to protect Mom's new reputation."

"Good woman." Lauren nodded and rolled a circle of salami. "Never let them see you sweat."

Chapter 25

What's in the Guest Room?

On Saturday morning, Olivia stood in her driveway swinging a bucket of cleaning supplies. She'd spent the whole of Friday catching up on Ellen's bills, paying her own, and cleaning the house. Friday was change-the-sheets day: three loads worth. Her mother always said that company should stay through only one set of linens. If the sheets required changing, the guests had overstayed their welcome. But her sisters weren't company; they kept her company. Having them both around filled the house with life and laughter again.

"Do we have to do this today, Liv?" Lauren groused, inching close to a whine. "We need to do Mom's house too. I go back to work on Monday."

"There's plenty of time to do Mom's," Olivia said.

Lauren gave her a guilty glance. "I can almost hear Mom commenting under the lid whenever I put something in my mouth."

Olivia laughed, envisioning the urn on the breakfast table. She had the same sense too.

"Where's Danny?" Lauren asked. "She's supposed to help us."

"At Mom's, packing up more clothes to take over to Ryan's. Then she's checking out the availability of an apartment at River Towers, the senior place Ardy mentioned. She wants to make sure they accept dogs."

"You should be doing that stuff. You're his *executrix*." Lauren dropped her cigarette on the driveway and twisted her sneaker over it.

Olivia grimaced and stared at the flattened filter.

Lauren stooped to pick it up but changed her mind. "I'll get it on the way back."

"Let's get going. Ardy's house needs to be shipshape before we bring him home on Monday."

"You couldn't say no to that sweet old man, could you?"

"I have my doubts on the sweet part."

As Olivia led Lauren along the paving stones to the side of Ardy's house, Lauren inspected the plaster siding. "This is a cherry little property, Liv. Ardy's going to tuck away a bundle when he sells."

"Why don't you buy it if Mom's book deal comes through?" Olivia suggested, wanting Lauren's reaction. The only response was crunching gravel as they entered the courtyard. "You could have all kinds of herb planters back here."

"Did you hear back from Karen?" Lauren asked, disguising the question as an answer.

"Not yet."

"Huh . . . A good sign or a bad one?"

"Means they're in discussion. A good sign."

With the toe of her sneaker, Lauren flipped up the mat in front of the French doors. The spare house key glinted in the morning sunlight. "Right where Ardy said. All the goddamned hoopla from the other night was unnecessary."

"I called a glass company to come while we're here. They'll be coming out in an hour to replace this window." Olivia stepped inside. "I'll tackle the kitchen while you run the vacuum."

For over two hours, Olivia scrubbed the dated avocado-toned appliances to their original luster and emptied the refrigerator of expired condiments. Lauren ran the old Hoover and washed the downstairs windows. After the glass company finished replacing the pane in the back door, Olivia met up with Lauren in the entryway, their hair wet with sweat.

"If I buy this place, I'm putting in air-conditioning," Lauren said. She wiped her forehead, making her dark bangs stand straight out like an awning.

"I want to check out what's in the room upstairs," Olivia whispered, telling herself she was just curious about Ardy's story. She threw a cleaning rag over her shoulder and started up the stairs.

Lauren followed. "I'm glad you said it first. I couldn't think of anything else as I pushed around that monster vacuum. He wanted you to clean everything but that bedroom? Why?"

"Let's find out."

Olivia flipped the switch in the spare bedroom. The bulb in the sconce illuminated to a dull, dusty glow. She batted at the dust strands with the towel. When on her original hunt for Ardy, she hadn't noticed the additional boxes, magazines, and piles of papers littering the corners of this room. Olivia plopped herself, crossed-legged, in front of two boxes and reached for a stack of yellowed newspapers. Lauren did the same.

Olivia thumbed through the front pages of the top three. "They're all from the *Philadelphia Inquirer*." She read one of the headlines from 1992: "'Mobster Felix Fazziano Shot to Death in His Car in South Philly.'"

Lauren shimmied on her rump to be closer to the newspapers. "Here's another one. 'For Nearly Fifty Years, Fazziano Was An Underworld Player.'" Lauren read aloud the blurb under the headline:

If you've strolled down East Passyunk Avenue at nine o'clock in the morning, you've, no doubt, smiled and waved at the friendly old man walking his dog. At the same time each day, Felix Fazziano left his South Philadelphia apartment, crossed the street for a newspaper, and entered the café for a cup of coffee with his dachshund named Oggie. But this man, according to authorities, was no one to mess with. For nearly fifty years, Felix Fazziano was a long-time member of the Philadelphia mob. He made his living as an extortionist, gambler, and swindler. Yesterday, at the age of 73, Fazziano's career came to a violent end.

"Ardy moved into this house in 1992, right before Adam and I got here," Olivia recalled. "I remember . . . he had a dachshund too." She turned to Lauren. "The dog's name was Oggie."

"Liv, this is giving me the creeps. These are all about gangsters in Philadelphia. Why does he have this stuff in here? You think that Fazziano guy is Ardy?"

"Sounds like. This article describes him to a tee."

"Except for the dead part." Lauren shook her finger. "You check that box; I'll check this one."

Cardboard rustled as they both struggled to open the flaps. Paper crinkled as they dug through the boxes.

Olivia rested her wrists on the sides and turned to Lauren. "More cuttings from Philadelphia newspapers. These go back to the eighties. There's one in here about some guy named Antonio Nunzio." Olivia spit dust from her mouth. "Plenty of research material in here for a book, though."

"Liv?"

"What?"

"Check out this third box."

Olivia scooted over to Lauren and peered over her shoulder. Her breath caught in her throat. "Oh my God!"

Inside the box were stacks of cash: twenties, fifties, and hundred-dollar bills, held in one-inch clumps with dirty red rubber bands.

Lauren picked out a stack and bounced it, assessing the weight. She fanned the bills, all hundreds, for a quick count. "I'll bet there's five thousand bucks in this one alone."

"Don't touch it! Put it back!" Olivia lowered her voice as if they were being bugged. "You'll get your fingerprints on it. I don't want to bail your butt out of jail. What should we do?" She studied Lauren's face for a plan. When none was forthcoming, she said: "Maybe we should call Ryan."

"But we shouldn't have been snooping in Ardy's stuff. We can't tip our hand. He's an old man. He's ninety-three, for crying out loud!"

Olivia gave her sister a tired look. "Lauren . . . you were the one who lectured Jeff Rovinski at the meeting. Something about treating me differently because I'm *old*?"

"Not me. Danny said it."

"Yeah . . . well."

"Let's go call Ryan."

~ · ~ · ~

At four o'clock, with the cleaning bucket on her arm, Olivia opened the mailbox while Lauren fiddled with her copy of the key to the front door. She sent Lauren back to the driveway to pick up her cigarette butt. Physical and emotional exhaustion took over as Olivia flipped through the envelopes: cable bill, more final closure notifications of her mother's accounts, and an envelope from Sloane Publishing.

"I'll get in the shower while you call Ryan," Lauren said and stepped inside. She flapped her arms in the entryway. "Air-conditioning. Thank you! Thank you!"

"If you want to pit out your blouse, check this," Olivia teased. She held up the manila envelope.

"No way! The contract?" Lauren inspected the logo on the return address.

"I doubt it's the actual contract. Their lawyers don't work quite that fast." Olivia ripped the flap and pulled out five pages fastened with a paperclip. "It's a letter of intent. We're one step closer."

"I might not be able to handle living next door to you. My blood pressure is out of control. Do I still have wine in my box in the fridge?"

"I put an extra one in the garage."

Lauren dashed up the stairs and disappeared into the guest bathroom. Olivia set the cleaning bucket in the laundry room and trotted to the den. Sitting at her desk, she pulled on the front of her T-shirt, which had stuck to her chest with sweat. She picked up the phone and called Ryan's mobile number. He answered.

"Hey, Olivia. Danny's putting her clothes away. You want to talk to her?" Ryan's voice sounded buoyant. "She's taken over my closet, and Pogo's claimed the bed."

"No, Ryan, I'm calling to talk to *you*." She hesitated. "I need you and Danny to come over as soon as you can."

"You sound worried. Is everything all right?"

"It's about Ardy. He's okay, but we found something when we were cleaning his house. I can't mention what it is on the phone."

"We're on our way. Give us twenty minutes."

Olivia set the phone in the charging stand and glanced at her watch. She had time for a shower, provided Lauren hadn't used up the hot water. Conflicted emotions filled her with each step to her bedroom: sadness at her mother's conspicuous absence and comfort for her sisters to be by her side; fear for Ardy's safety and eagerness to write his story. Layered beneath her skin was elation, too, at the prospect of Lauren living next door and the Rovinskis sitting in a jail cell. Freesia—without a care in the world—stretched out on her bed, belly up.

With the drapes closed, the room was cool, quiet, and dark. She resisted the temptation to stretch out on the soft pillows and close her eyes. Instead, she meandered into her bathroom and turned on the shower. With her sweaty clothes in a heap on the floor, she stepped inside the stall. Surrounded by protective tile, Olivia let the cool water wash over her until it steamed with heat.

Chapter 26

The Book Deal

Ryan and Danny sat on the living room couch and listened as Olivia and Lauren paced around Pogo, attempting to explain what they'd found in the box in Ardy's house. Exhausted from the afternoon's training and play session with Danny and Ryan in Laurelhurst Park, Pogo lay prone in the center of the carpet. Freesia had slunk downstairs and sniffed Pogo's oversize paws without the dog's knowledge and jumped on Danny's lap. At the chime of wine o'clock, Lauren broke off from the pace and headed toward the kitchen to twist the nozzle on her box in the refrigerator.

"I can't believe all that cash was sitting on the floor upstairs with the back door broken," Olivia said. "The glass company fixed it this afternoon."

"Where's the cash now?" Ryan asked, taking notes.

"Still in the house," Lauren interjected, returning to the living room with her tumbler. "We didn't want anything to do with it."

"So R. D.'s going to be released on Monday?"

"We're picking him up."

"He's doing fine but he wants to move into a senior apartment." Olivia nodded for emphasis. "Ardy's been packing. Keeping up the house is too much for him."

"He's selling the house," Lauren added.

"Who *is* Ardy, Ryan?" Olivia pressed. "I mean—what did he do?"

Ryan hesitated. "Not for me to say. I don't even know the details myself."

"Is he in the Witness Protection Program? He must be connected, in some way, to the mob. Those newspaper articles pretty much screamed that declaration to the rafters."

"Yeah. He is—was. The less all of us know the better."

Frustration mounted. Olivia wanted to be in the loop of information when expectations were on the line. Ardy counted on her to deliver. "But one of the articles described someone named Felix Fazziano who sounded just like Ardy. The man was murdered. Ardy wants me to write a book and publish his story after he's dead. I have to do research. None of this makes any sense."

"You need to talk to R. D. about his life," Ryan deflected. "Leave me out of the story part. I'll deal with the money. The Feds—the ones who came to the house when we found him—will need to be notified. The cash could very well be legit. R. D. may just be paranoid about checks or credit cards." Ryan stood. "Talk among yourselves. Olivia, can I use your den to make a call?"

"Of course."

When Ryan left the living room, Danny set Freesia on the floor and slapped her hands on her knees. "Why do I miss all the good stuff with you two!?" Freesia commenced a stalk-walk toward Pogo. She sat and scowled at the sleeping dog, watching his paws flex in a dream run in the park.

"You're better off. What you're calling 'good stuff' is creepy and weird," Lauren said. "Trust me; you didn't want to run into it. I wasn't prepared."

"I'm ecstatic," Olivia countered. "An unbelievable memoir is in those boxes."

"Speaking of books . . . Olivia's got good news to share."

As the three of them streamed into the kitchen, Olivia grimaced at Lauren to keep quiet.

Danny slumped in one of the counter chairs. "I hope your news is better than mine."

"What?" Lauren's smile evaporated as she pulled out a chair.

"None of the three senior communities on the river has any availability. Ardy will need to go on a waiting list. Two of them were knocked out because he wouldn't be able to keep Pogo. They only allow dogs under twenty pounds. What's your news?"

Lauren nodded to Olivia and spread her hands. "Full disclosure, Liv."

"I got a letter of intent on Mom's book." Olivia plucked the envelope from the breakfast table and tapped the top of her mother's urn with it. "Here, Danny. Read this."

She studied Danny's expression, her sister's features loosening as she flipped through the letter.

Lauren tiptoed to the den and leaned her ear against the pocket door. Olivia waved her back to the kitchen and pointed to the counter chair.

"Two point one million?" Danny said, raising her eyes. "I'd better read this book."

"Yeah, you'd better. I'll print off a copy for you," Olivia offered. "Lauren read the original, but the paper's old and Pogo did a number on some of pages."

"Send it to me as an e-book." Danny acted as though the manuscript had already been published.

"We have a ways to go, toots." Olivia scoffed at her naïveté. "Like I said, I'll print you one the old-fashioned way or give you a PDF of the scanned version."

"Go ahead and print me one. I'll read it in bed."

"Speaking of paper, the three of us need to sign the third page of that letter to move forward."

Danny held out her hand and wiggled her fingers for a pen. Olivia rummaged in her utility drawer, the only one in her kitchen not organized—just like her mother's. She plucked out a black ballpoint and handed it to her.

"Hey, Lauren?" Danny clicked the pen several times, a signal of conspiratorial thinking. "Why don't *you* buy Ardy's house? He can take over the lease on your apartment. Pull a switch. Your complex allows dogs. You'll be able to afford to buy his house when this book deal is done." She tapped the paper. "And Ardy won't have to pay the real estate commission. Have Ted arrange for an appraisal and draw up the real estate contract, so Ardy has assurance he's not getting screwed. I'll help Ardy with what he needs after he moves in."

Lauren turned to Olivia and stuck her thumb toward Danny. "Where does she come up with this stuff? I can't find anything to bitch about with that plan."

Danny fluffed the bottom of her pageboy. "I got it going on."

She scrawled her full name, making a wide loop of the final *E* in Dushane. Lauren signed her name with two loopy *Ls*: Lauren Lyndale. Olivia added hers in flowing script and made an exaggerated gesture of dropping the pen back in the drawer.

"As soon as Ryan comes out of the den, I'll scan a copy for each of you and e-mail one back to Sloane."

Olivia turned and opened a bottle of wine. She poured a glass for Danny, Ryan, and herself. Lauren gripped her tumbler.

The three of them sat in silence. Their gazes crossed and tangled as if a dreamcatcher hung in the kitchen window. The longer they waited, the more Olivia worried.

"What's taking so long?" Danny asked.

"This is stupid," Lauren griped, reaching for her tumbler. She took a sip.

Olivia flinched when the pocket door slid open in the den. Ryan emerged through the doorway of the kitchen, his expression grim.

"Riojas is on his way over," he said. "He thinks the cash was stolen before R. D. went into the Witness Protection Program."

Olivia straightened. "We need to go over to his house and get those newspapers. They're my research for the book. The Feds can take the money but not those *papers*!" She turned to Danny. "C'mon. We need your hands too."

"I don't think you should be—" Ryan's expression turned to alarm. "I'll go in."

"It's okay, the three of us can handle this," Danny assured.

Following Danny to the entryway, Olivia whirled on Ryan. "I don't want you to be compromised in your official capacity. Stay here with Pogo."

"The hell I will! You three are not going in that house alone."

~ · ~ · ~

Ryan held open Olivia's front door as the three sisters bumped the jamb, breathless, with two boxes of newspapers and as much ephemera as they could hold. Holding R. D. accountable at ninety-three while trying to protect him set up a complicated situation. And when Ryan added the Dushane sisters to the mix, complicated turned to chaos.

Ryan rubbed his face. "These papers might be considered evidence."

"Of what?" Lauren countered. "The Feds are well aware of whatever's in Ardy's background. The newspapers aren't news to them. Everything in them is public information."

"Let's set these in the den," Olivia said. "We'll talk to Ardy on Monday when we pick him up. He needs to know we have them."

"You're right, Lauren. This stuff is creepy," Danny said, dipping her head toward the newspapers piled in her arms. "You'll give Ardy's house way better karma."

"No more going in or coming out of R. D.'s house with *anything* until he's released from the hospital," Ryan warned. "I'm serious." When the three women were together, it was like trying to corral rambunctious puppies. Their collective energy was more than he could handle.

"These are important. Ardy wants me to write a book," Olivia defended. "He asked me to do it. This stuff is gold."

"He asked you to write a book, not dig through his personal possessions without his knowledge."

"Yeah . . . well . . . like Lauren says, desperate situations call for desperate measures."

Ryan stood at the dining room window. "Stay here—*all* of you. The Feds just pulled in front of R. D.'s house." He dashed outside and closed the front door.

As Ryan approached Riojas, he anticipated this conversation would be a delicate dance behind a shield of information on both sides.

"Mr. Griffin doing all right?" Riojas asked, shaking Ryan's hand. Even in casual attire, the man looked official.

"He is. Due to be released from the hospital on Monday."

"So why was the neighbor in the house? What's her name?"

"Olivia Novak. She's my future sister-in-law."

"The writer, right?" Riojas nodded as if a writer's vivid imagination could become a thorn.

"The same. My fiancé is her younger sister. We're taking care of Griffin's dog until he gets home."

"My wife reads Novak's books. Steamy stuff." Riojas's gaze rose to the second floor of Griffin's house. "How'd she find the money?"

"Olivia and her older sister, Lauren, went in to spruce up the place as a favor. Olivia's known Griffin since she moved in back the early nineties."

"Ninety-two." Riojas studied Ryan. "Are they aware of Griffin's background?"

"I don't know anything about the man myself. My involvement was limited to keeping an eye on him when the database breach happened."

"I think the old guy's harmless." Riojas locked his dark eyes on Ryan's. "But not thirty years ago. Did they find any weapons inside?"

"No. Olivia would have mentioned it, and I didn't see anything out of the ordinary when I went in with them."

"Let's take a look."

"We can go through the back. The key's under the mat." Ryan started down the path toward the back patio.

Riojas chuckled. "Under the mat. Classic."

~ · ~ · ~

With an eye to the peephole in the front door, Danny hovered on the balls of her feet to watch for Ryan. Pogo jumped and set his paws on her back. "Riojas came out of Ardy's house with the box," she reported. "He's opening the trunk of his car. Oh God."

Olivia and Lauren peeked through the drapes of the dining room window, trying to stay out of sight. "Riojas's face looks serious," Lauren whispered.

"Ardy's in big trouble." Danny joined Lauren and Olivia at the window, followed by Pogo. "We've got to protect him."

Lauren turned. "How?"

"He can't go to prison—not at ninety-three . . . and not without Pogo." Danny grimaced at Lauren. "You need to fix the color on your hair."

Lauren rolled her eyes and turned her gaze back to the window. "Ryan's walking back!"

Olivia flapped her hands. "In the kitchen. Quick! Talk normal."

Danny bolted to the kitchen and hopped onto a counter chair. Lauren slid on the tile floor in her socks, as if on ice, and picked up her tumbler. Olivia snatched up the signed letter from the counter and dashed to the den. Freesia streaked to the living room. Pogo turned in a circle, trying to decide which way to go.

The front door opened. Pogo's toenails scraped the hardwood floor as he trotted to Ryan out of obligation. He didn't even bark.

"I'll be right in!" Olivia called out from the den, a bit too loud. "I'm just sending off a letter." She fired up the printer and spit out three copies, then scanned them to her PC. After attaching the signed papers to the e-mail, she wrote a friendly, brief note to Karen and hit *send.* With the paper tray full, she started the print job on the manuscript. Olivia slowed her steps back to the kitchen, attempting to act casual.

"Olivia had to send something to her agent," Lauren said to Ryan, nervous.

"One for you . . . and you . . . and me." Olivia dealt the copies of the letters like playing cards. She turned to Ryan. "A deal's coming for Mom's book. This is our inheritance." She scratched her eyebrow and shifted. "So, how'd it go with Riojas?"

"The money's been confiscated," he said. "The serial numbers Riojas checked confirms the money was stolen from an evidence locker of a racketeering case in Atlantic City. It went missing right before R. D. entered into Witness Protection."

They all stared at each other to the background accompaniment of the faint *cachunk . . . zzzhhh . . . cachunk . . . zzzhhh* in the den. An image of her printer spitting out counterfeit bills set Olivia's nerves on edge, but she refused to cave in to suspicion.

"Ardy's going to be so pissed," Lauren said.

"He needs that money," Danny added.

"You know what?" Olivia set her hand on her hip. "I don't think so. I'll bet the cash was an albatross. His voice yesterday was full of regret."

"I hate to say this, guys," Ryan said, "but whatever he felt about the money, he likely needs it. His nest egg's in the back of a Fed car. If he did steal the money, though, this is a moot point. That cash wasn't his to begin with."

"Did Riojas say anything about who Ardy is—was?"

"Not a word." Ryan shook his head and pointed in sequence. "But I don't want you three going to the hospital to visit him without me."

Danny slid the letter in front of Ryan. "Read this."

He narrowed his eyes. "What now?" As Ryan scanned the pages, his eyes widened. "Are you kidding me?"

"Nope! Where should we go on our honeymoon?" Danny fingered his shirtsleeve.

"Well . . . as Ellen would say, 'Anywhere that doesn't smell bad'." Ryan laughed and held up the goblet.

"Here's to Mom, her fabulous book, and to bringing Ardy home," Olivia announced, clinking her glass in sequence. "And to a new book in the wings. My first serious one."

Cachunk . . . zzzhhh . . . cachunk . . . zzzhhh, agreed the printer.

"Hand me the phone, Liv." Lauren said, shaking her finger. "I want to go with you guys to pick up Ardy. I'm calling work to squeeze out one more day."

As Olivia held out the phone to Lauren, the printer went silent in the den.

"Okay, Danny. One hot *mom*uscript coming up."

Chapter 27

Danny and the Manuscript

On Sunday morning, chicken apple sausages sizzled in the pan as Olivia poked them with a fork. She nodded knowingly at Lauren when the stairs creaked. Danny and Ryan stumbled into the kitchen at eight o'clock. Ryan wandered toward the coffee pot, reaching for a cup as if he'd found the Holy Grail. Danny looked spent.

"Were you two doing the horizontal mambo all night?" Lauren teased. "The light was on at three o'clock this morning when I got up to go to the bathroom."

"Ask your sister," Ryan said, yawning. "I was sound asleep. She stayed up reading."

"Not even engaged a week and you're acting like an old married couple."

"So . . . what did you think of the story?" Olivia asked.

Danny ran her hand through her hair and shook her head. "No. The book doesn't read anything like Mom."

Olivia glanced at Lauren. "You mean . . . you don't think she wrote it?" She turned off the stove. "Sausages are ready. Push down the toast."

Depressing the lever on the toaster, Danny hesitated. "I'm sure she did . . . but the story's fiction. Mom would never be so vengeful and calculated. She wasn't that way."

"Did you like it?"

"No. And I'm not going to finish it. I lean toward historical fiction, like Mom." Danny raised her eyes to Ryan as she blew into her coffee mug. "Don't get me wrong, though. I'm thrilled at the possibility of the book being published." But her voice sounded less than thrilled.

Ryan stabbed a sausage and blew on it. He bit the end. "I haven't even read the darned thing, and I love it."

"That's what I'm talkin' about, Ryan," Lauren quipped. "A man who understands."

"Understands. None of you understands," Danny muttered. Her eyes glistened as they filled.

Olivia froze, suspending the fork over the pan. Lauren straightened and stared and Danny. Ryan stopped chewing and swallowed.

"Understands what?" Olivia asked, studying her younger sister with concern.

"I know you and Lauren think I was just running away from what happened with Ryan's run-in with that knife. You were right—at first—but after a month I realized Mom needed help. She was deteriorating fast. She couldn't remember when to take her meds, or even which ones she was supposed to take."

Olivia shifted her gaze to Lauren, embarrassed. Lauren turned away and blew out a breath. Danny kept going, attempting to tamp down her grief.

"The nurses and doctors started directing all their instructions for Mom's care to me. Mom couldn't keep anything straight, but she was bound and determined to stay in the house. I dealt with managing the prescriptions, getting her to the doctors' appointments, and watching her diet." Danny's voice turned to frustration. "I was pounded with questions: 'Did Ellen fast for her blood work?' and 'When was Ellen's last bowel movement?' Jesus! They treated her like a child. In many ways . . . she was." Danny put her head in her hands as Ryan embraced her. "How could I leave her? She couldn't be alone."

Olivia wiped the stream of guilt from her own cheek. "Why did you take this on yourself? You never reached out for help. How were Lauren and I to know?"

"Whenever I talked to Mom, she always said she was doing okay," Lauren said. "The only time she reached out was for an emergency."

"You heard that message I played for you both. She sounded fine. And that was just two weeks before she died."

Danny pulled away and straightened her shoulders. "You might think the Platters wrote 'The Great Pretender,' but Mom held the copyright on that one. She couldn't admit to you or Lauren that she wasn't the same old Mom."

"I owe you an apology, Danny," Lauren said and lit a cigarette. "You're right. To me, Mom was always the same old Mom. She's still messing with my head, especially with that book."

"I didn't want to believe Mom was failing," Olivia conceded. "But I should have faced the reality of her decline."

"You mean you were too obsessed with finding out who killed Adam and writing your books," Danny said. She held up her hands. "Believe me, I get it. Mom did too. She didn't want to add to your worry. Plus, she loved that you're a writer."

"I'm sorry too." Olivia glanced at the urn on the breakfast table. *I'm sorry, Mom.* "I should have visited more without a reason."

"There wasn't anything you could do."

"You did what *you* needed to do, Danny," Ryan said, "for Ellen. If my Mom was still alive, I would have done the same thing. I was an only child. You're lucky to have Lauren and Olivia by your side right now. And you have me."

Danny stroked Ryan's cheek; her fingers lingered over the scar. "Dad's, Adam's, and Mark's deaths—and your accident—messed with my head. Mom helped me through it. I owed her for that. But payback ended up being a full-time job. Can you imagine what being pulled in two different directions would have done to our relationship if we were married?"

"We would have gotten through it, Danny Girl."

"The sausages are getting cold," Danny muttered.

"C'mere," Lauren said.

Danny's bones turned to Jell-O in Lauren's arms. After Olivia joined the embrace, she turned to Ryan, who needed his own hug. Scratching at the patio doors caught her attention. Pogo wagged his hips outside in a canine rendition of the cha-cha.

Danny took a breath and wandered to the breakfast room to usher Pogo inside. "Forget it. What's on the docket today?"

Olivia patted Ryan's back. "Well . . . I'm diving into Ardy's newspapers in the den. I've got to piece together what all this fuss is about."

Lauren scooted off the counter chair. "I'll help you."

"Ryan and I will take Pogo to the park. A walk will do us good."

~ · ~ · ~

Olivia sat on the floor and began sorting through the piles of newspaper clippings by decade. Lauren wandered into the den with a cup of coffee.

Lauren took a sip from her mug and scanned the hundreds of books on the built-in shelves. She fingered a few of the spines. "I loved Carlos Ruiz Zafon's *Shadow of the Wind.* How can you go wrong with a secret museum of lost books?" She turned and glanced at Olivia.

"One of my favorite books. Just like the premise, I searched for as many copies as I could find to give to everyone as a gift."

"I treasure my copy," Lauren said. She groaned as she lowered herself to the rug, almost splashing her coffee but recovering at the last second. "I knew Danny wouldn't like Mom's book."

Olivia continued to study an article, but glanced at the rug. "To be fair, though, she didn't experience the truths we spotted in the story. And we didn't see Mom from Danny's side."

"It's a bitch to be old."

"What's even scarier are these articles." Olivia tapped the paper. "Fifteen murders, so far, in this box alone. This one's about Antonio Nunzio." She welcomed the twinge of a new obsession, and drawing

Lauren into her world held comfort, protection without boundaries.

"You serious? Who's Antonio Nunzio?" Lauren pushed back the flaps. She closed her eyes and picked out a different article.

"What am I going to say to Ardy on Monday?" Olivia stopped reading and stared at her sister.

"Deal with this head-on." Lauren studied the yellowed newsprint in her hand. "This one's from 1988; says Nicodemo 'Little Nicky' Palermo took over the Nunzio crime family in Philadelphia and was sentenced to forty-five years."

"Go check that name on the Internet."

Lauren stood and slid in the chair to Olivia's computer. Her familiar *clickety-clack* raced as she typed into the search engine. "Whoa! Palermo's still alive. Born in 1929. Makes Little Nicky about eight-five now. He's in prison."

"Still alive?"

"Still alive . . . " Lauren gulped. "What the hell did you get yourself into? I hope Little Nicky doesn't have a long memory. You think he knew Ardy?"

Nodding, Olivia's wheels turned. "No doubt in my mind." She stared out the window and watched a possum root around in her impatiens. "This is going to be a lot more serious than I thought."

"So what are you going to do?"

She needed guts to write this story. That's what separated average writers from groundbreaking authors. Chutzpah. Fearlessness. Olivia fingered the article in the quiet of the den as Lauren stared at her.

"Tell his story."

Chapter 28

The Service Dog

On Monday morning, Olivia and Lauren watched Danny breeze ahead of them through the glass doors of Milwaukie Hospital. Pogo pulled at his leash, sporting his fake service dog vest. Danny threw the volunteer a quick wave—a different woman—as she dashed past the information desk. Having gone ahead, Ryan waited for them in Ardy's room on the fifth floor.

Olivia swung her red satchel and peeked through the door, waiting outside with Lauren for her to finish sneaking a cigarette. "C'mon! Danny's on her way up. Let's go."

"We're not doing a mob hit, Liv." Lauren crushed her cigarette butt on the sidewalk. She picked up the flattened filter when Olivia pointed and tossed it in a nearby trash basket. "God forbid a nurse smells smoke on me."

Olivia stepped off the elevator and nodded to the mounted dispenser as she pumped three squirts of hand sanitizer. Lauren rolled her eyes and did the same.

Sitting quietly in the leather recliner chair by the window in Ardy's room, Ryan's fingers formed a steeple under his chin. He'd taken the day off, and while Ryan wasn't in uniform, Olivia did spot the lump of his Glock under his sweatshirt. Danny held down the bottom corner of the bed, bobbing her yellow sandal in rhythm to Pogo's thumping tail as he stretched out next to Ardy.

Olivia swung the door closed for privacy. She and Lauren each took one of the open guest chairs.

"We cleaned your house yesterday," Olivia said, her tone signaling something dirty lurked behind the words. She reached into her satchel and set a notepad and the folded pages of faded newspaper in her lap, a pen poised in her hand.

"'Preciate what you three done for me. You too, Eason." Ardy stroked Pogo's head, heavy on his chest.

"Don't thank us yet," Lauren warned.

Ardy threw her a wary glance and then rested his head on the pillow and closed his eyes. The wisps of his silver hair, in need of a wash, fanned like baby bird feathers. "You found the cash, didn't you?"

Olivia nodded. "It was sitting, plain as day, in the middle of room. Anyone could have found it. Not the safest way to keep money."

"It was insurance. So, I needed it close. Plus, don't trust bankers." He grimaced and avoided making eye contact.

"The house is clean, Ardy, but the money isn't. The Feds took the box."

Ardy's bushy eyebrows moved in opposite directions. Quite a feat of coordination. He'd realized he had more people to answer to than were sitting in the room.

"Where'd the money come from?" Ryan asked, leaning forward with interest.

Ardy blew out a breath of defeat. "Wondered why you hadn't said nothing since you came in, Eason. Money came from an Atlantic City racket. I had a policeman on the take. He lifted it for me before I went into protection. Parting gift, you might say." Ardy gave Ryan a tired glance. "Don't worry, Eason, that flatfoot's long dead."

Ryan leaned back in the chair, satisfied he'd heard the truth.

"Who was *this* guy?" Olivia asked, holding up a photo she'd found in one of Ardy's boxes. She pointed to the graphic AP photo of a bloodied and charred man in the front seat of a black burned-out

Oldsmobile. Then she held up a yellowed newspaper article showing a similar, albeit less graphic, depiction of the same scene. She read the name in the caption: "Felix 'Crow' Fazziano."

"Yours truly," Ardy muttered. He offered her a sad smile. "Feds were closing in on the Atlantic City operation. I had to cooperate, or I would-a ended up like that guy." He pointed to the newspaper. "I didn't want no part of leaving my dog. I had Oggie to think about, before Pogo here." He stroked the poodle's head. "Oggie was my dachshund . . . with me a long time. Had back problems and needed help with one-a them wheely carts to walk."

"But—" Olivia stared at the photo, stunned.

"After I testified, the Feds put a stiff—laying in the morgue from a different hit—in the car, said it was me. Lit the sucker on fire, so nobody could tell." He chuckled, as if the charade were all in a day's work. "I picked to come to Ore*gon* 'cause I thought it'd be good for Oggie. Cool . . . lots of trees." Ardy gazed down at Pogo. "Happens with those kind-a dogs."

"I remember Oggie when Adam and I moved in," Olivia said, nodding.

"Got Pogo here from the shelter. Didn't think I'd get another one after Oggie died, but the house was too damned quiet. Nobody should be all alone. A sin to get depressed." Ardy thumped the dog's rib cage. Pogo let out a groan in response.

"Why did you save those newspapers?" Danny interjected.

Danny's question prompted Ryan to lean forward again.

"Cover your ears, Danny," Ardy said. "I don't want you to think bad about me."

"Oh, stop. I'm sure your intentions were honorable."

Olivia pursed her lips. Lauren shifted in her chair and crossed her legs. Ryan rubbed the back of his neck, but never wavered in his focus on Ardy's face.

"Keeping tabs on my colleagues. Dying off—one by one by one." Ardy bounced his crooked forefinger. "Not for one minute did I trust I was safe until they was gone. I breathed easier when each one-a them wise guys was six feet under."

"Have there been attempts to find you or any threats?" Ryan asked.

"Hell no. I mean—not that I can tell. They have ways-a letting you know." Ardy shook his head and waved his hand. "I live pretty simple, uncomplicated. I keep one eye open, though."

"Do you feel safe in your house?" Lauren asked.

"Safe as anywhere, I guess. But it's too much for me anymore."

"How about you move into my apartment? I'll buy your house—at market, of course—so you can get your nest egg back in a legitimate way."

"And I'll write your story," Olivia added. "We'll do it together—gory details and all. I promise I won't send the manuscript to my agent until after you're gone. We'll have plenty of time, because you're not going anywhere any time soon." She held up her first three fingers of her right hand. "Girl Scouts' honor."

Danny flipped over Pogo's ear and inspected the soft skin inside, as if checking for ear mites. "Lauren's apartment complex allows dogs. I checked out three senior complexes on the river, but they all have a waiting list or restrictions on a dog's weight. Pogo's *way* over the size limit."

Ardy pondered the suggestion, rubbing his chin. "And I can keep Pogo, huh? Gotta keep Pogo. What about after I'm gone?"

All eyes focused on Ryan. Danny's gaze appeared to be more pleading than the others.

Outnumbered, Ryan nodded. "*Yes* . . . we'll take Pogo—*if* the time comes. Danny's made a project of him. She wants Pogo trained for the healing dog certification."

"The nurses think he's certified," Danny reiterated, beaming. "The patients love him. He knows to stay seven minutes in each room and move on."

"Hey!" Olivia interjected, snapping her fingers. "How about all the proceeds from your memoir be donated to a program for training therapy dogs? I only want to write the book, not profit from it. Let's do something good with the money. A charity angle would push sales."

Ardy gazed at the four of them in sequence. "You'd do that for me? Like forgiveness for what I done?"

Olivia tucked the newspapers under her notepad and slipped them back into her satchel. She stepped to the side of the bed and set her hand on his. "Yes, Ardy. I'm your executrix, remember? It's what we do: make things right. But in this case, the Dushane sisters can do much more while you're alive."

"I don't deserve this," he muttered.

"I thought you'd say that. Everyone has a story, Ardy. And I want to tell yours."

"Did the Feds take all the papers?"

"They're in my den. The three of us, under Ryan's supervision, went in to get them before the agent arrived."

"Riojas? Skidmore?"

Ryan nodded. "Riojas. You know him?"

"I check in every few months. He's a good kid."

"Speaking of good kids," Danny said, "time for this curly kid to get his butt out of bed and make some rounds. C'mon, Pogo!" The dog jumped from the bed and trotted to the doorway. He poked his head into the hall and looked both ways, as if deciding which patient to visit first.

"A lot to do." Olivia patted her case. "We'd better bust you outta here. Now—here's the way I'd like to work: I'll interview you one day a week—let's say Tuesdays—and then write for five. Sundays will be my free day. I'll bring you the pages I've written when we meet. You can read them, call me to argue and curse, and make changes as I work on the next chapter. We might have a manuscript by Halloween for you to put in a safe-deposit box. I'll rent one, and you'll have control of the key. We'll all sign confidentiality agreements. I'll set up an appointment with my lawyer to get the papers drawn, and make arrangements for a charitable trust. Let's call it the Pogo Charitable Trust. And with a book to be published, you *have* to have an iron-clad will drawn up."

Ardy blinked, processing the information assault. "Just write the damned thing."

"Oh no. We're doing this the proper way. Too much at stake."

Lauren stood and glanced at Olivia. "The proper way." She gave Ardy's blue-veined foot a gentle shake. "Get dressed. Let's check you out of this germ hotel. If you think your butt's sore now from laying in this bed, wait until Olivia starts nipping at your cheeks. You're gonna look like a baboon at the zoo."

~ · ~ · ~

Olivia, Lauren, and Ryan waited in the lobby for an orderly to deliver Ardy in the mandatory wheelchair and for Danny to finish her visiting rounds with Pogo. Olivia figured Ardy was giving the nurses the business about not walking under his own power. Ryan laughed about no one questioning the handwritten designation on Pogo's ill-fitting orange vest. His important work forgave the minor infraction. Danny wanted to follow through on her promise to get Pogo certified.

"When are you going to start writing Griffin's story?" Ryan asked of Olivia.

"As soon as I can. I hate to remind us of this, but since he's ninety-three, we need to spend as much time together as we can." Olivia shook her head. "Unbelievable! Felix '*Crow*' Fazziano?!"

"Any ideas for a title?"

"*Protection* popped into my head. I can't decide on whether I want to make it a memoir or a novel with a colorful plot. How does it get any better than a mob guy with a soft spot for dogs? The article in that old newspaper pretty much nailed the premise for me."

"Ooooo . . . I like the polarized personality angle," Lauren said. "I want to read the story as soon as the draft's done. Hurry up and write."

"Before I write one word, I need to get Mom's house squared away, finalize her book deal, make arrangements with Ted, and *then* I can start the interviews with Ardy. Why do I do this to myself?"

"Because you prefer things to be tangled up and complicated. I'll help you. When Danny comes down, we'll get Ardy settled with Pogo and go over to Mom's. We have to sort through the stuff today, because it's back to work for me tomorrow."

Ryan scratched his forehead as he gazed at both sisters. "I'm looking forward to going back to work. You guys are wearing me out."

Chapter 29

Back to Mom's House

Olivia felt better about leaving Ardy alone with Pogo after she programmed her mobile number into Ardy's home phone. He'd promised to keep it close at all times. Once he was settled in front of the television with Pogo and a sandwich, Olivia drove Lauren and Danny to Mom's. Ryan had more important plans: a few hours of recorded episodes of *Pawn Stars*. She didn't blame him for wanting solitude after spending several hours with Ardy, Pogo, and three women with varying levels of estrogen.

"Lauren, you tackle the closets since you're so fond of them. Danny, you get your room packed and cleaned. I'll tackle the kitchen and bathrooms."

"Let's do it," Lauren agreed.

"Ugh," Danny added and headed toward her bedroom.

Olivia recognized many of her own shortcomings in her mother, but one of the things on which they had been completely aligned was their passion for cleaning supplies. Under the kitchen sink, bottles and sprays waited, garnered from supersize promises on the Internet, info-mercials on television, and in-store demonstrations, all neatly lined up for every type of surface and purpose. Ellen was the first to whip out her credit card for outrageous claims. Some of the products even lived up to the hype. Olivia had her own penchant for powders, goo removers, stain eliminators, and anything labeled *scratchless*.

With the kitchen and bathrooms brought up to open-house level, Olivia met up with Lauren and Danny, who were rummaging through the closets. She'd given each of them small pads of sticky notes in bright colors: yellow for Lauren, neon pink for Danny. Olivia took a few minutes to stick a few of her vivid blue ones on a framed set of four Harold Altman prints in the entryway, given to her parents for their fortieth anniversary. Anything left over would be consigned, auctioned, or donated to charity.

Olivia aimed for their mother's bedroom. She set the cleaning bucket in the bathroom and returned to the bureau. The display under the mirror hadn't changed in twenty years: a bottle of White Shoulders perfume, wedding pictures of her and Adam and Lauren and Mark, and a posed beauty shot of Danny. Her face drooped at the sight of Ellen's jewelry box. The velvet compartments cradled the adornments—gifts from the three girls and their father—of a woman who wanted to be beautiful.

She was.

Dividing up the earrings, bracelets, necklaces, and pins by who gave Mom what, one piece drew her gaze . . . an earring with no mate. Ellen's favorites: each earring had been of two dangling silver hands holding a small pearl. The sisters had chipped in for the earrings as a birthday present back in the eighties. When Mom had lost one a few years ago, she'd griped, ad nauseam, about the loss. *Where's the earring? It has to be here. I know it's here.* Olivia had searched their father's car; Lauren had returned to the grocery store to walk the aisles; Danny had inspected the rows of vegetables in the garden. Mom had even picked through the vacuum cleaner bag. Nothing. She had vowed to turn the remaining earring into a lapel pin, but never found a jeweler who could tackle the job to her satisfaction. Olivia set the earring aside in the unclaimed portion of collected shiny memories. She gravitated to her sisters' voices in the hall.

"Tag it or it goes," Olivia warned. "How are you both coming along?"

"Pretty much done," Lauren said. "I'm excited about having Mom's vacuum cleaner. Mine spits out more than it sucks up."

"I made three piles of jewelry from Mom's box. Go check them out and switch them around. I divided up the pieces according to who gave them to her. But if you don't mind, I'd like to keep the one earring with the pearl we gave her."

"You mean the *drama* earring?" Danny said, rolling her eyes.

"The very one."

"Fine with me," Lauren said over a stack of terry cotton in her arms. "Mom's towels are soft and fluffy. How did she keep them so white? Mine look like they've been washed in coffee."

"The magic of bleach. Let's knock off." Olivia glanced at her watch. "It's four thirty. Mom has steaks in the freezer. We'll take them back to my house. I'll broil one up for Ardy too."

"I'll pick Mom's tomatoes for a Caprese salad," Danny offered. "They'll rot on the vine if we don't eat them. She still has basil too. There's mozzarella in the fridge."

Olivia eyed a box on the floor of the hall closet and tapped the side with her loafer. "What's in here?"

"I dunno." Lauren sighed. "I can't do any more today."

Unable to ignore a mystery box, especially after those from Ardy's house, Olivia leaned into the closet. The brittle tape crunched as she pulled back the flaps and peered inside. "Piles of pictures. Oh Lord." She plucked one from the top. "This is you, Lauren, at your high school graduation. You're standing with that skeevy boyfriend you had, the one with the Hitler mustache."

"Mom didn't like him," Lauren scoffed. She stared at the faded color picture from 1970, her face awash in memories. Taken with an old instant camera, Lauren's long dark-brown hair had been tied in pigtails, held with elastic bands stuck with floppy Gerber daisies.

"'In-a-Gadda-da-Vida!'" Olivia laughed, scissoring her fingers in front of her eyes. "We danced to that in the living room?"

"Led Zeppelin. 'Whole Lotta Love'." Lauren reached into the

box. "This is like a game of Feeley Meeley." Studying the next picture, she started laughing. "You, Olivia, showing off with your Easy Bake Oven. What? 1968?" She took off her glasses and squinted one eye. "You have a turd in your hand."

"I loved my oven!" Olivia studied the picture. "I cooked up one of those little chocolate hockey pucks, burned to a crisp under a sixty-watt lightbulb."

Danny stepped forward and pulled out a photo. "It's me. My sixteenth birthday party." The photograph showed Danny with a feathered cascade of sprayed hair, wearing spandex pants and a body-hugging wrapped top. Her lips were shiny, thick with gloss.

"God! I can hear Duran Duran playing." Olivia waved her hand. "Terrible years for music."

Lauren closed her eyes and reached deep into the box. A scalloped black-and-white photo emerged from its depths. "It's Mom and Dad by some lake with trees. Look how pretty Mom was. I bet none of us was born yet."

Olivia and Lauren gazed at the picture. Danny took in the scene between their shoulders.

"Life before us," Danny whispered.

"C'mon," Olivia said, refolding the flaps. "We'll take this home and split them up when we have more time."

~ · ~ · ~

After dinner, Olivia waved at Lauren as she drove their dad's Blazer back to her apartment, leaving her Ford Focus behind. The lack of proper brakes made her too nervous for Lauren to drive it. Danny left for Ryan's house, anxious to spend every waking moment with him. Throughout the evening, more pictures emerged from the box. Wine had been poured and corked—and uncorked again. The passage of time could no longer be denied. She felt old. The faded photos justified the emotion.

Olivia plodded across the driveway with a plate of leftover steak and Caprese salad for Ardy, an excuse to check on him. Pogo barked up a storm when she rang the doorbell but only whined and wagged his tail as Ardy opened the front door.

"You doing okay?" she asked. "Need anything?"

"Doing all right," Ardy said, appearing relieved to see her. Good to be home."

"I brought you some dinner. I thought you might like a snack before you go to bed."

Ardy took a whiff under the tin-foil covering. "'Preciate it. Needs more garlic. Want to get started on the book? Not doing nothing."

"I'm zonked tonight. Give me a week. I need to meet with my lawyer first. Setting up a charitable trust takes a lot of paperwork. How about we start next Tuesday?"

"Hate lawyers." Ardy raised the plate as Pogo sniffed the rim.

"But we can't go forward without one." She sighed. "Enjoy the dinner. I'll check back."

"We don't got to do this, Olivia," Ardy said. Disappointment crept behind his words.

"Oh no. It's not the book. We've been delving into our own history tonight. Going through old pictures of our family was fun at first—"

"Know what you mean. I been doing some thinking about what I'm gonna tell you . . . or not tell you."

"Full disclosure, mister." She shook her finger and smiled as Ardy closed the door.

As Olivia climbed her own steps, her mood grew even heavier with her tendency to replace grief with activity. The work didn't bother her, but the subject matter did. She'd obsessed about a killer for the past three years, and now she was about to obsess about another. Maybe she'd overcommitted on this one.

The house was empty of laughter. Aloneness threatened like a rolling fog. To the accompaniment of the Supremes belting out "You Can't Hurry Love," Olivia scraped the plates and set them in perfect formation inside the dishwasher. Her emotions vacillated between anticipation for the future and letting go of a past she didn't recognized anymore. The picture box sat on the den floor, next to Ardy's newspapers, holding tight to the memories of a family. Little square windows of time, visual keepers of personal moments, wishes, and dreams. Her mother had those same moments. So did Lauren and Danny. And she was about to tear away the ugly layers of Ardy's personal—and secret—life, one she wasn't sure she was ready to see. Writing something serious turned out to be a more serious business than she anticipated. How much was anyone prepared for the truth?

Olivia threw open the doors and windows in the breakfast room, breathing in the cool breeze and ushering in the evening's energy. The house filled with shouts of kids playing tag in yards, barking dogs, and bursts of laughter from neighboring patios, as if new picture-box images from other families sailed on the air's current into the kitchen. Olivia turned off the Motown CD and let the sounds of people's lives fill the gap in her own.

The pans had been put away. Freesia had long retired to Olivia's bed. Lauren would soon be living next door, if all the arrangements with Ardy worked out. Olivia stood in her beautiful kitchen, alone.

If she started to cry, the tears wouldn't stop without Adam to console her. Olivia had taken for granted the ordinary routines with Adam and her mother. She missed turning in early with Adam, reading together propped up on pillows, and longed to spar with her mother about her current reading list. Those discussions gave Olivia insight and direction into her own writing. Ellen had been an emotional parachute, under which she'd held tight to the rip cord. All Adam and Ellen had to do was to exist, doing nothing but being everything.

Refilling her wine glass, with more than she should have, Olivia grabbed two napkins from the holder on the counter and Lauren's forgotten red lighter. She sat at the round tiger-oak table in the breakfast room. The scented candle deserved a relight. A warm, fruity bouquet swirled in the breeze as the flame danced. Olivia slid the urn toward her and proceeded to tell her mother everything that had happened since she'd been poured inside.

Chapter 30

Get Busy Ted

At noon on Tuesday afternoon, Olivia waved at the receptionist as she rushed through the offices of Delaney and Beal with two plastic bags. Ten minutes late, she dropped into the guest chair in Ted Beal's office and distributed their contents. Bribes of lunch worked wonders for scheduling emergency appointments. To keep Ted's disciplined diet, their once-rich luncheons had changed to grilled chicken Caesar salads. She handed one of the bags to Ted and plopped a long, crunchy baguette between them. Not quite as tasty as the Yum Yum Shop's but close.

"Are you going to sue this Jeff Rovinski guy and his daughter for punitive damages, Liv?" Ted asked, wrestling the end piece from the bread. "I shouldn't be eating these carbs." He stuck the heel in his mouth.

"At least I buy the good stuff," she said and broke off the other end for herself. "Call me crazy, but no. The last thing I need is to drag this out with a legal hassle. Everybody ends up miserable if I go for the jugular, except for you lawyers." Olivia sighed. "Adam wasn't litigious. Suing won't bring him back."

"So is this a friendly visit to buy me lunch? Ellen's estate is pretty much wrapped up. Are we on or off the clock?"

"On the clock. You'll need to cancel your Palm Springs golf trip, because you're about to be too busy."

Ted nodded as he pulled out a notepad and whirled a fresh number-two pencil in the electric sharpener. He blew on the tip and pressed the button on a small electronic timer.

"Go. We're on the clock."

"Mom had a manuscript called *Indigo to Black*," she announced. "I'm getting it published."

"You don't say? Fiction or nonfiction?"

"Fiction—" *At least I think so*, she added silently. "It's good."

"What do you want to do?"

"I need to set up a new estate trust in Mom's name, with updated terms. Lauren, Danny, and I will be equal trustees. A big advance is coming and both installments will go into the account. The balance over thirty thousand and the ongoing royalties are to be distributed monthly, divided into thirds, and auto-deposited into each of our accounts. The reserve will be to pay the enormous bill you're about to send me. Also, we need a stash in case any of the three of us gets into trouble."

"Mmm-hmmm. Okay . . . " Ted stopped his pencil. "How much are we talking about?"

"Two point one million will come in two installments from Sloane Publishing, plus ongoing royalties once the sales exceed the advance."

Ted's eyes widened as he whistled. "Go, Ellen! That's more—a lot more—than any of your advances, Liv."

"Thanks for the poignant reminder."

"Only stating fact."

"We'll all sign a copy of the book for you, but we're not quite there yet. The contract is coming, so I'll need you to review the terms."

"Happy to. Pretty straightforward."

"Oh, and Danny and Ryan got engaged. He proposed at Mom's service—you missed a good one, Ted."

"Wow! *At* the service?"

"Right after the dog busted the piper's bagpipes. Priceless. Mom's and Dad's wedding rings set the wheels in motion. Danny will be making an appointment with you to put together her and Ryan's will. They're getting married in October."

"Smart. Good thinking with this book deal."

"I'm not done. A second charitable trust needs to be set up—for a different book—in the name of . . . " Olivia swallowed a chunk of lettuce, "the Estate of R. D. Griffin."

"Who?" Ted brushed breadcrumbs from his lined pad.

"Ardy, as he's known. He's my neighbor. I'm writing his life story. He wants me to publish it after he dies. The proceeds for Ardy's book—if it gets published—will go into the new Pogo Charitable Trust you're going to create."

"And you? I assume you'll own the copyright if you're the author."

"True . . . but I want all the profits to be a tax-deductible donation into the trust, in memory of R. D. Griffin."

"What's the timeline on this?"

"As soon as possible. Ardy is ninety-three. I'm his executrix, so he'll need a simple will drawn up in addition to the trust. He doesn't have much, but if you give me the forms he can get you started."

"Where's the money going to go once deposited in this Pogo Trust? Who, or what, is Pogo?" Ted shook his head, trying to keep up.

"Ardy's dog." Olivia stabbed a piece of chicken from her salad and grinned. "The trust is to be named after his standard poodle. Danny's getting Pogo trained as a certified therapy dog."

"I hope we're done, because I'll never get to play golf again."

"A few more." Olivia made a checkmark on her list; her other hand kept a forkful of chicken hovering near her mouth. "Lauren will need to come in to meet with one of your colleagues to put together a real estate contract for her. Once the advance on Mom's book is deposited, she's buying Mr. Griffin's house next door to me." She popped the chicken in her mouth, chewed, and swallowed. "Ardy's moving into Lauren's apartment. They're pulling a switcheroo. She would have been here today, but she had to go back to work."

"A referral's no problem. I understand the arrangement for

Ellen's book, but I still need to know what happens to the funds for this Pogo Trust?"

"We're going to create a partnership agreement with the Oregon Humane Society. For a modest salary, Danny will be the trust's director and execute activities with OHS. The funds will be used for expanding their programs to train shelter dogs as service companions."

Ted shoved his pencil in the sharpener to freshen the tip. "Okay. Keep going. Sounds like good work . . . and perfect for Danny too."

"We're almost done." Olivia had finished her salad; Ted hadn't touched his. "I need you to write up four—no five—simple confidentiality agreements, to be signed by Mr. Griffin, Ryan Eason, Lauren, Danny, and me."

Ted raised his gaze but not his head. "What's that about?"

"The memoir—maybe a novel—is Mr. Griffin's life story. It's to remain secret until after his death."

"Why the intrigue?"

"I can't tell you."

"C'mon, Liv." Ted spread his hands. "We go way back."

"The less you know about this particular writing project the better." She met his stare.

Ted chuckled, uncomfortable. "What? Are we going to find out who really killed *JFK*?"

Olivia shrugged and broke his gaze. She chased a lone cherry tomato around her container and finally stabbed it with her plastic fork. A gelatinous red blob of seeds shot across the desk and landed on Ted's notepad. He stared at the crimson slash across the words *Pogo Charitable Trust.* Ted reached over the desk and clawed the air for a tissue.

"Make it six confidentiality agreements, Ted," Olivia said, reaching the tissue for him. "You'll need to sign one too."

"Jesus . . . A week and a half without your mother and you've come up with all this?"

"Oh—and you need to update my will. Lauren and Danny will be my co-executrices. You can turn off the clock now."

Chapter 31

The Check Arrives

After Labor Day, the onslaught of paperwork streamed into Olivia's mailbox. She knew Ted had filed the application with the state of Oregon for the Pogo Charitable Trust, because interspersed in her mail were pleas for money addressed to the new entity. The causes ranged from replenishing the bee population to harvesting medicinal bark from Pacific yew trees for cancer research, and everything in between.

Olivia flipped through the stack. Her fingers stopped on an envelope from Sloane Publishing. The first installment of the advance had arrived, just as Karen promised. Olivia checked her watch: three ten. A deposit at the bank was still possible. The new account was set up and ready to go, and this was one account that would never be closed: the account for the Estate of Ellen Dushane. Olivia bounced to the kitchen, rehearsing her words to Lauren and Danny.

Freesia appeared at Olivia's side and rubbed against her leg, claiming ownership.

"You miss Pogo, don't you?" She chuckled. "Yeah, right."

Freesia followed her, twisting between Olivia's calves to charm her into an early dinner.

"Hold on. Give me a minute." She closed her eyes and opened

the envelope. She pulled out the letter and a check for the first half of the advance. The remainder would be paid upon publication of *Indigo to Black*, slated for April. Karen suggested a spring launch to kick off the summer reading season. Olivia had agreed—the sooner the better.

With mixed emotions, Olivia stared at the check. Her mother had finally received the stamp of approval she'd deserved. If Olivia had only known about the manuscript while Ellen was alive, her mother could have lived in a better house, traveled the world, and bought anything she had wanted. For Danny and Ryan's upcoming wedding, Ellen might have taken Danny aside in a special moment to hand over her and their father's rings. Ellen could have crowed to their father about her own achievements and assets.

But then again, her mother hadn't been comfortable with the social aspect of fame and glory; Ellen had lived her dreams of personal accomplishment through her kids. Olivia, in her usual way, would have pushed her mother beyond her comfort level. And Danny might not have reconnected with Ryan, remaining stuck in a layer of indecision or worse. A book tour, interviews, and public attention would have been nothing more than a stressful intrusion into Ellen's private world. Even with all the money, her mother likely would have lived the same way: puttering in her garden, smoking cigarettes, and cooking up BLTs, steaks, and sausages in her clean kitchen. What if . . . what if. Olivia shook her head. *Mom.*

Olivia took a breath and reached for the phone. "Lauren! Can you meet me at Mom's bank at four? The first installment is here."

"Are you serious? Don't joke, Liv. I swear to God, if you're—"

"I'm not! The check is in my hand. I'm staring at it. Says one million fifty thousand."

"Ted is worth every penny we pay him."

"He hauled ass on the book contract. I need to call Danny and get cleaned up. I gotta go." Olivia disconnected and called Danny's cell number.

"I hope you're sitting down," she said when Danny answered.

"I am now. I'm changing the sheets, and then I'm going to hang a gorgeous watercolor of Mom's. The tape on the back was falling apart, so I had it reframed."

"I don't remember ever seeing a watercolor."

"I found it in the closet in the guestroom and tagged it."

"What's it look like?"

"Small. A lake with trees in all their fall glory. Super old—forties or fifties."

Olivia raised her eyes to the ceiling. To Danny, "super old" meant anything before she was born. "Huh . . . interesting." Her wheels started to turn.

"The colors are perfect for our living room. You don't think it's the same lake in the book, do you?"

"Noooo," she scoffed, waving the check. "An inspiration maybe. Can you meet me at the bank in forty minutes? The first installment of the advance came in the mail today."

"I'm there in fifteen minutes."

"On second thought . . . bring the watercolor with you. I may want to take the piece out of the frame."

"Why?"

"To send to the publisher. The image might make a perfect book cover. Meet you at Mom's bank, Danny Girl."

Olivia ended the call and stared at the phone. She tried to swallow, but her mouth had gone dry. Another clue.

The realization rang like a bell. Her mother had left the old manuscript for Olivia to find, by design. Like a mother bear with three female cubs, Ellen had acted on animal instinct: she taught Lauren, the strongest, to fight and survive; protected Danny, the most fragile, by offering the plumpest teat and softest paw; and unable to corral the independent one, she had left a trail for Olivia to find her way home.

~ · ~ · ~

An hour before closing, Lauren, Olivia, and Danny sat in front of the manager of their mother's bank. A fiduciary novice in his thirties, the man had one of those practiced smiles, the overly warm one that came with retaining customers after their deaths. He handed each of them a new silver pen with *Premier Customer* etched in looping letters.

"I'm so glad Ellen will be staying with us," he said. "I'd be thrilled if the three of you signed a copy of her book for me when it's published."

"With this fancy pen," Olivia said, rocking the shiny instrument back and forth.

The manager collected the forms. "As soon as the check clears, we'll make the transfers into each of these accounts in the amount of three hundred forty thousand, leaving your requested reserve of thirty thousand. The deposits will be funded in five business days." He smiled again, showing off his veneered teeth. Too white. "I'll be right back, ladies."

Danny turned to Olivia. "Why the reserve?"

"In case one of us makes a bonehead move and needs the money in an emergency," Olivia said. "Plus, Ted's bill will be a whopper."

"What if something happens and the book doesn't get published?"

"Don't go on a wild spend-a-thon, Danny, but the contract says we don't have to give back any *paid* part of the advance if the manuscript is delivered—which it has been. If Sloane decides not to move forward, we won't get the final installment, but then Karen is free to shop the book to another publishing house."

Lauren grimaced. "All this money and the damned government will take most of it. Criminal! And now we have to wait a week for the check to clear. The bank wants to sit on the cash."

"Considered inherited income," Olivia chided. "This falls into a different tax structure, and as of right now we're under the exclusion for Federal taxes. I can't promise what will happen for the royalties down the road if the book's a runaway hit. That income might end up being taxable."

"Yeah . . . well." Lauren narrowed her eyes. She turned in the chair and stuck out her foot. "I might get a new pair of shoes after the governor pays for a fancy fund-raising party—with *my* tax dollars."

"Oh, stop. Get some new underwear instead."

"Now, you can move forward to buy Ardy's house," Danny interjected.

"We've started negotiating," Lauren scratched her lip. "That sweet old man is eating my lunch. Even at ninety-three, Ardy's ruthless. No concessions. *I'm* the one making concessions."

"I'm not surprised." Olivia chuckled and turned to Danny. "What will you do first?"

"Get my wedding dress altered and pay for the honeymoon." Danny glanced at her sisters with a precocious grin.

"Aren't you going to show it to us?"

"Not until it's done. I want it to be a surprise."

"Where are you and Ryan going?" Lauren asked. "And don't say the Grand Canyon or Niagara Falls."

"Fishing. We've reserved a cabin in Vermont on Indigo Lake as a nod to Mom's book. October will be gorgeous, just like the watercolor. It's in the car for you to send to the publisher, Liv."

Olivia gulped. "I thought you didn't like Mom's book."

"I never said I didn't like the setting. And the book is paying for the honeymoon."

Lauren glimpsed at Olivia and spread her hands. "I'm not saying one damn word."

"It's a miracle."

The bank manager came back into the office. "We're all set." He shook each of their hands. "Keep the pens with my compliments. See you in a few months when you get the final installment."

Chapter 32

Ardy's Tuesday Interviews

By mid-September, Tuesday interviews with Ardy—now at his apartment—held top priority on Olivia's schedule. From Olivia's side, no publicity commitments for Mom's book were allowed on Tuesdays. From Ardy's, he was finally done with his one other major task: he had finally hammered out a deal with Lauren to buy his house. Ardy enjoyed pressing Lauren's buttons, but when he was satisfied he'd met his match, he caved to many of her demands. His old mobster negotiation tactics came out like brass knuckles: Ardy wanted to build future gains into the price; Lauren argued the price needed to be offset by the investment she'd need to make to install air-conditioning, paint the house, upgrade the kitchen appliances, and even scrub the oil stains from the driveway. Olivia refused to play referee. The final point of the negotiated terms called for Lauren and Danny to unpack Ardy's boxes in the apartment, while he sat on the couch with Pogo directing traffic.

Olivia planted herself across from that couch with her laptop, preparing for her next interview. The first two sessions were brutal, both in the process and the story. Ardy's childhood had been a Petri dish for breeding a life of crime: an absent, alcoholic father and an angry, bitter mother, both struggling immigrants. The tiny stray Jack

Russell puppy Ardy had found in an alley remained, to this day, the bright spot of his youth. He'd named the dog Felix after his former self. And so was born a lifelong love of dogs. With his little companion by his side, Ardy sought solace in making extra money as an errand boy for a union boss. At the age of seven, Ardy's first job entailed feeding loose change into a cigarette machine to buy the boss's unfiltered Pall Malls. Pennies grew into nickels; quarters churned into dollar bills. By age ten, loaning money at exorbitant interest rates became his specialty. Ardy called his take of the spoils "juice."

Olivia scooted Pogo's paws from her side of the cushion. Between his two-hour sessions of service dog training on Thursday mornings and his practice healing rounds at Milwaukie Hospital throughout the week, Danny kept Pogo hopping on all fours before returning him home to Ardy in the evenings. Olivia's Tuesday interviews were the dog's only day off, which he spent eavesdropping under Ardy's touch.

"I just remembered: keep the screen door to the balcony closed; the squirrels will jump in from the tree," Lauren called out from the kitchen. "How do you like the place?"

"Real good. Pogo's happy," he said. "You know, Lauren, you could've paid *me* every month for the house instead of the bank." Ardy winked at Olivia. "I'd-a given you a better rate."

"Ohhh . . . no. Your pedigree as a banker makes me nervous."

Ardy chuckled. "I wouldn't screw you, Lauren. I'd keep the juice running so you never paid off the principal." He slapped his knee as Lauren peered around the corner of the kitchen and stuck out her tongue.

"Okay, let's stay on task," Olivia instructed. "After Lauren organized the newspaper articles, I've mapped out forty-six murders. Since we're doing this in chronological order, we've discussed your early childhood of pickpocketing and running errands to when you got involved with the mob"—she checked her notes—"which appears to be 1936, right before the murder of John Avena."

"Big Nose."

"Excuse me?"

"Everybody called Avena 'Big Nose.' The Lanzetti brothers shot him. Corner of Washington and Passyunk. Nowadays, they call it a drive by." He laughed with a wheeze and started coughing.

"Why?" Olivia's fingers paused on the keyboard.

"Let's just say things got a bit tight within the family over a gambling racket. I specialized in extortion and loan sharking." Ardy stuck his nose toward the ceiling. "Hear that, Lauren?"

"I heard it," she called back. "What'd I tell ya!"

Ardy nodded, satisfied he'd delivered one final jab. "Me and Tony Nunzio"—he crossed his fingers—"right together. I didn't go for the drug dealing. We was nice family guys until he killed my wife."

Olivia's mouth froze open as Lauren entered the small living room, followed by Danny.

"Everything's put away in the kitchen," Lauren announced. "Now, I have to go and unpack *my* stuff."

"The new bed's made up with fresh sheets, Ardy," Danny added as she emerged from the short hallway. "The last of Mom's vegetables are in the fridge."

Pogo lifted his head and gazed at Danny with doughy eyes, as if to say, *Please don't make me get up*. Danny leaned over the couch and kissed the soft spot on the back of his ear with a loud smooch. "You're a good boy, Pogo. Tomorrow, you need to visit Mr. Freeman with the bad owie." She turned toward Olivia and lowered her voice as the dog licked her fingers. "Brain tumor."

"You wise guys go on ahead," Olivia suggested, distracted by Ardy's last comment. "I won't be too much longer here. I'll meet you back at the house."

"Thanks, you two. You girls are swell." Ardy waited for the front door to click shut and turned back to Olivia. He thumped Pogo's rib cage. "Where were we?"

"Nunzio had your wife killed," Olivia muttered, barely able to get the words out.

"Let's hold off on that."

Relieved—but compelled to hear more—Olivia had given up on

the organized approach to the story. She let Ardy ramble without rules, expounding on whatever popped into his head. The chronology could be pieced together later. "Tell me about Antonio Nunzio. The 1980 article of his murder said Antonio led the family for a long time, since 1959."

"A sweetheart, but the man had rules." Ardy stuck up his crooked forefinger and shook it. "Tony didn't go for drug dealing. Put his foot down. Had ethics. Was what you could call . . . 'conservative' in his endeavors."

"Like?"

"Gambling, sharking, labor rackets. And if someone had to be killed—which *did* have to happen now and again—the hit was clean, squeaky clean."

Olivia put her emotions in neutral to speak. "Did you ever kill anyone yourself?"

Ardy gazed down at Pogo's head in his lap. "C'mon, Olivia. What do you think?"

"This isn't about what I think," she argued. "You're the one who wanted your story recorded. Don't sugarcoat the facts." Olivia stared at him as her fingers rested on air.

"On my eighteenth birthday, I did the first one—back in thirty-eight. Like it was yesterday. A guy didn't pay up. Tony was initiating me." He glanced at Olivia, his eyes tortured with recall. "Don't even remember the sap's name, to be honest. Told me to kill his dog—Australian shepherd mix. Beautiful. I sure remember that dog's name: Salgado—Sal for short. Tony knew I loved dogs."

Olivia's stomach clenched to hold back a shout, a shriek, a yell, and imagined her hands around Ardy's neck. "Did you?" she whispered.

Ardy didn't offer an immediate answer. He shifted. He crossed his legs and rubbed his chin. He scratched the gray stubble on his cheek, as if the inside of his mouth itched.

"Looked right at me with trusting eyes . . . pleading eyes," he muttered. "Had to, or I'd be killed myself. Got to have moxie. Be a big man. Show respect." Pogo let out a groan as Ardy stroked his ears. "I was nothing after that day. *Nothing* inside."

Olivia couldn't get a breath. "Jesus God . . . *no*. You've had to live with this all these years? You waited for decades to get away, didn't you?"

"Decades and decades."

Ardy wouldn't meet her eyes. Instead, he closed his and squeezed the creased olive skin between his bushy eyebrows with his fingers.

"I don't know what to say," she said, her voice cracking.

"Don't talk. Write."

"I thought I knew how to write, but *this*—"

"Enough for today, Olivia. Enough."

So it went—hour upon hour—each Tuesday afternoon. Human moments grew from gut-wrenching confessions of unspeakable crimes. Every major milestone of Ardy's life had been punctuated with a murder. And every Tuesday afternoon, Olivia left the apartment in silence, twisting the knob to make sure she secured the lock. She wanted to slap Ardy's face . . . and then give him a hug.

Chapter 33

The Pearl Earring

For the entire following week, Olivia toggled between working on the draft of Ardy's manuscript and getting Ellen's house ready for sale. Both tasks took their toll. It had been difficult for her to witness the untagged furniture and knickknacks being carried out to the truck for their trek to the auction house. While Danny had gathered up the contents of Ellen's closet, making several trips to the drop offs of local charities, Olivia and Lauren cleaned. Neither one of them wanted to face the disposition of their mother's clothes. They had parted with Adam's and Mark's wardrobes and couldn't go through the process again. Clothes carried a scent that brought to life the small moments, the special moments, of the person who wore them. The berry-colored stain from a jelly doughnut on Ellen's favorite knit sweater had reduced Lauren to tears. Olivia had fled to stand out on the back deck. She'd picked several leaves of her mother's basil and rolled them in her fingers, inhaling the licorice aroma like an anesthetic.

None of them had the stomach for conducting an estate sale on their own. Lauren wanted no part of spending her weekend in negotiations over the worth of their mother with someone who would turn around and sell her mementos on eBay. She preferred to give away the everyday items to charity. So they did.

Today was the final step. Lauren had arranged for the three of them to meet the realtor at their mother's empty house. Tracy Meldrum, a top sales agent at Lauren's realty office, would handle the listing. Ardy might be a loan shark, but Tracy was a land shark, closing properties before buyers and sellers could change their minds. Olivia stood with Lauren and Danny in the kitchen as Tracy assessed the house. She emerged with a smile on her face.

"The place looks *fab*ulous," Tracy announced. The woman's energy exceeded that of the three of them combined. "Here's the contract. Once you sign, we'll be off and running. We need to get the house on the market. School is back in session, which puts us at a disadvantage."

Tracy's phone rang out the tune "This Land Is Your Land." She held out her pen to Lauren and pointed to the papers on the counter. Lauren plucked it from her fingers as Tracy gravitated to the living room to take the call.

Lauren gazed at Olivia and Danny "Well, no going back now."

"After this, we're done," Olivia said.

"I thought I was ready. Maybe I should have bought this house, not Ardy's."

"Not a good idea to do business with family. Plus, you're impossible to negotiate with." Olivia gazed around the kitchen. "This will always be Mom's house. It never would have felt like your own."

"I know, but—"

"You've done something wonderful for Ardy," Danny reiterated. "I lived here with Mom for three years, Lauren. Not for one day did this ever feel like my home. But the minute I stepped back into Ryan's house, it felt right. You said the same thing when you did the final walk-through at Ardy's."

Olivia nodded in agreement as she signed the document. She set the pen on the counter. "Speaking of walk-throughs, I'll be right back."

Olivia turned and wandered through the empty house, while Tracy talked on her phone at the front window in the living room. The walls still breathed with the unstoppable energy of Ellen Dushane.

Even after scrubbing every surface, vacuuming the carpets, and mopping the floors, Olivia picked up the lingering powdery aroma of her mother's perfume, applied each morning after her shower.

Continuing down the hall to get away from the chatter of Tracy's next deal, Olivia meandered into her mother's barren bedroom. The heavy insulated drapes she'd hemmed for Ellen, to keep out the chill, hung closed over the windows. As she pulled them open to let in the light, the pucker of the mistake in the hem drew her gaze. She remembered knotting the thread too tight. Her mother never noticed, or at least hadn't mentioned the gaffe to Olivia. No doubt, she'd said something to Danny about it. Ellen's way.

A glint from something shiny at the baseboard caught her eye. She knelt on the floor. The muscles in Olivia's face slackened. Hooked in a loop of the carpet was an earring: two silver hands holding a freshwater pearl. Its lonely mate waited for a reunion in Olivia's own jewelry drawer. No need to carry out Ellen's wish to turn it into a lapel pin. Some things repair themselves.

"All this time . . . right here," she whispered. "Oh, Mom. Are you seeing this?" She squeezed the earring in her hand like a talisman.

In a daze, Olivia drifted back into the kitchen to find Lauren, Danny, and Tracy waiting for her. She held out her palm.

"I found it," she said, her voice catching in her throat.

Danny touched the small pearl as if it might come alive. "A sign."

Lauren glanced at Danny, expecting more. "Of what?"

"Mom is okay with us selling the house."

The declaration made Olivia's shoulders relax. "I think you're right, Danny."

"So do I," Tracy interjected, holding out her pen. "Olivia, your mother said you left the date blank."

Olivia chuckled and entered the date. "We're ready to go." She pushed the front door key across the tile counter toward Tracy.

"I've never seen a house so clean." Tracy gazed at the open kitchen and small den with a fireplace. "The place sparkles."

"Our Olivia," Lauren said. "Born with sponges for hands. You could call her Edward Spongyhands. I told you there wouldn't be a need to hire a professional cleaning service."

"Can I contract you to clean my listings before they go on the market?"

Olivia locked her gaze on Lauren. They both burst out laughing.

"No, I'm serious!" Tracy insisted.

"Priceless," Lauren choked, trying to catch her breath. "I'm sending this one to the tabloids. 'Hotshot writer reduced to scrubbing toilets for sister's realty firm'!"

Chapter 34

Two Books Are Better than One

A blaze of color ushered in the first Tuesday morning of October, but Olivia was oblivious to the change of month. The ringing phone in the kitchen jolted her awake. She'd fallen asleep on the living room couch. At some point in the night, Freesia had crawled up and slept on her chest. She pulled the end of the cat's tail from her mouth. Pages from the draft of Ardy's manuscript crinkled as she set the cat on the floor. Piles of paper scattered at her feet as she stood.

"I'm coming! Hold your damn horses!" Olivia stumbled as Freesia raced ahead of her to the kitchen. She glanced at her watch: nine twenty. "No wonder you're hungry," she said as she picked up the phone. Olivia gave the caller an audible yawn instead of an identifying greeting.

"Did I wake you? You need to get up." A woman's voice. A New York accent.

"Who is this?" Olivia pulled the receiver away to inspect the caller ID.

"What? Excuse me, but I happen to be the agent who's making you and your sisters millionaires, that's who!"

"Karen! I'm sorry. I've been up all night editing." Olivia flinched when she realized it was Tuesday. Her next interview with Ardy was at one o'clock. She also remembered that the Rovinskis were being sentenced at the same time as her meeting with Ardy.

"What I like to hear, Liv. And I hate to say this, but shut down your computer because everything's on track with *Indigo*. Sloane is set for the April release. We'll be jamming through the holidays to get preorders."

"Oh, right. *Indigo*. Pretty fast." Olivia pressed the button to start the coffeepot.

"The publicist will be e-mailing you an interview schedule. Don't stress; most are phone-ins, but go to the salon and get a fluff up. A few are local morning shows who want to talk with all three of you as a group. There are requests for appearances at some writing conferences too."

Karen's words finally registered. "Wait! Starting when?"

"The ARCs are going out to bookstores by Thanksgiving. Buzz-a-buzz-buzz, Liv. Get your butt in gear."

"Lord, help me . . . " Olivia ran her hand through the tangles in her hair. The thought of the advanced reader copies of her mother's book being released for public scrutiny made the whole ordeal real, not just a family drama. "Are they keeping the cover art from the galley I reviewed?"

"The same. They love the image, and so do I," Karen raved. "The watercolor of Indigo Lake is perfect. They're sending the original back in a few weeks."

"Fine . . . " Olivia closed her eyes, envisioning the warm wash of turning leaves and sparkling water. If it hadn't been for Danny finding the art piece in the closet, Olivia would never have known of the watercolor's existence. She shuddered at the thought of the charming work ending up at the auction house.

"At least sound excited, Olivia. I'm working my ass off here."

"I am . . . It's been a long week."

"Rest up. Once you get the publicity schedule, call me to review the dates with your calendar."

Olivia straightened. "Remember, I can't do anything on Tuesdays.

Nonnegotiable, Karen."

"I know. I know. You told me a thousand times. Sounds ominous. Any hints of a forthcoming gem?"

Olivia shifted. "My little sister's getting married on Saturday."

"What's that got to do with Tuesdays? Would it kill you to tell me what you're working on?"

"I hope not, Karen."

~ · ~ · ~

As Olivia backed out of the garage for her final interview appointment with Ardy, Lauren pulled into her own driveway in a brand-new red Honda Accord. Not the flashiest of cars but flashy for Lauren. Olivia shut off the engine and stepped from her car. The combination of elation and guilt in her sister's expression made her chuckle.

"What do you think, Liv? She's a beauty, am I right?" Lauren beamed as she swept her hand like a model on *The Price Is Right.*

"Do the brakes work?" Olivia joked and pointed to the three-month-old dent in her garage door.

"At least my car and Dad's Blazer are out of your hair. I traded in both those pieces of crap."

"I love the car. Did you leave the salesman licking his wounds?"

"Always tell 'em you want to finance to get the price down. Then, pay cash. Works like a charm."

"Things are popping on Mom's book, by the way. It'll be out in early April."

Lauren's face lit up with pride. "I can't wait to hold one. I'm so proud of her."

"The big publicity push starts soon. You and Danny are expected to participate. At least your hair's all one color now, but you might want to get your roots done—professionally."

"No way. Uh-uh. You're not putting me in front of a microphone or a TV camera. Plus, I need to help you with Ardy's manuscript. The articles are all cataloged and organized—two binders worth. How's the draft coming along?"

"Today's my final interview to clarify some facts. I'm going over to his apartment now. We're pretty much done."

"Oh, wait!" Lauren trotted toward the front steps. "A package came yesterday for Ardy. Looks like he ordered something."

"What is it?"

Lauren shrugged and disappeared inside the house. She came out with a puffy manila envelope.

"Here, take this with you." Lauren handed Olivia the package. "How are you holding up?"

"Exhausted. Ardy lived his whole life trying to keep his head from being blown off. You can't imagine what he's told me." Olivia gazed out across the lawn. The maple leaves were well into their journey to bright red. A chill pushed away summer. "Pretty tough stuff."

"Are you having doubts?"

"The Pogo Charitable Trust is too important. Doing something good with the whole mess of his past keeps Ardy going. Danny's work with Pogo keeps him looking forward too."

"Your face looks funny, Liv. What's the matter?"

"The Rovinskis' sentencing is today."

"Are you going to go?"

"No," she said. "When I said I was done, I meant it. My focus now is on this book and Mom's book."

"Ardy's story is getting you obsessed again. Take a break and clear your head."

"I can't. I worry that . . . something might happen"—Olivia hesitated and focused on a squirrel razoring through the casing of a chestnut—"before I finish the manuscript."

"Ardy's tougher than you think. Believe me. Try buying a house from him. He makes the car salesman, who chewed me up an hour ago, look like Mother Teresa."

"I hope so." Olivia squeezed the spongy envelope. "I gotta go. Ardy's waiting for me."

Chapter 35

The Last Interview

R. D. stepped through the door to the apartment and looped Pogo's leash over a hook, one dedicated for the purpose. Olivia would be coming in about fifteen minutes for their last interview. He had to admit, walks with Pogo were easier after the training sessions with Danny. Healing dog. R. D. shook his head and chuckled. Danny couldn't imagine how much healing Pogo had done.

R. D. gravitated to the galley kitchen. After he washed and refilled Pogo's water bowl, he lined up his afternoon pills on the counter: blood thinner, blood pressure stabilizer, blood cleaner, and a blood orange for a snack to keep from throwing up all those pills. Getting old wasn't some big reward. People worked so damned hard to live longer, but when they got there the body turned longevity into a punishment. R. D. flexed his stiff fingers, a reminder to add an arthritis pill to the regimen.

Pogo sensed the time. An internal clock prompted the dog to take his place on the couch to hold down his white towel. R. D. would miss this routine when the manuscript was done.

Olivia was a damn good writer; she wrote from the heart. Must be why she was made so much coin with those romances. Good racket. Good people . . . and her sisters too. Olivia almost made him out to be a good person, underneath all the crap. R. D. had learned a lot about himself from reading the early draft of the manuscript, things he had never realized until the milestones of his life were put together. One thing led to another to justify his actions. The mob became a surrogate family, instilling their own set of morals and values. Now, all those wise guys' kids had kids of their own. Olivia and her sisters were like his kids.

R. D. gazed at Pogo on the couch. And Danny; she should have Pogo if something happened. All it took was for him to forget to take his meds.

Tap. Tap. Tap. "Me, Ardy!" Olivia's voice. His shoulders relaxed. When would he ever stop thinking of a knock or a doorbell as a death knell? Never.

R. D. shuffled down the short hallway to the front door. He unhooked the chain and turned the deadbolt. "Come on in. Want something hot? Cold?" Olivia carried that red satchel of hers. Looked like devil business—his devil business.

"Water, thanks. Today might be short, Ardy. I'm pretty much done with the draft. Only a few more questions."

"Then what?" he asked and pulled a plastic bottle from the door of the refrigerator.

"Well . . . a whole lotta nothing for a long time, I hope." Olivia sat on her usual end of the couch in the small living room. Pogo thumped his tail when she patted his back. With the sliding door open, a crisp breeze fluttered the pages of the *Oregonian* on the coffee table. "You get the sole copy of the final manuscript. Then, I'll drive you to Cascade Bank with all the newspaper articles, and we'll put the whole shebang in the safe-deposit box. You keep the only key." Olivia dug in her purse. "In fact, here." She pulled out the small steel key and handed it to him.

"No other copies nowhere?" R. D. narrowed his eyes as he handed her the water bottle in trade for the key. He dropped it in the breast pocket of his plaid flannel shirt. *Don't give nothing without getting more in return.*

"Nope. Any working copies will be shredded before I give you the final." Olivia twisted the cap on the water bottle and took a sip.

R. D. studied her. "Anybody else read it?"

"Not yet. Only Lauren will. I'll need her to edit and proof for typos. She has a good pair of eyes, no matter how much she gripes that she can't see anything."

"Okay, but don't let Danny read it. I got a soft spot for her. She'll get the wrong idea about me." He threw Olivia a quick glance. "You know . . . she asked me to give her away for her wedding."

"I can't think of anybody better to take her arm down the aisle. Danny's a grown woman. She can handle the truth. But no, she doesn't know all the details. She loves you, Ardy, no matter what."

R. D. winced as he sat on the couch. He let out a sigh upon landing. "What you got?" Pogo licked R. D.'s fingers, as if sensing the pain.

Fishing through her case, Olivia pulled out several pages and a notepad. "Here's the last chapter. We end with the trial where you testify, then we move to the process of your going into the Witness Protection Program. We won't give details of where you are now. Your name will be changed." She turned to face him. "But . . . Ardy?"

He raised his gaze from the pages, his mind swimming with the vicious faces at the trial. "Yeah?"

"I want you to write the epilogue—your own words, not mine. Only one or two pages, no more than five hundred words."

"Me? I don't write so good. What's an epilogue?"

"It's a follow-up to what happened in the story. The end after the end. I think readers need to experience your voice. It's about authenticity, a verification you were alive and well at the time this book was written."

"Can't I just tell you, and you write 'the end'?"

Olivia groaned. "All right, we'll do one more session after this, but you need to think about what you want to say. Your words, not mine. Don't rattle something off the top of your head, either, like you always do. Spend some time with your thoughts." She poised her fancy pen over the notepad. "Okay, imagine yourself back on the witness stand.

Tell me your interpretation of the expressions and actions of each person at the trial."

"Pretty simple. If Palermo had a gun in his hand, he would-a shot me between the peepers." R. D. rubbed his forehead, as if an imaginary hole had opened in his skull. "I had to point out Little Nicky Palermo when they asked me to identify him. My finger might as well-a been a gun. The anger didn't get to me, though—I could deal with that—but the betrayal and disappointment on his face . . . faith being blown to bits. So wrong, but so right."

"Good . . . this is good." Olivia's pen scratched on the paper, churning his words and spinning them into something readable. "When you looked into their eyes, did you regret the choice you'd made to cooperate with the Feds?"

"No." R. D. shook his head for emphasis. "I was a dead man . . . and now, thirty years later, I'm sitting here talking with you. Not a bad choice, Olivia."

Olivia stopped writing and raised her eyes to him, as though they were smiling. "I think you just gave me the last line of the book."

"Are we done?"

"I think so. I know a good last line when I hear it." Olivia capped the pen. "Oh . . . I almost forgot." She pulled out a small package from her case. "Lauren wanted me to give this to you. She said it came to the house the other day."

R. D. set the last chapter pages on the coffee table and took the squishy envelope, the plastic bubbles crinkling inside as he squeezed. "No idea."

"Maybe something you ordered before you knew you were moving? The mail can be slow. I have to go." Olivia stood and moved to the door. "I want to rewrite the final pages while they're fresh."

"When you coming back?"

"Give me a few days. I have to do some interviews for my mother's book, but Danny will be by on Thursday to pick up you and Pogo for his graduation. Let's keep our regular Tuesday meeting after Danny's wedding. I'll bring lunch to celebrate." Olivia reached out to him. "Read those pages and let me know what you think. And don't forget to rip them up when you're done."

R. D. wanted to remember her hugs for the rest of his life. She always acted like he'd break if she hugged too tight. Silly girl. Hugs couldn't be too tight.

"Go on, now. Finish her up. You done good."

"Do you have a suit for the wedding? I can take you to the tux rental place."

"I got one. My casket suit." R. D. laughed and scooted her toward the front door.

"Don't talk like that. You'll look like a million bucks, whatever you wear."

With her parting words, R. D. turned the deadbolt and hooked the chain. The package in his hand felt weighty, clanky, like something metal. His old address was written with a black marker. No return. No postmark, either. He didn't remember ordering anything. Agent Riojas arranged for all his mail to be forwarded.

R. D. stared at the package, attempting to shake off the ingrained response of suspicion to anything new. He headed to the kitchen.

"Big prize!" he joked. "Tell 'em what the old man won, boys!" He chuckled as he rummaged through the utensil drawer. He pulled out the scissors. Cutting across the top of the envelope, the bubbles popped from right to left. He squished the sides, turned the package over, and shook out the contents.

A leather dog collar, cracked with age, clattered to the counter with the clang of a metal identification tag. The pounding of his heart caused R. D.'s hand to tremor as he fingered the scratched and worn steel tag. One word: *Salgado.*

"Sal," he whispered, barely able to utter the word. "No, no, no, no . . . " R. D. pulled out his wallet and plucked Riojas' card from an inner sleeve. He reached for the phone and called the secure number.

"I know you see it's me on your screen," R. D. said, his voice shaky.

"Verified," Riojas answered.

"Got something in the mail. *Fiddledeedee.*"

He'd never uttered the code phrase before, so simple and harmless, but the four syllables would set off a chain of covert plans that were now far from his control.

"Where was it delivered?"

"My old house on Thirty-Fourth."

"They don't know where you are. Sit tight! Stay put! You know what to do. I'll have Skidmore at the apartment in twenty minutes. He'll stay with you for the next thirty-six hours while I make the arrangements."

R. D. hung up without responding. He set the phone on the counter next to the collar and shuffled to the living room, his steps leaden. Riojas's instructions might as well have been dog commands. *Obey. Stay put. Stay alive.* He pulled the sliding glass door closed, struggling to secure the latch. He slid the drapes until the room darkened. He rushed, as fast as could, down the hall to the bedroom and locked the window. He double-checked the chain and deadbolt on the front door. He turned off the lights.

Taking a seat on the couch next to Pogo, R. D. waited for Skidmore to arrive. He set his gnarled hand on the dog's rib cage. Pogo was sound asleep, worn out, tired of running.

The apartment rested in shadowed silence, except for the tick of the swinging pendulum on the wall clock in the dining nook. In thirty-six hours, after Danny picked up Pogo on Thursday morning, he'd be off to someplace new. Riojas was scrambling to make plans. He hoped the next place wasn't going to be too hot or cold.

"You like your Danny, don't ya, big fella?" A hollow thump released in time with the clock's rhythm as he patted Pogo. Then he patted his shirt pocket to make sure the key was still safe. "I'm gonna be fine . . . just fine."

In the silence, R. D. picked up the draft of the last chapter of the book from the coffee table and started to read. He figured he might as well come up with his parting thoughts for Olivia. Epilogue she called it. Nothing too long. He didn't even need all those five hundred words.

Chapter 36

Disappointment Comes in Many Forms

On Thursday morning. Danny's wedding invitation sat on R. D.'s dining table like a Ouija board—yes, no, goodbye. Salgado's old and cracked leather dog collar sat next to the calligraphied announcement. The rust-stained stitching had frayed with the passing of so many years.

"No other option," Riojas said, sighing as he pulled an envelope from his suit jacket pocket. "Here's your new birth certificate, social security and Medicare cards, and ID. We skipped the driver's license. You shouldn't be driving anymore."

"Iowa, huh?"

"Senior living complex. Progressive care, if you should need it. Nice. You can stay independent in your own apartment."

"Cold in Iowa in the winter. You sure I can't take my dog?"

"Afraid not. Too big," Skidmore said. "They wouldn't bend on the weight limit."

"And too hot in the summer for Pogo, I guess," R. D. mumbled with resignation. The bullet being planned for his brain couldn't be worse than this. He raised his eyes to Riojas. "You gotta watch my old house. Lauren's there . . . and Olivia."

"Ahead of you. We got it covered."

"The flight leaves PDX at two," Skidmore said. "As soon as Danielle picks up Pogo, the movers will pack and load the truck. They're waiting on the next street." Skidmore checked his wristwatch. "What time is she coming?"

R. D. continued to stare at the table. "Eight thirty. Pogo graduates his class today. Told Danny I'd go."

Riojas inspected the identification tag on the collar. "Not worth the risk, Mr. Griffin—I mean Mr. Milner. Tell her you don't feel well or something."

R. D. rested his head in his hands and leaned on his calloused elbows, supporting the weight of heavy thoughts. The wedding invitation drew his gaze. He slid the cream-colored notecard forward and studied the gold curlicue lettering: *Danielle Dushane and Ryan Eason request the honor of your presence . . .* "Supposed to give Danny away at her wedding on Saturday. She'll be disappointed."

"Not a word." Riojas rolled the dog collar into a tight coil and slipped it into a plastic evidence bag. He tucked it into the inner breast pocket. "Sorry, old man. You're not getting killed on our watch."

A vigorous tap of the doorknocker made the three of them freeze. Skidmore reached for his semiautomatic in his body holster. Riojas stood and made a serpentine movement down the hall, his own gun trained on the front door.

"She's early, or—"

Pogo barked and leaped from the couch. He trotted to his leash dangling from the hook and pulled on the strap until it fell to the floor. Picking up the lead with his teeth, the dog sat and whined as his tail thumped the ceramic tile. He was ready to go.

"Ardy? You awake?" asked the muffled female voice. *Tap. Tap. Tap.*

With a squint through the peephole, Riojas confirmed Danny's arrival and motioned Skidmore into the bedroom. He waved his gun for R. D. to answer the door.

The chain clattered as R. D. unhooked the latch and turned the deadbolt. He nodded for Riojas to join Skidmore before he pressed the handle.

"Morning," R. D. said, trying to keep his voice upbeat.

"Today's the big day!" Danny announced and raised her sunglasses to hold back her hair. Her expression radiated promise. "Right, Pogo?" Danny leaned into the dog's side and rubbed his head.

"Yep. Big day." R. D. turned away, his steps stiff as he moved toward the kitchen. He didn't want Danny to see his face. "You two have fun."

"Aren't you coming with us? You promised."

"Got a lot to do today, Danny."

"Ohhh, *Ardyyy*," she moaned. "If you need me to pick up anything, I can—" Danny's sneakers squeaked on the linoleum as she followed close at his heels.

"No. No. This day is about you and Pogo." Danny moved to stand in front of him. There it was: disappointment. Not her last. Danny had those puppy-dog eyes, pleading eyes, the kind of eyes that were hard to deny. R. D. pulled an envelope from the breast pocket of his flannel shirt. "Give this to Olivia, will ya? She wanted me to write something for the book."

"Sure. No problem." Danny slipped the envelope into her purse but not without studying him, suspicious. She returned to the front door where Pogo waited, impatient. As she hooked the clasp to his collar, she said, "C'mon, boy. Time to go get certified. We're making an honest dog out of you."

"Go on, now," R. D. instructed, shaking his finger.

Danny gazed at him, as if she wanted to insist he go with her but thought better of it. "I'll have him home by four thirty. I have a ton of errands to run after Pogo's ceremony." She lowered her sunglasses as she stepped outside. "I'm picking up my wedding dress this afternoon."

R. D. stooped and placed his hands on each side of Pogo's muzzle but continued to address Danny. "Real good. A day to remember. You'll be pretty as a picture."

Danny hesitated at the threshold. "Ardy?"

As he let go of Pogo, R. D. tried to raise his eyes but his throat constricted, as if choking hands cut off his air supply. He stood, but all he could utter was a breathy, "Yeah?"

"Are you okay?" Danny studied his face.

"Scoot."

Danny leaned inside to kiss him on the cheek. At the third step, Pogo pulled on his leash. The tender peck lingered for a few seconds on his tough skin as she raced behind the dog.

"Danny?" he called out, his voice reaching out to her with invisible arms. She stopped and fixed on him from behind her sunglasses. "Take good care-a Pogo. You do that for me, won't ya?"

"Of course. What a silly thing to ask." Danny fanned her hand and shook her head at the request. Pogo pranced down the walkway toward the parking area, forcing her to keep pace.

R. D. stared, his limbs limp, as Danny secured Pogo into the shoulder harness in the rear seat of her Sebring. Danny waved and smiled as she drove away. A new identity waited for Pogo too—certified, legitimate. Pogo gazed out the window in R.D.'s direction; their eyes met for the briefest of moments. The car disappeared.

As the door clicked shut, R. D. tried to think of the last time he'd cried. He hadn't blubbered since finding his wife on the kitchen floor with three bullet holes in her chest, back in eight-one. Behind a blur of tears, he struggled to turn the deadbolt, fought to slide the chain.

Atonement? Penance? Bullshit. This was hell.

Riojas emerged from the bedroom, pressing buttons on his cell phone. "Let's move."

Chapter 37

Tricks Are For Kids

On Thursday afternoon, Olivia sat at Lauren's breakfast table with a cup of hot tea, watching her sister through the open French doors of her new house. In the courtyard, Lauren paced in broad circles around her new patio set, puffing away on her cigarette.

"What are you doing?" Olivia asked.

"I got a Fitbit," Lauren announced. "You know, the wristband that counts steps and calories? I'm getting healthy."

"Then put out your cigarette." Olivia shook her head and flipped over the pages of Ardy's manuscript. "How many steps so far today?"

"Five hundred."

"Not enough."

"I walked around my car in the driveway ten times—almost two hundred steps." Lauren stopped in the doorway and pointed at the manuscript. "Sticks in my craw you wouldn't let me read the early drafts before you shredded them. Don't you trust me?"

"This isn't about trust," Olivia said. "The story needed to be tightened up and waiting for you to read would've slowed me down. I won't have these daytime hours when Mom's book comes out. As it is, the publicity schedule's cutting into my writing time." Olivia circled a typo. "You can have this copy. It needs your editing touch, so be brutal. Not too smooth, though. I want it to have a gritty edge."

"How am I supposed to get my steps in if I'm doing edits?"

"Twerk while you work." Olivia tried not to laugh.

"What the hell are you talking about?"

"You know, bend forward and wiggle your hips as fast as you can. It's good for the thigh muscles."

"I haven't used those muscles in years." Lauren grimaced. "What am I supposed to do, stop and twerk at the bumper of the car?" She turned in the doorway, leaned forward, and jiggled her hips. "I loooove my new car. How's that?" Her new flowered underpants peeked over the top of her jeans.

"Pretty. . . "

Lauren wrinkled her nose and pointed to the manuscript. "Are you going to let Ardy read that?"

"I'll print the final version for him to put in the safe-deposit box and shred this working copy after I make your changes." She peered over the papers. "You need to work up to ten thousand steps. And while you're at it, walk to the salon and get your hair done before the wedding. No bottle jobs."

Olivia straightened when the doorbell rang.

Lauren stubbed out her cigarette. "I'll bet that's Danny. She was picking up her wedding dress after she took Pogo to his last training session. Get the door."

"You get the door. You need the steps."

Lauren pointed. Olivia slapped down Ardy's manuscript.

Marching down the short hall to the entryway, Olivia spotted Danny and Pogo through the side window. In oversize black sunglasses with her dark hair behind her ears, Danny held a zippered bag on a hanger over her shoulder. Pogo held his leash in his mouth, wearing his yellow service dog vest—a real one.

As soon as Olivia opened the front door, Danny rushed past her, squeaking out quick steps to the kitchen in her sneakers. Pogo jingled after her. According to Danny, the official vest gave her carte blanche to take the dog into stores in the warmer weather. She wouldn't hear of leaving Pogo in the car. Olivia likened the vest to misusing the handicapped parking permit Danny had snatched from their father's Blazer.

"I'm running so behind," Danny huffed. "I have one full day left to get all this last-minute stuff done. Try finding fresh tulips in October. I switched to gardenias. They smell better."

Olivia trotted behind her and Pogo to keep up. "Gardenias will be gorgeous."

"And it's a good thing I called to pay in full at the resort at Indigo Lake. The place is sold out. Since word about the book got out, everybody and his brother are going up there." Danny unzipped the garment bag. "You ready?"

"Hit us with all you got," Lauren said.

Olivia set both hands on her cheeks as Danny pulled out the dress in a dramatic sweeping motion. "Oh, Danny," she exclaimed. "Mom's wedding dress!"

"Do you think Ardy will like it? Should I rent him a tux?"

Olivia chuckled. "He's got one."

"Isn't it sweet of him to give me away?"

"Ohhh . . . he's sweet, all right."

Lauren's fingers grazed the tiny pearls on the taupe linen, embroidered in a swirl pattern over the entire mid-length skirt. A rim of piping along the scooped neckline complemented the fitted bodice of cream-colored satin. "You'll be as beautiful as Mom was in this."

"I found it in the cedar chest with the family plaid," Danny said. "A bit small, so I had the seamstress add some breathing room. Mom had quite the figure on her wedding day."

"You want to borrow her earrings?" Olivia offered.

"I would, but Ryan gave me these pearls as an engagement gift." Danny pulled back her hair to show off the lustrous orbs.

"Now that you have the dress and Olivia and I have our outfits, I don't know why you're stressing so much," Lauren said.

"I'm sorry," Danny stood with her fist on her hip, "but you guys are *not* the center of the universe. Ryan and I have friends, you know."

"Speaking of the center of the universe . . . " Olivia hesitated. "Do you want to scatter Mom's ashes before you leave for your honeymoon or wait until Mom's book comes out in April?"

"When the book gets published. That's the right time. I'll be too stressed out before then." Danny waved her hand. "Once we're back from Vermont, we'll have Thanksgiving and Christmas, and Mt. Hood will be snowed in. Let's wait until April."

"I'll mark the calendar to make a reservation for lunch at Timberline Lodge. *Lauren's* buying."

Sporting his official yellow vest, Pogo sauntered into the familiar kitchen with his leash in his mouth, continuing his sniffs of the new scents in the house. Danny smiled and pulled a folded piece of parchment paper from her purse. She held up the certificate. "Pogo graduated. He's now a certified healing dog!" She clapped her hands. "Come Pogo! Sit."

Lauren and Olivia glanced at each other in amazement as Pogo planted himself next to Danny. With military precision, Pogo held his head erect and back straight, waiting for instructions. Danny slipped him a kibble treat.

"What a transformation!" Olivia said. "He's a show dog."

"Our little star. Pogo stole the ceremony. Two hospitals and three senior centers signed him. He's going to be a busy boy. And if you think that's amazing, check *this* out. I've never seen Ryan laugh so hard. I can't wait to show Ardy." Danny reached into the fruit bowl on the breakfast table and picked out a banana. With a vigorous wag of his tail, Pogo stood straight and poised. "I taught him this one."

Danny set the banana between Pogo's ears. As she started to sing "The Girl from Ipanema," the dog took three steps forward and three steps back, swinging his hips in rhythm. The fruit remained still.

Olivia busted up and couldn't catch a breath.

Lauren bent over the kitchen counter. "I'm gonna wet my pants," she squealed, wheezing and crossing her legs. "He's a dancing bumble bee!"

Danny plucked the banana from Pogo's head and peeled back the skin. "That's my boy!" She took a bite. "C'mon, Pogs. Time to get you home to Ardy." She reached into her purse. "I almost forgot. When I picked Pogo up this morning, Ardy wanted me to give you this. He said something about writing something for you."

"Right," Olivia confirmed. "We're supposed to meet on Tuesday. He wanted to dictate it to me because he didn't feel confident about his writing."

"Well, he must have changed his mind." Danny handed Olivia the sealed envelope.

~ · ~ · ~

After Danny left with Pogo, Olivia and Lauren continued their chuckle about the dog's antics, until Lauren started to read Ardy's manuscript. Olivia watched her sister's face turn serious as she went deeper into the first chapter.

Olivia tapped the envelope in her hand. She unsealed the flap. Inside, a folded piece of notebook paper held few words, no more than a short paragraph:

Lock all the doors. Turn off the lights. Even that don't keep the bad deeds out. So you got to open the place up and let the good deeds in to cover it all up. Fiddledeedee. Fiddledeedee.

"Huh?" Olivia stared at the ruled paper, convinced the words meant something she didn't understand. She read the note again, liking the rhythm of the poetry. "Here, Lauren, look at Ardy's last words for the book. Maybe I'll use this as a quote under the dedication to Pogo. What do you think?"

Lauren set the manuscript on the breakfast table and read the message. "Sounds like Ardy, all right. But I don't know what the hell it means."

Olivia glanced at her watch. "Keep reading while I go check on the mail. What are you planning for dinner?"

"Mmmm . . . mmm." Lauren had resumed reading the manuscript.

The former creak of fear in the oak floors of Ardy's house had been replaced with the fearlessness of Lauren. She made the spooky place a home. Olivia still pinched herself that Lauren lived next door. And Danny started anew with Ryan because of what the three of them had done—what their mother had done. Life wasn't just for the young. But the note nagged at her.

Olivia stepped across the driveway, glancing at the old oil stain from Ardy's Datsun. Ardy insisted on continuing to drive, even though he shouldn't. He believed the privilege to be his last remaining freedom. She was afraid he'd hit someone, unintentionally, of course.

A thick bundle of envelopes popped the top of Olivia's mailbox. Ted Beal had been a relentless legal beagle. Three pieces in the stack bore his law firm's name, which might be related to her updated will or the papers for the Pogo Charitable Trust. No rush. Ardy was doing fine. Her fingers stopped on the last piece. She pulled out a small envelope, the size of a greeting card. Shaky handwriting. No indication of the sender. Even more curious was the lack of a postmark or stamp. The weight of something metal, like a coin, slid around inside when she gave the envelope a quick shake.

"Olivia!" Lauren shouted, waving from her front door. "Hurry!"

With the stack of mail pressed to her chest, Olivia rushed toward Lauren's house. As she got closer, she spotted the phone at her sister's ear.

Danny, Lauren mouthed and pointed to the receiver. "Calm down! Let me put you on speaker. Olivia's here now."

Olivia followed Lauren into the kitchen and tossed her mail on the counter by the gas stove.

Between gulps and crying, Danny tried to speak. "Ardy's gone! I knocked . . . on the door . . . to bring Pogo back. There was no answer, so I—"

"Gone, like dead? Or gone, like disappeared?" Lauren grilled, trying not to overreact.

"Di . . . disappeared."

"Call Ryan!" Olivia ordered. "Ardy may have fallen inside."

"I did. Pogo was so upset. Ryan met me at the manager's office to see if someone could open Ardy's door. Pogo knew something was wrong."

"And?" Lauren said.

"We took the manager back to Ardy's, and when we went in . . ."

"What Danny?!" Olivia shouted into the phone.

"The apartment was . . . empty. No furniture. No nothing."

"What the hell happened?"

"The only thing Ryan could think of was that somebody from Ardy's past threatened him, maybe found out where he lived."

"But how? We did everything—*everything*—to make sure not one word of the book leaked out."

"Ryan said this might not have anything to do with the book."

"Get over here with Pogo. Have Ryan follow you. I don't want you anywhere near Ardy's apartment," Olivia demanded. "Now, Danny!"

Silence streamed from the receiver for a few seconds. "Liv . . . you don't think—"

"*Please,* Danny." Olivia's mind raced with an inventory of possible culprits from Ardy's past who might pose a threat. Danny didn't know about any of those juicy details, and Lauren was about to read them.

"I'll be there in ten minutes. Ryan needs to stay here with the manager. He's making a statement. I told him to call me at your house, Liv."

Olivia ended the call. Her gaze locked on Lauren's, too stunned to be able to say anything. They both leaned on the kitchen counter with the phone between them. Lauren hissed air through her teeth. Olivia drummed her fingers on the tile counter.

Breaking the tense silence, Lauren said, "I packed his stuff to move him into my apartment because he was old and frail. And he moves out since Danny picked up Pogo this morning? Doesn't make sense. I don't buy it."

"He had help. A lot of help. He wouldn't up and leave, unless this was about saving himself or his dog. I've spent hours talking to the man. The one thing he would never do is . . . jeopardize . . . Pogo." Olivia straightened. "Wait a minute . . . "

Her pile of mail, tossed by the stove, fanned in a line on the counter. The small envelope drew her fingers. Ripping the flap, a key clattered to the tile counter as she pulled out the note:

Don't try to find me. Been moved. Have Pogo stay with Danny and Ryan. He loves them. Keep the key. You'll know when it's time.

Olivia's mouth went dry as she stared at the words. Her hand shook as she held out the note to Lauren. "From Ardy. He's alive. This was hand-delivered sometime today."

Lauren picked the card from Olivia's fingers, skeptical. She read the note. "He's giving you responsibility for the book *and* the key?"

"He trusts me."

"Of course he trusts you. We all do. He trusts Danny and Ryan too."

"He trusted you, too—enough to sell you his house."

"Come out here for a minute." Lauren padded to the patio table in the courtyard.

"What are you going to do?" Olivia followed.

Lauren reached into the pocket of her jeans and pulled out a disposable lighter. Holding the note over the ashtray, she set the paper on fire. An orange flame crept across the handwritten words in a disintegrating wave. As it approached her fingertips, Lauren dropped the blackening corner.

"You never received this note, Liv. We have to honor Ardy's trust. This note could be deadly to you, me, and Ardy if someone found it. We know nothing."

"There was a time with Mom's book when you didn't trust me," Olivia whispered, holding up the small key.

"Yeah . . . well. That was different."

Olivia inhaled at the sound of two car doors shutting in front of the house, followed by a jingle. "Danny and Pogo are here. Thank *God.*"

"You think this had anything to do with the package that came here for Ardy?"

"I doubt it." Olivia's stomach disagreed. Something might well have been in that package. "Don't freak yourself out." What disturbed Olivia most was that it had been delivered to Lauren's address.

Lauren counted off her steps aloud as she trudged to the refrigerator and shook her wine box to assess the level of the contents. "Wine o'clock. Let's all go over to your house and wait for Ryan to call. We can tackle the picture box. For some reason, those are important to me right now. Plus, I can get in another sixty-two steps from my door to yours."

"Do a few more laps around your car on the way over."

"In case anyone's watching the house, I'll twerk. That'll scare 'em away."

Olivia didn't laugh as she gathered the rest of her mail and tucked Ardy's manuscript under her arm.

Chapter 38

The Credible Threat

"He ain't living here, Boss." Little Frankie Jr. said as he admired his gold pinky ring. "I been sitting down the street for two hours, and I'm telling you he ain't *here.*" Little Frankie gazed at the small Tudor and thought the house was a nicer than his. Crow didn't deserve a house like this.

"Give me the license plate on the red Honda," the gruff voice ordered on the other end of the line. "Cheesesteak is good at finding out who owns cars. The kid can do anything on the computer." Nicolai "Cheesesteak" Romov got his name from his lunch. The kid was never without a string of yesterday's cheese stuck in his scruffy beard.

Little Frankie recited three numbers and three letters. "Ore*gon* plates. New." Frankie leaned on Oregon's third syllable like someone who didn't know what a hazelnut was. Tapping the steering wheel, he waited. This whole trip might be a waste of his time. He doubted Crow even drove anymore. But Nicky Palermo still called the shots from inside the slammer.

"What, Cheese? Got it." The voice turned back to the receiver. "Some broad named Lauren Lyndale."

"Yeah, I think I saw her. The crazy bitch came outside and walked in circles around the car. I counted. Ten times."

"What's that about?"

"Dunno. Some other broad showed up too. Had a bunch of papers and a lotta hair. She's still inside. And then, another one pulled up and went in the front door with a big black dog. A looker."

"The dog?"

"No, the gal."

"Cheesesteak thinks the damn Feds put the wrong address in the Witness database on purpose. Sneaky bastards."

"So . . . what do you want me to do now?"

Silence.

Little Frankie straightened and tightened his grip on the gun in his lap. "Wait. They're coming out of the house with the dog. The old one's locking the door."

"You think it's Crow in disguise?" the voice asked. "Dressing like some old woman in drag?"

"Naaaah," Frankie scoffed. "Hair like hay? Big knockers like that? She's old but not *that* old." He snickered. "Damned if she ain't walking in circles around the Honda again, with a box of cheap wine too. Stuff's nasty. Now she's acting like she got bugs in her pants. Maybe a bell up there she's trying to ring." Little Frankie stared, fascinated, as Lauren did four laps, stopping at the front and back bumper to jiggle her hips. "The three of them and the damned dog are going next door. These West Coast people are a bunch of crazies."

"We're calling off the hit," the craggy voice said. "What a friggin' mess. Go to the airport. Come on back to Philly."

Little Frankie Jr. hung up and tossed his phone on the passenger seat. "All this way for nothing." He set the safety on the gun and turned the key in the ignition. "I should-a blown up that damn red Honda."

~ · ~ · ~

Riojas removed the headphones, his gaze focused on the gunmetal-gray Lincoln that filled the video screen. He grabbed his mobile and called Skidmore.

"Little Frankie is on his way to the airport. I'll follow him. I need backup to take him down. Have the team intercept the Lincoln at the rental agency when he returns the car. I don't want him to get anywhere near the terminal. You got the conversation recorded?"

"Clear as a bell," Skidmore said, chuckling.

"Where's Griffin—Milner—now?"

"About to land in Iowa. The team in Des Moines is ready for the hand off. He's fine. Was that Palermo on the other end of the line?"

"No doubt. Still calling the shots from prison. Did you leave the card for Novak next door like Griffin wanted?"

"Least I could do. Nothing in the note will cause any problems. Harmless. I have a craving for a Cheesesteak with a side of Little Frankie. We owe these gals for putting Griffin in that apartment."

"And for adopting the dog. Let's go eat these guys' lunch."

Chapter 39

The Picture Box

With his belly full, Pogo stretched out on an oversize spa towel Olivia had thrown over her living room couch. Eyes partially closed, Freesia's head hung over the back cushion. Her paw now rested on the top of Pogo's head, as if she could prevent the dog from getting up. Olivia, Lauren, and Danny sat around the picture box. With the phone within reach, Olivia waited for a call from Ryan about Ardy. By the second glass of wine, Danny's tears over Ardy's abandonment had quieted with the exchange of old black-and-white baby photos. To keep her distracted, Lauren filled in the age gap with obscure stories of the family before Danny had been born. Olivia glanced at the phone every few minutes.

A picture of Olivia in a birthday hat made Lauren lose her balance from laughing. She spilled her pink wine on the area rug. "A toothless clown with a funnel on your head!"

Olivia grimaced as she raced to the kitchen and came back with a box of baking soda and a hand towel. She sprinkled the spill and pressed the wet spot with a hand towel. "Goes in my pile."

Danny inspected a candid picture of Lauren dancing with Mark at their wedding. "I can't believe you had red, white, and blue as your colors. And those *hats*."

"Damn straight. Bicentennial wedding—1976 was a banner year!" Lauren stilled as she gazed at her husband; so young, so healthy. She blew out a breath. "Goes in my pile."

Olivia stood and folded the hand towel. "I'm glad you let us pick out what we'll wear for your wedding, Danny. Your blue and taupe colors will be beautiful. Back in 1979, my bridesmaids' dresses were cheap maroon polyester. Lauren had major visible panty lines."

"Yeah, you could see a zit on an elephant's butt in those synthetic gowns," Lauren teased. "Hose 'em down, though, if you spilled anything."

"I wish this rug were made of polyester," Olivia griped, studying the wet spot.

All movement stopped when the phone rang. Olivia glanced at the caller ID before answering. She moved to the entryway and kept her voice low.

"Ryan! What'd you find out?"

"I talked with Riojas." Ryan's voice sounded officious. "Ardy's been moved. They traced the database breach to Philadelphia."

"Was he threatened?"

"Riojas wouldn't say if anything specific happened, but my guess is yes."

"Where is he? Is he okay?"

"He's all right. His name's been changed again. Riojas wouldn't say what it is or where he's been relocated to."

"Makes sense, but . . . I'm his executrix. How I am supposed to handle his affairs if something happens?"

"Maybe through your lawyer, since he wrote R. D.'s will. Is the manuscript you're writing in the safe-deposit box yet? What about all those newspaper clippings?"

"Lauren's reading it. She's proofing, but it's here at the house. I intended to hand the final version over to Ardy." Olivia debated whether to tell Ryan about Ardy's farewell note and the key. Since the message didn't exist anymore, she chose to keep mum. Her job as his executrix included protecting *Protection*. "The safe-deposit box will hold the manuscript and the binders of clippings too." She hesitated. "Ardy gave me the key."

"Go to the bank in the morning. Get Griffin's manuscript out of your possession."

"Are you okay, Ryan?"

"I should have done a better job of protecting him, Liv."

"Quite the opposite," Olivia countered. "Ardy would've died in that Murphy bed if you hadn't been there. You might have prevented a crime from happening to Danny at Ardy's apartment. We'll never know, but at least he's alive . . . because of you and Danny and Lauren and me. We all protected him. He's a lucky man."

"Send Danny home with Pogo when you guys are done. If she drinks too much wine, though, make her spend the night with you."

"Why don't you come over and both of you stay here tonight. I'd feel better with a flatfoot in the house." Olivia tried to keep her voice casual, but the statement rang all too true.

"Give me an hour."

Olivia hung up and returned to the living room. She sat on the floor. "Ryan's coming over. We think it's a good idea for the four of us to be together tonight. He talked with Riojas. They moved Ardy. Ryan doesn't know where."

"Is he okay?" Danny asked, relieved.

"For now, yes. The breach was traced to Philadelphia. Ryan assured me the move was only a precaution. But it looks like Pogo is your and Ryan's dog now, Danny. Trust me, it's what Ardy wanted."

Lauren nodded her approval of the information. Softened truth.

"Poor Ardy. That's why he was acting so weird this morning. He *knew*. It must have killed him to leave Pogo."

"The whole point, Danny. Ardy wanted to make sure Pogo was safe. Because of you, he is."

Olivia glanced at Lauren, who winked.

"I guess so." Danny tucked her hair behind her ears.

"It says a lot about what he thinks of you to entrust you with his most precious asset."

Olivia peered at the remaining pictures in the box. "Let's dump these out and divide them up. We can trade them like bubblegum cards later."

"Perfect," Lauren said. She turned over the box, their family cascading to the carpet. Two yellowed newspaper articles, cut from the *Boston Globe*, settled on top of the pile. "Hey . . . what are those?"

Lauren picked up one; Olivia reached for the other.

Danny waited, taking a sip of her wine. "Ardy, Ardy, I'm so glad you're okay," she whispered and inspected her toes. "I should have gotten a pedicure. Now I don't have time."

The living room remained silent as Olivia and Lauren each read an article.

"Lauren?" Olivia muttered, never lifting her gaze.

"Liv?" Lauren answered.

Blood raced in Olivia's veins, making her face tingle. She stared at the headline from September 1947:

Promising Young Med Student Poisoned at Fraternity House

Lauren snatched the one in Olivia's hand; Olivia took the one Lauren had read. The second one was from November 1947:

No Clues in Poisoning Death of Boston University Med Student

They handed both articles to Danny. Her jaw dropped as she read them. She stared at her sisters. "You don't think—"

"I don't know," Lauren stammered, "what I think."

"I'll tell you what I think." Olivia stood and flipped the towel over her shoulder. She held out her hand to Lauren. "Give me your lighter and follow me. Danny, bring those with you."

Olivia marched into the kitchen with the lighter and her empty wine glass. She threw the wine-soaked towel in the sink and splashed some cabernet into her goblet. Danny held out hers. Lauren leaned into the refrigerator and filled her glass from the wine box.

"I can't believe it," Danny whispered, handing the articles to Olivia.

"I *don't* believe it." Olivia shook the clippings. "These prove nothing. Someone could jump to conclusions, and I, for one, will *not* have our mother's good name tarnished."

Lauren stared, wide-eyed, at Olivia. "What's the statute of limitations on murder?"

"Death . . . " Olivia held the yellowed and faded newsprint over the ashtray and lit the words on fire. She stared at the flaming headlines as the paper curled and charred. When the embers extinguished, Olivia's shoulders relaxed. "This stays with the three of us. Not one word to Ryan. He loved Ellen, and that's the way it will stay. Do we have a deal?"

"A blood deal," Danny said. "Rumors aren't real. Ryan would be the first to agree. There's not one shred of evidence. Those articles are only circumstantial."

"That's right," Lauren agreed. She held up her tumbler. "Mom protected us. We need to protect her."

Three glasses collided in a toast.

Danny shook her head as she swallowed. "Oh, c'mon. Have you two considered you're blowing this out of proportion? We're the ones who're jumping to conclusions."

Lauren lit a cigarette and tossed the pack on the counter. "What do you mean?"

Olivia turned on the stove fan and studied Danny, ready to hear what wisdom would pop from her mouth.

"I mean . . . what if those articles were the inspiration for the book and not the other way around? Mom might have written a fictional story about something real that happened but not to *her*—after the fact. Don't most authors do that? Base fiction on true events? The articles don't prove *she* did the crime. What if Mom went to school with the guy or knew him through someone else? Maybe she didn't know him at all and just thought the story would make a good book."

Olivia volleyed a defensive look between Lauren and Danny, uncomfortable. With her hand on her hip, Olivia unhooked her gaze from her sisters and settled it on the pile of cinders spilling over the crystal ashtray. Danny's explanation made sense. Did she want it to be true because it was a good story? Drama and intrigue was more interesting than the drudgery of daily life.

Lauren stuck her forefinger in the ashes and swirled the blackened wisps.

"Give me that." Olivia took the ashtray and marched to the breakfast table where Ellen's urn had become a familiar centerpiece. Lifting the lid and opening the inner plastic bag of her mother's ashes, she shook their suspicions inside.

At the long *bong* of the doorbell, Danny fluttered her hands. "Ryan's here!"

Olivia scrambled to reassemble the urn.

Chapter 40

The Safety-Deposit Box

On Friday morning, Ryan sat with Lauren at Olivia's kitchen island, waiting for Danny to get up. Olivia started to unload the dishwasher from last night's late dinner of pasta primavera. She turned to face Ryan with a plate in her hand.

"I never got to talk to Ardy about the note he left me."

Ryan straightened. "What note?"

"We talked about him making a personal statement in his own words for the epilogue. He gave a note that was meant for me to Danny when she picked up Pogo yesterday." Olivia put away the plate and reached into her purse hanging on the back of the counter chair. She handed the note to Ryan. "I'm putting this in the book."

He read the short message. "Huh . . . Sounds like he's describing what happened. Something spooked R. D. The Feds too."

"It reads like poetry—sort of."

"Did R. D. act strange or give you any reason to suspect he might be in danger?"

"Noooo . . . " Olivia hedged. "Not with me, but Danny said he acted weird when she picked up Pogo yesterday."

"Yeah. She told me."

Changing the direction of the conversation, Lauren said, "You ready for tomorrow, Ryan?"

Ryan flushed pink. "I love your sister. She needs me and I need her. I can't wait to marry her."

"The way it's supposed to be."

"By the way, Olivia. I didn't see you at the Rovinskis' sentencing on Tuesday. I waited for you to call me."

Olivia fidgeted. "What happened? I couldn't go. I had my last interview with Ardy for the book." An excuse. She could have rescheduled the meeting with Ardy, but with all that had transpired she now appreciated how important that last meeting with him was.

"Melissa got two years' probation with community service," Ryan said, his voice filled with disappointment. "As an adult, Jeff got one year for tampering with evidence."

"Pffbbtt . . . " she scoffed. "The spoiled brat will pick up her life as if nothing happened."

"It'll follow her on her record, but she was a minor at the time of the accident." Ryan eyed her. "They were both apologetic in front of the judge. Helped their cases."

"Fine. Even better." Olivia sprayed bleach cleaner on a sponge with a rapid-fire trigger finger.

"Liv . . . I hate to bring this up," Ryan said, cautious, "but you're protecting R. D., and look how many people he killed. You're being awfully quick to forgive him. I hope writing this book will allow you the same level of forgiveness about Adam's death."

Olivia glanced at Lauren. She pursed her lips. Olivia turned and cleaned the fingerprints off the microwave. "Yeah . . . well. That's different."

Lauren turned to Ryan. "I use that line, too, when logic makes too much sense."

"Where's R. D.'s manuscript?" Ryan took a sip of coffee, studying both sisters over his mug.

"I finished reading it last night," Lauren said. "I didn't sleep, even with too much wine. It's good, Liv. Don't change one damn thing." She stuck her thumb over her shoulder. "On the library table in the front hall."

"The bank opens at ten," Olivia said. "There's no rush."

"You didn't write the book under your own name, did you?" Ryan stood and set his mug in the sink.

"I thought about it, but haven't decided. We have time to figure it out."

Lauren took a sip of her coffee and eyed Olivia over the rim. "How about Della Pinkham?"

"Hey! I like it. Della . . . Pinkham. The funny thing is that it sounds even more like a romance writer than Olivia Novak."

Ryan remained undeterred. "Where are the binders with the newspaper articles?"

"In the den." Olivia's smile faded at Ryan's serious tone.

"Get 'em." Ryan grabbed his keys on the counter. "I'll take you to the bank in the cruiser. I don't want you driving with this stuff by yourself. Which bank?"

Olivia hesitated. "Cascade . . . in Sellwood."

"You *can't* be serious."

~ · ~ · ~

With her arms full, Olivia stood at the front door of Cascade Bank. She turned and attempted to raise her thumb at Ryan as he waited for her in the cruiser. He nodded and made a shooing motion.

Right at the stroke of ten o'clock, the bank manager waved for patience as he turned the lock on the glass front doors. Olivia gripped the petite key, balancing two binders of newspaper articles and a thick manila envelope. At this particular bank, she wasn't only known for being an author but also for being a victim of an ex-employee. When she opened the account, the staff had treated her with kid gloves.

Olivia chose to set up the box in both Ardy's and her names at a bank other than Ardy's, her mother's, her sisters' . . . or her own. She wanted no connection to be made to anyone in her family. As soon as Ryan had told her that Jeff Rovinski had worked at this branch of

Cascade Bank in Sellwood, Olivia decided to rent the box at this location.

"I need to put something in my safe-deposit box," she said and stepped inside.

"I'll be right with you, Mrs. Novak," he said. "Give me a minute to open the vault and get the second key."

"No rush . . . " But she was in a rush. Ryan's concern had her spooked. Holding tight to the binders and Ardy's manuscript, Olivia's gaze swept the lobby. The tellers scattered to act busy when they recognized her. Although she'd never visited this bank when Jeff worked here, Olivia sensed the atmosphere had been exorcised.

The manager opened the thick, full-length steel door behind the teller stations, revealing a room lined with metal compartments. She stepped forward. He followed her inside with the bank's copy of the key.

The air changed the instant she entered the vault. The aroma filled her mouth with an unpleasant taste of metal. An image of the manager slamming the door and spinning the lock triggered a sense of urgency. The dense combination of steel and personal secrets squeezed her chest, limiting her ability to take in a full breath. *Third row up, fourth over.* Her gaze settled on the box number matching the one etched on the key: 304. Olivia would open this compartment only one more time after today, and when she did, Ardy's story would be released to the world by an author named Della Pinkham. This wasn't about fame and glory; this was about a helluva story.

The manager turned the second lock with the bank's copy of the key. "I'll wait out here to give you some privacy."

"I'll only be a minute."

So much work. So many hours. Olivia inhaled as she slid the thick envelope and two binders inside the drawer. She re-secured the lock.

Protection was now protected. She closed her eyes, hoping Ardy was as well. When she pulled out the key, the steel warmed in her palm. Olivia turned and breezed past the waiting bank manager.

"Thank you. I'm done."

Chapter 41

Vows for the Future

The anticipation and hope inspired by wedding days differed from the feelings evoked by other special days. Christmas came close. On this crisp October Saturday morning, pots of bright white and purple chrysanthemums lined the steps of St. John's Church. Water droplets shimmered on the fall leaves of the maple trees after an early-morning drizzle, the sun popping the autumn color to a vibrant dazzle.

Olivia checked the satin-covered buttons on the back of her mother's wedding dress as Danny sucked in a breath. "Perfect. You're beautiful." Olivia gave her sister's shoulders three quick pats.

It gave Danny a familiar comfort to hold the ceremony in this small church in downtown Milwaukie, south of Sellwood. Every Sunday, Danny had accompanied Ellen to the quaint service. No Bible thumping or fire and brimstone took place here, only an outpouring of community spirit to help those less fortunate.

The guest list had been cut off at twenty-five to keep an intimate atmosphere for the exchange of their private vows. Most of the guests were policemen and their spouses. Ryan was not only admired as a colleague but as a friend. Lining the front pews were Ted Beal and his wife, Danny's therapist, and members of her support group.

"I saw Ryan out there, Danny," Olivia said. "Doesn't get more handsome."

"I'm so lucky," Danny said. "We should have been married years ago."

"Don't do that to yourself," Lauren chided. "Mom needed you as much as you needed her." Lauren handed Danny the simple bouquet of gardenias and miniature grape hyacinths. "You have the neck of a damn swan. Right off the cover of a *Vogue* from 1950."

Olivia rippled her fingers over the tiny pearls on Danny's skirt, hearing the voice of her mother in her head. *Don't spill anything, but if Danny does, do you have a laundry detergent stick in your purse?* Olivia glanced in the front pocket of her satin purse for the orange tube of Tide to Go. *Yes, Mom.*

"You're both beautiful too." Danny fluffed her sheer, shoulder-length veil.

"I look fat." Lauren adjusted the drape of her dusty-blue silk jacket. She picked at her freshly dyed chestnut bangs. "My feet hurt. Liv made me buy these pumps. I swear I'll never put them on again."

"You do *not* look fat," Olivia countered. "And you can't wear orthopedic shoes with that gorgeous suit."

"Forty-two steps down the aisle." Lauren held up her wrist, showing off her Fitbit monitor like expensive jewelry. "And where's Pogo?"

"Won't get you to ten thousand," Danny said. "Pogo's waiting for me at the back of the church. And remember, I'll give the signal when it's time for him to start walking. Pogo goes first, then you and Liv."

"Got it. Let's go. The music's getting louder."

"I need a minute." Danny turned to the mirror to admire the dress. Standing behind her, Olivia smiled at her little sister's reflection. Danny waved her unadorned left hand. "You're going to make me cry and ruin my makeup."

Olivia rested her hand on Danny's shoulder. She was given pause at the image of her sister. At forty-five, she was every inch a bride. Danny resembled her mother, even more so in her wedding dress. Soon, she would be wearing Ellen's ring. Olivia thought it would be downright scary if Danny had been a writer too. "Come out when you're ready."

Olivia left the small reception room at the back of the church to join Lauren. She took a whiff of her nosegay of gardenias. The sweet aroma nearly reduced her to tears, but she held them back. Pogo's tail thumped the red carpet as she approached.

"Check out the front pew," Lauren said, pointing to the front of the church.

Leaning to get a better view, Olivia spotted two empty places cordoned off with taupe satin ribbon and tied with gardenias. "Who are they for?"

"Mom and Ardy." Lauren's lip quivered.

Olivia's face fell as she turned back to Lauren. "So sweet . . . Danny's full of surprises."

The photographer rushed toward the two of them. A flash caught the moment.

"Don't you dare make me cry, Liv. I swear to God, I'll never be able to look at these pictures again."

Danny's eyes appeared to be a bit glassy as she joined Olivia and Lauren. "Got the rings?" she asked and straightened her shoulders.

"Right here." Lauren held up a small drawstring pouch of taupe satin.

"Give it to Pogo."

Olivia glanced at Danny, suspicious. "He was good at the rehearsal, but what if he eats it? He's been known to do worse."

"If he does," Lauren said, "it'd be really romantic if the rings come out at the same time—fecalogically speaking."

Danny wrinkled her nose. "He knows what to do."

Lauren bent down to the dog, whose curly, mounded head had been given extra pouf. "Why am I hearing the soundtrack to *Super Fly*? What'd you do to his hair?"

"I took him to Show Dogs. It's a doggie salon in North Portland."

Lauren rolled her eyes as she flattened her hand. The pouch dangled from a finger. "Sit. Stay. Eat this, Pogo."

"Don't encourage him," Olivia chided. "He's being so good."

With a delicate pluck, Pogo grasped the pouch in his front teeth. The small bag resembled a silky tongue. Pogo's dark eyes shifted as Danny adjusted his satin vest, with the words *Wedding Ring Service Dog* embroidered in contrasting navy blue script.

The lilting organ introduction of "Simple Gifts" started, a prompt for the guests to stand. All eyes gazed at Danny in her last moments as Danielle Dushane. They delighted in watching the majestic stance of the impressive poodle, the leader of the group. Danny gave the hand signal for Pogo to start his trek.

Pogo led the procession in measured steps, pausing for the outstretched hands to give him a pat as he passed. As Olivia followed Lauren down the carpet, she caught Ted Beal's eye and pointed at the dog. *Pogo*, she mouthed. The empty square of flowered ribbon drew her gaze. The space was too small to contain the larger-than-life presences of both her mother and Ardy, who might as well have been in the building. She imagined Ellen turning; her mother's smile a reflection of the closure that comes from letting go. Ardy was alive, somewhere, but surely wishing he had his arm laced through Danny's to walk her down the aisle. Indeed, this moment was a simple gift.

While everyone chuckled at the curly black bearer of the rings, Olivia beamed at the way Ryan's gaze stretched to Danny. To him, no one else existed.

Chapter 42

Sunday Book Review

Strong *Indigo to Black* preorders through the holidays and healthy initial sales figures kept the glasses clinking at Sloane Publishing. True to her word, Lauren bowed out of the publicity appearances. Her excuse had been the need to work up to ten thousand steps. While the count went up, her weight remained the same. Danny, however, glowed. Marriage agreed with her. But no word from Ardy, or whoever he was now. Olivia chose to interpret the lack of contact as a good sign.

Today was the day for the long-anticipated April review of *Indigo to Black*. To celebrate—or lick their wounds—the three sisters and Ryan decided to gather with Pogo for a nine o'clock Sunday breakfast to honor Ellen.

On her way down 99E to Milwaukie, Olivia stopped at Starbucks to purchase four thick copies of the Sunday *New York Times*. She gasped when she pulled into the lot. A white Suburban sat parked in front of the entrance. A familiar twinge shot through her chest, a burned-in body response. She fought the instinct to reach for the Journal of Agony, every entry a blind accusation of a stranger's guilt, but the notebook was gone forever. When she glanced at the license plate, her shoulders slumped with embarrassment: *AVN-CLNG*.

As she opened the front door of the coffeehouse, a faint scent of citrus perfume floated above the aroma of freshly ground coffee beans. *Avon.* Olivia's gaze swept the tables, all empty with exception of one. A young girl of about six sat across from her mother at a small round table by the window, coloring in a Barbie book with intent. She'd outgrown the Hello Kitty barrettes in favor of ones with silk flowers interspersed with blue crystals. The glass gems sparkled in the sun's reflection off her long blonde hair, a mirrored vision of her mother, who poked at the mound of froth on her cappuccino. Olivia moved closer to the condiment station to eavesdrop on their conversation. As the child made quick strokes with an orange crayon, she expounded on the virtues of her school teacher: her outfits, her hair, and how pretty her handwriting was. Olivia took four newspapers to the cash register.

"Just the papers?" the clerk asked.

"Yes—I mean no." Olivia pointed to the glass case. "Add one of those lemon bars with the squiggles."

"For here or to go?"

"For here."

Abandoning the newspapers on the counter, Olivia took the ceramic plate from the clerk. The lemon bar rested on a laced paper doily with a princess-like presentation, complete with an extra dusting of powdered sugar. Olivia set the plate on the table between the pair.

"This is for you," Olivia said, offering an accompanying smile. "Enjoy."

The woman raised her eyes with a questioning gaze. "Thank you, but—"

"Just a random act of kindness on a Sunday morning." Olivia said and returned to the register. She handed the clerk a twenty dollar bill. "Keep the change."

Gathering the newspapers, she waved and headed to the door with an extra bounce in her step. At the last minute, she pulled out the advertising supplements and threw them in the recycle bin. She wanted the papers to feel as light as she did.

Olivia pulled into the parking lot of Hale's Restaurant in Milwaukie, a breakfast hangout popular with policemen, aficionados of eggs with Spartan Sauce or nuclear waffles with slabs of butter and whipped cream—and the Dushane family. It had been Ellen's favorite restaurant because of the authentic German sausages and house-smoked bacon.

Ryan's cruiser sat in the parking lot. The waxy words *Just Married* had long ago worn off the back window, but the two cartoon dog bones showed up when it rained, their outlines beaded with droplets. Pogo had settled into his new life, celebrating his own union with his humans by accompanying Danny and Ryan on their two-week honeymoon in Vermont. Lauren's red Honda sat next to the cruiser. Olivia parked next to it. They were all inside, waiting for her grand entrance with the pile of newspapers. But this day wasn't about her; it was about their mother. Tomorrow's scattering of the ashes was about Mom too.

Olivia shut off the engine and bundled the four fresh newspapers under her arm, vowing not to peek. Tempted, but she didn't dare. A slight smile cracked as she fingered her mother's pearl earrings. Both of them. She quickened her steps to the entrance.

"I think my party's been seated." She smiled at the host. "A cop with two biddies and a service dog."

"Right this way," the woman chuckled as she led Olivia toward the back of the restaurant. She glanced over her shoulder. "Pogo wanted a booth."

Every table and booth in the restaurant was full: multiple generations of families at breakfast, some with only a remaining Mom or Dad; others with grandparents. Sunday was the day to celebrate stories with visual remembrances in picture boxes. Olivia filled with warmth at the four heads, one curly and black, in the booth by the window. She held up the stack of newspapers.

"There she is!" Ryan declared and stood. Mom would have said, *He's been raised right.* "We're starving."

"I got 'em!" Olivia announced. "I hope it'll be worth the wait," She scooted next to Lauren and slapped the papers on the laminate table. "I swear I didn't look."

Next to Danny, Pogo sat in the window spot, proud to be wearing his yellow vest. Always working, that one. Olivia reached over the table and gave his head a scrub.

"He can go anywhere now," Danny crowed. "He's such a good boy,"

"We have to talk about the sleeping arrangements, though," Ryan added and sat. "Let's just say he's a bed hog."

Lauren tightened her grip on Olivia's arm. "Better be good. This review determines whether we're all eating steak or munching on Spam for the rest of our lives."

Olivia took a deep breath and handed each of them a newspaper. Frantic rustling of print replaced their voices. In synchronized movements, the four of them leaned back in the booth as the fifty-year career server poured coffee without spilling a drop.

"Hey Madge," Ryan said to the server without raising his eyes.

"You ready to order?" she asked. Madge raised her blue-shadowed eyes from the order pad without moving her head. "I read . . . Ellen's book."

Olivia abandoned her hunt for the review, wanting more. Lauren, Danny, and Ryan did the same. "And?"

"Loved the story. Couldn't put the darned thing down. That Becky character made the hair on my arms stand on end. Glad she wasn't my daughter, but I never thought I could root for a killer. I cheered on the poor little thing. That bastard deserved what he got for standing up poor Becky. Just think, Becky grew up, got married, and had three nice kids." Madge bobbed her pencil. "Still waters ran deep in Ellen to write a story like that. You never can tell who's livin' right next door." She nodded for emphasis and flipped to a fresh page on her pad. "The usual? Veggie scrambles all around?"

Five pairs of eyes stared. The server smiled at Pogo, as if he were about to request something off the menu, with specific instructions for how his eggs should be prepared.

"Yeah . . . sounds good," Ryan muttered, crinkling his forehead.

"Wait . . . no potatoes, toast, or butter for Pogo. We're watching his weight." Danny nodded in agreement and patted Ryan's arm.

Olivia's gaze trailed Madge as she sashayed toward the kitchen, her confident steps showing everyone in the restaurant she harbored inside information.

"Found it!" Danny declared. "Page three."

Once again, the pages crinkled as Olivia, Lauren, and Ryan flipped the pages and folded the Sunday Book Review section like a racing form.

Danny read the headline aloud and then, hearing no objection from the others, kept going:

Debut Author Has New Take on Being Jilted

It took over 60 years to discover the brilliance of Ellen Dushane. Her debut novel, Indigo to Black, *gives us a rare glimpse into the mind of a 17-year-old young woman in the 1950s—from a different side.*

Dushane's character of Becky Haines is both the antagonist and the protagonist of the story, a tricky feat to pull off. Dushane achieves the goal by making Becky a real girl with real emotions, in an era when young women were wrapped in a shroud of unrealistic expectations. Lurking beneath the surface are Becky's own expectations for love at a deeper level. And she's going to get it, one way or another.

Among the birches and maples of Vermont at a summer camp on Indigo Lake, Becky finds love with a medical student: he's handsome, attentive and seemingly dedicated to her. Vowing to reunite the next summer at an exact time and place, they part. Long months pass with the squeeze of overwhelming infatuation. They write. They call. They wait. And when the day arrives, Becky waits . . . and waits some more. The love of her life never shows up. Only a note delivered by his buddy, says, "I can't."

But Becky can. The reader jumps on the freight train of Becky's emotional journey through devastation, grief, anger and finally . . . revenge.

Ellen Dushane's death brought Indigo to Black *to life. We will never know the story of the story. Her daughter, Olivia Novak, a best-selling author in her own right, discovered the manuscript in her mother's safe after her death. With agreement from her siblings, Novak delivered Dushane's poignant and disturbing literary triumph to the world. We, as readers, are grateful she did.*

"I'd say it's pretty darned good." Danny raised her eyes to assess the others' responses.

"Damn skippy!" Ryan agreed.

"This guy is usually mean," Lauren added. "At least he acknowledged you're a best-selling author."

Olivia stared at the article. "I'd kill for a review like this."

Lauren turned to her. "No, you wouldn't."

"I'll bet you'll get a good one, Liv," Danny said, "when you finally publish *Protection.*"

"Now, how could you possibly know?" Olivia asked, her nose still buried in the review. "You haven't even read it."

"You wouldn't let me."

"Keep your voice down. I'm protecting you from reading some pretty terrible things about Ardy. They'd just get you upset."

"Well, I've read it," Lauren said, lowering her voice. "Hang on to your Spanks when that review comes out."

Ryan chuckled. "Better loosen yours. Here comes breakfast."

"Veggie scrambles!" Madge announced with a large tray balanced on one hand. "Hope you're hungry! No carbs for the dog." She eyed the newspaper as she distributed the plates. "Ellen's write-up?"

"Yep. Want to read it?" Olivia held out her copy.

Danny blew on Pogo's veggie scramble as she spread the egg and vegetables out across the plate. She tucked a white napkin in his collar and stuck her finger into the egg. "Okay, Pogo. Cool enough. Good to go."

"Honey, pick out the peppers," Ryan chided. "Trust me on this."

Madge stood reading in silence, drinking in every word of the review as knives scraped butter on the toast in washboard rhythm. Olivia studied the server's face. Pursed lips challenged the edges of her lipstick. When Madge finished reading, the brown penciled lines that were once her eyebrows raised as she tapped the paper. "I'd bet y'all's breakfast Ellen's story is real. *That's* why she hid the manuscript in the safe."

"I hate to disappoint you," Lauren interjected, "but no way. Ellen was an open book."

Danny nodded in agreement. "I lived with her. Not a chance."

Fascinated with the conversation, Olivia remained quiet. She hung on the woman's every word.

"What about you, copper?" Madge batted Ryan's shoulder with the newspaper, her other hand on her hip. "You knew Ellen. What do you think?"

Ryan shook his head. "Ellen was a protector, not a killer."

Madge grimaced. "Shoot. Would a made for a good scandal. My copy's in the car. If I bring in the book, will all three of you gals sign it for me?"

Danny pulled her *Premier Customer* pen from her purse. "Ready when you are!" She handed over Pogo's empty plate.

Chapter 43

Protection

Clouds shrouded Timberline Lodge on Monday afternoon. Ryan agreed to take Pogo for the day while the girls conducted their private ceremony of scattering Ellen's ashes. April could be risky for weather on Mt. Hood, but the sisters didn't want to wait any longer to set their mother free. The three of them and Ellen's urn had wound up the mountain road, passing through bright sunshine, blooming spring color, and crisp alpine air. As the trees thinned, thick clouds sparkled with ice crystals. By the time Olivia had pulled into the parking lot of the massive Cascadian structure, the air had turned into a blanket of cold fog, masking the silent, snow-capped peak of the mountain's summit. It loomed five thousand more feet above them, and they were already six thousand feet above sea level. The aroma of pines charged the senses.

Built in 1937 as part of a WPA project, the building tipped its hat to Oregon's pioneer design aesthetic. The historic hotel and ski lodge had been restored to its original glory in the late fifties, right down to the hand-hewn burl animal sculptures gracing the banisters of the numerous creaky staircases. The patina of aged wood punctuated the authenticity of the artful details, too numerous to appreciate in one visit.

In the lodge's formal Cascade Dining Room, Olivia set Ellen's urn next to her, at the fourth place at the table. Lauren and Danny took seats across from her.

"This day's been a long time coming," Olivia announced. "A lot has happened in nine months."

"Can't accuse you of exaggerating that one," Danny added.

"Can you believe I had to get a permit to scatter Mom up here?"

"We didn't have to pay to scatter Mark, Adam, or Dad. Is that new?"

"This whole area is considered part of the National Park Service." Olivia rolled her eyes. "Now they charge for everything to beef up their budgets. But we're legal."

"Just like the damned government," Lauren groused. "A scatter tax. The juice starts running the minute you're born and keeps racking up until you die. They get you coming and going. It's like the mob."

"You and your rules, Liv. How do you know this stuff?" Danny asked.

"Because I'm old." Olivia pretended to peruse the selections on the menu. "Right, Lauren? You know more than I do."

"Don't remind me." Lauren opened the menu. "I'm buying, Danny. I had to break into my retirement account to eat here, so we might as well chow down."

Olivia rummaged in her purse when her cell phone rang. She'd changed the chirp to the ring of an old-fashioned bicycle bell. She raised her eyes from the screen. "It's Ted."

Lauren grimaced and swished her hand. "I hate cell phones. So rude. Take the damned thing out of the restaurant."

Olivia rushed to the catwalk that circled the upper level of the lodge. She gazed up at the two-ton beams supporting the roof.

"Ted? Is everything okay?"

"Well . . . I'm not sure," he said, his voice crackly from the mountain's altitude. The concern could easily be heard, and it caught her attention. "I got a call from the administrator of a senior home in Iowa. The woman had a message for you."

"She did? What could she possibly want with me?"

"A Mr. Gerald Milner passed away this morning—about two hours ago. Instructions were left that, upon his death, you were to know, quote, 'it's okay to go. Fiddledeedee.' What the hell is that supposed to mean?"

Olivia closed her eyes. *Milner! Iowa!* "Did she say how Mr. Milner died?"

"In his sleep. The woman said it was peaceful." Ted paused. "Is he . . . R. D. Griffin, Liv?"

"Without a doubt."

"Okay . . . You'd better come in. We can go through the details."

"Please call the woman back," Olivia choked, her eyes welling with tears. "Tell her I want Mr. Milner's body shipped here to Oregon, to the Willoughby Funeral Home. The three of us and Fred will make sure he has a proper service. If anyone can write his obituary, it's me."

"Will do. I know this isn't the news you wanted, today of all days."

Olivia steadied herself by grabbing the rail. The forty-foot drop to the main floor had a dizzying effect with the swirl of Ted's words.

"Thank you for telling me. I'll come in tomorrow . . . or sometime this week," she said. "I need to get back. Rude to leave Mom sitting on the table in a restaurant."

Ted gave an obligatory chuckle before Olivia hung up. She gazed at nothing. The safe-deposit box key sat in a zippered pocket in her wallet. As she turned and stared into the dining room, Lauren and Danny chattered with the server as they placed their orders. Lauren pointed at Olivia's empty seat. She figured an order had been placed for her. But it wasn't important. Important were the two people who sat at the table with Mom, laughing over etched bacon and tomatoes. The three of them had a hopeful future, a future she could have never predicted nine months ago. She held tight to the thought.

As Olivia slid back into her seat, she took a sip of the raspberry iced tea, untouched in front of her place. Her mouth had gone dry with indecision.

"We ordered a salad for you," Lauren said. "We need to get this show over the cliff."

Danny took a sip of her tea as she studied Olivia's face. "What's the matter? Everything all right? Something about the book?"

"Not Mom's book." Olivia dug in her purse and pulled out the key. She held up the small cut piece of glinting steel, which carried huge implications. "Ardy passed away this morning."

~ · ~ · ~

In clearer weather, standing anywhere outside of Timberline Lodge offered a panoramic view of the Cascade Mountains. Now, Olivia and her sisters were engulfed in cold mist, the temperature plummeting by the minute. A continuous push of dense air rustled through the branches behind them. The arms of Lauren's jacket swished as she zipped the knit collar tighter around her neck. Puffs of steam emanated from Danny's mouth as she tried to accept Olivia's news of Ardy's death and what they were about to do. Their spot at the edge of the wooded area overlooking the cliff was familiar. The three of them had stood here before for the lost men in their lives, with the exception of Ryan. They would return soon for Ardy. He needed a final home with a family.

"I'm freezing my butt off," Lauren griped.

Danny blew into her cupped hands. "Feels like it's going to dump snow any minute. We should get back down the mountain soon."

Olivia gripped the urn in the crook of her left arm. She removed the lid and held it out to Danny. "Here. Hold this." Olivia pulled off her right leather glove.

"What are you going to do about *Protection*, Liv?" Lauren asked.

"I can't undo this bag inside with these gloves on."

"Noooo . . . I mean Ardy's book."

"Today isn't about Ardy. Today is about Mom." Olivia set her glove on the rail as she pulled the plastic bag from the urn. "Ready?"

Lauren and Danny each set a hand on Olivia's as the three of them shook the ashes into the wind. Looking all together like tendrils of smoke, the beige particles of Ellen sailed over the side of the cliff. The cindered flecks of the blackened newspaper articles, lighter than the rest of their mother, floated on the current after her. Insignificant in comparison.

In a line, the sisters peered over the safety rail as the dust disappeared. Silence accompanied the flurries of snow that had started to fall, as if the mountain, too, released its grief for Ellen Dushane, their father, Adam, and Mark. All here for a brief moment together . . . and then gone.

"I can't do it," Olivia said. "I'm not willing to compromise what the three of us have."

Lauren turned and stared at her, incredulous. "*Protection*?"

"Yeah . . . " Olivia continued to lean over the guard rail. "We'd be looking over our shoulders for the rest of our lives if Ardy's memoir hit the market."

"What about the Pogo Charitable Trust?" Danny asked, grasping Olivia's arm.

"I'll fund it myself with half my share of royalties from Mom's book."

"I'll put in half of my share with you," Lauren offered.

"Me too," Danny agreed. "Pogo's work is too important. I'll bet Mom's book will outsell what Ardy's story would do, anyway." She turned with a sheepish grin. "No offense, Liv."

Olivia closed her eyes, forming words she couldn't utter to anyone but her sisters. "At least . . . not while we're alive." She handed the empty urn to Danny as she rummaged in her purse. Unzipping the pocket in her billfold, she lifted out the safe-deposit box key. "This is the last time the three of us will lay eyes on this." The metal turned cold in her hand.

"Why? You worked so hard," Lauren said, flexing her fingers.

"Even under a pen name, I underestimated the threat. A lot of people need to die before Ardy's book can be published"—A gust of wind caught her glove, sailing it over the cliff and into the mist. Olivia inhaled—"and that includes us."

"Your glove," Danny whispered.

Lauren stared over the steep drop. "Forget the glove. Olivia's walking away from her first serious book."

Olivia straightened and smiled. "Not entirely. I'll let Ted's law firm figure it out. I have a different book in mind." An image of her fan at Powell's Books filled her mind. Olivia had seen her own face in the woman's countenance and couldn't shake the empathetic expression.

"About what?"

"The three of us. My name's going to be Valerie. I'll dedicate it to Mom and the two of you."

"Sounds boring. What are you going to call it?" Snowflakes passed through the steam from Lauren's words.

"*The Executrix*."

Epilogue

One Year Later

Olivia waited in the lobby of New York's Waldorf Astoria Hotel for Lauren and Danny to emerge from the bank of elevators. Every *ding* made her head turn toward the doors, hand-forged with Art Deco designs. Three invitations to the annual National Book Critics Circle Awards Ceremony at the New School in Soho went damp in her hand. *Indigo to Black* had won in the fiction category. Yesterday had been the public reading; tonight was for shaking hands and extolling the literary accomplishment of Ellen Dushane.

Having never, herself, won an award for her writing, Olivia embraced the accolades through a blood connection. Books had the DNA of their authors, and that was enough for her. The need to protect Ellen's memory superseded her own quest for glory. A year ago, Olivia might have thought the scenario would be different, but Ellen had taught her that not all stories were worth the emotional cost of the telling. In a similar way, Ardy had taught her that not all stories were worth the physical cost.

Olivia had changed her will, with agreement from Lauren and Danny. Upon the death of the last sister, the instructions in each of their wills permitted a representative of the law firm of Delaney and Beal to open the safe-deposit box at Cascade Bank. The manuscript and binders for Ardy's story were to be sent to Karen's literary agency, or her deemed representative. As Ardy's executrix, Olivia would keep her word—only a little longer than they'd planned. While Olivia wouldn't enjoy the benefits of the publication of *Protection*, its literary legacy would add to the funds of the Pogo Charitable Trust, allowing the continuance of its healing work long after the three sisters were gone. Maybe *The Executrix* would add to the legacy too. A draft of *The Executrix* was done and had been handed off to Lauren for the final edits. Karen had already started the hounding process to read the first fifty pages.

Stepping across the shiny marble floor of the main lobby, Olivia peered down the staircase to the entrance and spotted the limousine waiting for them outside. She glanced at her watch. The crystal buttons of her black silk suit danced in the light of the chandelier. The mint of the Listerine strip stung her mouth as she swished her tongue over her teeth.

Ding!

Lauren stepped out of the elevator in a ginger-colored jacket and dressy black slacks. With a fresh haircut and color, she stood straighter and with confidence. But Lauren's expression still screamed, *Do I have to do this?* She carried her everyday purse instead of an evening bag. So Lauren. She'd rather be home in her house dress and socks. Behind her, Danny was picture-perfect in a knee-length black dress, unadorned and elegant in its off-the-shoulder drape. On the outside, Danny was ready for the paparazzi; on the inside, Olivia suspected she stressed about finding Ryan and Pogo in the crowd when they arrived at the New School. As a service dog, Pogo went everywhere with them, even to the extent of having his own seat on the plane. But in truth, Ryan and Pogo would be hunting for Danny, so excited he was for her.

Olivia beamed at her two sisters as they joined her. At the top of the stairs, flanked by two giant urns, she pointed to the limousine outside.

"Good God," Lauren said, "We're going to a funeral!"

"Or a celebration." Olivia handed each of them their invitation.

Lauren ran her fingers over the embossed title on the cream-colored paper; a mixture of pride and sadness washed across her face. She raised her eyes to Olivia. "Do I look fat?"

"No, you're fabulous." Olivia laughed and squeaked out an air kiss at Lauren.

"Mom would have been proud of us," Danny said. "I miss her."

"Me too," Olivia echoed. "Time to get in the car and go honor her." She pointed to the revolving door.

Danny floated down the stairs to the entrance, as if on an escalator. Lauren pushed against Olivia's heels as they each slipped into the whirling wedge of the revolving door. The three of them ejected onto the sidewalk and were met with a smile from the limo driver. He waited by the open back door.

"You want a cigarette before we go?" Olivia asked of Lauren.

"Nope. I quit twelve hours ago. I'm about to chew through wood, though."

"Ladies? You ready?" the driver said, sweeping a hand to the lit interior.

Olivia shooed Danny into the car and scooted in the seat after her. Lauren stuck her foot out to get into the car, and as she did so, revealed ginger-colored orthopedic loafers. "What the hell is up with those shoes? They look like curried sausages!"

"They match!" Lauren exclaimed. "Nobody can see them when I'm standing. My feet are killing me."

Their mother's ring on Danny's hand flashed in the bright lights from the hotel's entrance. Olivia couldn't help but notice. *Smile for the cameras, Mom.*

As the driver closed the door, Olivia grasped Danny's and Lauren's hands and squeezed their entwined fingers, the three of them connected in blood, laughter, and tears.

Author's Note

I hope you enjoyed *The Executrix*. At the time of this book's publication, I'm pleased to say that my mother is alive and well at the age of eighty-one. She is such a good sport and has a wonderful sense of humor. Mom wrote a book once, but she assures me the manuscript doesn't exist. Unfortunately, no *Indigo to Black* is lurking in the safe—at least, I don't think so.

A Portland gem, Powell's Books is an inspiration to any writer. While signings for romance writers are a rare occurrence at Powell's, I took the liberty of holding my character's event there.

Hale's Restaurant in Milwaukie, Oregon is always jammed. The mix of locals and policemen make for a fun breakfast.

A few items in the fictitious book *Indigo to Black* are tidbits from my life. The Yum Yum Shop in downtown Wolfeboro, New Hampshire is a real bakery. I have such fond memories of this delectable shop, having spent summers in Wolfeboro. If you're ever in town to experience the amazing New England fall color, stop by for something yummy. You won't be disappointed.

Our family found several Lydia Pinkham's Elixir bottles on my grandfather's farm in New Hampshire. At the turn of the century, women spent at least five days a month wonky-wired on Lydia Pinkham's Elixir . . . 18% alcohol.

The character of R. D. Griffin (a.k.a Felix "Crow" Fazziano) is fictitious. However, he was inspired by an actual Philadelphia crime figure, Felix "Tom Mix" Bocchino, who was shot and killed in his car in 1992. Bocchino was known for walking his dog, thought to be a poodle.

The newspaper articles in the family picture box are fictitious and are the product of a vivid imagination.

Lastly, help the old man next door. An act of kindness can change your life.

The Dushane sisters will be back . . . stay tuned!

About the Author

Courtney Pierce lives in Milwaukie, Oregon, with her husband and bossy cat. Following a twenty-year career as an executive in the Broadway entertainment industry, she published a trilogy of literary magical realism, *Stitches, Brushes*, and *Riffs*. She became transformed by the magic of fiction from a theater seat, observing what made audiences laugh, cry, or walk out the door. Courtney has also published two short stories: *1313 Huidekoper Place*, for the 2013 NIWA Short Story Anthology *Thirteen Tales of Speculative Fiction*, and *The Nest*, for the Windtree Press anthology *The Gift of Christmas*. Courtney is active in the writing community. She is a member of Willamette Writers, Pacific Northwest Writers Association, and Northwest Independent Writers Association.

Follow Courtney's books at her website: **www.courtney-pierce.com**

38776525R00178

Made in the USA
Charleston, SC
15 February 2015